NIGHTS
BY
SARA ORWIG

AND

HER TYCOON
TO TAME
BY
EMILIE ROSE

"What I want in life has changed since I left Texas," Maddie said again.

"What I want in life has changed, too, Maddie. We want different things, have different needs now than we did back then." He tilted her chin up and leaned close again. "All I know is that you should watch out, because I intend to cater to the part of you that still responds to me when we kiss."

"It's sheer foolishness that there are moments I can't resist you," she replied. His words made her heart pound, and now she was ensnared in his crystal blue gaze. Panic gripped her. She was tumbling rapidly into a situation she'd hoped to avoid. There was the matter of their *daughter*— who he knew nothing about. "We're not going to rekindle what we had. We've both moved on and our lives have changed."

He ran his index finger down her cheek. "Some things haven't changed at all."

Dear Reader,

Once again, I have set another book in Texas with its glittering, down-to-earth, friendly people and larger-than-life ways. This last story in my series about the handsome millionaires who have been friends since earliest childhood focuses on Gabriel Benton, Jake's younger brother. It is a story of reunion involving Gabe, the handsome blue-eyed rancher, and Madeline Halliday, a woman he has grown up knowing and once viewed as his best friend.

Their romance encompasses the triumph of love and forgiveness, qualities that belong in the deepest and longest-lasting relationships. I've said before that families are close to my heart and enter into the themes of my books, including this one. Family has a big influence on our lives, and that is true of Maddie and Gabe.

Friends and former lovers, the two encounter each other along a Texas highway. Gabe, a man accustomed to getting his way, cannot resist wanting to be with Maddie and talks her into dinner. He re-enters her life, stirring passion, guilt and—finally—the revelation of the secret that changes both their lives.

This book is a farewell to the four CEOs who all wear Stetsons, call Texas home and fall in love with exciting women.

Thank you for selecting my book.

Best wishes,

Sara Orwig

Libraries and Information

This book should be returned by the last date stamped above.
You may renew the loan personally, by post or telephone for a
further period if the book is not required by another reader.

wakefieldcouncil *working for you*

Published in Great Britain 2012
by Mills & Boon, an imprint of Harlequin (UK) Limited,
Eton House, 18-24 Paradise Road, Richmond, Surrey TW9 1SR

© Sara Orwig 2011

ISBN: 978 0 263 89150 8

51-0312

Harlequin (UK) policy is to use papers that are natural, renewable and recyclable products and made from wood grown in sustainable forests. The logging and manufacturing processes conform to the legal environmental regulations of the country of origin.

Printed and bound in Spain
by Blackprint CPI, Barcelona

Sara Orwig lives in Oklahoma. She has a patient husband who will take her on research trips anywhere from big cities to old forts. She is an avid collector of Western history books. With a master's degree in English, Sara has written historical romance, mainstream fiction and contemporary romance. Books are beloved treasures that take Sara to magical worlds, and she loves both reading and writing them.

To my family with all my love.

One

Gabe Benton spotted the car pulled off the straight
West Texas highway—a speck on the flat, mesquite-
covered horizon—and he pulled to a stop expecting to
find a stranger.

When he stepped out of his car, the woman, who'd
been changing a flat tire, glanced over her shoulder. A
thick blond braid hung beneath her baseball cap. She
wore jeans and a short sleeved, cotton shirt.

"Got trouble?" he inquired.

She stood. "Gabe?" she asked in disbelief.

"Maddie?"

His heart missed a few beats. Startled to hear a voice
he knew as well as his own, he looked at the woman
more closely. Yes, it was Madeline Halliday, and she
was even better looking now than she had been at
twenty-one.

The curves shaping her white blouse were lush,

her waist tiny, her legs as long as he remembered. Her skin was creamy, stirring a vivid memory of how she had looked naked in his arms. His pulse sped up. His breathing altered. She was a knockout, now more than ever.

He was shocked at how glad he was to see her. It took an effort to resist closing the distance between them. And then he couldn't hold back. In two strides, he reached her, wrapping his arms around her, fighting the temptation to kiss her long and hard.

Their last tense week together had been six long years ago. But now Maddie was back in his life.

She was soft, warm and sweet smelling. He held her tighter, his pulse racing. When she embraced him in return and stepped back, he wanted to pull her into his arms again.

"It's great to see you," Gabe said. "You look terrific."

"Thanks, Gabe," she said.

"I'm sorry about the loss of your grandfather," he added, looking into dark brown eyes surrounded by thick lashes. After their breakup, Maddie had moved to Florida.

"Thank you. And thank you for the flowers you sent."

"The flowers were in lieu of my offering condolences in person. I'm sorry I missed the memorial, but I was in Wyoming buying cattle. By the time I got word, I couldn't have made it home in time."

"Some things don't change. You're still traveling for business," she said, and for a moment her smile faded.

"Not as much these days. Sorry I wasn't here. Sorry, too, about the loss of your father. I didn't know about his death three years ago until a year later."

"Thanks. Dad's loss was difficult. My mom has

adjusted pretty well. When I came for Granddad's memorial, there was a big crowd. Since my family has lived here almost as long as yours, there were lots of people from the area."

"What brings you back again after only three months?"

"Mom and I inherited the ranch. Neither of us wants it, so I'm here to make the arrangements to place it on the market."

"That's a surprise. I hope you've given it some thought," he said, easily falling into the closeness he had once felt with her, "because that's a fine ranch."

"We're sure about what we want to do. I hope to be back in Florida by next week and have this place sold by July."

When he grasped her hand and looked at her bare fingers, relief flooded him. "No wedding ring."

She smiled again. "No. I've been too busy with work. Let me guess—you're not wearing one either."

He grinned. "You know me too well. Will you be here long?"

"Just long enough to get everything arranged to sell. I'll stay at the ranch while I'm getting the house ready and while I find an agency to deal with the property."

"I'll finish changing your tire and then let's go where we can talk. I'll take you to dinner tonight."

She glanced at her watch. "I shouldn't—"

"Come on. You can give one evening to an old friend," he said, gazing into eyes that could, apparently, still make him weak in the knees.

"I never could resist you," she replied, smiling. "Yes," she added, and turned away, walking back to the car before he could reply.

You resisted me once was what he wanted to say, but

he kept quiet. His pulse jumped another notch now that he was reassured she was not carrying a grudge about the way they'd ended things six years ago. Already, he was anticipating the evening with her and thinking about dinner. He hurried to get to the tire before she did.

"We've lost touch," he said as he hunkered down to remove the flat. "I heard you got that business degree."

"Yes. I transferred to the University of Florida in Gainesville where I majored in business. Now I work for Clirksonie Realty in Miami."

"Like it?" he asked while he dropped a lug bolt onto the hubcap lying on the ground.

"Very much. I'm busy. I heard you moved back to the family ranch."

"I did. That year after you left, I spent more and more time there. Finally, I retired to the ranch last year. I was restless in my job and wanted the move. Maybe life wasn't the same without you here," he said, giving her a crooked grin.

She smiled, shaking her head in disbelief.

"I can't imagine you leaving your Dallas job for the ranch, but that is what you always said you wanted. I'm glad to be away from our spread. Ranching is hard work."

"Not when you love doing it. If I recall accurately, you always wanted to get away from here. Hard for me to understand. You're in Miami? No way is it as peaceful as it is out here."

She smiled. "We could argue that one forever. The ocean can be peaceful. I love the beach. I love the activity of a big city, too. Miami, Houston, Dallas— they're all exhilarating to me. I'm surprised you don't miss the office."

He shrugged. "Sometimes I do," he said. "You have grandparents in Miami, don't you?"

"Yes. My mom's parents. They're both still there and Mom is. We all live close to each other, so that's nice."

In the silence, as he worked on the flat, he couldn't help reflecting on their breakup. Maddie had been getting serious while he hadn't wanted to. When she broke off their relationship, she wouldn't talk to him or tell him why. At the time, the only disagreement between them had been his decision to accept a temporary position in Nigeria, where his company wanted to send him, rather than agree to stay in Texas with her.

It was while he was in Nigeria that he heard she'd moved to Florida. As far as he knew, the only time she'd returned to Texas was for her grandfather's memorial service.

He stood and brushed off his hands. "There," he said, carrying the flat tire to her trunk. "You picked up a nail somewhere."

"I can't imagine. This is a brand-new rental from Dallas. I got it at the airport and definitely didn't expect a flat. I've called them. They're sending out a replacement tomorrow and they'll drive this car back."

"Good deal."

"Thanks for stopping to help," she said, gazing up at him. She had pushed the baseball cap back and he looked down into her dark eyes. Strands of blond hair fluttered around her face.

"Wouldn't have missed you for the world. I'm glad to see you again. I'll pick you up at your grandfather's ranch about six."

"That's fine," she said. "Thanks again, Gabe."

He nodded and fell into step beside her as she walked

to the front of the car. He reached ahead to open the door for her, his gaze running over her as she climbed into the driver's side. After closing the door, he leaned down, speaking to her through the open window. "I'm glad you're back."

"It's only for a short time," she replied solemnly.

"I'll get you to stay longer," he said, deciding that's what he wanted.

"Still so totally confident," she said with a smile. "Another thing that hasn't changed."

"I'll see to it that you're *glad* to stay longer," he stated, smiling, but beneath his light tone, he wanted her to know that he intended to do what he said. "See you in a little while." When he stepped back, she turned the key in the ignition.

Driving home, all he could think about was Maddie. Recollections of summer evenings spent with her came back with clarity. After she'd left, it had taken him a while to admit to himself how much he missed her. He had always expected her to return home, but she never had. Until now.

Six o'clock. Would she have let him know she was back in Texas if he hadn't happened to pass her on the road? He suspected she would not have contacted him. Even so, eagerness filled him and he looked forward to the evening with her.

His ranch house loomed into sight. He'd had the place built a mile from his brother's house, which had been the family home. His brother Jake liked to stay on the ranch some of the time and they both owned shares in the ranch operation.

Gabe looked at his sprawling house. The main hall and one wing were finished. They were still working on the other wing. The roof of the house sloped over a screened-in porch, giving the structure an old-fashioned look, which he thought suited him. Every time he saw the house, it gave him satisfaction. Enough that he could almost forget that he sometimes missed Dallas.

He parked in the back and hurried to the kitchen to see what food he had stocked. He wasn't taking Maddie out to eat. Anywhere in the county she would be besieged by old friends and he wouldn't get time alone with her. She used to be warm, loving, ready for fun. He wondered how much she had changed.

God knew he'd changed in the past six years. At one time, he'd avoided all serious relationships, even with Maddie. But this past year, more and more, he'd been thinking about marriage. He'd begun avoiding long, empty nights by himself on the ranch.

His brother and his brother's friends were all married now and appeared happier than ever. His closest friend, Luke Tarkington, had married last year and Gabe saw less of him. Gabe had recently had another birthday. He was in his thirties and he'd felt a growing restlessness, an urge to settle down, but there was no one in his life he wanted to settle with.

Now, here was Maddie. He couldn't help imagining the possibilities.

When Maddie parted from Gabe, she had glanced in her rearview mirror as he walked back to his car. The same purposeful stride, the same lanky, long legs covering the ground easily. His black Stetson rested squarely on his head, the brim rolled in the typical fashion for their area of Texas. His shoulders looked broader than she remembered and she knew his lean look was deceptive, because he was stronger than a lot of men who were heavier. A persistent knot in her chest ached and she held tightly to the steering wheel as if it were a lifeline.

As she drove away, she focused on the stretch of flat highway ahead, seeing heat waves shimmer beneath the afternoon sun, too aware that Gabe was not far behind her. She waved when she turned into the Halliday ranch.

Tonight she was having dinner with Gabe.

She had always let him take charge and get his way, but she was a grown woman now and she should have refused the date.

When she had turned from her flat tire to find him standing behind her, her pulse had jumped. He was still the most handsome man she'd ever known with his startling blue eyes fringed with brown lashes. She had intended to avoid him while she was here. She definitely had not planned to spend any time with him. There was too much unresolved between them.

They had been friends since she was a kid. Later, it became so much more. Sometimes she wished she'd guarded her heart, but then she wouldn't have Rebecca. And she wouldn't have known what it was to love Gabe.

Their last summer still pained her when she thought about him walking away without making arrangements to see her again. While they had been arguing about the future, she had received the shock of her life.

The final week Gabe had been in Texas, before he'd traveled to Nigeria, she had learned she was pregnant with his baby.

Memories rushed at her now: the first shock of learning she was pregnant; the thrill of knowing she was carrying Gabe's baby. She had shared her life with Gabe since she'd been about eight, and she'd loved him almost as long. So, in some ways, the pregnancy was joyous news. It had been a bond with Gabe that was forged for life.

When she'd realized what she had to do—keep the baby a secret from him—she had been devastated. But always, no matter how she looked at the situation, the best thing for both of them had been to keep the news to herself. Gabe hadn't been ready for fatherhood or marriage or a binding commitment. He wouldn't even commit to a serious relationship with her before the pregnancy! Even now, she was still convinced that revealing the truth would have been disastrous to Gabe. She had saved them both. She'd saved Gabe from a marriage and responsibility he hadn't wanted. She'd saved herself from settling for life on the ranch when she wanted something more.

As she drove the familiar road to the home where she had grown up, she tried to ignore the tingly feeling that had started the moment she'd seen him and continued even now.

At the first sight of him her palms had gone damp and her breathing had altered. After all this time how could he still do this to her?

Memories of being in his arms, of making love to him, tormented her. Memories she had tried to forget through the years. But now that she'd seen him, they came tumbling back as fresh as if they had happened yesterday.

"I won't get involved with you again." She whispered the promise to herself, knowing that in some ways she would always be involved with him. There was Rebecca. And it had taken only one look into his blue eyes for the years to fall away. Could she still love him?

When she neared her family home, she looked at the tall wooden house that had belonged to her family for generations. She didn't mind selling it. While she had been happy here, she didn't want to move back. In Miami, she had a great place, with a big patio and a great bay-front view in a thriving metropolis she loved.

Stepping out of the car, she heard someone call her name.

She waited, watching a lanky, brown-haired man jog across the driveway toward her. Smiling, she waved.

"Maddie, welcome home."

"Thanks, Sol. You look the same as ever," she said, stepping forward to give the foreman a hug.

"Older now. It's good to have you here." He smiled at her and pushed his broad-brimmed Western hat back on his head. "How's your mom?"

"She's fine, so are my grandparents."

"You should have brought your mom with you. Tell her hello from all of us."

"I will. This is a fast business trip and then I need to get back to my work in Florida. It was easier to come by myself."

"Let me get your things. You leave all this to me." He moved past her to take her bags from the car after she opened the trunk. She shouldered a bag and picked up a suitcase.

"Leave those, Maddie. I'll get everything."

"Thanks, Sol. I'll bring this much. You can get the rest. I'm going in anyway so there's no need to go empty-handed."

"Things are in pretty good shape here. When will you have somebody out to look at the place?" he asked as they walked to the house.

"I have an appointment this afternoon in Lubbock with an agency. Tomorrow I'm meeting a broker who is driving here from Fort Worth. I have a third appointment with a representative from another agency in Dallas. I'll choose one to handle the sale and then I'll better know the schedule for placing the ranch on the market. I'm glad you've found a job you want." She entered a side door, smelling a vacant, stuffy odor as she turned off the alarm.

"Hard to leave this place, but life changes," he said, glancing around. "It's not the same with your granddad gone."

"I know it's not. It was good of you to stay for as long as I need you. It'll be a lot easier if we can sell the place as is, with cattle included and some of the furniture still in the house. If we can't sell it that way, then we'll do what we have to do. I don't know how long it'll take, but I hope we sell quickly."

"I'll pass the word along. We're down to a skeleton crew now. Most hands have taken jobs elsewhere. Some have been hired on places with the stipulation that they can't start until you've sold the ranch."

"I appreciate that," she said. "Leave the bags here at the foot of the stairs. I can get them."

"I'll take them to your room," he said, moving past her to carry the bags upstairs.

"Would you like a cup of coffee? I can have a pot brewed in no time," she called after him.

"Thanks. I'll come have coffee later if that's all right. I have to get back to work now."

She returned to the kitchen to get a glass of water and followed him to the back door. "Thanks so much for unloading my car. I'm not certain how long the arrangements will take, but I hope to get everything done this week and head back to Florida."

"The men want to say hello to you, but most of them

are out in the field right now. It's good to have you home. Sorry it isn't the happiest occasion."

"Thanks again, Sol," she said to the man who had been their ranch foreman since she was two years old.

He left, striding across the porch, jamming his hat farther down on his head.

She hurried up to the room that was still hers—white furniture, frilly white curtains, a view of the front and the big oaks that had been planted years ago by her grandfather.

She paused to stare at her canopied bed. Swamped with memories, she could envision making love in that bed with Gabe the summer she had been twenty-one. They'd had the house to themselves and she had wanted to show Gabe her home. In her bedroom, he had prowled around the room looking at everything until he drew her into his embrace for a kiss. They had made love right here, in her bedroom.

She thought now about the result of that afternoon, Rebecca. At this point in time, she couldn't guess how Gabe would feel if he discovered the truth. She suspected he'd feel the same as he would have six years ago.

Except for himself, Gabe had never really had any responsibilities. He was immensely wealthy, a millionaire; his older brother had grown up running interference between Gabe and their strong-willed father. She'd worried over her decision countless times, but she always came to the same conclusion—for her sake and for Gabe's, to save them both and to save their child from upheaval and unhappiness, Rebecca would remain a secret.

An ache deep inside started and she gave herself a small shake, closing her eyes as if that would shut out all memories of him. She busied herself unpacking and getting ready for her appointment with the agency in Lubbock.

Picking up her phone, she called home. First, she talked to her mother and then she listened to her daughter's high-pitched voice as she came on the phone.

"I miss you, Mommy," Rebecca said.

"I miss you, too," Maddie replied, feeling her insides clutch. She always hated to be away from Rebecca, especially overnight, and she missed her daughter intensely. It had been a couple of hours since the call she made after landing at DFW. She could imagine Rebecca's big blue eyes, her brown hair falling almost to her shoulders. It was Rebecca's blue eyes that would give away the truth if Gabe ever saw her. "I miss you terribly," she said.

"Come home."

"I will as soon as I can. Grandma is with you and she said you are baking cookies. You will get a cookie soon."

Maddie sat in a rocker and talked to her five-year-old for the next twenty minutes. Finally, Rebecca said goodbye and Maddie's mother, Tracie, came back on the phone. They talked another fifteen minutes before Maddie ended the call.

Touching her phone, Maddie looked at Rebecca's picture, clutching it to her heart for a moment and then staring intently at it. Long ago she had locked away wishful thinking. She had stopped imagining what might be between her and Rebecca's father, always reminding herself that Gabe was not ready for fatherhood or marriage. He probably never would be. And she had her own dreams, for a career and a life in the city. She didn't want to spend her adult life on a ranch.

These painful thoughts and memories were what she had dreaded about this trip. She'd hoped she wouldn't encounter Gabe, and now that she had, she was still certain it was best he didn't learn about his daughter. If she could get through this week, she would leave Texas for good and her heartache over Gabe would fade, as it had before.

Maddie reassured herself that she could spend this evening surrounded by old friends, cut the time short and tell Gabe goodbye early. If so, their time together would be over and she wouldn't see him again.

Two

Gabe walked across the familiar porch, remembering all the times before when he'd taken the same walk to pick up Maddie. Now, when she swung open the door, his heart pounded just as it had six years ago. She wore a dark blue, knee-length, sleeveless dress with a scoop neckline that revealed gorgeous curves. Her blond hair was caught up high on her head and fell freely in back.

His mouth went dry and he thought again that she was far more beautiful now than she had been at twenty-one. "You look fantastic," he said in a husky tone.

"Thank you. You look rather nice yourself," she added, sounding polite. "I have my purse and I'm ready to go."

Why hadn't he visited her after she moved away? He had always remembered her bitterness when they had parted and he had worked at trying to forget her. Now memories of the good times bombarded him. He'd always liked being with her. She had been gorgeous since she turned eighteen. Now she was devastating.

He inhaled an exotic scent he could not identify.

"I want to hear about the years since I last saw you," he said as he climbed into the car.

He listened while she talked about her job, her graduation from the university in Gainesville and settling in Miami where her grandparents lived. She barely mentioned her family, but he knew from past conversations that they were important to her.

"I'm still surprised to find you here. We should have kept in touch, Maddie."

"We're far apart, in years, in geographical areas, in lifestyles, in goals."

"We have a friendship that can bridge all that, and we have this attraction between us. Now that you're grown up, the years no longer matter."

"Gabe, where are we going?" she asked, looking out the side window as he turned through the front gate. "This is your ranch."

"Yep, it is. I thought I'd cook tonight. If I take you out anywhere in this county, or any of the surrounding ones, you'll have other people welcoming you back all night and guys wanting to dance and talk. I don't care to sit and watch."

She laughed. "You can't be jealous. And I know you're never bored."

"Maybe I can be."

"Which? Bored or jealous?" she asked, drawing out the word *jealous*. When he glanced at her, she smiled.

"I would be green with jealousy," he replied, flirting with her. "You're here and I want you with me exclusively. Those other guys can wait for their chances to find you with a flat tire. I'm not sharing."

She laughed, a merry sound he hadn't heard in too long. "Don't be ridiculous. You haven't seen me at all for the past six years. You have no idea who I see or if half a dozen guys are in my life."

"They aren't. You told me so earlier today," he said, grinning at her. "And for now, I know that I'm in your life and that's that."

"Still arrogant, Gabe."

"You're a gorgeous brown-eyed blonde who makes me weak in the knees. I'm not letting you out of my sight."

"I know better than to believe that 'weak in the knees' stuff."

"All right. Maybe not weak in the knees. But my heart pounds and I can't get my breath and my palms are sweaty—"

"Stop!" she exclaimed. "That's laying it on too thick."

"Or maybe I remember what great times we had together."

"We did have those," she replied with a wistful note in her voice.

"Yet I don't hear one word about you wanting to be with me, or being glad I want you all to myself, or finding this evening exciting, or anything else I would like to hear."

"I said all that when I was eighteen, nineteen and twenty," she remarked drily.

"Not enough, you didn't," he said. His insides roiled. He had been kidding and flirting, but her reaction was having a surprisingly deep impact on him.

"It's been too long, Maddie. Why didn't you come see your grandfather?"

"There was no need. He came to Florida several

times a year. He'd stay a month at a time, sometimes. The older he got the more often he came and the longer he stayed. Mom tried to get him to move there to be with all of us, but he wouldn't leave Texas. Probably felt the same way about it that you do."

"I should have called you."

"I really figured you had moved on with your life. I moved on with mine."

"You're finally a grown woman and I don't have to worry about going out with someone too young."

"As if you ever worried about that," she remarked. "It didn't keep you from asking me out."

"You were irresistible and you still are. I'm glad you're here. You're absolutely certain you don't want to keep the ranch so you can come back sometimes?"

"Positive. You know my dream has always been to get away from it."

"When you leave this time, you won't be coming back, will you?"

"No. There's no reason to return, and I wouldn't have any place to stay."

"I intend to give you a reason to want to return," he stated. "Besides, darlin', you can always bunk with me," he drawled in a husky voice, holding her hand in his. Her skin was smooth, her hand warm and soft.

"Sure, I can." She laughed, and he gave her a glance before quickly returning his attention to the ranch road. "Someday, Gabe, you might actually marry. I don't believe a wife would welcome me with open arms."

"I would," he said.

"You're still not ready to settle. Some things never change," she said. "I'm sure you're the fun loving, carefree guy you've always been."

"You say that like you're declaring I have measles.

You might be surprised. Time changes people." He looked down at her bare hand. "You haven't settled either, Maddie."

"More than you have," she said, staring out the car window.

"It will surprise you to know that I've built my own home out here."

"Now that I'll be happy to see. So you don't live with the family in the main house?"

"No. Jake and I bought Dad's shares of the ranch. I'm building because I want my own place," he said as they passed within sight of Jake's house.

"I understand that. And with your money, you don't have to worry about maintaining it or even doing your own cooking. Your dad lost interest in the ranch?"

"Dad bought a place on a lake in the Hill Country. The original house is now Jake's."

"Oh, my gosh! Is that your house?"

"Yes, it is," Gabe said.

"It's the size of a hotel," she said as he wound up the front driveway. "And they're still building," she added, staring at his home. "This is never what I would have imagined for you."

"That's interesting. What did you expect to see?"

"Something much smaller, very rustic, very masculine. You have a beautiful, old-fashioned, warm looking mansion. An enormous mansion. You can't possibly need all that space. You must be planning on marriage."

"I'm older, Maddie. Maybe it's time to settle down," he said. She turned to him. He looked at her and then back at the road. "You're shocked by my answer. A lot of space suits me and I'll have what I want in the future. It gives me room. That's one reason I love the ranch—open space. Cities feel crowded, closed in. Out here, there's peace and quiet."

"There's that, all right. You can sit and watch the grass grow. Your mansion amazes me."

"I'll have what I want in it, a theater room, a gym, an office. I'll show it to you."

"I would never have guessed you wanted something as lavish as this. Especially out here on the ranch. Landscaping, fountains. I'm sure you have a swimming pool."

"You're right. See, you don't totally have me figured out."

"I can say the same," she replied, turning to give him a direct look. As his attention swung back to the road, he wondered how much she had changed while she had been away.

He parked in front of his house, cut the engine and turned to her. "So we still have a lot to discover about each other," he said quietly.

"Don't get ideas, Gabe. It isn't going to happen. I plan to take care of business and then I'm gone forever."

"Maybe. Sometimes life can surprise you."

"May I quote you on that one?"

Her answer startled him and his eyes narrowed. "You've changed, Maddie."

"How so?"

He continued to study her, looking into her dark eyes. "You're more sophisticated, less open."

"Time and experience, I guess," she replied. While he gazed at her, silence stretched between them. For the first time since he'd known her, Maddie had an air of mystery about her. She had always been totally open with him, pouring out all her feelings. That was over.

She was poised, self-contained and self-assured, and he was more intrigued than ever.

"Come have a look at my home," he said, and climbed out of the car, hurrying to open her door. As they walked up the front steps, she looked around.

"This is a beautiful porch. A bit old-fashioned, which surprises me again," she said.

"See. There are still facets of my personality for you to discover."

"Only if I want to learn more. Because of our past, you're assuming that I do. I'm not twenty-one anymore. I grew up."

"Did you ever, Maddie," he said, his husky tone returning. "You're a gorgeous woman. My pulse doesn't stop racing when I'm around you."

"We're old friends, Gabe. That's it," she stated in such a no-nonsense tone that he felt an invisible wall between them.

"We're a hell of a lot more than that," he said, unlocking his door and turning off the alarm. He stepped back out and picked her up.

With a yelp, she wrapped an arm around his neck. "What do you think you're doing?"

"I'm carrying you across the threshold of my house as a way to welcome you. I know you're not my bride," he said, relishing holding her and breaking through the barrier she wanted to erect between them. Big brown eyes only inches from his face gazed back at him. He could detect the exotic scent she wore. Warm and soft, she was light in his arms and he didn't want to set her down. The air between them crackled with awareness and desire. The temperature in the entrance hall climbed.

Her eyes held fire in their dark depths and her lips

parted slightly. With their gazes locked, he stood her on her feet. They faced each other with only inches separating them. For him, time didn't exist. It was as if the past six years had vanished. He wanted to kiss her and she looked as if she wanted him to.

When he framed her face with his hands, she caught his wrists in each hand. "Gabe, we shouldn't go back there," she whispered.

"It's a welcome home kiss," he said, lowering his hands to her waist. He leaned closer and his mouth covered hers.

Maddie closed her eyes. She did not have the willpower to say no. She wanted his kiss, even though she knew what a hazard it would be to her peace of mind. To her whole life. She *couldn't* get involved with him again.

Yet she wrapped her arms around his waist and kissed him in return, soaring in a dizzying spiral while heat started low inside her, filling her.

Delight and desire roiled in her. Years fell away and no longer mattered. For a moment, the only significance was Gabe's mouth on hers. The man she loved—he always had been, from her first crush. In that moment, with his lips on hers, she had to face the fact that she loved him still.

Longing consumed her while his kisses enticed her to toss away caution. Her erratic breathing matched his. It was Gabe in her arms. Her tongue thrust deep. She wanted to set him ablaze as he did her.

She moaned softly in pleasure, feeling his hand drift across her shoulders. His caresses down her back and over her bottom brought her back to her senses.

"Gabe," she whispered. "We have to stop."

He raised his head slightly, the look in his blue eyes

stabbing her. "Why? You're not committed to anyone else. Neither am I. This kiss is for old times' sake and a welcome back to Texas."

She moved out of his embrace. "Don't complicate my life. I'm selling the ranch, returning to Florida and not coming back here. Don't make me want to return Texas. I don't want ties here," she said, too aware that she already had a tie to Gabe that she could never unravel.

"Those are strong words, Maddie. As if you have a grudge."

"No. I have a satisfying life in Florida that I love. I don't want it upset."

"It was only a few welcome-back kisses. You didn't want to return when it was hell of a lot more," he said. His breathing was still ragged, his blue gaze smoldering. "Come on. I'll show you around and then we'll have a drink and I'll cook steaks."

"That's fine," she answered, trying to regain her composure. She walked past him, heading for the first open door off the entrance hall. She entered a dining room. Centered below a crystal chandelier stood a table surrounded by sixteen chairs. "This is a beautiful room," she remarked.

"Don't sound so shocked. Even after you saw the exterior, you expected something rustic, didn't you?"

"Actually, yes. You've always been so into being a cowboy."

"My family room is where I went with Western furnishings. I'll show you. We'll go through the kitchen on the way."

She walked beside him through the dining room and into a spacious white kitchen. At the far end was a cozy breakfast area with another large table, a sofa and chairs, and a huge brick fireplace.

"This is wonderful, Gabe. You've done a good job. Did you plan all this yourself?"

"I had a decorator. I explained what I'd like and she did the rest. I had final approval, of course, but most of her choices suited me fine."

"This room is grand."

"Thank you. I'm glad you like it, Maddie. My office is close to the kitchen. Let me show you."

He took her down a wide hallway into a large room. He watched as Maddie surveyed the room.

"Gabe, this is amazing. Two desks. Why do you have six computers?" Without waiting for an answer, she turned to look at the rest of the room. "You have everything. Television, fax machines, copiers. You don't need this for ranching."

"I do my own investments, and I keep up with world markets. I enjoy it, and I've had some success with it."

She turned to study him. "You've surprised me again."

"I think on this one, I might have surprised my family, too."

"Does Jake consult you about investments?" she asked as her eyes narrowed.

"As a matter of fact, he does. I did a little investing for him at first. Now I do all of his personal investments."

"That's impressive."

"Not really. It's something I like, and I've been lucky. Jake and I will be worth more than Dad soon."

She inhaled, thinking about Rebecca. Gabe could do so much for his daughter. Was she doing the wrong thing, keeping Rebecca hidden from him?

"I thought we'd eat on the patio," he said, leading her back through the kitchen and outside. She stepped out to a partially enclosed, air-conditioned patio that overlooked an Olympic-size swimming pool.

"This is beautiful, too, Gabe," she said with a smile. "You can go ahead and say it. I thought I knew what kind of house you would like, but you've surprised me. A very pleasant surprise, I might add. You had an excellent decorator."

"Thanks, I think. So how different is my place from yours?"

She laughed. "My little house would fit in your dining room and kitchen. It's small and the decor is far less expensive."

"That isn't what I meant."

"It's the same style of decor."

"That's why you're so shocked. Just because I love ranching and you've always wanted to get away from Texas, you thought we were opposites in everything. What would you like to drink? I have a well stocked bar."

"How about iced tea?"

"Coming right up," he said, walking behind a bar.

She climbed on one of the high stools in front of him, crossed her legs and looked around. "You have fancy outdoor furniture, too. Do you spend a lot of time out here?" she asked, turning back and catching him looking at her legs.

"I swim often," he replied, his gaze holding hers for a long moment. While they talked about his house in a very ordinary conversation, she could still feel the tension and sparks between them. "I enjoy the patio and pool, and I'm sure I will even more as time passes."

"Except you'll be working. You'll work on the ranch and you won't relax and enjoy this any more than you do now."

"You might be right on that one. What kind of hours do you have when you're in Florida?"

"Long," she remarked drily as he handed her the iced tea. She took a sip, watching him pour his own drink and thinking of how their daughter had Gabe's coloring. What would he be like with a child? She had never seen him interacting with children.

"Let's go sit where it's more comfortable," he said.

They crossed the patio to a thickly cushioned redwood sofa. She sat in a corner and he moved close to face her.

"Tell me about your life in Miami and how it's so different from being here."

"Monday through Friday morning, I go into the office. I show houses, my time fluctuates. It's an exciting, varied job and I love it," she said, aware they sat with knees touching. Gabe had stretched out one long arm to play with locks of her hair. Each tug on her scalp made her tingle.

It was difficult to ignore the effect he had on her. Had he noticed the slight breathlessness in her voice? While she wanted to kiss him again, she couldn't afford to fall more deeply in love with him. She kept busy in Florida, finding it easier as time passed to avoid thinking about Gabe. She remembered now that when she was around him, she had little resistance. It had never occurred to her that he would bring her to his house for dinner where it would only be the two of them. A whole evening with Gabe, while her insides fizzed with excitement. She reminded herself to keep up her guard. Any feelings he created in her now would only disturb ghosts of the past she did not want disturbed.

"There has to be more than that to your life for you to love Florida so much," he said.

"Often I spend free time at the beach. My family is all nearby and I have friends. I love it. I love the city and the activity."

"Don't you still have close friends in Dallas? I remember you used to."

"Yes, I do. We keep in touch. I've even had two excellent job offers from there, one right after I graduated and one more recently."

"Did you give them any consideration?"

"Not really. I'm happy where I am. I like Dallas, and at one point in time, I would have accepted work there, but not now."

They sat and talked until Gabe put the steaks on. She strolled to the cooker with him. In minutes, spirals of gray smoke escaped from the covered grill while Gabe put bowls of tossed green salad on the table. Next, he retrieved two potatoes from the oven and they each fixed their own with butter, chives and sour cream. By the time he had steamed asparagus, the steaks were ready. They sat near a fountain on the patio.

"I'm amazed. I've never seen you do all this yourself," she said, waving her hand over the table and the food.

"I still say you don't know me as well as you think you do. Time changes people. I want to get to know you all over again, Maddie."

"Sorry, Gabe. There isn't time for it. We have tonight. That's all."

"Maybe," he said, his blue eyes intent on her.

"I had forgotten you have a stubborn streak in you."

"I think it might match the one you have," he replied with a smile. He raised his glass. "Here's to memories and new discoveries."

"Here's to seeing an old friend and wishing you a wonderful future. You're a nice guy, Gabe Benton."

One corner of his mouth lifted in a slight smile. "You keep trying to hold me at arm's length. We've been friends too long for this 'I barely know you' attitude. I'm getting past it, Maddie." On the last word, his voice lowered and the look she received made her tingle.

"Maybe. In the meantime, dinner is getting cold."

After the first bite of steak, she smiled. "This is heavenly."

"I'd rather watch you than eat," he stated.

"That's ridiculous," she replied, hating the breathlessness that fairly shouted her true reaction to him. "Besides, I'll bet you said that to the last person you invited out here."

"Truthfully, I've never said that to anyone before."

She drew in a deep breath. "It's not going to get you anywhere saying it now," she stated, glad her voice had gained a note of aloofness.

He smiled at her, shattering any illusion she might have had about him cooling his flirting.

"This is a delicious steak," she said, hoping to keep the topic neutral.

"Not nearly as delicious as your kisses."

She closed her eyes and chewed, feeling her face flush because of his remark. "I'm not listening to you. I'm eating this steak," she said. They were skirting dangerous territory. She had gotten over the past and shut Gabe out of her life. It had taken time, and it had not been easy. Now, with his flirting and charm, he was trying to get back into her life, but she had no place for him there.

"You're not looking at me, but I know you hear me," he said, laughter in his voice. "Your kisses are delicious and have taken away my appetite for what's on this table. If I hadn't found you on the highway, would you have come to Texas and then gone home to Florida without seeing me?"

As soon as he asked, her eyes flew open. She felt ensnared in his gaze. "Yes, I would have."

To her surprise, he winced. "Was it because of the way we parted?"

"Since the last summer we were together, our lives have changed. I'm different and you're different. We're really strangers now, except for childhood memories."

He leaned across the table and caught her hand lightly, rubbing his thumb over the inside of her wrist. "There's no way we're strangers, and we have a hell of a lot more than 'childhood memories' between us. You know better than that. Holding you in my arms, making love for hours under the stars—those were not childish memories," he said in a husky voice that wrapped her in a blanket of intimacy. "I thought our last summer was fantastic."

She couldn't get her breath, and she forgot about dinner. She tried to regain her composure and keep a wall up between them. She slipped her hand out of his and leaned back a fraction.

"What I want in life has changed since I left here," she said, again glad her voice held a firmness she wasn't actually feeling. She looked down at her plate blankly and then took a bite, even though her appetite had fled.

"What I want in life is changing, too, Maddie. We're older. We want different things, have different needs now than we did then. We know each other, and we don't know each other at the same time. Discovery and reunion are both great."

"Don't, Gabe," she said, shaking her head and placing her fork on her plate.

"I think that's part of you talking to me. There's still part of you who is happy to be with me."

"True enough. But the part of me that is cautious about this reunion is the intelligent, reasoning part. The part that rules my life."

He tilted her chin up and leaned close again. "Then watch out, Maddie, because I intend to cater to the other part, the emotional part that responds to me when we kiss."

"It's sheer foolishness that there are moments I can't resist you," she replied. His words had made her heart pound and now she was caught in his crystal blue gaze. Panic gripped her because she was tumbling rapidly into something she'd hoped to avoid. "We're not going to rekindle what we had. We've both moved on and our lives have changed."

"Some things haven't changed at all," he replied, running his index finger lightly down her cheek.

"I never thought we'd be having an intimate one-on-one dinner at your house tonight. You know what I expected."

"Disappointed so far?"

"You know I'm not. I want to eat and talk and remain friends. I don't want to return to being lovers."

"You eat what you want. We have the whole evening."

"I can see the plans in your eyes," she said, and shook her head. "It won't happen, Gabe."

"What do you think you can see?"

"Seduction," she stated bluntly. Her cell phone rang, and she saw it was a call from home, sending another chill down her spine. She didn't want to take the call in front of Gabe. "Will you excuse me for a moment?"

He nodded and she got up to walk away, aware he could hear the first part of her conversation as Rebecca said hello.

"Mommy, I miss you."

"Hi. What are you doing?" she asked, going into the kitchen. Her heart lurched with love at the sound of her daughter's voice. She missed Rebecca and wished she could hold her.

"I'm talking to you."

"I know you're talking to me. Are you having fun?" Maddie asked softly, assured of the answer, because Rebecca loved to spend time with her grandmother.

Maddie heard a clatter and then her mother said hello.

"Sorry, Maddie, Rebecca got the phone and called while I was running her bath. She knows which number is your one-digit call."

"That's all right. I'm eating dinner. Is everything okay?"

"We're fine. I'm getting her ready for bed. She wanted to talk to you. Now she's getting out her bath toys."

"It's always great to talk." Maddie checked over her shoulder, hoping Gabe could not hear her now.

"Are you through for today?"

"Yes. I'm out for dinner with Gabe," she said, avoiding any mention of eating at his ranch.

"Is that wise?"

She wanted to answer no, it wasn't smart at all, but she would never admit that she hadn't been able to resist his invitation. Instead, she reported the events of the day to her mother. She glanced back outside at Gabe, who sat relaxed, sipping his drink, his profile clear to her. She turned her back on him.

"I'll let you tell Rebecca good-night."

"Night, Mommy. I love you," Rebecca said.

Maddie smiled. "Night, sweet baby. I love you, too, and I miss you so-o-o much. Oodles of hugs to you," she added in a low tone.

"Come home."

"I will soon, I promise," she said, feeling an ache. Rarely away from Rebecca overnight, she missed her daughter. She switched off her phone and returned to the table, seeing the curious expression on Gabe's face.

"Call from a close friend?"

"My mother, actually," she said, sitting to finish her dinner. "She expected to find me alone."

"Do you live close to your mother?" he asked, and she noticed he was not eating.

"Very close. She's next door."

"That makes it easy," he said.

"I heard your brother married Caitlin Santerre."

"That's right. Jake is very happily married as of this past winter. Caitlin is a freelance photographer with her own galleries. She's very good. And, yes, she is a Santerre."

"That was a shock. I thought maybe someone got it wrong. A Benton marrying a Santerre. End of the feud."

"Unless Will Santerre returns to Texas, but he told Jake he never would. He sold the family ranch to Jake and now we've got an oil well."

"Which I'm sure fell into your line of work."

"Yes, it did. Jake was getting to be a menace to himself at work, he was so crazy in love."

"Which you've always managed to avoid."

"Maybe I was waiting for you to come home," he said, leaning closer to run his finger along her cheek again.

She wrinkled her nose at him. "I know better than

that, too. There's really only one person in your life, and that is Gabriel Benton."

"I'm a bachelor. It goes with the territory."

"So when you decided to retire from the corporate world and live on the ranch, name the people you consulted about your decision?"

He shook his head. "You got me on that one. I didn't consult anyone."

"That's right. Gabriel Benton is the only one involved. Enough said."

"I don't recall you being tough or cynical. I remember someone sweet as sugar."

"I've been out in the real world a while."

"If you're through eating, let's move elsewhere."

"It was a wonderful dinner. What a good husband you'll make someday," she said with amusement.

"I'm glad to hear you admit that," he answered. "Bring your drink and let me show you something else."

Perplexed, wondering where they were going, she picked up her iced tea and followed him down the hall. They entered a large billiard room with polished oak floors. A billiard table stood to one side of the room. Gabe switched on a few low lights and turned on music.

He crossed the room to take her drink and set it on a table. "Let's dance."

A two-step played. She hadn't danced one in years, so she faced him and they danced on the open floor beside the billiard table.

He spun her around and pulled her close, his boots scraping on the oak floor.

When the dance ended she laughed. "That was great, Gabe. I haven't danced a two-step in too long to remember."

"A polka's up next."

Maddie's cell phone rang and she pulled it out of a pocket and waved it at him. "If you'll excuse me," she said, turning and walking into the hall to talk.

When she returned, a ballad was playing. Gabe stepped close. He put one hand on her waist and he held her hand with his other one.

"Sorry about the call," she said. "Work."

"That's fine. Take all the calls you want. I don't mind."

"Thanks." As they danced, she looked up and was mesmerized. She was dancing in Gabe's arms again. It brought back too many memories.

"Things were good between us, Maddie," he said solemnly.

"I know they were, until we parted. Then they weren't. Soon I had left here and you did, too."

"I remember when you were a little kid. When your dad brought you to our ranch, you'd follow me everywhere I went."

"Thank heavens I outgrew that!"

He smiled at her. "I'd be happy for you to follow me everywhere now."

"I don't think you mean that for one second. It won't happen anyway, so we'll never really know."

He turned a long lock of Maddie's blond hair in his fingers. "Your hair was probably the envy of all the girls in school."

"I don't think so."

"It's gorgeous now."

"Thank you."

"Remember when we'd meet and have those early morning rides at sunrise—something I haven't done in years."

"Neither have I, but that I don't miss. Life changes, Gabe."

He pulled her closer and they danced in silence. They had always danced well together. She remembered how easy it had been to follow his lead. Being in his arms, dancing with him, spending time with him—every moment reawakened memories and brought back ties she thought she had severed. *Get through the night and tell him goodbye.*

When the ballad ended and another began, Gabe looked down at her. Their gazes met and the air between them crackled with electricity. His arm around her waist tightened, and he started to kiss her.

"This is where I need to say no, no, no, although I can't imagine it would have any effect if I did," she whispered.

"You don't really want to say no," he said, and then kissed her. His arms banded her waist while she wrapped hers around his neck. His tongue went deeply into her mouth, stroking, stirring memories, creating new ones.

Time spun away while they kissed. She wanted him more with each breath, but she knew she couldn't get involved with him. Her future—Rebecca's future— depended on avoiding that.

He ran his hand down her back, caressing her bottom lightly. His hand drifted up again while he continued to kiss her senseless.

How long they kissed, she didn't know. Still kissing her, Gabe picked her up and carried her to the sofa. He sat, cradling her on his lap.

Her heart pounded and she ached inside, deep down. Physically, she wanted him with all her being. But logically, it was the cold, hard truth that getting

entangled with Gabe would ruin the life she'd built. She
had a secret child to keep from him. Intimacy would
only lead him to discover the truth.

Gabe caressed her nape and passion once more
consumed her. She wound her fingers in his thick hair
and unfastened the buttons of his white shirt with her
other hand. In minutes, she'd pushed away the white
shirt and toyed with his brown chest hair while they
continued kissing.

Gabe's hand moved to her throat and then slipped
lower, following the curve of the neckline of her dress.

She gasped with pleasure and then moaned softly.
For a moment, she relished his caresses. She was with
the man she had loved all her life. How easy it would
be to pick up where they'd left off. And how disastrous.
She gripped his wrist, moving his hand.

"This has to stop," she declared, gasping for breath.
"That summer you left—I won't go through that again."
She sat up, straightening her dress. His blue eyes were
filled with fire. Locks of his brown hair tumbled on his
forehead.

"It was only a few kisses," he said quietly. "It's not
the same as that summer. And back then, I needed to
leave, for my job."

"That's over and done, but I don't ever want to feel
that way again." She stood and smoothed her dress.

"I was only in Nigeria for eight months. You could
have continued your education at Tech, and when I
returned, I'd have been there for you."

"Gabe, it's ridiculous to argue now, but you would
not have 'been there for me,'" she said. "You were never
into commitment, and you certainly weren't at that point
in your life. And I was."

"I suppose you're right on all counts," he admitted,

surprising her. He stood. "I'll get our drinks. Come sit here and we can talk."

She returned to the sofa. Gabe picked up his cold bottle of beer and joined her, sitting close. He took a sip and turned to face her.

They sat and talked until almost midnight. She asked about the last rodeo he had participated in, listening and laughing as he talked about his bronc riding. That led to what she had been doing and she told him about her family trip to France and Italy and how much she had enjoyed the cathedrals she had seen. Finally, when she saw it was only minutes until midnight, she said, "I should get home now. I don't usually stay out late. If my family should call me, they would be in a panic if I'm not home."

"Your mother surely won't call at this hour. Besides, she obviously knows to try your cell phone. I remember she kept close track of you, but you're a grown woman now."

"She still worries. She wasn't happy about my plans to stay alone at the ranch. I think she's forgotten how safe it is here."

"You know you can stay right here with me."

"Oh, right. As if that would be a peaceful night's rest."

She gave him an exasperated glare.

He threw up his hands. "Okay. I know that look. I'll take you back to your ranch now."

She smiled. "I knew you'd do what I asked. Thank you, Gabe," she said sweetly.

He picked her up and spun her around. She yelped while she clung to his shoulders. "Hey!"

"I'm glad to see you and wanted to do that one more time. I wanted to hold you and have you hold me. I wanted to hear you laugh. Maddie, I'm glad you're back," he said, suddenly sounding earnest. Her heart lurched.

"I'm not really back. I left your life a long time ago," she replied, feeling the tension escalate between them once again.

He inhaled deeply. "I'm going to change your mind about leaving again." The note of steel in his tone made her heart beat faster. Once, she would have been thrilled to hear those words from him. Now, they threatened her peaceful life.

"Don't try to make a project of me. Besides, you haven't missed me."

"I did miss you," he said. "I just didn't realize how much. You've been in my life even when we were both kids. When you moved away, you left a void."

His words wrapped around her, binding her heart to him in ways she wouldn't be able to forget. In ways she couldn't deal with now. "Gabe, you don't mean it. You would have come after me if you'd felt that strongly."

"It took a long time for me to realize the cause of my dissatisfaction. Even longer to face that my life had changed because you were no longer in it."

"I need to get home," she said abruptly. She didn't want another broken heart. It had taken her years to mend her last one.

He leaned forward to touch her lips with his again, a fiery, possessive kiss that bound her heart as tightly as his words had.

When he raised his head, she looked into determined blue eyes. He set her on her feet and their gazes still held. With an effort, she turned toward the door.

They walked through the house together and out to his car. When they stepped into the cool night, Gabe draped his arm across her shoulders and pulled her close against him.

"Anyone who works for you staying at the house with you?"

"No, there's no one staying with me."

"In all seriousness, you could stay here, you know. You can have a separate bedroom, and you'll have all the peace and quiet and privacy you want."

"I better stay at my place," she replied, doing the smart thing. "I've always felt safe at home. Besides, I have a direct line to Sol's house."

"That's good to know. He'd come on the run if you needed him."

At the car, Gabe turned her to face him, keeping his arm around her.

"Let me take you to dinner again tomorrow night. I won't bring you over here. We'll go somewhere special."

"Thanks, Gabe. Tonight was great. You know I had a great time—"

"Maddie, let's have another few hours together," he said, interrupting what she had been about to say. "A dinner is harmless. You'll sell the place soon. You could sell it by the weekend, and then you'll return to Florida. Let's go out together again before you leave," he said, bending his knees so he could look into her eyes.

She argued with herself, a tiny voice screaming to turn him down. That voice was being drowned out by another inner voice shouting yes. And Gabe was looking at her with those sexy blue eyes that spun a magic spell.

"Yes, Gabe. Against all logic and good judgment, I'll have dinner with you again."

He gave her a tiny squeeze. "I'm glad. We'll have a super time." He leaned forward to brush a kiss on her forehead, then her lips.

He held open the passenger-side door for her, closed it and strode around the car to slide behind the wheel. They talked all the way to her ranch and then sat in the driveway talking for another hour. It was into the early-morning hours when he walked her to the door.

He entered with her and waited while she switched off her alarm and turned on the lights. "It's been a great evening, Maddie. I'm glad you're back, even if it's temporary." Stepping closer, he brushed another kiss on her lips. His mouth was warm, enticing, coaxing more kisses.

"Gabe," she said, ending the kiss.

He looked over her head to the room beyond her. "This is a big house out in a remote spot. You're accustomed to a big city, a house with neighbors, your mother close by. I'll sleep down here on the couch."

"Sol is not far away."

"He's about four minutes if he comes on a dead run. I can stretch out on the sofa and you'll never know I'm here."

"I'm not a little kid any longer. You don't have to protect me and hover around."

"I'll be the one to decide about hovering and I know you are definitely not a little kid any longer. I've known that since you were seventeen," he drawled in a softer tone that caused her belly to flutter.

"In the morning, I have an appointment in town at nine o'clock."

"I can call you way earlier than that. Or I can tiptoe out before you wake up."

"Gabe, I'll be fine."

"I know, but I'll worry. Your mother will feel better—even Sol would say it's a good idea. Now, no more arguments. I'm on the sofa."

She shook her head. "If you get kinks in your back, it's your own fault. There's nothing yummy here for breakfast because I drink coffee and orange juice and eat a piece of toast. Without butter."

"Fine with me."

She stood with her hands on her hips, staring at him in consternation, certain she would not shake him out of the house tonight. "Gabe, you know it's as safe here as if I were sleeping in the middle of the sheriff's office."

"It will be, with me here," he replied, grinning.

She shook her head in exasperation. "I'll lock up and then I'm going upstairs to bed."

"Fine and dandy. I'll stay downstairs. I remember my way around."

"Do you really?" she asked, surprised. She threw up her hands. "Stay. I'll be up at six. I'll let you out and lock the door behind you. I'm not getting you a pillow or anything, Gabe. I don't want you doing this."

He smiled. "I won't worry. Sol won't worry, because he'll see my car and you can tell him that I slept on the sofa."

"I'm not telling Sol anything."

"Suit yourself, Maddie. 'Night." Gabe brushed a kiss on her lips and headed off to the front living room.

She shook her head, locked up and went upstairs, leaving the downstairs lights on for Gabe to worry with.

She was going out with him again. She rubbed her forehead and glanced over her shoulder, seeing the light still spilling from the front room. He'd always been so protective! He had a strong sense of duty. Six years ago, she had been certain that if she told him about her pregnancy, he would have insisted they marry out of a misguided sense of honor. He would have been far more stubborn and insistent about that than he had been about staying tonight. And her future would have been as ruined as his. Even after seeing how much he'd changed, and even though she wished Rebecca knew her father, she still felt justified in her actions.

The evening had been exciting—and dangerous to her heart. Gabe was older now and, to her surprise, he had grown more responsible, even more appealing than he had been before. He had changed. His house had been a big shock, not at all what she'd expected. And he'd missed her—she was still trying to hold that at bay.

Maybe they both had grown up during their years of separation. And if it turned out Gabe *had* grown up, she might have to rethink the future.

She thought of Rebecca again, unable to keep from wondering what it would be like if the three of them were together.

Three

Stretched out on the sofa, Gabe reflected on what he had admitted to Maddie—something he had never said aloud before in his life. Not even to his brother, Jake, the person he was the closest to. He hadn't wanted to face the truth six years ago: that Maddie's departure was the source of his dissatisfaction with life. It had taken him a long time to realize that his restlessness had only started after he'd returned home to find that Maddie had moved to Florida.

He didn't know whether or not she had believed him tonight, but he had been truthful. He had missed her. He hadn't gone after her because, at first, she'd ended the relationship before either of them left West Texas. And, then, he had thought she'd come back to Texas. Once time had passed, he hadn't been sure of his welcome. But now he knew that she still responded to him physically. He expected to overcome the barriers she kept putting between them.

Maddie had emphatically declared there was no man in her life, but he wondered. Each time she had answered her cell phone, she had spoken in a soft, guarded voice. She had not been talking to her mother, or a grandmother either. Not in that deep, soft tone. Both calls had come from someone she cared about.

His thoughts shifted to the coming day. He was meeting his brother and his brother's best friends for breakfast in Dallas at seven. He'd have to take his small plane. And he'd have to get out of Maddie's house before six, but night would be over.

Six o'clock was only a few hours away, but sleep wouldn't come. He couldn't get Maddie out of his thoughts. If she sold the ranch and left, he would go to Florida to see her this time. He wouldn't let her disappear from his life again.

With that determination still fresh in his mind, Gabe left for Dallas the next morning without waking Maddie.

He walked into the restaurant several minutes late and spotted his brother and friends sitting at a large round table in the corner. Gabe had always tagged along with Jake and his buddies. Growing up, he had been the younger brother and they had put up with him. Once grown, the slight difference in their ages no longer mattered. Gabe had become close friends with Tony Ryder, a driven, near-billionaire hotel magnate who had recently married. With thick, unruly black curls and dark eyes, Tony looked more like a Vegas roulette dealer than the tough businessman he was.

Nick Rafford had been the first in the group to marry and had wed the woman who had adopted his deceased brother's baby. Now they had their own little girl and Nick seemed more relaxed, happier. Gabe wondered if that would happen to Jake because of his marriage.

As Gabe hurried to join them, Jake saw him coming and stood to greet him. "Good morning. Here's my cowboy brother," he said, smiling at Gabe, who had dressed in slacks, but wore his broad-brimmed hat and his Western boots. Gabe shook hands with his older brother, feeling as close to Jake as he thought it was possible to feel. Jake had always included Gabe in things he did.

Dressed in suits, the others would leave for work as soon as breakfast was over. Gabe went around the table to shake hands with each man

"Sorry, I got a little delayed."

"We're used to it. Brother even ordered for you," Nick remarked drily.

Gabe turned to Jake. "So what did you order?"

"Your usual—pancakes, poached egg, bacon, orange juice."

"Sounds good, thanks. How are all the families?" he asked, and listened as each one answered, with Nick producing pictures of his two children, Michael and Emily.

"Jake, tell him your news before one of us does," Tony said.

"What don't I know that everyone else does?" Gabe asked his brother, realizing Jake hadn't stopped smiling since saying hello.

"Caitlin is expecting a child," Jake said, grinning broadly. "You're going to be an uncle, kid brother."

"Congratulations!" Gabe said, delighted. "Imagine, me—an uncle." He grinned nearly as broadly as Jake. "That is fantastic news! Astounding."

"I didn't expect this much enthusiasm from a guy who knows nothing about babies." Jake studied his brother.

"I like Nick's kids. Michael is cute, and Emily is a little doll."

"Thanks. I have to agree," Nick replied with a grin.

"Maybe you're growing up, Gabe," Jake said, still focusing on his brother.

Gabe laughed. "This baby is different, too. This will be my nephew. Or niece," he added. "I might have a niece. Wow. If we weren't in this relatively quiet restaurant, I would let out a whoop."

"Hold it in, little brother," Jake drawled. "I know you, and you're not kidding. If you do that in this place, we'll get booted out before we get breakfast. Celebrate when you get outside."

"Let's have a toast," Gabe said, raising his glass of water. "To my brother and to Caitlin. Congratulations to the new mom and dad. May you always remember not to meddle unnecessarily in your baby's life."

"Hear, hear," Nick said, smiling as they all clinked glasses of water against Jake's goblet.

"Amen to that one," Tony added. "With all our interfering fathers, I hope we have learned to stay out of our children's lives when we should. Course, our control freak dads were what made us all such close friends through the years. Because of them, we have a bond that most men don't. But as much as I like y'all, I'd rather not have that tie with you."

"Well, thank goodness Dad still leaves me alone," Gabe said as he set down his glass.

"He sees you as the baby brother and doesn't realize time is passing. When you take the plunge and propose, he'll go into shock," Jake said with another smile.

"You're right," Gabe replied, thinking about Maddie. He glanced around the table and looked at three happy men who were more relaxed than they used to be in their single days. "I will have to admit, marriage seems to agree with the three of you."

"That and the recent investments you've made for us," Tony said, raising his glass to Gabe. "You've made us all richer. I knew there must be a good reason I put up with you tagging along all those years. Who knew then you'd grow up to be a shrewd investor?"

"Maybe his brother," Nick said. "Jake always has had faith in you. Thanks, Gabe. You've really turned a dollar for us."

"See, I kept telling y'all if you put up with him, you'd be glad someday," Jake said, and they all laughed.

"I'm glad everyone is happy," Gabe said, looking up as the waitstaff brought big trays loaded with breakfast.

"Thanks again for ordering for me, Jake."

"You're welcome. You're predictable when it comes to breakfast. About the only thing predictable in your life."

Gabe grinned. "Speaking of unpredictability, Maddie Halliday is back. She's come home to sell the Halliday ranch. Don't get a gleam in your eye, Jake. You own more land than one man should right now."

"I may not be able to resist looking at the ranch, *Dad*," Jake said.

"I deserve that one. Buy the Halliday place if you want it. It isn't close to yours though."

"That won't matter. I'll look into it. Is it on the market?"

"Not yet. That's what Maddie's here to do. I happened along yesterday when she was on her way to the ranch and had a flat on her brand-new rental car."

"What's she up to? Is she married?"

"No, she's not."

"Well, well," Jake said, studying his younger brother.

"I can see the wheels turning, Jake. She loves Florida and her job there. Her mother and maternal grandparents all live there. She can't wait to put the ranch on the market and get out of here forever."

"No, I don't guess there will be anything between the two of you, then. Her determination to leave Texas would kill any interest you would have in her," Jake said.

Conversation changed and Gabe was happy to eat in silence and avoid more questions about Maddie. For now, he wasn't sharing his thoughts with Jake.

When the group had finished eating and broken up to go to work, Jake walked out with Gabe.

"I wasn't kidding about looking at the Halliday ranch," Jake said. "Actually, I'm surprised you don't want it. It's closer to your half of the ranch than mine."

"Jake, I'm spending more time with my investments. And yours, I might add. I'd rather do that than worry about increasing my land holdings."

"I'd rather you did, too. You're a damn fine petroleum engineer, but you've got the knack for investments—that's your real talent. Just keep it up. You're going to make me wealthier than Dad and probably yourself, too. He'll go into shock when he realizes the extent of how your wealth has increased. I've told him a little, and he gets very quiet."

"I like the work, Jake. Anyway, I don't have to own half of West Texas to be satisfied. Our ranch is big enough, and we've got income from other sources. To me, it just looks like a lot more work. The Halliday ranch may turn a tidy profit, but I can't see why you'd want to deal with it. "

Jake studied him a moment. "The door is always open at the office. You know I'd like to have you on a consulting basis if you don't want to come back full-time."

"Thanks."

"The guys were talking before you arrived today. They are really happy, Gabe. You've done a great job for them."

"I'm doing all right for myself. Investing is a way to prove myself, beyond the family business and the ranch. I'm no longer 'Jake's little brother.' It's one thing that I've done all on my own, with no family involvement other than the fact that you are one of my clients."

"You hardly have to prove yourself."

"Sometimes I feel I do. Jake, I've always been your little brother. That's how people know me. This is something I can do that is totally apart from the family business or the family ranch or your expertise. I'm on my own."

"Well, if it makes you feel better, you've been damned good at it. You're making both of us billionaires. I think it's only a matter of time until Dad asks you to handle some of his personal investments."

"I wouldn't mind that," Gabe said, and then he wanted to change the subject. "I'm thrilled for you and Caitlin. The baby is really great news."

Jake grinned. "We think so. We're excited. Actually, Mom and Dad are far more worked up than I thought they'd be."

"Mom, I'm not surprised. Now Dad—he'll be a granddad. I wonder if that gave him a jolt."

"Didn't seem to. So far he hasn't tried to interfere, but I expect an account to open soon for our baby."

"Oh, sure. He'll do all sorts of things. Tell Caitlin I'm happy for both of you. And thrilled for me. An uncle. Most amazing. Can't wait to spoil him or her. Dad may not be the only one starting to do things for the baby."

Jake laughed. "You surprise me more all the time. Could it be my baby brother is growing up?"

"Maybe it's time, Jake," Gabe answered a little more sharply than he'd intended.

"How do I get in touch with Maddie?" Jake asked.

"I have her cell phone number," Gabe replied, fishing in his pocket for his billfold and pulling out a slip of paper with her number. "Here, call her on my phone, and I'll talk to her after you've finished."

"Sure," Jake replied, making the call and setting up an appointment with her to discuss the ranch. He handed the phone to Gabe. "Thanks. She's waiting. See you, Gabe."

Gabe nodded as he said hello to Maddie, watching his brother walk away and thinking about the baby news. Jake would be a dad, and he would be an uncle.

He sauntered to his car and climbed in, sitting and talking to Maddie, reminding her they were going to have dinner at a local place where she would see a lot of her friends.

Maddie had an appointment, so as soon as they finished their call, Gabe drove to a local jewelry store to find a baby gift for Jake and Caitlin, finally settling on a Dresden calliope music box that he had gift wrapped. Whistling, he drove to the office, still amazed that he would soon be an uncle, something he had never thought about and hadn't expected to have happen for a long time.

Maddie would be as surprised as he. An hour after lunch, Gabe was already wanting to leave early so he could get ready to see her and tell her the good news.

Maddie dressed in new jeans and a blue Western shirt. She looked forward to the evening and getting out where she could see old friends. She tried to keep that prospect as her focus and avoid thinking about Gabe, but it was impossible.

"Foolish, foolish woman," she admonished herself, speaking aloud in the empty room. When she had come home for her grandfather's funeral, six men had asked her out. She had turned each one down. She hadn't wanted to go out with them, but even if she had, she still would have refused to do so. Any relationship in these parts would complicate her life too much. Besides, next to Gabe, the men all paled in comparison.

"Why can't you fall in love with someone else?" she asked herself, thinking about Gabe.

The doorbell rang and she hurried downstairs to open the front door. Looking great, Gabe stepped inside.

"Oh, my word." Her gaze raked over his blue shirt and his tight jeans and Western boots. "We're dressed alike," she observed, making him flash a wicked grin.

"We think alike," he said.

"Oh, no we don't. I know better than that. I'll run and change my shirt. You stay right here. Or go sit in that front room where you used to wait for me."

He gripped her wrist. "Forget it. You look great and I'm happy for us to be dressed alike. Maybe it'll send a message to the locals to stay away from you."

She stared at him a few seconds before she spoke. "I cannot understand you. You act like you want a relationship between us, yet I know you don't."

"Oh, yes, I do. I keep telling you—time and people change. You're different now, and I am, too. So let's explore the differences."

Sighing, she shook her head. "Gabe, don't try to dredge up what's over."

"We can talk in the limo. Are you ready to go?"

"I suppose, although I think we'll look silly dressed alike."

His grin returned. "I like it. Makes you my woman."

"If that doesn't sound like a Neanderthal, I don't know what would. You're not going to ruin my evening out, are you?"

"No, I'm going to stand back and watch every single guy in the county want to dance with you."

She had to smile. "I suspect a few ladies will see to it that you don't get lonesome while I'm on the dance floor."

They both laughed, and he squeezed her hand lightly. "It's great to be together again," he said. His words twisted her insides. She didn't want to have fun with him, fall into old habits and find him as charming as ever. Why did he always seem larger than life to her? It had made sense when she had been eight years old and he had been thirteen. Back then, she had thought of him as the big brother she wished she had. She stopped seeing him as a substitute brother when she was about twelve years old. By that time, she thought Gabe was the cutest boy in the next dozen counties.

As they sped along the highway, Maddie talked about the agencies she'd interviewed earlier that day, and Gabe told her what he knew about each and which one his family used.

"Enough about me and my day. How was yours?"

He flashed her a broad grin, and she wondered

if he had made some highly rewarding deal. "What happened? You look like the proverbial cat."

"Happier than any cat. I got some really great news. Jake is going to be a father, which means I will be an uncle."

While he shot her another quick smile, she stared in surprise. "That's really great," she said.

"You don't sound like you actually think so," he said, giving her another quick look.

"Again, you shock me. I'm amazed you're so delighted. What do you know about babies or being an uncle?" she asked with a sharp note in her voice.

"Nothing," he replied cheerfully, "but I'll learn and it'll be fun. I'm excited to be an uncle." He gave her another quick look. "Sorry, Maddie. For a moment I forgot you're an only child, so you won't be an aunt."

"I'm not worried about that. I could marry someone who is an uncle, and then I would be an aunt by marriage. I'm amazed that you find a baby really great news. I figured you wouldn't care."

"Maybe a few years ago I would have been that way, but this spring I volunteered to help with a shelter after a tornado, and those little kids were cute. Then I got involved in a community project where we took two kids to work on the ranch, and I dealt with them pretty much on a daily basis. I enjoyed both projects."

"Well, another surprise. I didn't know you were into good deeds, and I'm astounded you enjoyed working with the kids."

"See, I've been telling you since yesterday, there are facets to me that you don't know."

"Maybe there are, Gabe," she said, looking at him intently, wondering if he had changed. She had known him extremely well by the time she moved away from Texas. At that time, he had no interest in kids, commitment or charitable deeds.

"Now, I can't imagine my brother as a father, but Jake will be a good one, I'm sure," Gabe said.

"I'm sure, too. He's been like a father to you," she said.

It was hard to imagine the Gabe she used to know donating his time to help storm victims and enjoying spending time with kids. Also, the project that had involved kids at his ranch would have meant an even stronger mentorship with the kids. Had he matured and grown up in the years she hadn't seen him? Would his feelings toward his own status as a dad be different now than they would have been six years ago?

For the first time, she began to seriously question the stand she had taken to keep Rebecca's existence a secret from her father. If Gabe had changed, her decision to keep Rebecca a secret would have to transform, too. She glanced at his profile and wondered again about the depth of his feelings about the expected baby arriving in his family.

Her world had suddenly shifted. She was at a loss and needed to regain her composure before Gabe noticed. He used to be able to read all of her feelings.

"Have you talked to Caitlin yet?"

"No, but I will soon. I got a baby present this morning, and I had it gift wrapped. If I'd thought a minute, I would have held off on the wrapping and shown it to you."

"One more surprise. What did you buy?"

"It's a fancy calliope music box from Starling's Jewelry."

"I'll bet it's beautiful. The baby can't touch it, but

that's sweet, Gabe. Caitlin and Jake can play it for the little one. That was being a good uncle."

"I can't wait. A nephew would be fun. A niece—that would be a huge delight."

Thinking instantly of Rebecca, Maddie's heart thudded. She drew a deep breath. Again, she questioned her decision to keep Rebecca from her father. If Gabe was this way about Jake's baby, what would he be like about his own? Had she made a terrible mistake? Or had Gabe matured over the past six years?

He kept talking to her, but she couldn't focus on what he was saying. Her ears rang, and she felt light-headed. She tried to get a grip on her emotions. Gabe had shocked her deeply, and he was going to realize something was amiss if she didn't begin to act like herself.

After a few more seconds, she picked up the thread of conversation.

Gabe drove her to a local place where musicians were already playing fiddles and people were doing the two-step. They hadn't gone three feet from the front door before old friends greeted and hugged Maddie.

Gabe left her with friends and managed to get a table. He ordered an iced tea for her and a cold beer for him then returned to stand near her.

Finally, they made it to their table. Gabe glanced at his watch. "That only took a half hour. Think I'll get to dance with you tonight?"

Smiling, she grasped his hand. "Let's go dance now."

They entered the dance floor while a two-step was playing. Gabe was a great partner, and she loved dancing with him. With work and Rebecca, she had missed going dancing. When Gabe faced her, his blue-eyed gaze blazed with desire. She couldn't look away.

Her racing heartbeat and breathlessness were not from dancing.

They finished the dance and another couple hurried over to greet her. She hugged Sophie, her closest friend from early childhood, and then received a light hug from Sophie's husband, Tyler Randolph, another local she had known most of her life. Her past was secret from old Texas friends, which always gave her a twinge of guilt. Her grandfather had been a man with secrets and he kept them well, including the one concerning his granddaughter.

They chatted until music started again.

The next dance was claimed by another local she had grown up with. While she danced with Dan Emerson and caught up on his life, she saw Gabe dance by with another acquaintance. Molly was laughing at something Gabe was telling her, and he was smiling. He looked as if he were having the time of his life. This was Gabe as she had always known him—fun, carefree, charming, enjoying life to the hilt. And not a man for marriage, babies, responsibility—as carefree as the wind. Was she missing what was really there? Had life and time made changes in him?

Later in the evening, they ordered ribs, but she could barely get through her dinner for people coming over to talk to her. They soon had half a dozen chairs around their table.

It was midnight when she finally agreed to leave. Not until they were in his pickup, did Gabe give her a long look. "I've finally got you to myself."

"Sorry, Gabe. Is it really that important to you to have me to yourself? I had a wonderful time seeing old friends."

"I'm glad you did, even though I wanted your undivided attention."

"It was nice to see everyone. Except for a few close friends in Dallas, I only kept in touch with Granddad. My family ties here are severed. By the way, I meant to tell you, your brother and I have an appointment. He said you knew that he was interested in our ranch."

"That's right. Jake is buying up Texas."

She smiled. "Funny he's doing that when he doesn't even live out here all the time and doesn't sound enthused about ranch life the way you do."

"No, he doesn't love it to the extent I do, but Jake loves being on the ranch as a getaway. He can relax out here. This land grab is Jake's means of going after oil, gas and water—natural resources that he expects to become more valuable each year."

"Your brother has the Midas touch. I hope that you inherited it, too."

"Enough to keep me happy. Jake does the work of two men. Since his marriage, he's a little better about taking time off. Would you object to selling to him?"

"Not at all if the price is right. I'd be happy to sell to your brother, and it would probably have pleased my grandfather. I want to be rid of the ranch and go home."

"I'll never understand your attitude about Texas. You were happy growing up here."

"I love the bustle and excitement of a big city so much more. I always have. I love Dallas, Houston, Miami. Had I stayed in Texas, I would have settled in Dallas most likely."

"I wish you had. I have a feeling you'll make the sale soon and be gone. I'll come see you in Florida this time," he promised.

"If you come, I think you'll be disappointed because I give myself completely to my work."

Her cell phone rang, and she looked at it. "I need to answer this call." She spoke softly, but knew Gabe could hear her easily. "Good night. That's great. I miss you, too," she said in almost a whisper. "Is everything okay?" She listened to Rebecca talking and then said her farewell. "I love you, too. 'Night."

"Your mother really misses you, doesn't she?" Gabe asked, sounding nonchalant, but she could tell he didn't think she had been talking to her mother.

"Yes, she does," Maddie answered. "We have always been close."

"Nice, that you two are close. I wouldn't want to be so close with my parents. I love them, but they meddle. Especially with Jake's life."

"Is your dad still doing that?" she asked, hoping to divert the conversation away from her phone call. "I remember some of the times you told me about the grief he gave your brother."

"My dad laid down an ultimatum for my brother last year. Jake had to marry within the year or he would be disinherited."

"Good heavens. That's dreadful," she said. "I remember you complaining sometimes about your dad interfering with you, but nothing that drastic. Is he interfering with you now?"

"No. Not so far. He's always concentrated on Jake."

"Why did he want Jake to marry so badly? Did he want a grandbaby?" she asked, tilting her head to one side to study Gabe.

"I'm sure. Now that Jake and Caitlin have announced they're expecting, my parents will have their first grandchild and be focused on that. I expect my dad to stop meddling with Jake and hopefully never start with me."

Gabe parked in the driveway near the back entrance to her house. Porch lights were on and a tall yard lamp spilled yellow light in a large circle over where they had parked.

As soon as she unlocked the door and they stepped inside, Gabe drew her into his embrace and kissed her. She clung to him tightly, too many memories pressing in, desire running wildly rampant.

"Maddie," he whispered.

Her insides heated. She wanted him with a desperation charged with six years of empty nights and tormenting dreams. After being reminded of all she'd left behind tonight, now, Gabe was in her arms, kissing her and she didn't want to let him go. For a few minutes, she stopped thinking with logic and reason. Instead, she took what she wanted and gave herself to him.

He raised his head, combing his fingers into her hair, pushing out her pins and letting it fall freely. "Ah, Maddie, this is what's right, the way it should be," he whispered, showering kisses on her as her hair cascaded over her shoulders.

She had to stop, but not yet. For now, she relished being in Gabe's arms, kissing him, touching him and being touched by him.

"I can't go back into an intimate relationship," she whispered. "We—"

His mouth ended her talk.

She caressed his nape, his throat while she swiftly unbuttoned his shirt and pushed it off his shoulders to run her hands over his muscled, broad shoulders. He had filled out since he was twenty-seven. He was more muscular, firm, sleek and enticing.

She wrapped her arms around his neck again to kiss him, because this was Gabe, the love of her life. On fire with wanting him, she closed her eyes and stopped thinking, giving herself to heightened awareness of his mouth on hers, his hands moving over her, his strong, powerful body.

"This is right. You belong with me," he whispered, startling her. He had never before made such a remark.

"This can't happen," she whispered. "I wanted to avoid this."

"You won't have regrets," he said.

"You were always too arrogant. There is no way I 'belong' to you, Gabe," she said, meaning it, yet unable to stop kissing him.

Gabe kissed her again, and logic spun away. While she held him tightly, relishing the moment, she drew one hand down his smooth, muscled back. She felt his fingers at the buttons of her shirt and in seconds he'd tugged it off and tossed it aside. He unfastened her lace bra, discarding it before he cupped her breasts with his hands.

His gaze traveled over her. "You're gorgeous, Maddie." He leaned down to take her breast in his mouth, his tongue slowly drawing circles on a taut bud.

She moaned with pleasure, running one hand through his hair, her other hand caressing his body. He was the only man she loved or had ever loved. She had no intention of admitting it to him or openly acknowledging it in any way. Except for Rebecca, who was proof of that love.

Gabe had no idea about her feelings. Gabe was wonderful, but most of his relationships were superficial. He had been superficial with her that summer six years ago.

Now, though she still wasn't sure if he'd changed, nothing he did felt superficial.

He cupped both breasts and drew slow circles with his thumbs.

She moaned again with pleasure, hearing her voice only dimly because her pulse thundered in her ears. She wanted Gabe with all her heart, but when his hands were at her buttons, ready to unfasten her jeans, she gripped his wrists.

"Gabe, wait. This is too fast for me. I can't go back to intimacy with you. It tore me up when we broke up."

He was breathing as hard as she while he gazed at her with half-lidded eyes.

"Maddie, I want you to be mine."

She shook her head. "I'm not a woman who has flings," she said, pulling her clothing in place swiftly, her hands shaking while emotion tore at her. She ached with wanting him, yet giving in was the way to catastrophe. "Especially not with you, someone I loved. You know I was getting serious that summer. I wanted commitment. You didn't. And you're not ready now."

Something flickered in the depths of his eyes. He inhaled deeply.

"You don't know that, Maddie. Maybe I'm ready to settle down. I want you. I want to make love to you all night long. You're not disappearing out of my life this time, like you did before. I know that was my own fault," he added swiftly. "I let you go when I shouldn't have because I wasn't ready for a serious commitment."

"You always knew what I wanted," she whispered.

"We were too young, Maddie. You were just twenty-one."

"Maybe. Maybe not, Gabe."

"I let you go, too, because I thought you'd come back

here. It never occurred to me you would leave the state and stay away."

"You didn't come after me," she said solemnly.

"I promise, that won't happen again."

Startled by his admission, she was momentarily taken aback. "Shh. Don't say that," she whispered. Hoping to get her emotions under control, she walked away from him. "It's late, Gabe. I can stay here alone tonight. You go on home."

"Nope. While you're here, I stay on the sofa. I don't want to worry about you in this big house by yourself."

"Suit yourself."

"Maddie, I want to take you out again tomorrow night."

"I'm having lunch and spending the afternoon with three of my friends in Dallas tomorrow," she replied stiffly, hurting, torn between wanting him and being angry with him about the past.

He walked over to place his hands on her shoulders. "I'll fly you to Dallas in the morning, and we can stay at my condo, which is large enough you'll have plenty of freedom and privacy. I can put a limo at your use."

The tension left her, and she had to laugh. "That is an irresistible proposition. Limo, Dallas condo, private flight—I will accept. One question first, you're not thinking of joining us for lunch are you?"

"Oh, please. You should know me better than that. I'll be at the office. Once we get to Dallas, you won't even know I'm there until dinner."

"Gabe, if you're within a city block, I will know you're there, but thanks. I'll accept your offer."

"Good. Come sit and talk. I'll keep my distance."

"You didn't dance a lot tonight."

"I was waiting on a certain blonde to be free," he said, and she smiled.

Maddie's cell phone rang, a dim sound, but she could hear it and so could Gabe.

"That's my phone. This late at night, I better take the call," she said. She yanked up her jacket to retrieve her cell and walked away to take the call, aware she was disheveled, her mouth still tingling from his kisses.

"Maddie, I'm sorry to call so late," her mother said. "Everything is all right. Rebecca had a nightmare. I put her in my bed, and she had another one. She's crying and wants to talk to you."

Aware of Gabe nearby, who was watching her and listening, Maddie started walking down the hall.

"Put her on the phone." She could hear sniffles. Her heart lurched when she heard Rebecca's high-pitched voice.

"Mommy."

"Sweetie, I love you and everything is all right. Get Grandma to read a story to you. What story would you like tonight?" Maddie smoothed her hair from her face as she talked.

"Come home."

"Honey, I'll be home as quickly as I can. It won't be tonight or tomorrow. Get Grandma to read to you."

"Okay. I love you."

"I love you, too, honey," she said, relieved to hear Rebecca's voice growing calmer. She missed her daughter badly and wanted to hold her close and comfort her. "I miss you oodles and oodles and will come home just as soon as I possibly can. When I do I will read six stories to you. How's that?"

"Good," Rebecca said. "I love you."

"I love you, too, sweetie. Good night."

Tracie came back on the phone, and Maddie talked to her for a few minutes then ended the call. When she turned around, Gabe was waiting. He had pulled on his shirt and buttoned the last two buttons at his waist.

"Who were you talking to, Maddie?"

Four

"Only family, Gabe. Not a guy. There really isn't one in my life."

"How I'd like to fill that void," he said lightly, not pressing her about the call. But she knew Gabe hadn't put it out of his mind and was curious about who she had talked to.

"Let's have a nightcap and talk. It's not that late," he said, draping his arm across her shoulders.

"We do have some cold beer, milk, tea and there's a wine rack filled with bottles that have been here awhile."

"Cold beer sounds fine."

"And I'll have milk. Tell me about the boys who worked on your ranch, and how you got into that," she said. "I don't recall you doing volunteer projects when I was here."

"I didn't. Tony Ryder got involved with the project

and he talked to Jake, who talked to me about helping because I'm the one on the ranch the most. It's through a nonprofit and involves boys who've had a little trouble with the law, but not enough to incarcerate them. The kids have dropped out of school, or have family problems. That type of thing. The organization tries to get help for them, place them on ranches where they can work and be around good people, around animals. It seems to help. Anyway, I volunteered to take two of them—one was thirteen and the other fourteen. The boys stayed with one of our families who live here on the ranch, and that was additional support for them. It worked out well. They're in school now. I keep up with them."

She turned wide eyes on him. "Gabe, I'm truly surprised. I can't imagine you doing this. You're the youngest in your family. You don't know kids."

"It's not that big a deal, Maddie. Those two kids needed some support and guidance, and I could give that easily. I've got the ranch and the time and the money. Neither kid had ever been on a horse. It was kind of funny and pitiful at first, but they took to it. The transformation in them has been awesome. That's one time the word 'awesome' really fits. The guys out here were great. Those boys took to ranch life as if they had been born to it. It was fun to see the changes in them. I got tutors for them in math and reading and their grades have jumped. I have high hopes for both of them. If they get their grades up and keep them up, I'll send them to college."

"I'm impressed," she said, truly meaning it. She stared at him because the Gabe she had left six years ago would not have tied up his life in any such manner.

"They say leopards never change their spots, but I guess leopards do grow up."

He leaned close to her. "Are you accusing me of being shallow and immature?"

She gazed into the bluest eyes she had ever known. "To be truthful, yes. When I left here I sort of thought you were. Not shallow, but a wee bit immature. That particular year, I don't think you would have taken in two boys who needed help," she said carefully, thinking about Gabe and wondering about the depth of the changes in him.

He stared back intently at her. "You are probably right, Maddie," he admitted.

"You always have been honest."

"I guess I had some growing up to do."

"Maybe we all did, Gabe," she added, remembering how she'd had to grow up quickly when she had a baby. If Gabe had helped those two boys and continued to care about them, how much more would he be interested in his own child? Could she forgive Gabe enough for walking out on her to share her daughter with him? Would Gabe forgive her for withholding that he had a daughter?

She ran her hand across her forehead and tried to focus on what he was telling her. She needed to shove aside her questions and think about them later.

"Have you heard one word I've said?" he asked, studying her, looking amused, but also curious.

"I'm sorry, Gabe. It's been a long day and night."

"Anything I can help with?"

"No, but thanks," she said, smiling at him. "I should take my glass of milk and go to bed. Tomorrow will be another busy day. Take one of the bedrooms upstairs and stay out of my hair."

He grinned. "Yes, ma'am," he said, grabbing up a handful of silky locks and running them along his jaw, "but it's going to be a strain."

"Watch out, Gabe, or you'll be staying downstairs again, on the sofa."

As she reached for her glass of milk, Gabe took her wrist to stop her. "Sure you don't want to sit a minute and talk?"

She shook her head. "Sorry. I'm sure. Maybe another time," she said, knowing that most likely there would be no other time. "I'll turn off the lights."

"I'll get them," he said, moving quickly to switch them off. He dropped his arm casually across her shoulders and they checked the doors and the alarm and then climbed the stairs together. How natural it seemed.

He selected the bedroom closest to hers.

"You have your own bathroom. I'll see you in the morning in the kitchen," she said.

"Yes, you will. I'll be more than happy to tuck you in."

"Forget it, Gabe," she snapped.

He laughed, pulling her into his embrace.

"Okay, only a good-night kiss." He kissed away her protest and in no time she had her arms wrapped around him as she kissed him deeply in return, hot kisses that stirred fantasies instead of assuaging desire.

When she stepped away, they were both gasping for breath. "Tomorrow, Gabe." She entered her bedroom and closed her door, setting her glass of milk on a table.

She heard his boots scrape the bare wood floors and then he was gone. He had not closed his door.

Later, she lay in the dark, her thoughts in turmoil.

She had always felt so right about her decision to keep Rebecca a secret. Revealing the truth would have messed up both their lives, at the time, but now—Gabe had changed and she had too.

Becoming a mother and being in the business world had changed her. She was mature enough now to know she wouldn't have to marry Gabe, even if he tried to pressure her into it. And he would try. Gabe had an old-fashioned streak as solid and real as the old-fashioned mansion he had built.

Now she was strong enough in her own right to be able to turn him down. Gabe had faced challenges and grown. And how thrilled he had been over becoming an uncle. To go right out and buy a baby gift, the coming event had to be important to him. To consider sending two boys to college—that had been a reminder of how much he could do for Rebecca. The question persisted— if he helped kids who weren't his, how much more would he care about his own child?

Questions haunted her and drove away sleep.

While she was here, with him, she needed to take a long look, make an assessment.

She wanted to take some time before giving up the secret that would change so many lives. Her mother and grandparents would not want her to reveal the truth to Gabe. It would mean they would have to share Rebecca and lose precious time with her.

And Maddie had to forgive Gabe for walking out that summer. He had never made promises to her about commitment. She had fallen in love; he had not. She'd thought she wasn't carrying a grudge, but maybe she had been. And maybe it was time to forgive him. As for the bigger issue—maybe it was time to tell him about Rebecca.

* * *

The next morning, Gabe moved quietly around the kitchen. As he made breakfast and tried to avoid clattering dishes, he couldn't keep from thinking about her phone calls. He hadn't heard what she'd said last night, only the tone of her voice, but she'd obviously been talking to someone very special.

The Maddie he had known all his life until her move to Florida would have told him who had called. She had always confided her secrets. He was certain that was no longer the case. Far from it. He was certain she didn't want him to know.

At the same time, she had insisted it wasn't a guy. She had said family. He found that difficult to believe, but she had never lied to him before. If not a guy, who was it? He didn't think she had been talking to her mother, grandmother or grandfather, so who? For that matter, if it *had* been a guy, why not tell him?

And if it hadn't been a guy, why was it so private?

Gabe stared out the window without really seeing the yard. He was totally puzzled. The truth hit home that she had a life far away from him and he was no longer any part of it. Why had he always believed she would come back to Texas?

For the first time since her return, he faced the fact that he had always felt their time together really wasn't over. Now, he saw that notion had been a mistake. She had cut all ties, except with the grandfather who visited her instead of her coming back to Texas to visit him. Maddie would leave this time and never return, and she had made it clear that she didn't want Gabe to come to Florida.

There had to be a guy, he thought. The realization made his insides clench. He didn't want another man to be in her life. He knew the feeling was totally ridiculous. He had no claim on Maddie. But he wanted one. The more he thought about marriage and Maddie, the more he wanted it. They fit perfectly—except for her love of Florida and his love of Texas.

Annoyed at his own thoughts, he worked in silence, finally pouring coffee and sitting near the window to wait for her to wake up. He heard a scrape and looked around. Maddie entered the kitchen, and his gloom dissipated.

"Good morning," he said, ensnared. She wore cream-colored slacks and a matching blouse. Her hair was loose, falling over her shoulders in a golden cascade. He wanted to cross the room, wrap her in his embrace and make love.

Instead, he stood rooted to the spot, watching her. He poured chilled orange juice for her, then crossed to her, holding out the drink. But at the last minute, he couldn't resist. He set the drink on the nearby counter and wrapped his arms around her and kissed her.

Each time he held her, she hesitated for a few seconds before returning his kiss passionately. He desired her with an intensity that startled him. He wanted to make love with her for hours. In spite of her fiery kisses, he felt he was light-years away from getting to do so.

Her hair was silky, smelling fresh and clean. She was soft, warm, pliant in his arms. He leaned over her, kissing her deeply, wanting to seduce her, knowing he couldn't get through to her the way he once had. Regret tore at him.

She wriggled away, smoothing her slacks, which were flawless. "We better stick to schedule, Gabe. I have my day booked. Once I arrive in Dallas I have every moment planned. I do need to get there on time."

"Sure. Have some breakfast."

He served her and sat with her, sipping his cup of steaming coffee while she ate toast and drank orange juice.

"Do you have any appointments today?" she asked.

"I have an appointment this morning with Jake, and I'll be at the stockyards later. You like city life. Tonight I'll show you Dallas. You haven't seen it for six years, have you?"

"Actually, no."

"Great. I'll make dinner reservations."

He pulled a key out of his pocket. "Here's a key to my condo. When we get to Dallas, I'll have the limo drop me at my office. It will take you where you want to go for the rest of the day, and we can meet at my condo in time for dinner. How's that?"

"Sounds grand," she said, flashing a warm smile that made him anticipate the evening.

His hand brushed hers as she took the key and slipped it into her pocket. Quickly, she finished her breakfast. Excusing herself and stepping to the window, she called Sol to tell him her plans.

Gabe could easily hear her. She made no effort to speak softly. Whoever she had talked to in Florida, the person had been far more important to her than Sol, and Sol was a lifelong employee and friend. The puzzle grew, and Gabe was at more of a loss than ever.

"I can be ready in ten minutes, Gabe. Is that too soon to leave?"

"Not at all," he replied, pulling out his cell phone. "My pilot already has an approximate time for our departure. I'll let him know."

She rinsed her dishes and placed them in the

dishwasher alongside Gabe's. She hurried out of the kitchen and was gone.

He stared after her, realizing just how big the changes in her were. She had moved on. He shouldn't expect her to pick up where they'd left off, but somehow he *had* expected the same close friendship they'd once shared, even if they were not lovers. Growing up, she had always shadowed him, done whatever he was doing, kept in constant touch with him. That sharing seemed to be over. The changes in her shouldn't continue to surprise him, but they did.

From the moment he had recognized her on the side of the road, she had been one surprise after another. So many unexpected differences now. She was more poised, confident, and didn't need him the way she used to.

He got ready to go and waited for her at the back door. She entered the room, her long blond hair swinging gently across her shoulders with each step.

He watched while she set the alarm, and then they left.

They chatted through the drive to the airport and then on board the family jet. He had taken women on the jet half a dozen times before, and they had always been impressed with the private plane, even women who came from families that owned their own planes. It was plush, with an elegant interior. He noticed Maddie paid little attention to it, making him wonder about her own lifestyle and how accustomed she was to luxury and to flying.

"Maddie, I want you to visit Texas again," he said, leaning closer, putting his elbows on his knees. Her skin was flawless. He could look at her all day. Her beauty took his breath.

She smiled, looking cool and reserved, and he knew what her answer would be before she shook her head.

"Gabe, I told you, I don't plan to return anytime soon. I have a busy life."

"I can't believe you're that wrapped up in your work. There's no man?"

"Absolutely not. And it's not all work. I'm wrapped up in my life there. I have family, friends."

"Your mom doesn't miss Texas?"

"Actually, she does. Mom's two lifetime best friends are in Dallas. She visits them several times a year, and she would see Granddad while she was here. She'll keep seeing them."

"Maybe I ought to call and prevail on her to bring you along."

"I've outgrown that. I doubt if you will miss me much or often. We're almost strangers now."

He reached up to touch her silky hair. "Strangers with you? Not ever. I know so much about you, Maddie, as you do about me. For years we were friends and then it became much, much more," he said, his voice dropping in timbre as he looked into her wide, brown eyes. Her lips parted, and she drew a deep breath. He wanted to slip the pale buttons free of her blouse and pull her onto his lap. "I know so much about you. I know how you look in passionate moments—"

"Gabe, I walked into that one. So, okay, we still know each other," she said, gulping for air and obviously trying to make her voice firm. "No, I won't be back, and, no, you won't miss me," she said, surprising him with the note of steel in her reply. "I have a life. It's over a thousand miles away and does not involve you. You've been fine with that for the past six years so don't tell me it's different now."

He caught her chin in his hand and slipped his other arm around her waist suddenly, turning her to look into his eyes. "Then why does your heart pound when I touch you? Why are you breathless? Why are your kisses hot? Why do you cling to me when I kiss you?" he demanded.

He could see anger flash in her eyes. Was she upset that he could see so easily the effect he had on her? When her lips parted, he moved his head to close the last inch between them. He placed his mouth on hers as he kissed her.

She responded, kissing him in return, and he flipped free her seat belt and lifted her to his lap, holding her against him as he continued to kiss her.

When she finally broke away and slipped back to her seat, she buckled up, looking shaken. With a lift to her shoulders, she raised her head to look him straight in the eye.

"So I'm physically attracted to you. I'm vulnerable because I haven't been kissed in a long time. I can't resist you physically. But it's only attraction, Gabe. It's meaningless, so don't put stock in my response to you. I mean what I say about leaving Texas."

"And I mean what I say about getting you to stay longer," he said, leaning close again. "I want to make love with you, Maddie."

"It's not going to happen," she whispered. "Where's the lavatory?"

He pointed, telling her. He watched as she walked away, her hips swaying slightly. She was holding back. He had known her too well and for too long. There was something she wasn't telling him. Whatever it was, it was tied to those phone calls she had taken.

She was gone a long time. When she returned, she

looked composed. For the remainder of the flight she managed to keep their conversation turning constantly to impersonal topics.

In Dallas, they took a limo to the headquarters of the Benton family business. Gabe brushed her cheek with a light kiss and climbed out. "See you tonight," he said, closing the door.

He watched the limo drive away and then entered the office building, already thinking about the evening and where he would make reservations for dinner. It was Saturday. She hadn't settled on an agency yet to handle selling the ranch, which meant she would be here at least through next week. He hoped longer. He wanted to change her mind about coming back to Texas for a visit. He wanted to change her mind about inviting him to Florida. Most of all, he wanted to change her mind about making love. She set him ablaze. Right now, he wanted to be with her and he had a feeling he wouldn't be able to concentrate on anything else.

Maddie spent the morning shopping for gifts to take to Rebecca, to her mother and to her grandparents. She met her friends for lunch, which extended into a long afternoon. At half-past four, the group broke up and she took the limo back to Gabe's condo.

She called him on her cell phone and learned he would be there within the hour.

Using his key, she let herself in and dropped her purchases on a sofa. She walked through the elegant condo that looked untouched. How much time did Gabe actually spend here? Someone probably cleaned for him—often. The hardwood floors gleamed and the dark mahogany furniture held the faint scent of furniture polish. Thick area rugs in deep blues were in various living areas. The view of Dallas would be spectacular at night. She touched the piano, wondering why he had one. She knew he didn't play a note. She paused at the door of the master bedroom and then roamed around inside. There were a few pictures of Gabe with his brother and his deceased sister, Brittany. There was a picture of Jake, Gabe and Caitlin Santerre, now Caitlin Benton. Maddie had known Caitlin as far back as she could remember because they had gone to school together.

She glanced at the big bed, wondering about Gabe and the women who had been in his life. She was certain there had been women. Gabe was a fun-loving man who liked women, and they liked him.

Maddie left the room, examining each bedroom and finally picking the one the farthest from Gabe's. After gathering her purchases and carrying them to the bedroom she had chosen, she closed the door. All day she had avoided thinking about Gabe and Rebecca. She would finish her business here and get back to Florida before disaster befell her. She could stop worrying about whether or not she was doing the right thing, or trying to figure out if Gabe had changed and matured.

She should take this evening and enjoy him. But could she do that and not tell him about Rebecca? If she could, then she'd be on her way back home to Florida with her heart intact and her family at peace. Gabe would never know.

It wasn't that simple. Not after all she had learned about Gabe since being home. He had changed.

Yet when she even speculated about telling Gabe the truth, her insides knotted. He was a take-charge person, a man of action. Once she revealed the truth, there would be no turning back.

Gabe was arrogant. He could have a dig-in-your-heels

attitude. His wishes might not coincide with hers at all. If she revealed the truth to him, she had to be sure that was what she wanted. It would tie her life with Gabe's forever. Was that what she really wanted?

On the other hand, if Gabe had truly changed, grown more responsible, more interested in kids, didn't Rebecca deserve to know her father? He was a wonderful man. And Gabe deserved to know his daughter.

Who knew what Gabe would want to do? And once he decided, he'd never let up. He had far more wealth than she did. There was no way she could fight him in court or any other way. He had the money, the time, the contacts.

She sat on a chair by a window and called home, getting her mother first and then Rebecca. When she ended the call, she gazed out the window without seeing anything, simply thinking about telling Gabe the truth. She didn't want to. Yet each time she thought about returning to Florida without him knowing, she didn't feel right.

She thought about the pregnancy and childbirth she had gone through when she had been twenty-one. During that time, she had wanted Gabe with all her heart. The most joyous moments in her life had also been bitter, because Gabe had walked out on her that summer.

More questions came instead of easy solutions. If she told Gabe about Rebecca, Maddie faced another formidable question. Could she bear to watch him marry someone else while their lives were intertwined? No matter how hot the attraction, she and Gabe could never make a relationship work, because she wouldn't leave Florida and he wouldn't leave Texas. Gabe wasn't the type to settle for a long-distance marriage. So he would marry. He had already mentioned settling down and he was building his home. Then she would have to cooperate with Gabe and his wife. That situation would hurt. Gabe was the only man she had ever loved. She suspected that would be true for the rest of her life.

She still hesitated to reveal Rebecca because it would mean huge changes in her life, along with upheaval in her family's lives. Changes that would be far-reaching and permanent. It would mean countless trips between Texas and Florida. There would be no leaving Texas behind forever. No matter what happened between her and Gabe during this current trip, revealing the truth would mean her life would be connected to Gabe's irrevocably. She wasn't sure she wanted to deal with that.

Thinking of the possibilities, asking herself the tough questions, Maddie frowned as she struggled for decisions.

"Tell him," she whispered to the empty room, knowing she would have to, yet still dreading it. Taking a deep breath, she walked toward the closed door while arguments battled silently within her.

Yet she kept coming back to one fact. Rebecca had a right to know her father, who would love her.

Gabe and Rebecca both deserved the truth.

Filled with dread, she got ready to shower and change.

When she finally emerged from the shower, she had a towel wrapped around herself and she had blow-dried her hair.

As she crossed to the boxes she had placed on the bed, there was a knock on the door.

"I'm not dressed."

"Can I come in anyway?" Gabe called, opening the door a crack. "Are you presentable?" he asked while he was still out of sight.

"Not really. I'm in a towel."

"Hey, great," he said, opening the door and stepping inside. He held a dozen red roses in a crystal vase. "I brought these for you."

"They're beautiful and should last far beyond the next few minutes." She smiled. "Do you understand 'not dressed' and I'm 'not presentable'?"

He paused to let his gaze roam slowly over her. "I understand, but you're wrong. You're absolutely, gorgeously presentable, and you're covered more than you would be on the beach or at the pool. Which, speaking of, want to swim?"

"Thank you, I'll pass."

He set down the flowers and walked over to place his hands on her bare shoulders. The contact sent streams of fire through her insides.

"Gabe, I'll see you in a little while."

"One kiss while I can hold you close, with only a towel between us," he said softly. His husky voice set her pulse racing as he wrapped her in his arms and kissed her.

She shouldn't, yet how to resist him? Resistance was impossible when it was Gabe. She wanted to toss aside wisdom and caution and kiss him in return. She wanted to let go and for one brief moment, she did, relishing the feel of him against her. She ached to forget everything and drop the towel, but instead, she stepped away.

"Now you have to go," she whispered, unable to find her voice. Her heart pounded. She wanted him with an intensity that shook her.

She didn't want to leave Texas with her heart in knots

once again over Gabe. And she didn't want to rekindle anything between them. If she had to tell him about Rebecca, then it was imperative to have distance between them so she could keep her wits about her. Once he knew the truth, Gabe would come after her with marriage on his mind, no matter what he felt in his heart. He hadn't changed that much in all the years.

"I have to dress, Gabe. I'll see you in about half an hour."

His heated gaze raked over her again, making her tingle as if his fingers had drifted over her. He was aroused, studying her intently, standing with his fists clenched.

"You don't know what you do to me, Maddie," he said in a deep, hoarse voice.

"There was a time when I would have melted had I heard you say that," she admitted. "But not any longer, Gabe. That time is gone. I'll see you shortly for dinner."

They stood in tense silence, their gazes locked. Desire flamed in the depths of his eyes. She felt hot, tingling, wanting him beyond anything she had thought possible. Yet she stood rooted to the floor, resisting what her body clamored to have.

He turned and was gone, closing the door behind him.

She sagged and gulped deep breaths. Longing shook her.

She'd resolved to tell him the truth about his child. Now she would have to find the right moment to do so.

Five

Gabe showered and dressed in a charcoal suit with a white shirt and red tie. Gold cuff links gleamed in his French cuffs. With mounting anticipation, he waited in the living area of the condo, gazing at the city spread below.

When Maddie entered the room, his heart missed beats. In a simple red, sleeveless dress that ended above her knees, she crossed the room. Her blond hair was caught up on her head and pinned, hanging loosely in back. The vee neck of the dress revealed luscious curves and her long, shapely legs were as gorgeous as he remembered.

Drawn to her, he approached. "You look stunning," he said in a husky voice. Big brown eyes held his gaze, and her full lips were an invitation. He could sit and look at her all evening long.

"Thank you. You look quite handsome yourself," she

said in a subdued voice, and he focused more intently on her.

She looked stunning, composed and poised, yet he had the feeling something was dreadfully wrong. Maddie wasn't the open book she used to be. She no longer shared her life. Not any of it, least of all her concerns. He couldn't shake the feeling there was something he had missed and the feeling strengthened as he faced her.

"Ready for an evening out in a dazzling city?"

She gave him a glorious smile that almost made him think he was making a mistake about her feelings. "Ever so eager to see the sights," she replied lightly.

He walked up to wrap his arms around her. "I want you, Maddie. More than ever."

She shook her head. "Don't, Gabe. No matter how I may feel about you, there's no future between us. I love Miami as much as you love the ranch. That says it all."

He inhaled deeply. "I want you anyway. We can make love with no thought of tomorrow or Texas or Florida."

"That sounds like the Gabe I know," she said, smiling at him and stepping away. "One of us will cling to reason and logic. Now, I'm ready for this night on the town."

He took her arm, and they left, going to the waiting limo.

Gabe took her to a private club high above the city. The place suited him tonight, with its candlelight, roses on linen-covered tables and a combo playing old ballads as a few couples moved about a small dance floor. Adding to the ambiance, the view of the city was spectacular. Lights twinkled, and in the far western sky, the last rose streaks of sunset splashed across a darkening horizon.

As soon as they were seated at a table by a floor-to-ceiling window, Gabe ordered drinks and stood to take her hand. "Let's dance, Maddie."

When she walked into his arms, he drew her close, dancing to a ballad he knew she liked. She smelled like roses and lilacs, and she was soft and warm in his embrace. The dress was a thin barrier. He ached to make love to her. And he wished he knew how to get her to tell him what worries she had. He hoped she had meant what she said. Once upon a time, he wouldn't have questioned whether or not she meant what she said.

"Maddie, what's worrying you?" he asked quietly. "You used to share your joys and concerns with me."

She gazed at him with eyes that told him nothing about her feelings. "I have things back home on my mind, Gabe. I have never been away from work for long. I can do a few things long-distance, but not much. I'd like to wind up the business with the ranch and get that behind me. I had another talk with an agency this morning. I think I've decided to go with the one you suggested. Mr. Trockburn has been helpful."

"Ed's a hard worker and efficient. He'll do a good job for you."

"I think so. He's coming to the ranch Monday morning."

"Is that all?" he asked, searching her face for some clue, wishing she would share everything with him the way she used to do.

"Yes. Since when did you start worrying about me?" she asked too sharply, making him wonder if she had truly forgiven him for walking out. "You haven't known the problems I've faced over these past six years," she added.

"No," he answered. "I'm beginning to regret more

and more about the past, and that's one of the things I wish I could change. I want you in my life now, Maddie. I really do," he said, meaning it with all his heart.

"Don't be silly, Gabe. That's your physical reaction talking. You weren't thinking about me while we were separated, so it's ridiculous to look back over it in regret now. We both made our choices."

"Doesn't mean I might not regret some of the ones I made."

The music ended and a faster number played. She began to dance, smiling at him with an inscrutable look. Tantalized, he wanted her more than ever. He danced with her, both of them moving fast, her hips swaying.

He could feel beads of sweat on his forehead, but he didn't think it was from dancing. It was from watching Maddie. She was a flame, sexy and taunting. She slanted him a hot look, filled with temptation. She was flirting with him now, with her sultry glances, her sensuous moves. He had to control the urge to yank her into his embrace and kiss her.

He unbuttoned his coat, moving around her. When the number ended, he caught her, spinning her around and dipping her low. She wrapped her arms around him as she looked up into his eyes.

Their gazes locked as he raised her slowly. If he could, he would take her out of here right now, back to his condo and into his bed. He knew she would not consent, so he didn't attempt anything. She stood facing him, their gazes still holding. He drew her to him. Only inches away, she stopped.

Another ballad started and wordlessly they began to dance. She followed his lead, moving into his embrace. They were in perfect rhythm, falling into patterns they had practiced so many times through the years.

She was light as a feather and followed his lead perfectly. He knew so much about her and also so little. In some ways, she might as well be a stranger he had just met. In other ways, she was closer to him than any woman had ever been.

When the music ended, he took her hand. "Let's sit out a few." At their table he held her chair, letting his fingers drift across her nape and brush her shoulder lightly.

Gabe sat facing her. As they sipped their glasses of wine, several times she caught him studying her intently. He knew her too well. His questions indicated he sensed something amiss in her life, and knowing Gabe, he perceived it included him. He had always been sensitive to her feelings. She'd been right to have assumed he would still be that way.

It used to make her feel close to him. Now it disturbed her that he could read her so well. Once again, urgency tugged at her. She needed to tell him about Rebecca. But it had to be the right moment. She suspected when she told him everything, it would change how he felt about her. He might not forgive her. It might mean the end of her friendship with him.

He still made her heart pound just looking at him. He looked incredibly handsome. Always appealing to her, he was even more so in the charcoal suit with his impeccable white monogrammed shirt and gold cuff links. He looked what he was—a multimillionaire filled with self-confidence and a zest for life.

Tonight, there was a sober side to him, but she suspected it was because he thought something was bothering her.

She wished she could stop thinking about their

situation for the night. She longed to relax and enjoy being with Gabe. But it was impossible to turn off one of the most pressing problems she had ever had.

It was difficult to keep her mind on Gabe's conversation, but she tried to concentrate. If he realized how worried she really was, he wouldn't let up until he got some kind of answer.

"Maddie, dammit. What the hell is bothering you?" Gabe asked quietly.

She blinked and realized she had been so wrapped in her thoughts she hadn't heard a word he had said.

"Sorry, Gabe. I really am having a great time. Selling the ranch is pressing, and I got lost in my thoughts about it."

"I think it's more than that. You'll sell the ranch."

She smiled at him, trying to push her dilemma out of her mind and concentrate on giving all her attention to Gabe. "You're right. I shouldn't worry about the sale."

"You used to share every little joy and sorrow with me, and I guess I still expect you to do that. It worries me when you don't. Old habits are hard to break."

"Maybe you're too much of a take-charge person for me to share my worries with tonight. You'd step in and rearrange my life."

He held his wineglass and studied her. "I couldn't possibly step in and rearrange your life unless you asked me to," he said, and she wished she could take back her words. She could see Gabe mulling over what she had told him.

"Here comes our waiter to take our order."

After they had ordered, Gabe stood and came around to hold her chair. "Dancing is always good. I can hold you and it helps to move around and work off steam."

To her relief, it was a fast number and it did help to

move and stop thinking for a few minutes. She wanted to be in his arms, wanted to kiss him. She had fought this attraction since he had pulled her into his embrace to kiss her their first night together, but she wanted to make love with him. Just one more time. She was already in love with him. Making love would not change her feelings for him. But after she told him the truth, everything else *would* change.

She danced around him, watching him, seeing her desire mirrored in his eyes. He wanted her, there was no question or doubt. He had made that clear since that first moment on the highway.

Brushing against him, she circled him. His blue eyes flamed with blatant lust. Some locks of her hair fell free, and she shook them from her face.

Gabe reached out to take her wrist, turning her then holding her hand as they danced. He pulled her close for another dip that left her clinging to him, gazing into his eyes and thinking about kissing him.

The music ended and he slowly raised her up. He wanted to kiss, and she did, too, but they were in a public place. She didn't want to make a spectacle. She turned to walk back to their table, but a ballad started and Gabe drew her into his embrace, holding her close to his heated body.

"You're hot."

"Not half as hot as you are," he said, giving the word a whole different meaning. "You burn me to ashes by dancing around me, tempting me, teasing me."

"I didn't hear a protest at the time."

"Never a protest. I want you alone with me. I want to peel you out of that red dress and kiss you until you're as on fire as I am," he whispered in her ear. Her heartbeat raced, and she wondered if he could feel it.

"Kiss you all over. From your head to your toes. Slowly," he continued, barely moving, his warm breath tickling her ear as he whispered to her.

"Stop trying to seduce me," she said, twisting to look up at him.

"I think you want the same thing I do. You dance as if you do. Your eyes are filled with desire. Your body language says loving is what you want."

"So you're right. That doesn't mean it will happen."

He placed one hand on her cheek. "I'm going to love you, Maddie. We'll make love together, I promise you, before you try to walk out of my life again. I'm going to tie your heart to mine so you won't want to say goodbye."

She drew in a deep breath. His words thrilled her. She couldn't help but respond to the note of steel in his voice. Revealing the truth about Rebecca would forever change her relationship with Gabe. She wanted this one night with him. One night of loving Gabe and being loved by him. Before she confessed, she wanted a memory she could hold forever.

He took his hand from her cheek.

"Gabe, you know I want the same thing you do, but it makes parting hurt more." Even as she spoke, she thought of Rebecca. Maddie had a future with Gabe, but not one filled with love and shared joys.

"There's no way we can predict what the future holds."

The music ended and Gabe took her hand. "Our dinners are served. I saw the server stop at our table."

When they sat to eat, Gabe barely touched his dinner while he talked to her. She ate a thick, juicy steak that was delicious.

"I don't eat as much beef in Florida as I do seafood,

but here, the steaks are wonderful," she said, thinking more about Gabe's blue eyes than about her dinner. "You haven't eaten much of yours."

"I'm hungry for something else," he drawled.

She sipped her water, gazing over the rim of her glass at him, knowing both of them were thinking about hot kisses and making love.

Her cell phone rang and when she stood, Gabe came to his feet.

"Sorry, Gabe. I need to take this call. I'll be back." She fished out her cell phone and left, trying to put some distance between them before she answered the call from home.

When she finished talking to Rebecca, she left the lobby and returned to the table. Gabe had eaten a little more of his dinner.

She kept the conversation impersonal while they finished their meal and then they returned to dancing. An hour later, when the musicians took a break, Gabe took her arm. "Let's go somewhere else. I told you I'd show you Dallas."

"You have. The views here and at your condo are spectacular. I saw a lot today. I shopped and bought this dress for tonight."

"You did well. It's gorgeous. I've told you what I think about it. Or have you forgotten?"

"Yes, you've told me, and no, I haven't forgotten. That wouldn't be possible." Since she would have only one night with him, she wanted it to last. She hoped to draw it out and make each moment a memory that she could hold forever.

They left the club, and he drove to another one. Before he stepped out of the car, he shed his coat and tie and unbuttoned the top button of his shirt. "Put your purse in the trunk. You won't hear your cell phone anyway."

She did as he asked and walked with him toward the entrance. Lights glittered on the outside, and a flashing neon arrow pointed downstairs to a basement area where the rock beat blared loud and fast.

The place was dark, packed, with strobe lights blinking. She laughed when they danced. He looked at her quizzically.

"What?" he shouted above the deafening music.

"You. Here," she shouted back, dancing around him. "The cowboy—not your usual."

As he grinned, he unfastened more buttons of his shirt. She removed the remaining pins from her hair, letting it fall free while she gyrated to the heavy beat. The music prohibited conversation.

It was sexy and fun to dance wildly, to let go and forget everything else. Gabe was too appealing, locks of his brown hair falling across his forehead. With his shirt unbuttoned and his steamy moves, he wove a web of seduction. Even in his fancy black Western boots, he was a dream dancer, light on his feet, his obvious enjoyment contagious.

One piece led into another without pause, and she lost all sense of time.

Finally, Gabe took her hand and jerked his head toward the door. She followed him as they threaded through the crowd and then stepped into cool, fresh air.

She laughed. "That was exhilarating."

"We can go back to the club, drive around and take in the city then get a nightcap or go to my condo."

"I'll opt for the last choice," she said.

"What I wanted exactly," he said with obvious

satisfaction as he held the car door for her to climb inside.

They arrived at his condo and she settled for her usual nighttime drink of milk while Gabe had a cold beer. They had a balcony with a spectacular view and the evening air had cooled. A faint breeze made the balcony even more comfortable.

Gabe pulled his chair close to hers, holding her hand while they reminisced.

"Will you take anything back to Florida from your childhood home?" he asked.

"Sure. I've been packing boxes. I'll have them shipped. It's expensive, but not as costly as driving here and back to get them. There's no furniture that I want. Mom took the few things that I would have been interested in." While she talked, Gabe released her hand to play with strands of her hair. She tingled with awareness of his touch.

They continued talking about incidental things and events, local people and what they were doing, but she was more aware of Gabe's fingers brushing her shoulder and nape, turning locks of her hair in his hand. His white shirt was still open by several buttons, revealing glimpses of his muscled chest and brown chest curls. He was incredibly handsome, more so now than when they were younger. She looked at his mouth, remembering his kisses, wanting to kiss him now.

"Do you have any furniture from your family home?" she asked.

"Actually, I do. When Jake made the deal with Dad about the house, Mom asked me to pick out what I would really like to have and talk to Jake about what was agreeable with him. There really was not that much I wanted, so it worked out fine."

"You'll live on the ranch, go out with local ladies, marry one and settle for ranch life forever," she said, unable to resist combing stray locks of brown hair off his forehead simply because she wanted to touch him.

Gabe leaned close and picked her up, swiftly lifting her to place her in his lap. "Maddie, I want you in my future."

Her protest died when she looked into Gabe's eyes. They conveyed his desire. Her mouth opened, but words failed her. Then he covered her mouth with his.

Her heart thudded. Winding her arms around his neck, she kissed him while she tossed aside worries. She would take this night with Gabe. She would pour out her love. One night with the man she had always loved.

One night before she finally told him the truth.

Six

Maddie's heart pounded while she kissed Gabe passionately. Just tonight, she had told herself while dancing. Only once to show him how much she loved him, to rediscover and store up a memory that she could hold forever.

It had only been since she'd returned to Texas that she had faced the fact that she didn't think she could ever love anyone except Gabe. In the six years she'd been away from him, she hadn't realized that she still loved him. She had always reassured herself she was over him, her memories had faded and she didn't care. During that time, no other man had ever really appealed to her. With his first kiss, six long years of trying to forget Gabe crumbled into nonexistence. She had to face the truth.

He was the sole love of her life.

Tomorrow, she would tell him about his child. Gabe

took family seriously. He was close to Jake and had been close to his sister, Brittany. He was close to his parents. When he learned he had a daughter born five years ago, he might not forgive her for keeping Rebecca's birth a secret.

No matter her good intentions, fathers had rights, and she had violated Gabe's. He might not understand why she'd done it. Gabe had an old-fashioned streak in him and it showed up in all aspects of his life. There was a chance he would be angry, bitter and unforgiving about Rebecca.

Tonight was the time to make love with him, if ever. To love and be loved again by the one man who truly owned her heart.

She kissed him passionately, wanting this night to be the most memorable of all.

Gabe cradled her against his shoulder while his kisses scalded her and made her want more.

"We're outside. This balcony is public."

"Not really," he said, lifting her easily as he stood. "But we'll go inside," he said, and returned to kissing her. She paid no attention to where he carried her until he set her on her feet near a bed.

He never stopped kissing her, only now his hands were free. He caressed her. His hands roamed over her, down her back and over her bottom, his other hand on her hip, moving lower to her thigh.

He found the zipper to her dress and pulled it down enough to slip the top off. It fell to her waist, and she slipped her arms out of it while they continued to kiss.

Gabe's kisses set her ablaze. How much she loved him!

He held her away from him so he could look at her. As soon as he flipped free the catch to the wisp of a bra she wore, he cupped her breasts with his hands, his thumbs drawing lazy circles on her nipples. "You are beautiful, Maddie. So beautiful. More than you used to be." He pushed away the dress, letting it fall to the floor with a whisper of cool air on her ankles.

Holding his arms, she closed her eyes while sensations rocked her. She opened her eyes to finish unbuttoning his shirt and tug it out of his pants. In seconds, she pushed it away, letting it fall unheeded to the floor.

Holding his narrow waist, she ran one hand over his bare, muscled chest, tangling her fingers in his chest hair. She moaned with pleasure from his caresses and kisses.

"You're gorgeous," he whispered thickly. He leaned down to kiss her, taking one breast in his mouth, his tongue circling where his thumb had been. "Maddie, how I've dreamed about this. How I've wanted you! You can't ever know how much I've wanted you. I want you here in my bed. In my arms. I don't want you to leave. I want you to stay here with me."

"That won't happen," she whispered, wondering if he even heard what she said to him.

"You don't know what you do to me." He showered kisses on her temple, down to her throat, then to her ear.

His deep breath made his chest expand. She stood in low cut, lace panties and no stockings, because of the summer weather.

He peeled down her panties, and she stepped out of them.

"You're totally gorgeous. The most beautiful woman on earth. Maddie," he said, longing in his expression as he enveloped her in his embrace and kissed her passionately.

She unfastened and pulled away his belt. Then her fingers went to his trousers, which soon fell around his feet. He kicked them away. She gasped for breath, taking in the sight of him. He was tall, strong, aroused. Ready for her. She ran her hands across his broad shoulders, feeling the taut muscles, relishing the hardness, the strength of him.

"You make me melt to look at you," she whispered.

She clung to him, only his briefs between them. He was warm, hard, muscled. His body was perfection and she was on fire with wanting him to love her. She peeled away his briefs, freeing him, running her hands over his hips and along his thighs, then up again to wrap her arms around his neck.

"I'm the one on fire from looking. I've dreamed of this moment. Six years ago you were a beautiful girl. Now you're a breathtaking woman, all grown up, perfection. It's dazzling to look at you, Maddie."

"It's been so long," she said.

"I told you I wanted to kiss you from head to toe," he whispered in her ear. He picked her up, pausing to sweep back the covers before placing her on the bed. Then he knelt beside her, pushing her down gently and turning her onto her belly.

He began at her feet and left slow, hot kisses up over her calves and the backs of her thighs, taking his time, a sweet torment that increased her tension and made her want him more than ever.

Digging her fingers into the bed, she relished his touches. It was reality and not a dream. She was with Gabe. Gabe kissing her. Gabe caressing her. Gabe making her melt. She couldn't get enough, and she couldn't stop feeling as if it were a dream she would wake from.

Looking over her shoulder at him, she saw that his blue eyes had darkened with desire and his gaze was hot, intense. Each kiss added to the storm that swept her. She already ached for him, wanting to be one with him if only for tonight.

His hands played over her bottom as he roamed higher. His hands and hot breath were at the juncture at the back of her thighs, and she opened her legs to give him access.

When she moaned softly and attempted to roll over, he pushed her against the bed and continued kissing her back and nape. She rolled over, looking up into his eyes, which held consuming desire.

Scooping her into his arms, he kissed her. She returned his kiss while rubbing her body lightly against his. Their kisses muffled his moan.

"This is the way it should be, Maddie. You belong in my arms. Your heart belongs to me and always has."

"Shh. Take tonight. It's what we have," she said, trying to avoid giving credence to what he said, words that thrilled her even when she couldn't believe them.

He caught one hand in her hair while his other arm banded her waist. "It doesn't have to be just tonight. It doesn't at all, Maddie. That's your choice."

She pulled him close, trying to win his heart with hot kisses that he couldn't resist.

"You'll miss me. I'm part of your life. Just as you're part of mine now, and forever."

As she kissed him and ended his words, he held her tightly. She could feel his pounding heart against her own. While she ran her hands over his chest, she continued kissing him.

"I've missed you, badly," she whispered, knowing she shouldn't admit her feelings to him but unable to hold back the words. She showered kisses over his face and throat, feeling his faint beard stubble. Her hands ran across his shoulders and down his smooth, muscled back. She couldn't get enough of him. And then, as if he had the same thought about her, he pushed her down on the bed and started again at her feet. Working his way up with a tantalizing slowness, so deliberate, he watched her while she watched him in return, trying to resist grabbing him and kissing him.

His brown hair was a tangle now, locks falling over his forehead. He still looked powerful, sexy, appealing. His hands were a torment, caressing her as he moved up her inner thighs until she opened her legs to give him access.

Then she was lost in sensation. He trailed kisses over her breasts while his hands played between her legs and she spread them wider for him.

"Gabe, I want you," she whispered, pulling him to her.

He kissed her, silencing her words.

She sat up to kiss and caress him as he had her. She stroked him, letting her tongue run freely over him to pleasure him in every way.

She relished rediscovery. She wanted to create a night he would remember. This was transient, a shared moment that would not happen again, and she wanted it to be all it could possibly be for him, because it already was for her.

"Gabe," she breathed, suddenly, sitting up and framing his face with her hands to kiss him deeply, passionately.

He crushed her close in his embrace, and she could feel his heart racing as hers was.

She moved astride him, fondling him. As she ran her hands over him, she committed the feel of him to memory, pouring out her love for him.

With a growl deep in his throat, he swung her onto her back and moved between her legs to begin loving her all over again, his hands and mouth giving her pleasure.

Desire built with each touch and kiss until she was gasping, on fire with need.

His breath was as ragged as hers.

"Gabe," she whispered. "I'm not protected."

He stepped off the bed and crossed the room to pick up his trousers and get a packet from his billfold. He removed it and returned. She climbed out of bed to meet him, wrapping her arms around him when they kissed.

Lifting her to the bed, he knelt between her legs.

She watched while he put on the condom. He came down to kiss her, keeping his weight from settling fully on her.

He entered her slowly, teasing and making her arch against him. Her hips thrust and she ran her hands on his hard bottom and muscled thighs. He slowly filled her, withdrawing and entering again. Crying out with pleasure, she thrashed beneath him.

"I want you now." She held him tightly, her long legs locked around him. He eased into her again and then moved slowly, building the tension. When sensations rocked her, he kept iron control. Sweat beaded his shoulders and chest. She moved wildly, clinging to him.

"Gabe, now," she whispered.

The roaring of her own pulse drowned out any other

noise. She tugged at him while he drew out the loving as long as possible.

Finally, he lost control, groaning deeply when he thrust hard and fast and she moved with him. They rocked together, pleasure soaring. As they burst over a brink, he shuddered with his release and rapture enveloped her.

She gasped for breath while waves of ecstasy rocked her. "Ah, Gabe."

"Maddie, you're perfection," he whispered hoarsely. Even as his thrusts slowed, she clung to him.

"I've wanted that since you stood on the road and told me hello," he gasped. "Can you stay in bed with me tomorrow?"

She laughed. "That's a question I never expected to hear. We plan a whole day in bed—"

"Most definitely," he replied. "The whole day and tomorrow night, too. Ranch or here, I don't care, but if here, we don't have to dress and go out at all."

"That's ridiculous," she whispered, in euphoria, refusing to think about anything except enjoying how she felt and remembering the past few minutes.

For now, she was in Gabe's arms, one with him, in paradise. This was perfection, and she didn't want to think beyond this moment with him.

She brushed damp locks of hair back from his forehead while he did the same for her.

"You're beautiful. You take my breath away," he said.

"You definitely take mine, you handsome man," she said lightly.

He rolled on his side, taking her with him and holding her close. He smiled at her. "This is the best. This is the way it was meant to be and more. So much more." He showered kisses on her temple, down to her ear and then on her throat. "Ah, Maddie, I can't tell you how great it is to make love, to hold you in my arms, to have you here close to my heart."

Wonderful words, but not the ones she had always wished he would say, although now she didn't feel so strongly about wanting to hear them because it wouldn't matter whether they loved each other or not. Their lifestyles were set and neither wanted to change. She could no more give up her life than Gabe could give up his precious ranch.

He raised up on an elbow. "Will you?"

She laughed as she caressed his jaw, sliding her hand down to his chest to tangle her fingers in the mat of curls. "Will I what?"

"Stay here tomorrow with me?"

She sighed. "Don't intrude with talk about tomorrow just yet. We'll talk in the morning."

"Deal," he said, smiling. "I want to make you want to come back to Texas. Your roots are here. I'm here."

She placed her finger on his lips. "If you want me to stay tomorrow, you'll stop right now with the arguments."

"What arguments? I've spent the most fantastic— Hour? Two hours? I have no idea how much time, but it was fabulous. I want to hold you close and kiss you a little and touch you a lot."

She laughed as he wrapped an arm around her, smiling at her with satisfaction.

"I'll never forget this night, Maddie. It was magic."

"I quite agree and I don't want the world to intrude in any way." She paused, suddenly overwhelmed by emotion. "Gabe, forgive me when I disappoint you."

He smiled. "You won't disappoint me and I'll always—"

"Just remember I asked you to forgive me," she whispered, placing her fingers on his lips and stopping his words. "We go way back, and we've been through a lot together."

"True. Remember when I taught you to ride your new bicycle?"

"My dad was involved with the ranch and kept putting off teaching me."

"You were cute and bright and did what I told you. I felt sorry for you after catching you crying when you crashed on your new bike, smashing a bed of your mom's flowers. I thought you'd kill your bike before you learned to ride it."

She smiled. "You got me out of a lot of scrapes."

"Show me your gratitude," he said in a husky voice.

She smiled and pulled his head down to kiss him.

They spent the night making love and it was dawn when they finally slept, wrapped in each other's arms. Maddie stirred, opening her eyes to look at Gabe. His dark lashes were on his cheeks. He was too handsome. She took in the sight of him, feeling so full of love for him that she ached. They had no future. Worse, he might be forever unhappy with her. She suspected he would never see that she had acted to save them both.

Today, he wanted her to stay in bed with him—too tempting to pass up. This was an idyll she intended to take, knowing it wouldn't happen again. Today, she had to confess the truth. Their worlds would turn topsy-turvy, and she couldn't guess what would happen to their relationship. Next week she would be home, the ranch sold, the house and contents with their new owners. She would leave Texas, but now she knew it would not be forever.

She ran her fingers over Gabe's shoulder, feeling the bulge of solid muscle, and thinking again that she loved him with all her heart.

His eyes opened, gazing into hers. He was instantly awake. "That's the best way to wake up. You in my arms, and your hands on me," he said, pulling her close to kiss her. It was a sweet good-morning kiss that swiftly changed into steamy passion. They made love for the next two hours.

The room was filled with sunshine when she lay in his arms, catching her breath. "I think it is time to get out of bed. I'll shower."

"Stop right there. I have a much better idea."

"I might as well give up on my plans."

After a half hour, she was in a huge tub of hot water, in his arms, as they sponged each other and talked.

"Shortly, we will get out of here and call the restaurant next door and have breakfast delivered. And then I will carry you back to bed."

"I would love to eat on the balcony. The view is grand and the early morning should be nice before the heat sets in."

He chuckled. "I've got news for you," he said. "It is definitely not 'early morning.' Also, you didn't want to discuss it last night and I probably should go with the flow, but I have to know… Will you spend today here with me?"

"Yes, I will," she replied.

"I'm a happy man. My wish has come true."

"You're easy to please."

"I'll show you how easy," he whispered, caressing her. "See, your reaction is enough to give me all kinds of pleasure."

"I can tell," she said, aware he was becoming aroused

again. "Before I lose my train of thought completely, don't you have to be at the ranch or let someone know where you are?"

"I'll send another text shortly. I told them yesterday that I wouldn't be in this morning."

She twisted around to look at him. "You knew how easy I would be, didn't you?"

"Of course not. But I had high hopes."

They both smiled at each other, and he leaned down to brush a kiss on her mouth.

"Maddie, this is where you belong."

He stood, pulling her up with him. They dried each other and before they'd finished, he had pulled her into his arms to make love again.

It was noon before they had food delivered. She had dressed in jeans and a blue T-shirt. Gabe wore jeans and a navy knit shirt. They sat on the balcony to eat, having a spread of both breakfast and lunch items.

She gazed at the platter of fruit, another of sandwiches, scrambled eggs, bacon, hot rolls.

"Gabe, this is as decadent as making love for hours on end. We can't possibly eat all this."

"One of us may come close. I'm starving. It's been a long time since that steak last night."

She laughed and helped herself to a bowl of fruit. "Well, the fruit looks luscious."

"I'll tell you what looks luscious," he said, gazing intently at her.

She smiled. "Don't start until we eat a bite."

"I'll try to restrain myself, but when the most beautiful blonde in Texas is sitting only a few feet away and has let me make love to her all night—"

"Will you stop!" she exclaimed. "Eat something while you can."

"Want coffee?" he asked.

"No thanks. I'll have milk. I love milk."

"So I noticed." He poured a cup of steaming coffee.

They lingered over brunch, but within the hour they were back in bed and in each other's arms.

They spent Saturday and Sunday making love. On Monday morning, while Gabe dozed, she shifted to look at him. She had put off telling him about Rebecca. But It was time to get back to the real world. This afternoon she would tell him the truth.

Later that morning as they ate breakfast inside, she toyed with her glass of orange juice. "Gabe, I need to get back to the ranch today. I've put things off so we could have this weekend, but I should return and get ready for tomorrow."

"I don't want to, but sure. We'll fly home." He pulled out his cell phone and called his pilot. "All done. I'll have you back at the ranch by four."

"Thanks," she said as her cell phone rang. She answered and heard Rebecca's high-pitched voice. She stood, glancing across the table at Gabe, who came to his feet when she did.

She motioned to her phone and left him, walking out on the balcony to talk to her daughter and then her mother.

When she said goodbye and ended the call, she turned to face Gabe. He had stepped out onto the balcony and stood by the door. His tan knit shirt fluttered slightly with the summer breeze. He was in his jeans and boots and looked relaxed, except his blue eyes were focused intently on her.

Her heart thudded, and she couldn't get her breath.

"What did you hear?" she blurted out, shocked to find him standing there.

"Sorry, Maddie, to intrude, but we've spent more than twenty-four hours in intimacy. As close as I've always felt to you, I know there's something you're hiding from me. Is there some kind of problem at home? If you're in any trouble, if you need money, you know I'll help any way I can."

She let out her breath the minute she learned that he thought she needed money. "So you didn't hear my conversation?"

"No, I didn't."

Her breathing returned to normal, but her nerves prickled. It really wouldn't have mattered whether he had heard her end of the call or not. He would never have figured out who she had spoken to.

"I'm not in any trouble. I definitely don't need money," she said, picking her words carefully. "I do need to talk to you, and I've put off doing so."

"Whenever you want," he said quietly, still studying her as if he had never seen her before.

"Let's go inside where there aren't distractions," she said, trying to compose herself.

"Sure," he said, holding the door for her. As soon as they were inside, he turned her to face him, resting both hands on her shoulders.

"Maddie, we've known each other a long time. Whatever is bothering you, you can tell me."

"I hope you feel that way after we talk. This isn't going to be easy. Let's sit, Gabe," she said, still trying to buy some time. She had decided to tell Gabe, but she hadn't given a lot of thought to how to go about it.

When she sat in a wing chair, he sat close to her on the sofa.

"Gabe, this could make a difference in our friendship."

"No, it won't. Nothing can."

"How I wish," she said. "But I don't think you'll feel that way shortly," she added, and his eyes narrowed.

Leaning forward, she locked her fingers together. "There's no easy way to do this."

Seven

Gabe sat waiting, unable to imagine what disturbed her so much He couldn't conceive of anything that would end their friendship, particularly after this weekend together, yet her apprehension showed in her brown eyes and in the slight frown that furrowed her brow. Her knuckles were white—something he had never seen on Maddie before. Through all their childhood scrapes, the arguments that last summer, he had never seen her as tense as she appeared to be this moment.

"Maddie, relax. It's me, Gabe."

"First, I want you to understand that I did what I thought was best."

"I can understand that," he said, wondering what she had done that made her think he would be so critical. He felt relaxed and curious, unable to guess what could possibly be the problem.

"I did what I thought would save us both. Promise me that you'll try to remember that," she repeated.

"This is something that concerns me?" he asked, startled. His puzzlement grew because he couldn't imagine one thing that Maddie was involved in that also concerned him.

"Yes, it does," she said, taking a deep breath.

"Say it, Maddie. We'll still be friends," he said, now anxious to have her spit it out. He was totally at a loss. How could all those phone calls concern something that involved him? He could not imagine what tie he would have to Maddie and whoever she had talked to, much less talked to in that caring, low-voiced tone.

"Gabe, I have a daughter, Rebecca. That's who I've been talking to on the phone."

Stunned, he stared at her. "A daughter? Why didn't you tell me? You said you're not married. And what does that have to do with me?" he asked. The minute the words spilled out of his mouth, he stared at her in shock. "You have a daughter and this concerns me?" he said, unable to get his breath.

Maddie's face had paled, and her hands were locked even more tightly together. She bit her lower lip.

He felt like ice. "How old is your daughter?" he asked quietly, thinking there could be only one possible, incredible, tie here.

"Rebecca is five years old now. Her birthday was in April. Gabe, Rebecca is your daughter."

Feeling as if he'd received a blow to his midsection, he lost his breath. He came to his feet, raking his hand through his hair, stunned by her news and equally shocked that Maddie had never told him.

"I have a daughter. You got pregnant that summer. Is that why you wanted me to stay so badly? Is that why you left and wouldn't talk to me?" The questions poured out. He stared at her as if he were looking at a stranger.

"To answer your questions—at first that was not why I wanted you to stay. At first, I didn't know I was pregnant. I didn't want you leaving the country when I didn't think you really needed to go."

"I have a five-year-old daughter. Five years, Maddie. This is my daughter?"

"Yes, Gabe. Rebecca is your daughter."

"Why in hell didn't you tell me?" he asked, and she flinched.

"I debated with myself for hours, days, upon end. I moved away for both our sakes."

"I don't understand how you can say that," he said, stunned, trying to think back to that summer. "Why didn't you give me some choices here? I've lost five years of her life." He paced the room without waiting for Maddie's answers. He was the father of a little girl. His child. His baby. He turned to stare at Maddie, who wiped away tears. He tried to control his anger, which simmered and threatened to erupt. Why hadn't she told him?

"Maddie, you kept the most important event of my life from me." He couldn't hold back his remarks about what she'd done. He hurt, and anger shook him beyond anything he had ever experienced. "How could you?"

"I know I kept it from you," she said, coming to her feet to stare at him. "But, back then, would you have said that her birth was the most important event of your life? Would you have wanted the responsibility of a baby? Or of marriage?"

"Hell, I don't know. If I had known I was going to be a father, I would have done the right thing. I would have married you and taken responsibility. Why didn't you give me that chance?"

"Because I thought I was saving us both. I knew you so well. Whether you wanted marriage or not, I knew you'd ask me to marry you. At that time, Gabe, you had made it clear that you were not ready for commitment. You know you weren't," she said, clenching her fists, her arms stiffly at her sides. "You would have felt duty bound to propose. I was young and inexperienced, and I would have felt duty bound to accept your proposal."

"What would have been so bad about that?" he asked.

"You weren't ready for marriage, and I wanted to leave here. I wanted college and a career and to live in a city. You didn't want to be tied down."

"It didn't mean I wouldn't have done it. Maddie, if we'd married we both might have matured and worked things out."

"Maybe, but Gabe, you left. You let me go on my way when you went yours."

He sucked in his breath as his stomach knotted. "You're right about that, but if I'd known... I could have changed. You owed it to me to tell me," he said, glaring at her, for the first time in his life angry with her. "I'm a father, Maddie. Legally, I had a right to know. Didn't you know that?"

"Yes, I knew you had rights, but I did what I thought best for the reasons I just told you," she said, her chin jutting out stubbornly.

"I think the legal reasons outweigh your immature judgment on the matter."

"Maybe in retrospect it does, but every time I thought it over, I came back to the same conclusion. You weren't ready for responsibility and marriage. I wasn't ready to give up college and the career I had dreamed about."

He felt a tight knot of anger that he was trying to curb. "Do you have a picture of her?"

"Yes, I do," she said, her voice softening. "Rebecca has your blue eyes and brown hair, but she looks like my baby pictures."

"I'm a father. That takes some getting used to," he said to no one in particular, while Maddie got her purse and pulled out her cell phone. He walked over to take the phone from her and looked at a little girl with big blue eyes. His insides clenched as he stared at the picture. "My baby. This is her." After a moment he looked up. "Can we print this out?"

"I have pictures on my laptop. I can print one of those out," Maddie replied. "I don't have it with me."

Gabe took it and felt shaken, staring at the picture of a pretty, blue-eyed little girl smiling at the camera. "She's beautiful," he said, filled with amazement to think she was his. He was a father. "She's so pretty," he said, wishing he had known her from birth.

"I think so. She's sweet, Gabe." Maddie looked at him, and he stared back, still unable to comprehend how she could have kept his baby from him. From his whole family.

"Damn, Maddie," he said quietly, still trying to hang on to his temper. "My folks are so excited over Jake's news that Caitlin is expecting a baby. They've both called me. Now I have to break the news to them that they have a grandchild they've never seen."

"Gabe, I'm sorry," Maddie stated, turning away from him to wipe her eyes. "I keep telling you that I did what I thought was best for all of us."

"Your family had to know."

"Yes, they knew. Since you had left for Nigeria, they agreed with me," she said. He knew she was crying, but all he could feel was anger for being cut out of his daughter's life for all these years.

"I didn't get to see my baby."

"Gabe, I don't think you would have felt this way about her then." She spun around to face him. "That's why I'm telling you now. You've changed. We both have. We've grown up. You told me about working with those boys. You told me how you liked the little kids you worked with. Six years ago you wouldn't have felt that way. Take an honest and long look back at that summer and how you felt about commitment then."

He clamped his mouth closed tightly, thinking back. Raking his fingers through his hair, he shook his head. "I don't know how I would have felt then if you'd told me you were pregnant. I know I would have asked you to marry me."

"I know you would have, too, whether you wanted to or not. You've always had a high sense of honor and duty. You would have pressured me to marry you. I would have married you and sacrificed my education, my legal career."

"Even so, I still think you should have let me know," he persisted, trying to absorb her shocking news. "It wasn't right, Maddie. I've lost years."

"I haven't told my family yet that you know. I told Rebecca that her father went away and didn't come back. She's little and she accepted that."

"Dammit, Maddie," he repeated. "You should have shared this with me." He looked again at the picture. "I want to meet her. I want to fly you home and meet her."

"I figured you would."

"Legally, I don't know what I can do. I'll contact my lawyer and find out."

"Gabe, don't try to take her from me. I plan to share her with you. Please don't rush into something."

"At this point, Maddie, I don't think you have a right to ask me for any favors," he snapped, aware he was giving her a harsh answer, but she had kept his baby from him all these years! "You didn't think about hurting me."

Her eyes widened, and she bit her lip, looking uncertain and worried. He couldn't take back what he said because he had meant it. He wanted to meet his daughter. "I'll tell you, I intend to be part of her life from now on."

"I expected you to. Gabe, I've thought this over these past few days. I knew telling you meant I'd have to give her up part of the time. Just remember that."

"I've given her up for five years. I would never have left the country if I'd known. We should have married and stayed a family. We both would have grown up. I'll make arrangements to fly to Florida. How soon can you get away from here for a short trip?"

"I think the earliest would be Thursday."

"No. We're going before then. You can come back. We'll take the company jet. Also, I want to tell my family. Whatever we do, Maddie, we should marry and give her my name. If you don't want to be married, we can divorce or separate, but she'll have my name and legally be my responsibility and my heir."

"Gabe, this is a huge change in our lives for both of us. Take some time to think things through."

"I don't have to think through wanting to meet her. I don't have to think through wanting her to have my name and be my legal heir."

"Even if you marry someone else later and have a family?"

He looked at the picture once more. "She's my daughter. She'll be part of my life from now on, and I'll be part of hers."

"You aren't in love with me and weren't thinking about marriage. Be careful what you do. At least, don't try to rush into an unwanted marriage. Meet her and get to know her and then we'll talk about the future."

He nodded. "We'll see. I'll think about the options and what we should do. She's with your mother now?"

"Yes. Mom keeps her while I'm away or at work. I've rarely been out of town and never away from her overnight. She loves to go to Mom's house. My grandparents love her, and she loves them. She's a joy, Gabe."

He kept staring at the picture, thinking of the years he hadn't known her. He would meet her this week. His child. "What's her full name?"

"Actually, I didn't give her a middle name. It's Rebecca Halliday."

"Then I want to give her a middle name."

Maddie nodded without saying anything.

He couldn't look at Rebecca's picture enough, and it still shocked him to know this little girl was his. He wanted to share the news with Jake, and he had to tell his family, but when he told them, he wanted to have things lined up so he could inform them what he would do and when they would see her. He didn't want his dad stepping in and trying to take charge of the situation.

Still shocked, he stared at the picture. All these years. Florida was a long way from Texas. He would have to forgive Maddie, but right now, he couldn't. He believed what she had told him—she had thought she was doing what was best for all. What she should have seen was that it hadn't been her decision alone. She should have shared this with him.

He walked to a window to stare outside without seeing any of the view. He was lost in his thoughts, running plans and possibilities through his mind.

Finally, he went to his bedroom to change and get ready to take Maddie back to her ranch.

When he returned to the front room, she waited with her things collected and ready to go.

"Maddie, I've been thinking about all of this. I postponed the flight home today by a couple of hours. I'm going to see Jake and tell him. Then he'll understand why you're changing your appointment."

"That's fine, Gabe," she replied quietly. Looking solemn and worried, she sounded subdued.

"While I'm out, I want to pick up some gifts to take to Rebecca. What does she like? I don't know anything about her! What size does she wear?"

"She's dainty, very small-boned. She wears a Toddler Five. Sometimes even a Toddler Four. She's into princess toys right now. She likes dolls, teddy bears, books, play makeup and toy jewelry. She likes to paint, and she has a small toy computer she thinks is fun. She can read. She's bright and quick. I'm taking her paints that I've already bought."

He nodded. "I'll probably call you from the toy department. I'll see you after a while." He left, knowing Maddie was hurting, but he didn't feel like offering comfort. He was adjusting to her news, still fighting his anger at her for keeping his child from him all this time.

He drove to Jake's Dallas condo. Caitlin greeted him, ushering him inside. Her auburn hair was tied behind her head. Dressed in jeans and a T-shirt, she looked as slender as ever.

"Congratulations," he said, smiling at her. "Jake told me the news."

Jake sauntered up to put his arm around her waist, and she smiled, looking up at her tall husband.

"Thanks. We're both thrilled. Thank you for the present. It will be a keepsake."

"You are welcome. I was delighted to learn I am going to be an uncle," Gabe said, wanting to focus on their news before he went to his own.

"Come in and sit," Jake said while Caitlin stepped away.

"I'll leave you two to yourselves. I'm writing letters," she said. "I know, an antiquated pastime in our electronic world."

"Caitlin, I'll talk to Jake, but you might as well join us for a few minutes and hear what I have to say. In some ways it will have an effect on all of us."

"Now I'm curious. Let's go to the front room," Jake said.

Gabe followed them past the fountain in the large entryway, into a room with leather furniture and a wall of books. As soon as Jake and Caitlin were seated on the sofa, Gabe moved to the mantel and propped his elbow against it.

"What's up?" Jake asked. "You sound as if something has happened."

"Something has. I've been seeing Maddie. She's shared some news with me today. It affects me, and both of you. If you remember, she and I broke up six years ago, and she was angry with me for leaving the country because of my job."

"I remember. Caitlin, you remember Maddie Halliday, don't you?"

Caitlin nodded. "Sure I do. We were never close friends, but we were in school together. Our families knew each other."

"Maddie and I dated before she moved away," Gabe said.

"I remember that. I had heard you left Texas because of your work and she went back to Tech. I lost touch with her and haven't seen her since."

"What's going on?" Jake asked, tilting his head. "You don't look happy, so I don't think you're going to announce an engagement."

"No. I'm happy, but my news is a shock. What I'm not happy about is that I've learned about this years later."

"So?" Jake persisted.

"Ready?" he asked, looking at his brother. "This afternoon Maddie confessed that I have a daughter. She's five years old."

"I'll be damned," Jake said, standing and placing his hands on his hips.

"Congratulations to you," Caitlin said, standing also. "I think this is something the two of you need to talk about in private. I'll leave you alone, and Jake can fill me in."

"Caitlin, you're family. I don't mind if you stay."

Shaking her head, she walked to the open door. "No. You need to talk to Jake. That's a big surprise, Gabe, to learn you have a five-year-old daughter. I'll see you before you leave," she added, closing the door behind her.

"Why didn't Maddie tell you that summer she was pregnant? Was it because she was so angry with you for leaving Texas? You always said she was getting too serious, but if she had wanted a proposal from you, I'd think she would have told you she was pregnant."

"I thought she was getting too serious, but she said when she found out she was pregnant, she knew I'd feel duty bound to propose and it would have been for the wrong reason."

She had a point. "No wonder you sounded as if the world had dropped out from under you. What are you going to do?"

"Fly to Florida later today and meet my daughter. Can we get you to change the time of your meeting with Maddie about buying the ranch?"

"Sure. I've just called Ed to make a firm offer. I think she'll accept it. We should be able to move quickly, but I can adjust my schedule so you two can go to Florida. You a dad—will wonders never cease. And before I become one. Wow."

"She should have told me. But I know she's right. I would have proposed, even though I hadn't wanted a commitment."

"Yes, I can see you doing that. It's what I would have done under those circumstances."

"She also said that she would have accepted, even though she wasn't ready for marriage. She wanted an education and a career. She wanted to leave Texas."

"That's probably true, too. Both of you were younger. There's no way you—me, either, for that matter—were as mature five or six years ago as we are now."

"I don't know how we'll work this out. I'm going to get to know my daughter. That is one thing I'm certain about."

"Why did Maddie tell you about Rebecca now?" Jake asked, his blue eyes full of curiosity.

"We've been getting close. And I told her about working with the two kids who stayed at the ranch. I told her about the kids after the storm. Because of that, she thinks I've matured and am more responsible. Maybe her conscience got to her. Jake, I've been close to Maddie all my life, but I feel like this is a betrayal. She had no right to keep my daughter from me."

"You're right, but I can see her argument, Gabe. Six years ago, you didn't want to marry. You wouldn't have done so unless you felt duty bound. You told me yourself Maddie was getting more serious than you liked and you weren't ready for commitment. You spent an hour after a rodeo, drinking beer with me and relating how much you wanted to avoid commitment."

"I suppose I did, but I still think I had a right to know."

"She should have informed you. If I were in your place, I'd be unhappy, too, Thankfully, she's told you now. At this point, I'm surprised she told you. By the end of next week, she could be back in Florida and no one here would have known one thing about your daughter."

"You're right. I should be thankful she confessed. She'll have to share Rebecca with me, and I know that will hurt her and her family. It sounds as if they adore the child. She's called Maddie often. I'd guess there have been calls I haven't known about."

"Florida is a hell of a way from Texas, but you've got your own plane, which will make it easier to fly back and forth."

"The outlook isn't good. Also, I want everything arranged and in place concerning Rebecca before I tell Mom and Dad about this."

"Oh, hell, yes. This is one time Dad would step in

and meddle in your life big-time. I don't think your income from your investments would stop him in this situation."

"No, it wouldn't."

"Don't worry. They won't hear one word from me. You can count on Caitlin to keep quiet, too, until you're ready for everyone to hear the news."

"I appreciate that. I had to tell you."

"I'm glad, but I'm not sure what I can do to help you."

"You can listen. Before I call our attorney, I want to meet Rebecca and give this more thought. I don't even know what I want at this point, except to have Rebecca in my life and see to it that Maddie shares her with me."

"Are you going to propose to Maddie?"

"I told her I want to marry, if only temporarily, to give Rebecca the Benton name and make her my heir. It'll be a name-only wedding—a business contract. Maddie is as tied to Florida and her life there as I am to Texas and my life here."

"That's what you've said. Are you sure?"

"Why do you think she's selling the ranch? She doesn't want any part of life in West Texas. She can't wait to return to Miami. From the start of this visit, she has told me she would not be coming back here. Of course, that might have had something to do with the secret she was keeping from me, because that will have to change now. She'll have to come back. But I can't see a real marriage looming. I want to marry her, to give Rebecca my name and make her legally mine. Maddie may fight that. I don't know."

"You'll work it out. You two have been close forever."

"Yeah. I should get back. Now you're an uncle, Jake."

Jake smiled. "Indeed, I am. Little Rebecca will get a bundle of relatives and in seven months, she'll have a new cousin. Rebecca Benton, the newest Benton. It's great that you have a daughter, Gabe."

Gabe shook his head. "Damn straight, but I'm still in shock." He headed for the door. In the hall, Caitlin reappeared. Jake placed his arm around her once again.

"Congratulations," Caitlin said, smiling at him. "It's wonderful news."

"Thanks," Gabe said gruffly. He walked to the door with Jake.

"Take care of yourself and let me know how it goes. I'll rearrange the appointments I have. We can work that out easily."

"Thanks, Jake. I'll keep in touch on this trip, which will be quick."

In minutes, Gabe sped away toward a local mall, where he hoped to find presents. Then he'd go to Florida and meet his daughter. His stomach fluttered at the thought.

And he still needed to decide how he would deal with Maddie. Memories of the weekend returned. He was stunned, angry right now, but earlier he had been deliriously happy with her. Had he been falling in love with her?

This weekend, he'd been happier with her than with any other woman he had ever known. In bed she was hot and wild and eager. She was the closest friend he'd ever had, except for Jake, and in some ways, Gabe was far closer to Maddie. Even when she'd been keeping this shocking secret from him, he'd been able to read her distress.

He'd already considered marrying Maddie, dreamed of it, even. But, at the same time, there were reasons he didn't want to be in love with her. Without serious compromise, any relationship would have to be a long-distance one.

Maybe he was already in love with her. Maybe he had loved Maddie for years without acknowledging his feelings. Whatever he was feeling, he wanted to marry Maddie and give Rebecca the Benton name. Would he ever get Maddie to agree?

Eight

After watching Gabe drive away from his Dallas condo, Maddie sat on the balcony with her cell phone in hand. She had to make the call and the best time to do it was while Gabe was away. Reluctantly, she dialed her mother to break the news.

Over an hour later, she'd finished her call with her mother. Maddie sighed deeply, wiping her eyes. It had been an emotional call in a day filled with raw emotions. Her mother had cried. Maddie hated that she'd had to tell her the news over the phone, but she needed to warn her family before Gabe flew her home.

She, as well as her family, adored Rebecca, who was their world. Everything they did revolved around their little girl. Maddie rubbed her forehead. After she had told Gabe, she had wondered if she had made the mistake of her life in revealing the truth to Gabe. He was hurt and angry. Her mother was hurt and angry. Her grandparents would be also.

This situation had been a mess from the beginning, but at least she felt now that she had done the right thing. No matter what upheaval this revelation caused in their lives, Rebecca deserved to know her father and Gabe deserved to know his daughter. Gabe would be good to Rebecca. Gabe was already calculating the best way to take care of his daughter. Even going so far as to make plans for a marriage that revolved totally around the benefits for Rebecca.

Which was all right, Maddie realized. If Gabe had been head over heels in love with her, it would only mean more heartache. Neither of them wanted to compromise when it came to their lifestyles.

But he wasn't in love, so it would be easier to take a practical approach to whatever they did. She just hoped Gabe never realized the extent of her love for him.

She couldn't keep from crying when she thought about this morning and his anger. She had hurt him badly, far worse than any hurts stirred up that last summer they were together. She had been the one hurt then.

What a muddle she had made of things.

Maddie went to wash her face, hoping she could control her emotions by the time Gabe returned. And continue to contain them when she got home.

Studying herself in the mirror, she gazed at her image, but could only see Gabe's eyes, earlier today, flashing fire, his hands jammed in his pockets.

She heard a car and soon Gabe entered the condo. Looking fit and full of vitality, and carrying an armload of packages, he entered the front room. Her heartbeat quickened while regret tugged at her. She hated the rift that had come between them. After the weekend they had just shared, she wanted to walk into his arms and have him hold her tightly.

He paused to meet her gaze, staring at her in a long, solemn moment before he laid his gifts on the sofa. Anger still smoldered in the depths of his eyes, and she struggled to keep back tears.

"I bought some things," he said gruffly. She looked again at the mound of packages.

"Gabe, that looks like Christmas," she said.

"I wanted some presents. I want to see if you approve," he said, and the tension eased a fraction while she walked closer to look at the array of sacks and boxes.

"I'm sure they're great."

"Maddie, I know nothing about five-year-old little girls. Come check over this stuff and tell me if it's appropriate. If you think she won't like it, I'll send it back to the store."

Maddie had to smile. "Sure." She picked up a box with a beautiful princess doll in a beaded pink dress.

"Gabe, this alone will delight her. This doll must have cost a small fortune," she said, looking at the extravagant dress that had to have been hand sewn. "This is gorgeous, and she'll be delighted with it. Rebecca takes care of her things. Probably my mother's influence. She'll treasure it." Maddie looked at the array of packages again. "Save some of those for another time."

"Okay, the doll goes with us. Put it on the other end of the sofa. The rejects we'll put on the table."

Maddie smiled again. "This is sort of overkill."

"No, it isn't. What about this?" He handed her a

large box. She opened it to see a fuzzy, incredibly soft white bear.

"Gabe, it's perfect. You have two perfect gifts. Don't give her so much she can't take it all in. Giving a little less will make what you give her more meaningful."

"You think?" he asked, frowning.

"Yes, definitely," she said, feeling amused and hurting at the same time.

"All right. I got her a little necklace. Let me include that because it's not a toy." He rummaged in a sack and pulled out a box. "It's already wrapped, so I can't get your approval on this, but I took a picture of it." He pulled out his phone and showed her.

Maddie leaned close to look at a gold heart on a chain. "It's beautiful. She'll love it."

"Oh, one more thing. I can't go without giving her a book. A book is something important. I didn't know what she had, but the clerk said this is a newer one and it's been popular. You read it on the plane and see if it's right for her. If it is, I have a gift sack and they gave me some paper."

"All right. Now this has to be all." She turned to look at Gabe, who was only inches away, and for the first time since she had broken the news, he did not seem furious with her.

He glanced down at her and then plunged back into the sack. "Don't go away."

"I thought you were going to stop with these four," she said.

He fished around and came up with a box wrapped in silver paper, bound in white ribbon, with a spray of artificial flowers and beads tied into the bow.

Startled, she looked from the gift to Gabe, who gazed back at her with a somber expression.

"Maddie, eventually, I'll get over my anger. I know you made the best decision you could at the time. I wasn't ready to settle down that summer, something I told you over and over again. I never dreamed a baby would be involved."

Her eyes stung with tears, and she wanted to reach for him, but she still felt a coolness emanating from him. "I'm glad you can see why I didn't tell you. Gabe, I worried over that decision for a very long time, all during my pregnancy and for years afterward. I'm sorry to have hurt you, but I am glad you and Rebecca will be able to know each other now."

"In the meantime, we're going to have to work together. This is an offering to make amends."

She took the box and sat to open it, taking care with the beautiful wrappings and noting the name of an expensive jewelry store.

She opened the decorative box to find a plain black box inside. Surprised again, she opened it. A delicate, filigreed gold bracelet was inside. Small diamonds sparkled in the light.

"Gabe," she said, looking up at him. "The bracelet is beautiful. This isn't just 'making amends.'"

"Yes, it is, Maddie. You had my baby. I wasn't there to give you anything then. I want you to have this."

A knot hurt her throat. She wanted to throw her arms around him and feel Gabe's strong arms holding her. She wanted their world the way it had been this past weekend. And she didn't think it would ever be that way again. Instead, she ran her fingers lightly over the delicate gold. "This is so beautiful. I don't know what to say, except thank you."

"As long as you like it."

"Of course, I like it." She looked up at him. "I wish I could make things right between us."

"We have a lot to work out," he agreed. Once again she was ensnared in his steady gaze, and the tension between them increased.

"I called Mom. She'll tell my grandparents that you know about Rebecca. She knows we're coming to Florida."

"I suppose she didn't take it well."

"No, she didn't."

"I'm sorry for that, but she was part of the decision that led us to where we are today."

Maddie nodded. She had a lump in her throat again. She looked at the boxes and her bracelet, struggling to regain her composure. "The gifts are wonderful. You didn't need to do all this. Rebecca is so easy to please."

"That's good." They faced each other, the silence growing tense once more. She ached for his arms and his cheerful optimism. A chasm had opened between them, and she worried it would never be bridged.

Then he reached for her.

"Come here," he said, pulling her close.

"Gabe," she said, unable to keep back her tears. "I'm sorry for the way everything worked out."

"Me, too. But I know the truth now, and I'll get to see my daughter grow up. Even though I don't like it, I know you did what you thought was best for all of us."

She held him tightly, wondering if he could ever truly forgive her. At least they were making a start.

"I need your forgiveness, too, for walking out that summer," he admitted, making more tears come.

"I've forgiven you, long ago. We've both moved on. We'll need our friendship to get through this, Gabe. Rebecca and I have been so close. I've spent very few nights away from her. When I came for Granddad's funeral. This trip. Other than work, and an occasional evening out when she stays with Mom, I'm always there for her."

He ran his hand over her head lightly, twisting his fingers in her hair. "I'll be there for her too, now. And for you, Maddie. You'll have my friendship. I promise." He put his fingers beneath her chin to raise her face, and she wiped her eyes hurriedly. "Sorry."

"Don't apologize. And don't cry. I'm not taking her from you. We'll work things out."

"I hope so," she said, feeling slightly better. "Gabe, I want her to meet you and get to know you a little before I tell her who you are. I'd like to introduce you as my friend, first."

He gazed into her eyes while he thought it over. "Sort of ease into the announcement. We can see how it goes, Maddie. Just don't wait too long."

"Here. I want to wear my bracelet. Put it on me please."

She handed him the featherlight bracelet and held out her wrist, watching as he bent his head to fasten the clasp. His brown hair was thick, neatly combed. She could detect the scent of his aftershave—see his thick, long lashes as he looked down to finish his task.

"There."

"Thank you. It's gorgeous, and I'll treasure it."

"I should have been there to give you a gift when you were pregnant," he said. "Did you have morning sickness or anything?"

"No. A very uneventful pregnancy and a quick delivery," she answered, looking into his blue eyes and wishing their lives were different, more compatible. She ached with love for Gabe, and she wanted a life with him, but that was impossible. "Rebecca has always been a joy. You'll see."

"We might as well get ready to go. I'll leave the other presents for Rebecca until next time," he said.

"I'm packed and ready."

"It'll take me about five minutes. I brought something for your mother and your grandparents, so take those out to go with us. You'll be able to tell because of the way they are wrapped. For better or worse, we're going to be family."

His words tore at her heart. "You're right. Our lives will be forever linked."

A muscle worked in his jaw, and he gazed back at her in silence. His anger hadn't disappeared, but it had been tempered.

She hurt deep inside. By telling the truth, she had tied her life with Gabe's forever. By telling the lie in the first place, she may have lost him forever.

"I love her with all my heart. You will, too," she said, looking into his blue eyes, still wishing things could be as easy as they'd been this weekend. Their gazes locked and tension flared.

"Stop worrying, Maddie. I told you, we'll work through this."

"I hope so, Gabe," she said softly. As she watched, his blue eyes changed. The coldness vanished and he leaned down to kiss her tenderly. She held him tightly, relishing his kiss.

"Let's get ready to go."

Shortly, Gabe returned from the bedroom and his limo driver appeared to collect the luggage and the packages.

She could feel the tension in their silence as they rode to the airport. Yes, she hurt, but if she had to do it over again, she would still tell him. She had done the right thing. She believed that now just as much as she had believed that when she'd chosen to keep Rebecca a secret. She and Gabe had both changed.

Still, she couldn't imagine how they would work out sharing Rebecca when they lived more than a thousand miles apart. Gabe had resources at his disposal—a jet, a limo—but it was a huge distance and it would complicate their lives.

An hour later, they were airborne in the largest Benton jet. Gabe had paid someone in one of the airport stores to gift wrap the toys he was taking to Rebecca. He faced Maddie, who sat close enough that their knees almost touched.

Her silky hair was tied behind her head with a scarf. She wore pale blue slacks and a matching silk blouse and high-heeled sandals. She looked cool and poised and more like herself than she had earlier today. They would spend several nights in Florida and then fly back to Texas so she could take care of the closing of the ranch house and its contents and the sale of the land to Jake.

He studied Maddie now, desire stirring in spite of the emotional roller coaster of the day. His initial anger had subsided, and other emotions were surfacing. Desire flared, hot and insistent, as if a release for all the tension that had wound between them. She was enticing. He wanted to pull her into his lap and peel away the slacks and shirt and kiss her senseless. Aboard the jet, she wouldn't allow any such thing. At her house, he wondered whether she would put him in a separate bedroom. He hadn't asked her, and no matter what conflicts still stood between them, he hoped she didn't.

She turned big brown eyes on him. "What's on your mind?"

"Guess."

She smiled at him. "Forget I asked."

"There's a bedroom on this plane. Let me show it to you."

To his surprise she began to unbuckle her seat belt. He unfastened his quickly and stood, taking her hand and leading her back to the bedroom. He closed the door and pulled her into his arms, kissing her.

Clothing was shed and then he lifted her to the bed. He loved her with an intensity that built swiftly. Kissing and caressing him, she moved over him. "Sex is a bridge over the troubles and differences between us," she said. Her brown eyes were like midnight, her lips red and swollen from his kisses.

He pulled her down to him, and, with a groan, he rolled her over so he was above her. Then he stepped away to get protection, returning to make love to her with a frantic need that he hadn't shown before.

Release brought rapture. Gabe whispered to her, murmurings she couldn't understand because of her pounding heart. "It's good between us, Maddie. So damn good," he whispered, showering her with kisses on her throat and face. "Ah, darlin', we'll get over the rough spots. Maddie, I wish I had been with you."

"Gabe, I had to let go of the 'if onlys' long ago," she said quietly, running her finger along his jaw and then over his broad shoulder.

"My bracelet is beautiful," she said, holding up her arm and looking at the faint glimmer of gold. "I may not take it off."

Gabe stretched out a long arm and turned on a small lamp on the bedside table.

"You don't need to," he said. "It's a token, Maddie."

She rose up to look down at him. "I'll always love it because you gave it to me." She leaned down to kiss him. He wrapped his arm around her to hold her close while he kissed her in return.

She shifted and settled in his arms as he turned on his back and pulled her close against him. "This is better. I don't want problems between us."

"I don't either, Gabe."

"Then we'll try to avoid them," he said lightly. "Suppose she doesn't like me?"

"I can't believe you said that," Maddie said. "You are always so filled with confidence. Since when has there ever been a female who hasn't liked you? Besides that, she's yours, Gabe. She'll be like you, so she will like you."

"I hope so. It's scary. A baby has to accept you because you're all a baby knows or has, but a five-year-old—I'm certain she has definite likes and dislikes."

"I can't believe this," Maddie said. "You make deals worth millions. Never, ever, have I seen you uncertain around a woman, and I'll bet you weren't scared around those kids who worked with you."

"That is different from this. This is my one and only daughter and I don't want to blow it."

"You've always been so self-assured it borders on arrogance. You always want to take charge of every situation, which you have done here, I might add. This nervous uneasiness is totally amazing to me."

"You're really not helping me here," he said.

"You—asking me for help—mercy," she teased, half in jest and half incredulous because it was so unlike Gabe.

He suddenly rolled her over and was on top, holding

his weight on his elbows. "You think this is funny, Maddie?" She could see the amusement in his eyes, and she wound her fingers in his hair as she laughed.

"Stop worrying. She'll love you. I love you. Rebecca will love you." She said the words lightly, aware that was the first time she had ever said that to him, assuming he would think she was still teasing him.

Instead, his eyes narrowed. "You love me, Maddie?"

She drew a deep breath while her mind raced. "Maybe it's time to be honest about everything. Yes, I love you. I always have. There hasn't been anyone else, Gabe. Not once in all those six years."

He drew a deep breath, frowning slightly, and then he leaned down to close the distance between them and kissed her, hard and long.

Her heart thudded as she kissed him in return. He hadn't said *I love you*. But now he knew. Whatever happened between them, she had bared all her secrets.

She turned slightly. "Gabe, I tried to forget you. I really did. I thought I was succeeding—until this trip."

Still, he gazed at her intently, without saying what he was thinking. "I'm glad you couldn't forget me," he said finally. Then he kissed her again, a long, steamy kiss that became making love.

Later, as he held her close, she said, "I don't want to be in bed when this plane lands. It's time to dress and go back to our seats."

He glanced at his watch. "We have a little bit of time."

"One of us is returning to her seat," Maddie said, stepping out of bed.

When she was back in her seat, she realized that their lovemaking had shattered the tension between them. She hadn't felt this lighthearted in six years. She had revealed Rebecca's identity. She had revealed the truth in her own heart. But she knew tough times still lay ahead.

It was early evening when they parked in the driveway of a small house with palms and a well-kept yard. Beds of flowers bloomed, and the porch held pots of yellow bougainvillea and green banana plants.

Gabe's palms were sweaty. "Maddie, I've ridden giant bulls that didn't make me this nervous."

She patted his arm. "Relax, Gabe. You'll see. She's a sweetheart. You don't need to wear that suit coat. It's too hot. You don't have to be formal. Rebecca will never notice. We can leave my luggage until later, but I want the brown bag, because I have presents, too."

"I'll get them." He pulled off his coat before he got out of her car. He retrieved her luggage and his gifts from the backseat. They walked around the side of the house and entered through a back door.

"Mom! Rebecca!" Maddie called.

Setting down the luggage and gifts, Gabe stood behind her, never noticing his surroundings. All he could hear was the patter of feet and all he could see was the little girl dashing into the room.

Nine

Long brown hair swung with each step. She wore sandals and a pink shirt and shorts. Gabe's heart thudded. She was beautiful, even more so than in her picture. A live doll with creamy skin, thickly lashed blue eyes. Rosy cheeks complemented her big smile. She held out her arms as she ran for Maddie, who scooped her up into a hug.

He felt a tightness in his chest as he watched them. His daughter. He loved her without even knowing her. She was precious, beautiful, his baby. It was painfully obvious that she loved Maddie, and Maddie loved her.

In that moment, he knew he had to forgive Maddie for keeping the truth from him. Maddie was levelheaded. She always had been. She told him she had done what she thought was best for both of them, and, if he was honest about the young man he'd been, he'd admit she was right. He needed to accept that, and forgive her.

After all, he had walked out on her, and he needed a bit of forgiveness himself. From now on, he was in Rebecca's life and that was all that mattered. With emotion overtaking him, he wanted to walk over and wrap both of them in his embrace, but he couldn't. Rebecca had no idea who he really was.

Rebecca's thin arms had locked around Maddie's neck, and she squeezed tightly. "I missed you," she said in a high, childish voice.

Still holding Rebecca, Maddie faced Gabe. "Rebecca, I brought my friend with me. I want you to meet him."

Rebecca looked around her mother, and Gabe gazed into huge blue eyes that were the color of his own. His heart pounded more fiercely than it ever had as Rebecca smiled and gazed at him with curiosity.

"Hi, Rebecca," he said, feeling choked, and trying to get a grip on his emotions.

Maddie turned to her mother, who was standing in the kitchen doorway. "Mom, you remember Gabe."

It was an effort to tear his gaze from Rebecca.

"It's good to see you, Mrs. Halliday," he said. He could imagine her worry about losing Rebecca to him, yet she was quiet and probably resigned to his presence in their lives.

She merely nodded, her gaze resigned and sad.

Maddie patted her mother's arm and moved toward Rebecca. "I have presents. Let's get them out." She opened the brown carry-on and pulled out a wrapped gift. "Here's something for you, sweetie."

"Let's take them in the other room and sit where we can enjoy opening them," Tracie Halliday suggested.

Picking up packages, Gabe followed the women into a small living room. It was tastefully furnished in thickly cushioned upholstered furniture, cherrywood tables gleaming with polish and area rugs. After placing all the presents on one cushioned chair, he sat in another.

"Now you can open your presents," Maddie said.

With a big smile Rebecca tore into the wrapping and pulled out paints and a huge tablet. "Thank you," she said, running to kiss Maddie, who hugged her.

"Take a present to Grandma." Maddie picked up one tied with a large pink bow and Rebecca carried it to Tracie, whose face lost a bit of its sadness as she smiled at Rebecca.

"Help me open this, Rebecca," she said, letting her granddaughter tug free the bow. Together, they tore off the silver paper, and Tracie opened a box to hold up a sparkling Waterford crystal vase. "It's beautiful, Maddie. My flowers will be pretty in this. Thank you. Isn't this pretty, Rebecca?" she asked, turning it so Rebecca could see it. Rebecca ran her tiny fingers over it.

Gabe got his present. "Rebecca, I brought you a present today, too," he said, holding out the box with the doll.

She accepted it, removing the ribbon after a struggle and then tearing off the paper. She gasped with delight. "Mommy, look!" she exclaimed, hurriedly opening the box and trying to pull the doll out of it.

"Let me help you, Rebecca," Gabe said, moving to the sofa and looking at the contents of the box. The doll was held in by wire. Gabe carefully removed it, and when he finally handed it to Rebecca, she smiled broadly.

"Thank you," she said politely, her attention returning to the doll. She gazed at it with wide-eyed wonder while she lightly touched the dress. "She's beautiful. Mommy, look. Isn't she pretty?" She carried the doll first to her mother and then to her grandmother.

"She's very pretty," her grandmother said in a flat voice.

Gabe picked up the present for Tracie and carried it to her. "Mrs. Halliday, this is for you."

Startled, she looked up and then accepted the gift cautiously. She took out a gold chain spaced with diamonds.

"It's beautiful," she said, running her forefinger over it.

"Mom, that's gorgeous."

"You didn't need to do this," she said stiffly, looking as if she couldn't decide whether to keep it or not.

"I'll be part of Rebecca's life now, and part of your life. This is a token of appreciation, for sharing her with me," he said.

Her lips thinned in a tight smile. "Thank you," she said, looking down at the necklace.

"Let me put it on you," Maddie said, taking the necklace and fastening it around her mother's neck.

"It's beautiful," Tracie said again, sounding non-committal.

Rebecca played with her new doll, and Gabe turned to pick up another present. "Rebecca, I brought something else for you," he said, holding out another box that was wrapped in pink and blue paper and tied with a pink bow.

With sparkling eyes and a big smile, Rebecca took the package and tore it open, pulling out the white teddy bear to hug it.

"So what do you say?" Maddie prompted.

"Thank you," Rebecca said instantly, holding the bear tightly. "I like him."

"I'm glad you do," Gabe said. "You'll have to think about a name for him."

"What's your name?"

"Gabriel."

"Gabrel," she declared, smiling at Gabe.

He wanted to hold her close. Instead, he had to take it slowly and let her get accustomed to him. "Now, two more things for you, Rebecca." He held out the smaller packages. She took the larger and opened it to find the book, which she ran to show her mother.

"Maybe Gabe will read it to you later, if you want," she suggested. "What do you say to him?"

"Thank you," Rebecca stated politely before running to pick up the last present. When she opened it to reveal the necklace, she held it up. "It's pretty. Thank you," she said to Gabe. "Mommy, look." Again, she hurried to show Maddie, who put it on her daughter while Rebecca stood quietly.

"I'll put all this away," Tracie said, standing to gather up the discarded ribbons and wrapping paper. Maddie stood and offered to help, and together they finished picking up and left the room.

He knew Maddie had gone so he could have time alone with Rebecca. He got down on the floor. "Let's see Gabrel," he said, pronouncing the name as Rebecca had. Instantly, she was in a world of make-believe, with the doll and the bear.

While they sat on the floor and chatted, he tried to keep some of his attention on the conversation, but his focus was on Rebecca, who played with her new doll and teddy bear and obviously loved them.

He couldn't stop looking at his daughter, wanting to watch everything she did. He played with her, talking for the teddy bear while she earnestly held the doll and made conversation.

"Do you like to play with dolls?" Gabe asked when there was a lull.

"Yes. Want to see all my princess dolls?" Rebecca asked. "I cleaned my room for Mommy, since she was coming home. I'll show you."

Gabe followed her into a hall and past one bedroom. He could hear Maddie and her mother talking in the kitchen.

"See my dolls," Rebecca said, running across a room that was obviously hers. It had white furniture, splashes of pink in the pillows, cushions and bedding. There was a large dollhouse on one side of the room. On the other was a glass cabinet filled with beautiful dolls.

Maddie entered the room. "Are you looking at all the dolls?"

"Yes. We've been playing and talking," he said, wanting to put his arm around Maddie's waist, but holding back because of Rebecca.

He spent the next half hour looking at dolls and teddy bears and talking with Rebecca while Maddie hovered in the background and occasionally entered into their conversation.

Finally, she told Gabe they would get ready to go to dinner, and he returned to the living room to wait.

When everyone joined him, they got in a limo leased from a national agency he used when away from Texas.

Rebecca was fascinated with the limo and Gabe showed her everything, letting her climb around and touch things before the driver ever started the motor.

Dinner was long and Gabe tried to charm all three females. He had known Maddie's mother all his life, but not well, and it wasn't until dessert that he wrung the first full smile from her.

It was half-past ten and Rebecca had fallen asleep when they finally dropped off Tracie and the limo drove to Maddie's house.

Gabe carried Rebecca inside while Maddie switched on lights and locked the doors.

"I can drive my car tomorrow, Gabe," Maddie said.

He shook his head. "I have a limo at my disposal. You might as well let me provide your transportation this time."

"Very well. It will complicate your schedule."

"Not so much. You can go wherever and whenever you want. Just tell the driver. My schedule is flexible."

"Thanks," she replied.

He placed Rebecca in bed carefully. She was tiny, fragile and totally fascinating to him. As Maddie slipped off the girl's shoes, Gabe looked up at the mother of his child.

"She's beautiful, Maddie," he said, wanting them to be together, to be a family. "Forgive me. I shouldn't have left you. Unfortunately, I can't take it back now. I know you did what you thought was best, too."

She hugged him, closing her eyes. "I hope you do," she said. "She likes you, Gabe." She looked down at him. "I think I can tell her tomorrow who you are."

"That scares me more than anything else that's happened in my life."

"She'll love you. You did fine with her. Let me tuck her in, and we can go in the living room to talk."

He leaned down to brush a kiss on Rebecca's forehead, watching her sleep. He walked away, stopping at the door as Maddie tucked Rebecca in and kissed her lightly. When Maddie joined him, he put his arm around her waist.

They went to the front of the house to a living room that was filled with rattan and wicker furniture, plank floors and framed watercolors of seascapes and landscapes.

"See, we're not so different when it comes to decor," Maddie said. "Want anything to drink?" she asked.

He gazed down into her big, brown eyes and wanted her with all his being. "Maddie, come here," he said, ignoring her question. He drew her close to kiss her, forgetting everything else.

After a startled moment, she wrapped her arms around his neck and clung tightly to him, kissing him in return.

He didn't know how much later it was when he picked her up to carry her to her bedroom by way of her pointed directions.

Taking time, they made love. Gabe wanted her more than he ever had. Later, as his heartbeat returned to normal, he held her close and combed her hair from her face with his fingers. "This has been one of the greatest days of my life—to see and begin to know my daughter. But I don't think I'll ever win over your mother."

"I don't know. She's just scared she'll lose Rebecca."

"I'm not taking Rebecca away from her grand-mother!"

"Mom thawed some. Thanks in part to that spectacular gold and diamond necklace. You turning on the charm at dinner helped, too. She's scared of the changes that must happen now. So am I, Gabe," Maddie said solemnly, looking at him.

He gazed down at her. "I don't have answers yet. But

I know we will work something out. I want to know my daughter. I want her in my life. I want to give her things, to do things for her."

"Let's see what we can do before we call in the attorneys."

He nodded. "That's fine with me. I want Rebecca to know me before we change any of her routines. She wouldn't want to go anywhere with me right now because I'm a stranger to her."

"You're right. It's going to mean a lot of trips to Florida for you, Gabe. I can take her back to Texas with me when I go, to help you both get to know each other."

Maddie lay in his arms with her blond hair spread over his shoulder. She looked beautiful, warm, sexy. He wanted to forget the problems between them, forget everything except her.

"Gabe, I know I said we could tell Rebecca the truth tomorrow, but I'm thinking she may need more time."

"You're right. She needs to know me better, Maddie."

"I agree. Tomorrow morning I have to go into the office until noon, then I'll take off. We can spend the afternoon and evening with her here. When we return to Texas, I'll take her with me. I want to tell her about you when the time seems right. It may be a while before I can bring it up. If it doesn't seem okay tomorrow, I won't tell her. I want her to know and like you first."

"Whenever you tell her, it'll be a shock. She'll ask me why I left. That's what you said you told her—that I left and didn't come back."

"Yes, that's what I said. When she's older, I'll explain what really happened, but I think the full truth would be confusing to a five-year-old."

"I agree. I'll keep it simple and tell her I didn't know about her birth until now or I would have come back."

"And that's the truth in the most basic manner. I think she'll accept it. I don't know whether we'll have time on this trip, but when you do have time, I made scrapbooks and videos of Rebecca that I'll show you."

"We have time now," he said, sitting up, and she had to laugh.

"It's late, Gabe."

"Not that late. Let's see the scrapbooks."

Within the hour, they sat at the kitchen table with a stack of scrapbooks. He saw that the dates covered the time from Rebecca's birth to the present. Bare chested, Gabe wore jeans and Maddie had pulled on cutoffs and a shirt.

He lost awareness of time as he pored over the pictures, running his hand over some, feeling a knot in his throat several times. It hurt to know he hadn't been a part of Rebecca's life when the pictures were taken.

Next, Maddie got out DVDs she had made, and he watched pictures and listened to Rebecca's childish voice. He pulled Maddie onto his lap and held her close, trying in some small way to get back those years and be a part of their little family.

When the DVDs ended, she turned to him, nearly slipping off his lap. "Gabe, that's all."

He kissed her, a kiss that turned into passion, but when he began to unfasten her shirt, she stopped him and shook her head. "The rest of tonight, let's sleep in separate bedrooms."

He nodded, and she stood, moving away from him. "Gabe, it's after four in the morning."

"I know," he said, standing and helping her put things away and turn off lights.

At the door of the bedroom she had given him, he kissed her again.

In minutes, he was in bed, staring into the dark and trying to sort out the depth of his feelings for Maddie. He loved her. He wanted the relationship between them to go back to the way it had been before they'd both made mistakes. He couldn't stay angry with her, and he couldn't get her out of mind. The most logical thing to do was to get married—a real marriage, not a paper marriage just to give Rebecca his name.

He thought about the past weeks and his feelings for Maddie. He was in love. Even if there had been no baby, no Rebecca, he would still love her. As for marriage, he couldn't honestly say he wasn't influenced by the reality of the situation. Under the circumstances, it was the best solution to their problems. He loved Maddie and he wanted Rebecca to be a Benton.

On the plane, Maddie had admitted she loved him. She'd even said he had been the only man in her life. Maddie had to love him with all her heart to continue to feel that strongly about him through all the years, the separation and the upheaval in their lives. They loved each other—he wanted to marry her and they would be a family.

She was so damned independent and so damned determined to live in Miami. Could *he* make a change? Maybe there was a compromise he just hadn't figured out yet.

The next day they went to Tracie's house for breakfast. She was solemn, but not as quiet as when he had first arrived. While they left Rebecca with her grandmother, he had the limo drop Maddie at her office. He would pick her up for lunch, and she would take the rest of the afternoon off work.

Gabe drove to a jewelry store. When he left, he sat in the back of the limo and looked at the six-carat diamond he had purchased for Maddie. He couldn't guess her reaction.

At lunchtime, the limo parked in front of her building, and he waited, watching her step outside into the bright sunshine.

His pulse jumped at the sight of her. She had her hair piled on top of her head, pinned and looking businesslike. Her pale blue-and-white cotton suit and blue blouse also looked conservative, part of the business world. To his satisfaction, the suit skirt was short and her long legs were gorgeous. In her high-heeled sandals and short skirt, she turned heads as she crossed the sidewalk to the limo. The driver held the door for her, and she stepped inside, looking into Gabe's eyes as she smiled and sat beside him.

"Hi," she said.

He turned in the seat, pulling her into his arms and gazing into her eyes.

He kissed her before releasing her. "I want to see Rebecca, but I also want to be alone with you. I want it all."

"For now, we'll be with Rebecca."

They had a quick lunch, then stopped for lemonade and cookies with Tracie and Rebecca before taking Rebecca back to Maddie's house. They spent the afternoon together, and Gabe had a chance to talk and play with Rebecca all afternoon and early evening before Maddie declared it was bedtime.

Gabe got to read one bedtime story to Rebecca. Holding her on his lap, he read, letting her turn the pages. She smelled sweet, and he didn't want to tell her good-night.

He hurt whenever he thought about leaving them. It was going to be hard to return to the ranch and not see them. At least he didn't have to tell them goodbye this week because they would fly back to Texas with him, but too soon they would part. He'd been mulling it over all day, but as far as he could see, there was no way he could move to Florida. His business, his family—everything was in Texas. He and Maddie had some difficult decisions ahead.

Maddie sat across from Gabe and Rebecca, watching them read. Maddie's heart twisted. Rebecca liked Gabe. She had rarely warmed to a stranger so quickly. Maddie wanted Rebecca to know the truth, but it had to be revealed carefully. She couldn't rush into it.

When Gabe finished the story, he carried Rebecca to bed and tucked her in, brushing a light kiss on her forehead before leaving her with Maddie.

Maddie smoothed Rebecca's hair from her face, gazing at her daughter, wishing she could hold her close for hours. Reluctantly, she tiptoed out of the room. She had changed to cutoffs and a T-shirt in the early afternoon and her hair was in a thick braid down her back. Gabe was relaxing on the patio by the pool.

She sat with him, and he settled her into his lap.

"You have the intercom turned on so you can hear Rebecca?"

"Yes. Usually, she's a sound sleeper," she said, looking into Gabe's blue eyes, which were filled with desire. His gaze lowered to her mouth, and her heart beat faster. As she slipped her hand across his shoulder, his arms tightened around her and he drew her close.

Her heart thudded. She wanted him. They had spent such an idyllic day together, with Gabe pouring on the charm, looking appealing and sexy as he swam and played with Rebecca.

"Maddie, marry me. I mean, really marry me. I talked about marrying in name only, so Rebecca would be my legal heir, but this is different. I love you, Maddie," he said.

She was consumed by his intensity. His declaration of love was more important at the moment than his proposal, but even while it was indelibly etched in her memory, joy and regret mingled.

"I used to dream of hearing those words from you, Gabe. I didn't, so I went out and made a life for myself without you."

He winced. "Maddie, I've done some things the wrong way, made some wrong choices. But I know what I want now. I want you and Rebecca in my life. I love you. I want us to be a family."

She couldn't catch her breath. These words were what she had dreamed of hearing—six years ago. Now her life had changed. "I love you, too, Gabe. I always have and probably always will, but life isn't that simple. I can't just marry you and—"

He placed his finger lightly on her lips to stop her arguments.

"If we can't have a real marriage now, at least marry me for the legal reasons, for Rebecca's sake. We'll work out some kind of arrangement, but it will all be easier if we are husband and wife. Marry me, Maddie. We love each other and we both love her."

Maddie's heart pounded. Everything he said made sense and would be best for Rebecca, but without full commitment and compromise from both her and Gabe it would be a sham marriage. "Gabe, I can't give up my career and my life here. I want to live in the city and enjoy everything I've worked so hard for. I'm not a rancher's wife and never will be. You won't move to Florida, will you?"

Anger flashed in his eyes. When his jaw tightened, she had her answer, the answer she had known she'd receive.

"No, I can't give up Texas, my family, my roots and everything I've dreamed about all my life. But I still want to marry you, and I want you to accept my proposal, if only for Rebecca's sake."

She slipped off his lap to walk away from him and try to clear her thoughts. She turned around to find him standing by his chair.

"You still want to marry me, even when you'll be in Texas and I'll be in Florida?"

"It's a start."

"You can't go through life with that kind of marriage."

"I don't expect to be separated from you. I want you and Rebecca to visit, and I'll come see both of you. When I can't stand living long-distance, I'll let you know, but Rebecca will have my name forever. She's a Benton and I want her to be part of the family."

Maddie's heart pounded, her mind racing over the problems and the possibilities of his proposal.

But in the end, her heart won out.

Ten

"All right, Gabe. I'll marry you," she said breathlessly, remembering all the times she had dreamed about this moment. Now that it was here, because of the circumstances, it was bittersweet.

"Ah, Maddie," he said, striding across the patio, his blue eyes filled with desire. "That's good. You'll see. You're doing what's good for her, and what's good for us. I want you in my life, Maddie, as much as I want Rebecca in my life."

His kiss left no doubt about his wanting her.

He pulled away to look down at her, combing strands of her hair away from her face. "I have something here for you," he said, withdrawing something from his pocket and handing it to her.

Surprised, she looked at the small black box in his hand. She gasped when she opened it and removed the dazzling ring.

"Gabe, this is gorgeous," she said. He took it from her and held her hand lightly while he slipped the ring on her finger. "It's magnificent. I'm stunned," she said, all her tangled emotions intensifying.

"I love you, Maddie. I should have looked at my own feelings sooner."

She met his direct gaze, wondering if they would ever work out the differences between them.

Gabe's arms circled her and, for a moment, she forgot her worries and questions as she kissed him. He carried her to bed, and they spent the night in each other's arms.

Early the next morning, Maddie was in his arms when Gabe turned to face her.

"I have a small horse, a little mare that's gentle as can be. I want to give her to Rebecca. I'll walk her around or I'll ride with Rebecca if you'd prefer."

"Sure, Gabe," she said, amused that he had so many plans so quickly. "You taught me to ride, so you can teach our daughter."

"Good. Now, on to a more vital matter—let's marry soon. If you want a big wedding, that's fine with me. Big or small, I don't care. I want it to happen. Pick a date this morning."

"Under the circumstances, I want a small wedding. Only our family and our very closest friends. That's all. Less than fifty people if we can keep it to that number."

"We can if that's what you want."

"I know you told Jake and Caitlin about Rebecca, but you still have to tell your parents."

"I haven't told my parents yet because I wanted things worked out between us first. Otherwise, that's an open invitation for my dad to step in and try to take charge."

"I hope that doesn't happen," she said, having no intention of letting his parents run her life.

"He's always concentrated on Jake. With grandkids, I think both Mom and Dad will stop interfering so much, so don't worry. I want to stay here a few more days and get to know Rebecca better. When we go back to Texas, I'd like to take her with us, but also when we go, I would like her to know I'm her father."

"I'm still waiting for the right time to tell her."

"Whether you tell her before we go or after we get there, I know you'll choose the best time. When we return to Texas, we'll stay at my place. You can make your calls there and work on getting your house ready. I'll send a cleaning crew over, Maddie, and they'll have the place in fine shape. I can do the same for a yard crew and you'll have the place ready for sale."

"Thanks, that would be wonderful and save me a lot of work," she said, relieved, yet at the same time aware it would mean she would be free to return to Florida sooner.

"If you ever decide you want to give up your career, I can easily afford for you to do that. I'll set up an account for you, so you'll have your own money."

"I have my own money," she said with amusement. "I have a good job."

"So do I, Maddie, as you know. I've been dabbling in investments for a long time now. I've done okay. Better than okay. I'm approaching billionaire status."

Surprised, she raised up on an elbow to look at him. "I knew you were wealthy, but I didn't realize *how* wealthy!"

"If you have any money you want me to invest, I'll be happy to do it. I think I told you that I handle investments for Jake and a couple of his friends. I've actually thought about expanding my business slightly."

"That is very impressive, Gabe. You're multitalented."

"So are you," he said, swinging her down to kiss her.

Then thoughts and worries were gone as she focused on Gabe.

For the next two days, Gabe gave his full attention to Rebecca.

On Thursday, Gabe showered and went to the kitchen to cook breakfast while Maddie dressed. By the time she appeared with Rebecca, he had breakfast ready and he waited, sipping a glass of cold orange juice.

In blue cotton slacks and a pale blue, cotton, sleeveless shirt, Rebecca was ready to travel. She held her white teddy bear under one arm.

"Don't you look pretty this morning," Gabe said. "We're going on a big airplane today to fly a long way to Texas. Do you have your bag packed?"

"Yes, sir," she answered. "Gabrel is going to fly, too."

"I think Gabrel will have a lot of fun on his trip," Gabe said, smiling at her.

"Rebecca," Maddie said, pulling a chair closer to Gabe's and lifting Rebecca to her lap. "See what Mr. Benton gave me," Maddie said, showing Rebecca her engagement ring.

"That's pretty," Rebecca said, touching the ring lightly. "It's beautiful," she said in her childish voice. She looked at Gabe and smiled.

"I love your Mommy, and I love you," he said.

"Rebecca, Gabe has asked me to marry him."

For the first time, Rebecca's sunny countenance disappeared. "Are you going to leave me?"

"Heavens, no!" Maddie said, hugging Rebecca. "Not at all."

"Rebecca, I want your mommy to be my wife and you to be my little girl," Gabe said, meaning it with his whole heart.

Rebecca smiled broadly, and Gabe's heart skipped a beat. He leaned closer to her. "Will you let me be your daddy?"

Big blue eyes gazed into his while he held his breath. He only took a breath once before she smiled again. "Yes," she said shyly. Relief and warmth washed over him.

"I hope so. I love you and your mommy. I want you to come to Texas and see my house."

She nodded and looked at Rebecca. "You and Mr. Benton will have a wedding."

"Yes, we will, and you'll be part of it. We have to let Grandma know this morning. We'll go tell her together."

Gabe sat patiently while Maddie broke the news to her mother and Rebecca played with her teddy bear. Mrs. Halliday seemed even more impressed with the engagement ring than Maddie had been, studying it at length and giving him a faint smile. "So, Maddie, where will you live?"

"We have things to work out, Mom," Maddie said easily. "I've told you before."

Her mother nodded, giving him another inscrutable look, but there was more triumph in it than worry, and he wondered what Maddie and her mother had discussed.

They were soon on their way to the airport. When the plane took off, Gabe enjoyed watching Rebecca's enthusiasm for the flight. She was buckled securely in her seat, but she was excited, looking out the window and commenting on everything she saw.

Gabe reached over to take Maddie's hand, holding it and smiling at her. "She's happy. I hope you are."

"I am," she said, but her words weren't convincing. The worry was back in her brown eyes, and he wondered what lay ahead for them.

In the limo on the way to Gabe's ranch, Rebecca held her teddy bear up to the window, telling him about the land around them.

Finally, they reached Gabe's mansion. Men were working on the unfinished wing. Rebecca was curious about everything she saw.

Gabe gave Rebecca a tour of the finished part of the house. When they put their bags in the bedrooms, he stepped into one and turned to Maddie. "Your bedroom will adjoin this one, which will be for Rebecca. You can start planning how you want to redecorate. When we marry, you can do this over into a room for her, and you and Rebecca can discuss what she would like to have in here."

"Gabe—" Maddie started to say, and then closed her mouth, turning away while he talked to Rebecca to tell her this would one day be her room. Maddie wondered if Gabe had assumed she would come around to what he wanted. Rebecca would visit him some, but Maddie had no intention of spending a lot of time on the ranch.

When they were together in the kitchen after putting away their suitcases, he set out steaks to thaw.

"Rebecca, I have a horse for you. She will be your very own. Do you want to go see her?"

"Yes," she said, her eyes larger than ever and wonder in her voice.

"Maddie, why don't you come with us?"

She shook her head. "I've calls to make. You take Rebecca and show her the horse," she said, watching the two of them.

Gabe swung Rebecca up on his shoulders. As they left the room, Rebecca had her fingers wound in Gabe's hair. He held the little girl carefully and both of them laughed.

As they disappeared from her view, Maddie looked down at the huge, glittering diamond on her finger. She suspected she was in for a bigger hurt than she'd had six years earlier.

She had a wedding to plan, but it would be heartbreaking because she knew their marriage was not going to be the way she had dreamed it would be. No matter how she parsed it, there didn't seem to be a way they could compromise on their lifestyles.

Gabe was ever the optimist and accustomed to getting what he wanted. This time he wouldn't be able to. She tried to focus on the list of calls she needed to make. Sell the house and furniture, finish the deal with Jake and go back to Florida. Except leaving now meant that half of her heart would be left behind in Texas.

Through the week, they stayed in Texas. Tuesday night Maddie sat in the large family room while Gabe played a game with Rebecca. He was on the floor, making her laugh as they played, her constant giggles keeping a smile on Maddie's face. Rebecca had bathed and dressed in pink pajamas covered with panda bears. Her eyes sparkled.

The hall clock chimed. "Rebecca, it's story time and then bedtime, so you two wind up that game."

In minutes, they were finished and Gabe picked up

Rebecca. "I'll carry you to your room and read one story to you. How's that?"

"Good, if you will carry Gabrel, too."

"You hold on to Gabrel and to me." Gabe swung her up onto his shoulders and she grabbed fistfuls of his hair as they left for her room. Maddie followed, watching Gabe, thinking he was everything she'd ever wanted in a man. Intelligent, generous, fun, confident—and handsome. Right now he looked great in a knit shirt and jeans. He was also a cowboy at heart and wanted his ranching life as much as she wanted the life she had built in Miami. Florida was her home, just as this Texas ranch was Gabe's home. Irreconcilable differences.

She turned down the bed and tried not to rehash the same worries she'd had since meeting Gabe on that long stretch of highway two weeks ago. She watched while Gabe and Rebecca looked through books and Rebecca selected two for him to read. He sat in a rocker and pulled her onto his lap. Rebecca settled against him, looking at the pictures as he read.

Soon she yawned, then grew still and quiet. Locks of his brown hair had fallen over Gabe's forehead. His deep voice was soft, low as he read to his daughter.

When could she tell Maddie that Gabe was her real daddy?

Sunday night, Maddie was in Gabe's arms after making love. She caressed his throat, gazing into his eyes in the faint light from a small bedside lamp.

"Gabe, the ranch and house have been sold to Jake, so that responsibility is gone. Rebecca and I leave tomorrow for Florida. You and I haven't set a wedding date. At first I wasn't sure it would even happen."

"It's going to happen. I've been thinking about our

wedding. I'd like to have a bigger one. We both have family and close friends nearby, Maddie. I want them there when I marry you." Her heart pounded with his words. He toyed with strands of her hair. "We can marry in church. Having a ceremony will mean more to Rebecca, too."

Maddie nodded, glancing at her ring that sparkled in the dim light. "A church wedding—it's becoming real. A church wedding will push the date a little farther away because it will mean more planning."

"It'll be worth it."

"Gabe, my feelings about going home haven't changed," she said, worried that he thought these days on his ranch meant she was beginning to accept life here.

"I know, but I still want to have the wedding very soon. The sooner the better."

"I agree. It will be easier to tell Rebecca that you're her real father then."

"Can you take a week for a honeymoon?"

She knew she could. She could rearrange her schedule and make arrangements with an agent to cover for her. But did she want a week alone with Gabe to become addicted to spending so much time with him? She looked into his blue eyes. "Yes, I can take a week."

"You leave tomorrow. Come back next weekend."

"You come to Florida. Then I'll fly here later."

"All right," he said, sounding reluctant. They couldn't stop time, and they couldn't change their deepest desires and feelings.

"I'll pay all expenses, Maddie. Don't argue."

"Thank you," she said, trying to imagine that their marriage would be about more than just heartache and constant goodbyes.

Her fears were compounded the next day when she stood in the airport near the walkway for the big commercial jet that she had insisted on taking home. They still had no long-term plans for when she would return to Texas, or when Gabe could come to Florida, nothing beyond the next weekend. Maddie held Rebecca's hand and the little girl held her white teddy bear.

"Come back weekend after next," Gabe urged her. "I'll fly you here in my plane. I'll come get you and Rebecca Friday night and take you home Sunday."

The offer was tempting. "Will that be our relationship—only a few days together at a time?"

"I don't know, but I'll take what I can get. I want to be with you and Rebecca."

"I'll see, Gabe," she said, her spirits sinking. Now they faced the reality of their future. It was nothing like she imagined it would be.

When he kissed her goodbye, he held her long and tight.

When Gabe let go of Maddie, he picked up Rebecca and kissed her cheek. "See the big plane you'll be on. It's even a bit bigger than the one you flew on to come here."

"Come see us," Rebecca said.

While his heart lurched, he looked into her big blue eyes. "I want to visit you more than anything, and I wish you didn't have to go home now. Someday we'll have a home together, Rebecca, because I'm marrying Mommy. When I do, I'll be your daddy."

"Can I call you Daddy?" she asked shyly, making his heart clench again. He looked into Maddie's brown eyes and then back at Rebecca.

"I would love to hear you call me Daddy. You can start right now."

She smiled and hugged him, her thin arms wrapping around his neck as they called for passengers to begin boarding. "You're my friend," Rebecca said. "My daddy when you marry Mommy."

Seeing the love between Rebecca and Gabe, and wanting her daughter to have something special as she faced her first separation from her father, Maddie said, "Gabe, this may be as good a time as any." She moved closer and placed her arm around Rebecca so they stood in a tight group.

"Rebecca, Gabe is your real daddy. He's come back to be with us," she said.

Rebecca turned wide, blue eyes on him. "You're really my daddy?" she asked.

Gabe's heart skipped a beat.

"I'm really your daddy, darlin', and I'm here now. I will always be there for you," he said, feeling a knot in his throat.

Rebecca smiled again and kissed his cheek as she hugged him. He felt as if his heart would pound out of his chest. His gaze met Maddie's, and he wrapped an arm around her. He didn't care if they were in a busy airport or what was happening around them.

"I love you both more than anything else in my life," he said in a husky voice.

"I love you," Rebecca said. "I love Mommy."

"I love you both, too," Maddie said.

"We should go, Gabe, if we're going to get this flight." Maddie stepped back and he set Rebecca on her feet. She looked down at Rebecca, who was straightening a tie on her bear.

"That was easier to do than I thought it would be."

"I'm glad. Now I can tell my parents and everyone else. Maddie, I do love you both more than anything else," he said, hurting because they were leaving.

"Gabe—" She broke off as they announced boarding for her plane.

"It's time for us to board," she said. She hugged him and kissed him briefly. He held her tightly, kissing her until she moved away. "Goodbye, Gabe. We'll talk."

He watched them disappear down the walkway. Rebecca turned to wave at him and he waved back, and hurt. It felt too much like they were walking out of his life again.

Maddie was set about living life on her own terms and he didn't think she would change. That determination was something he loved about her, but he hurt badly because he wanted them to come back. The past few days had been the best of his life. It shook him to realize that he felt that way. He was more in love with Maddie every day. And he loved Rebecca with all his heart. Love wrapped him in chains that bound his heart to theirs. He saw now why Maddie had not welcomed other men into her life. It would have been impossible, since she had truly loved him.

"Dammit," he whispered, moving to the window to watch the plane. He wanted to run and escort them off, but he knew that would solve nothing. Maybe he could give up his life and move to Florida.

He could do investments full-time. He could work on a consulting basis for Jake, but he would always want to be back in Texas. He loved Maddie and Rebecca with all his heart, but his lifeblood was this place where he was born and raised. He couldn't imagine giving it up completely. It might work for a while, but then he would want to return.

Was where he lived more important than the loves in his life? He wasn't sure. All he knew was that he already wanted to be with them.

Heartbreak tore at Maddie. She fought back tears because she didn't want to cry in front of Rebecca.

Rebecca looked out the window, holding up the white bear so he could share the view.

Maddie loved Gabe. If only she could change. If only *Gabe* could change.

But both notions were foolishness. He probably hoped the same thing. Their lifestyles were disparate, and she saw no hope of working out any satisfying solution.

She loved Gabe with all her heart. Always had and always would. Rebecca loved him now, too. He was in their lives, and they would see him, but truly living together? She couldn't fathom how it would be possible.

As time passed and they moved back into their routine lives she just hoped they could stay as close as they had been these last few days.

A week later, Maddie still missed Gabe. He had planned to fly to Florida for the weekend and then business had kept him in Texas until it was pointless for him to try to come.

To her surprise, instead of learning to live without him, as she'd done before, she missed him more with each passing day. This time was even worse in many ways than that first big separation from him six years ago. Maybe she was more in love now. Maybe they were closer, now that they had both been fully honest about their feelings and mistakes.

Rebecca missed him and asked about him and talked each day to him on the phone. Maddie's calls to him lasted for hours and added to the longing that consumed her. She planned a wedding with her fiancé much too far away from her.

She cried herself to sleep at night, and her work began to suffer. She wasn't paying attention. She had lost her drive and her focus. Even her mother seemed to be worried about her. Tracie even surprised her by asking if Maddie had ever considered going back to Texas.

Gabe flew to see them the next weekend, and they had a whirlwind visit filled with laughter and family time during the day and nights of loving that held a sense of desperation for her. She loved him and didn't want to tell him goodbye, but deep down, she couldn't help but fear their long-distance arrangement would eventually come down to them parting ways.

They would marry, and Gabe would fly back and forth until he grew tired of it. Then there would be longer and longer gaps when they wouldn't see each other.

If only she didn't feel so isolated out on the ranch... she still felt strongly that she couldn't bear to live out there.

Their wedding was planned for mid-September, but with no date set. It was not as soon as Gabe wanted, but the first they could work out a time likely to work for both of them.

She would marry him for the reasons he had been so insistent on: for Rebecca's sake, to give her the Benton name and her real daddy.

Maddie could only hope the rest would fall into place.

* * *

Gabe had a project he was involved in that took him to Chicago, and he couldn't fly to Florida. He talked to Maddie and Rebecca, but two weeks passed without seeing them, and he had a feeling he was facing what his future would be like. How long would it be until one or the other of them ended the long-distance marriage?

He missed them more than ever and each phone conversation made him long to be with them until he was completely distracted. He was to the point of worrying about handling business deals, about how long it would be before he made a colossal mistake that cost him. He could understand now why Jake had been so befuddled when he had fallen in love with Caitlin.

There had to be a way to see them more often.

Suddenly he remembered remarks that Maddie had made about cities, about her life... She liked Dallas, and both Maddie and her mother still had friends there.

Could he give up living on the ranch and move to Dallas? He thought he could, if it meant having Maddie and Rebecca in his life.

Jake would take him back into the family business at any time. And he'd been wanting to expand... It occurred to Gabe that he could live in Dallas and deal in his investments full-time.

He'd be giving up the ranch, but not Texas. Maddie would be giving up Florida, but not city life.

He had dreamed, since he was a boy, about being a cowboy, living and working on the ranch.

Could he give up that dream for the love of his life?

Eleven

On Friday, Gabe intended to fly to Florida. He had worked in the Benton offices on Thursday and he was delayed leaving, finally closing his laptop and placing it in his backpack on the way out when his phone rang. Security at the front door told him he had a visitor waiting in the lobby, though the guard didn't get the name.

Gabe said he would be right down. He closed up so he could go on to his car without returning to the office and then he took the elevator downstairs.

In the lobby, he stepped out of the elevator bank and turned the corner for the reception desk.

Maddie stood waiting. Her blond hair was tied behind her head with a red scarf and she wore red slacks and a matching shirt. His heart thudded and he walked faster. Excitement swamped him, and he couldn't overcome the urge to grab her and kiss her, to make sure she wasn't an illusion, a figment of his wishful imagination.

He pulled her into his arms and kissed away her hello. When he finally released her, he said, "I'm shocked. This is a big surprise. Did you bring Rebecca?"

"No, she's with Mom."

"If you don't want to be thoroughly kissed in such a public place, we better go outside right now."

She smiled at him, and they walked outside and around the corner of the building where he pulled her into his arms to kiss her long and leisurely. She held him tightly, kissing him in return.

"Let's go to the condo," he said gruffly, and she nodded.

"I came in a cab. I don't have any transportation. I'm with you."

"Yes, you are," he said, taking her arm and heading to his car. "This is a surprise, Maddie. I'm scheduled to fly to Florida tomorrow, so what brought this on? And without you telling me?"

"Are you complaining?" she teased.

"Hell, no," he said as he drove.

"Gabe, slow down before you get a ticket."

"I want to be alone with you."

"That's what I wanted, too. I'll fly back to Florida with you tomorrow. This is an extra day."

He didn't believe that was her whole reason, but he accepted it. He didn't care, because he wanted to make love to her and hold her in his arms. His condo had never seemed as far from his office as it did right then.

When they finally stepped inside, he shut the door and pulled her to him.

* * *

It was almost nine that night before Gabe asked her if she wanted dinner and Maddie accepted. They had made love since Gabe had closed the door behind them that afternoon. They had showered, and he wore jeans. He'd given Maddie one of his robes.

They both went to the kitchen. As she watched him move around fixing sandwiches for them, she took a deep breath, but he cut off what she was about to say.

"I'm glad you're here and that there's only the two of us, because I want to talk to you," he said, cutting thin slices from tender roast beef.

"That's why I came," she said. "To talk to you."

His eyes narrowed. He stopped what he was doing to study her. He put down his knife, wiped his hands on a towel and walked over to place his hands on her shoulders.

"I want you and Rebecca in my life full-time, Maddie. I've been thinking about our future."

"So have I. I've been miserable, Gabe."

"Maddie, I've thought it over. Now listen and hear me out. I think I've found a compromise. If I opened an investment office in Dallas and we had a Dallas home, could you tear yourself out of Florida? I know you said you had some friends and contacts, there, even a job offer. It's a big city and you've—"

"Gabe!" she cried, throwing her arms around him to hug him.

He caught her, his arms tightening around her. "Hey!"

"That's why I'm here," she cried, feeling as if a crushing weight had lifted from her heart. "I was going to ask you if you could live in Dallas and commute to the ranch. I can get a job in Dallas."

He smiled. "I don't want to go through life with a long-distance marriage. I want you in my arms every night—or at least nearly every night. Jake asks me about every six months if I'd think about doing consulting for him. I'll have to travel some. I have some real estate investments to check on."

"I don't care, Gabe. That sounds great. I love you and Rebecca needs you," she said, the words tumbling out while she laughed and tears of joy filled her eyes.

"What about your family?"

"Rebecca will adjust. Children always do. My mom will probably come see us often. She may even move to Dallas herself."

"I have enough money I can get her a house of her own, and she can come and go when she wants. Or, we can build a big enough house that there will be room for your mother and your grandparents to come stay whenever and however long they want," he said. "Heck, they can live with us all the time! I just want us to be together, Maddie."

"That's what I want, too," she said, crying and smiling at the same time.

"You came here to ask me this same thing?" he asked.

"Yes," she cried.

"Stop crying," he said, kissing her. She held him tightly, her heart beating with joy that they had finally worked out a way to have part of their dreams and still be together. She leaned away, framing his face with her hands. "You really would work in Dallas? You can give up being a full-time cowboy?"

"I retired and moved to the ranch because I was unhappy after you left. I just didn't know why I felt so dissatisfied. I was a cowboy, but that didn't wipe out the empty feeling I had or the restlessness I couldn't shake. I just didn't recognize the depths of my feelings for you. I won't completely give up the ranch, but I don't have to live there."

"Gabe," she said, hugging him.

"We can go to the ranch some weekends. You and Rebecca can go with me. Will you do that?"

"Yes. Oh, yes. Gabe, I'm so happy," she said. "So, so happy you wanted to do this before I even asked you."

"I was going to lay out the plan this weekend. Maddie, this will make things better. If I have you and Rebecca in my life, everything else will be okay."

"I love you, Gabe."

He pulled her to him, holding her tightly as he kissed her and her heart beat wildly with joy.

He paused to look at her again. "Maddie, get a definite date set for our wedding. You might want to rethink again how big it will be. Now that we've worked this out, we may need a Texas-size wedding."

She smiled at him. "I think you're right."

Epilogue

Maddie's throat had a knot and tears of joy stung her eyes as Rebecca walked down the aisle, dropping rose petals along the way. Rebecca wore a deep blue dress that matched those of the six bridesmaids.

Maddie's white-silk strapless dress was tailored, clinging to her figure with a full cathedral train. While trumpets played, she walked down the aisle on her grandfather's arm. She paused to give her mother and grandmother roses and turned to give Gabe's mother a rose. His father smiled at her and both of Gabe's parents had made her feel welcome in their family. Then she looked into Gabe's eyes, and her heart raced with happiness.

Gabe stood tall, handsome and smiling at her, love showing in his blue eyes as her grandfather placed her hand in Gabe's warm, firm grasp. Looking handsome, Jake was Gabe's best man and Caitlin was a bridesmaid.

Maddie looked at the other groomsmen, who were Gabe's lifelong friends. And then her attention returned to her tall fiancé.

Gabe and Maddie stepped forward to repeat their vows.

Half an hour later they were introduced to the guests as Mr. and Mrs. Gabriel Benton, and then she hurried back up the aisle on Gabe's arm.

Later, at the country club reception, Maddie stood talking with her new sister-in-law. "We'll see a lot of each other," Caitlin said. "Jake and Gabe are close."

"I'm glad they are. Gabe's family has welcomed me, but then I've known all of you for most of my life."

"I'm glad for Jake and Gabe. I never had any such relationship with my half brother, Will."

"I really didn't know your brother. He was older."

"We don't keep in touch. Here comes Tony's wife, Isabelle, with Grace, Nick's wife."

"Caitlin, thank you again for the photographs you took of Rebecca and my bridal picture. I love them. You're very talented."

"Thanks. I was glad to do them. Rebecca is a doll, and she was great about posing. Jake's parents are so thrilled with her. When our baby is born, I'll have a million questions for you about baby care."

Maddie laughed. "I doubt if I'll remember. That was five years ago."

Isabelle Ryder and Grace Rafford joined them. "Maddie, you're a beautiful bride."

"Thank you," she said. "Here's who you should ask. Grace's Michael and Emily are younger than Rebecca."

"Ask me what?" Grace inquired, smiling at them.

"About babies," Caitlin said. "Maddie said it's been so long she doesn't remember."

Grace laughed, her green eyes twinkling. "I suspect it will come back to you fast enough."

"Not yet," Maddie said, smiling and glancing across the room at her handsome husband. She was ready to escape with him. He stood with close friends and his brother, but with the way he was looking at her, she guessed he wanted to get away as soon as they could, too.

"Jake, it finally happened," Nick said, grinning broadly. "You got your little brother married off." He turned to Gabe. "We never thought you'd do it and you didn't even have to be pushed into it by your dad."

"You became a dad before I did, too," Jake said.

"Which makes him the favorite with your folks," Nick added with good-natured teasing. "At least until you and Caitlin have your baby. Then you'll be the favorite son again."

"I doubt it," Jake said.

"Now that we're all married, we should take a weekend to get together and let our wives get to know each other better," Tony said. Jake agreed.

"You plan something, Tony," Nick said. "We'll have to work around football or wait until the first part of December for a fun getaway."

"Sounds good to me," Nick said.

"Y'all can plan away. Right now I have my own getaway to make. I'm going to collect my bride and see if we can't depart the premises," Gabe announced.

"Good luck," Tony said. "She'll want to stay for hours to be nice to the guests."

"He's right. Want to wager on how soon you get out of here?" Jake asked in fun, and they all laughed.

"Do what you want, I'm gone," Gabe said, walking away from them to get to Maddie. He saw her talking to his friends' wives. She was breathtakingly beautiful, but he couldn't wait to get her out of that stunning wedding gown, to take down her hair and make love to her all night.

He walked up to join the group for a few minutes. "Ladies, I'm going to steal my wife away now," he said, smiling at all of them. "If you'll excuse us. I want a dance."

They all politely agreed as he took Maddie's arm to walk toward the dance floor.

"Let's find Rebecca and our folks, tell them goodbye and get out of here," he said to her. "We can dance again on our honeymoon."

"You know we should stay for another couple of hours."

"Is that what you want to do?"

She smiled broadly. "Let's go."

They told their families goodbye, and Gabe picked up Rebecca to hold her.

"I'll miss you, Daddy," she said, smiling at him.

"I'll miss you, too, but then we'll all three go somewhere fun where you can see princesses and ride fun rides."

"I'll like that," she said.

"We'll all like it. Be a good girl," he said, kissing her cheek and setting her down.

"Bye, Tracie. Call us if you need anything," he said.

"I will," she said, smiling at him.

They left, rushing out to the waiting limo that

whisked them away before the crowd caught up with them.

As the limo drove through the Dallas streets and headed to the airport, Gabe pulled her into his arms. "I love you, Maddie. You and Rebecca are my life."

"I love you. I've always loved you," she said, wrapping her arms around him to kiss him.

When his fingers went to the buttons of her wedding dress, she caught his hands.

"Slow down, cowboy. We're still out in public."

"Not too public in here," he replied, removing a pin from her hair to let a curl fall free.

"Gabe, I have everything I could possibly dream of. We're married. We have Rebecca. Mom is moving back to Dallas. I was really surprised when my grandparents said they would move, too. I don't think they want to be away from any of us. There's only one more thing I can think of that I want," she said, twisting her fingers in her husband's thick brown hair.

"What's that? If I can give it to you, I will. I would give you the world, Maddie," he said, nuzzling her neck.

"Gabe, if we have another baby, it would be wonderful, and this time you would be..."

He kissed her hard, holding her tightly against him while desire flamed, and she kissed him in return.

They reached the airport before he released her. She straightened her dress. "Gabe, I will be a sight."

"Yes, you will. You'll turn heads everywhere you go."

"I'm so glad you have a private jet. As soon as we board the plane, I'm shedding this wedding dress."

"Fine with me. I'll unfasten the buttons."

"How kind of you," she said, smiling at him.

On the flight to their villa in the Caymans, Gabe

took her hand. As soon as they were airborne and could unbuckle their seat belts, he said, "Come here and we'll get you out of your wedding dress."

He took her to the luxurious bedroom and pulled her into his arms.

"I love you with all my heart," he said.

"Gabe, this is truly paradise. I've dreamed of this moment for too many years and then believed I had to give up my dream. But now it's come true."

"Maddie, I will try to make it up to you," he whispered as he showered kisses on her throat.

"You've already made it up to me," she replied. She framed his face with her hands. "You never answered me—do you want a baby?"

"Yes," he said. "That would be another dream come true for all of us."

"Then we'll work on getting one," she said, smiling at him.

He smiled in return as he lowered his head to kiss her.

She held him tightly, certain this was the happiest day of her life and expecting many more to come. She loved her handsome husband with all her heart, and now they would spend a lifetime together.

* * * * *

Greedy for a taste of her, Wyatt stroked his tongue across the lush, moist curve of Hannah's bottom lip.

Her flavour hit him with the punch of a straight shot of single malt whiskey, making his head spin and his body temperature spike.

Why her? Why did this woman who stood for everything he despised get to him? Hadn't he been burned by her type often enough to learn his lesson? Before he could make sense of her strange magnetism or get his fill, she jerked back, eyes wide and wary, and pressed her fingers over her mouth.

"You can't do that. You're my boss."

Reality slammed into him like an oncoming train. *Stupid move, Jacobs.* "You're right. A personal involvement would be unwise."

But even as he spoke the words he registered her heavy-lidded eyes, flushed cheeks and erect nipples—sure signs that her hormones were pumping as rampantly as his. And as impractical and ill-advised as it might be, he wanted her.

Dear Reader,

Horses were a huge part of my childhood, and I miss them terribly. If I ever win the lottery, you can be assured my first purchase will be a horse farm somewhere in central North Carolina.

Fortunately, Hannah and Wyatt's story gave me an opportunity to revisit one of my first loves, although my horse experiences were never anything as lavish as Grand Prix show jumping! There is nothing more breathtaking than watching a spindly legged foal take its first steps or taking those initial tentative steps into a new love.

I hope you enjoy the often unsteady steps of Wyatt and Hannah's journey. Let me know what you think. You can reach me online at my website, www.emilierose.com.

Happy reading!

Emilie Rose

HER TYCOON
TO TAME

BY
EMILIE ROSE

Published in Great Britain 2012
by Mills & Boon, an imprint of Harlequin (UK) Limited,
Eton House, 18-24 Paradise Road, Richmond, Surrey TW9 1SR

© Emilie Rose Cunningham 2011

ISBN: 978 0 263 89150 8

51-0312

Harlequin (UK) policy is to use papers that are natural, renewable and recyclable products and made from wood grown in sustainable forests. The logging and manufacturing processes conform to the legal environmental regulations of the country of origin.

Printed and bound in Spain
by Blackprint CPI, Barcelona

Bestselling Desire™ author and RITA® Award finalist **Emilie Rose** lives in her native North Carolina with her four sons and two adopted mutts. Writing is her third (and hopefully her last) career. She's managed a medical office and run a home day care, neither of which offers half as much satisfaction as plotting happy endings. Her hobbies include gardening and cooking (especially cheesecake). She's a rabid country music fan because she can find an entire book in almost any song. She is currently working her way through her own "bucket list," which includes learning to ride a Harley. Visit her website at www.emilierose.com or email EmilieRoseC@ aol.com. Letters can be mailed to PO Box 20145, Raleigh, NC 27619, USA.

To the Man upstairs for giving me more
time with my mom.
Each day is a blessing.

One

Hannah Sutherland pressed the pedal of the golf cart to the floorboard, racing the battery-powered machine up the long curving driveway toward the main house.

Guest. My office. N.O.W.

That had been her father's text, and as irritable as he'd been lately, she didn't dare keep him waiting. But who could be so important that she had to drop everything and hurry to the house?

When she reached the stairs leading to the back patio, she slammed on the brake, leaped from the vehicle and hustled into the house, straightening her hair and adjusting her hastily changed clothing as she crossed the black-and-white marbled foyer. The sound of her boots echoed off the vaulted ceiling.

At the sight of the closed office door, her step hitched. She hadn't seen that door closed since the day her mother had died. Apprehension climbed her spine like a spider.

She shook off her uneasiness and knocked on the glossy surface. A moment later, the panel opened revealing Al

Brinkley, the family's lawyer. He'd been her father's friend as well as his legal council for as long as Hannah could remember.

"Good to see you, Mr. Brinkley."

Brinkley's smile seemed forced. "Hello, Hannah. I swear you look more like your mother every day."

"So I've been told." Too bad looks were all she'd inherited from her mom. Hannah's life would have been so much easier if she'd picked up a few more traits.

His expression sobered, resurrecting Hannah's concern. "Come in."

Her father stood behind his desk, his face tense, a highball glass in his hand. It was a little early for cocktails.

Movement by the French doors overlooking the east paddock interrupted the thought. Tall and lean, the other occupant of the study smoothly pivoted in her direction.

His glossy brownish-black hair had been clipped short, but not short enough to hide a tendency to curl that did nothing to soften his uncompromisingly hard jaw and a square chin.

And while his features combined to form a tough but attractive face, nothing would soften those cool, distrusting eyes, and no amount of expensive tailoring could conceal his broad shoulders and firm, muscled body. He had the lean, mean, fighting machine look often displayed on military recruiting posters and an alert and dangerous air. She estimated his age as mid-thirties, but it was hard to say. He had old eyes.

"Come in, Hannah." The odd tension in her father's tone made her wary. "Brink, close the door."

The lawyer did as he was bid, sealing Hannah into the wainscoted room with the three men and a tense atmosphere. Private discussions were not the norm in the house. Nellie, who served as housekeeper, house manager and surrogate mother, was the only one who might overhear, and she was family in every way but blood. So why the secrecy?

"Wyatt, this is my daughter, Hannah. She's the veterinarian

overseeing Sutherland Farm's breeding operation. Hannah, Wyatt Jacobs."

Jacobs's searing scrutiny strangely repelled and yet attracted her. Duty compelled her into motion. She crossed the Aubusson carpet. Who was he and what kind of closed-door business could he have with the stable?

Judging by his expensive clothing and the platinum watch on his wrist, he had money, but then all of their visitors did. Grand Prix show jumping wasn't for paupers or even the middle class. Their clients ranged from nouveau riche to established royalty, spoiled brats to dedicated, die-hard horsemen. Where did Wyatt Jacobs fit in?

She'd bet he looked good on a horse with that erect, confident carriage. His eyes were the color of roasted coffee beans, the pupils barely discernible with the sun streaming through the French doors at his back.

"Welcome to Sutherland Farm, Mr. Jacobs," she recited by rote and extended her hand.

His long fingers closed around hers, and his firm, warm grip combined with the impact of that hard, dark gaze made it difficult to breathe. She might as well have had a girth cinched around her chest considering the sudden pressure on her lungs.

"Dr. Sutherland." His deep, slightly raspy and seriously sexy voice would be perfect for radio.

He held her hand, extending the contact and making her wish for a split second that she'd taken the time to freshen her makeup, unbraid and brush her hair and splash on some perfume to mask the scent of stables when she'd quickly changed from her soiled work clothes in her office. But she'd been rushing and done only the absolutely necessary repairs.

Stupid girl. He's a client. And you're not looking for romance, remember?

She tugged her hand and after a brief resistance he released her. She pressed her prickling palm to her thigh. She'd broken her engagement fifteen months ago and in that time she hadn't thought about sex even once. Until now. Wyatt Jacobs made her tingle in places that had been dormant for a long time.

Her father offered her a highball glass of amber liquid. "Dad, you know I can't drink when I'm working. I still have to deal with Commander this morning."

Her frustration with the stallion she'd left in the stables resurfaced. Commander wanted to kill everyone—especially the vet in charge of collecting his semen. In the arena he'd been a phenomenal competitor, but in the barn he was a bloodthirsty beast. His bloodline and list of championships meant she couldn't ignore him. His ejaculate was liquid gold. But she, her team and the stubborn stud had needed a cool-down period after an unproductive hour. Her father's interruption had actually come at a good time.

Her father set the glass on his desk beside her as if he expected her to change her mind, reactivating the warning itch on her nape. Hannah brushed aside her misgivings and returned her focus to their guest. Jacobs watched her with an unwavering, laser-like intensity that stirred a strange, volatile reaction inside her, and try as she might she couldn't look away.

She'd met movie stars, congressmen and royalty with less charisma. For pity's sake she'd dated and even kissed a few of them with no effect. So why did Jacobs rattle her cage?

Wait a minute. Was that anger lurking in his eyes?

There was only one way to find out.

"What brings you to our stables, Mr. Jacobs?"

"Luthor, would you care to explain why I'm here?" Jacobs deferred. Funny, she would have sworn on her mother's earrings that he wasn't the type to defer anything and doing so now appeared to irritate him.

When the silence stretched, she pried her eyes from Jacobs's handsome face and discovered her usually unflappable father looking defensive and uncomfortable, his pale features set—totally unlike his usual calm demeanor. He drained his glass in one gulp and set the tumbler on the desk with a thump.

Her anxiety level spiked. "Daddy, what's going on?"

"I've sold the farm, Hannah," her father stated baldly.

She blinked. Her father had never possessed a sense of humor. Odd time for him to find one. But the idea was too ludicrous to be anything but a bad joke. "Really?"

He glanced at Brinkley's stoic expression, then back. "I have places to go and things to see—none of which I can do if I'm tied to this business every single day of the year."

She searched her father's resolute face. He wasn't joking. The floor beneath her feet seemed to shift. She clutched the edge of the desk for balance. Her knuckles bumped the cold highball glass, but the chill of the crystal couldn't compare to the ice spreading through her veins.

She could feel her mouth opening and closing, but couldn't force out a sound. She shuddered in a breath then stuttered it out again while struggling to gather her shattered thoughts.

"You couldn't have sold the farm. You *wouldn't* have. You live for the stables." As far as she knew he had no other interests, no hobbies. Nothing except horses, winning and Sutherland Farm. He didn't even have friends outside the horse biz.

"Not anymore."

Something had to be wrong. Terribly wrong. Fear splintered through her and cold sweat beaded her lip.

Her neck felt like a rusty hinge as she forced her head to turn to Jacobs. "Would you excuse us a moment, Mr. Jacobs?"

Their visitor didn't budge. He studied her—as if trying to gauge and anticipate her reaction.

"Please." She hated the desperate edge of her voice. It verged on begging. And she never begged.

After a moment he nodded, crossed the room in purposeful strides and stepped through the doors out onto the veranda. A fresh-cut grass-scented breeze drifted in the open door, but the familiar aroma failed to do its usual job of soothing her.

"Would you like for me to go?" Brinkley asked.

Her father held up a hand. "Stay, Brink. Hannah might have questions only you can answer."

"Daddy, what's wrong? Are you ill?"

He sighed. "No, Hannah. I'm not sick."

"Then how could you do this? You promised Mom you'd keep the farm forever."

The lines in her father's face seemed to deepen. "That was nineteen years ago, Hannah, and she was dying. I said what I had to say to let her pass peacefully."

"But what about me? I promised Mom, too, and *I* meant it. I'm supposed to take over Sutherland Farm. I'm supposed to keep Grandma and Papa's property in the family and pass it on to my children."

"Children you don't have."

"Well, no, not yet, but one day—" She paused as an idea pierced her like a nail. "This is because I didn't marry Robert, isn't it?"

Disapproval clamped her father's mouth into a tight line. "He was perfect for you, and yet you refused to settle down."

"No, Dad, he was perfect for *you*. Robert was the son you always wished you'd had. Instead, you got me."

"Robert knew how to run a stable."

"So do I."

"Hannah, you don't ride. You don't compete. Your heart is not in this business, and you don't have the drive to keep Sutherland Farm at the top of the Grand Prix community. Instead you waste your time and money on animals that ought to be euthanized."

No matter how many times she heard it, the old attacks still chafed. She stuffed down her emotional response and focused on the facts. "Mom believed in rescuing horses, too, and my horse rehabilitation program is a success. If you'd take the time to look at the statistics and read the success stories—"

"Your operation runs in the red every quarter. You're careless with money because you've never had to fight and scratch for a living."

"I work."

He grunted in disgust. "A few hours a day."

"My job isn't the eight-hour-a-day variety."

"When your mother and I assumed responsibility for my parents' old tobacco farm, this place was losing money hand over fist. We built Sutherland Farm into the showplace it is today by fighting and clawing our way up the ranks. Your mother had ambition. You do not. Robert might have managed to talk some sense into you and divert your attention to more suitable hobbies. But that didn't work. Did it?"

She'd ended her engagement the day she'd realized Robert had loved the horses and farm more than he had her. He'd been willing to trample people in pursuit of the almighty dollar. But her father would never listen to that. The men were like peas in a pod—identical in their drive for success despite the costs.

Robert had been her father's ideal of the perfect son-in-law—aggressive in business and a star in the show ring—but ultimately, he wasn't her ideal husband or life partner. She would have come lagging in a distant third in his heart at best. But she could hardly tell her father the only time Robert was passionate was in the riding ring.

"Robert wasn't right for me."

"You're twenty-nine, Hannah, and no man has ever held your attention for more than a few months. You're too picky."

"Daddy, I'm sorry I didn't inherit mother's grace and ability on horseback or your competitive streak. But this farm was her dream. And now it's mine. I can run it. I may not know how to ride a champion, but I know how to breed one. I have what it takes."

"No, Hannah, you don't. You've had a few successes with your stock, but you lack fire and ambition and you have absolutely no head for business. You're never going to be ready to take the reins of Sutherland Farm."

She flinched. His cruel words only confirmed what she

knew he'd been thinking for years, but they still stung like the whip of a crop. "That's not true."

"I'm doing you no favors by continuing to coddle you." He paused and glanced at his friend. "I won't always be here to support you, Hannah. It's time you learned to take care of yourself."

"What do you mean?"

"I'm cutting you off."

Shock followed by a chaser of panic sent her staggering backward. "What do you mean?" she repeated.

"I will no longer support you or your lost causes."

"Why? What did I do? How will I survive?"

"You'll have to learn to live on your salary."

Hurt, fear and betrayal ignited like a barn fire beneath her breastbone. "Couldn't we have talked about this before you made such a drastic decision?"

Her father shrugged and realigned the pen beside a thick pile of papers on his desk. "What good would that have done?"

"I would have talked you out of it. Somebody should have talked you out of it." She shot an injured and confused glance at the attorney who shrugged apologetically. "This farm, this property has been in our family for generations. There are a lot of people depending on you and me and—"

"It's too late, Hannah." Her father sighed and suddenly the starch left his spine, making him look old and tired. He refilled his drink, then sank into the leather chair.

She turned to Brinkley. "Can he do this? What about my mother's share of the business?"

"Your grandparents put the farm in your father's name before he married your mother. Her name was never added to the deed. You received the only inheritance you'll get from her estate when you turned twenty-one."

And most of that was gone. She'd spent the money on her horses, confident in the belief that her father would continue to fund her efforts.

Then realization clicked, jolting Hannah out of her

stupefaction. Wyatt Jacobs must be the one who'd bought the farm right out from under her. The sneaky, conniving, inheritance-swindling bastard.

Cold eyes, cold heart, Nellie had always said.

Hannah's pulse galloped in her eardrums like stampeding hooves. If she couldn't make her father or Brinkley see sense, she'd have to talk to the jerk who had usurped her and convince him to renege on the deal. Then she'd figure out a way to change her father's mind before he found another buyer.

She stalked through the patio door and spotted the interloper at a table, calmly eating from a plate of Nellie's cookies and drinking a glass of milk as if he hadn't just blasted the foundation right out from under her life. She marched toward him and pulled up at his elbow.

"This is my home. You can't waltz in here and steal the property. My father is having a momentary bout of senility and—"

Jacobs rose to tower above her, his face like granite. "I didn't steal Sutherland Farm, doc. I paid more than fair market value."

He calmly lifted the cookie and took another bite. His insolence stung like a slap in the face. Then as she focused on the cookie she realized she wasn't the only one who would be blindsided by today's disastrous news. She swung to her father who had followed her onto the patio.

"What about Nellie? She's lived with us since Mom died. She has no other home, no other family. Just us. You can't turn her out to pasture. She's too young to retire, and jobs are hard to find right now."

"Wyatt has promised to continue employing Nellie."

Wyatt has promised. Right. And she trusted him about as far as she could throw all six feet plus and two hundred whatever rock-solid pounds of him. She glared at him. "What about the other employees, the clients' horses and the stables? Are you going to do a clean sweep?"

Most new owners brought in their own teams, and she

hated to think of the people she'd known and loved like an extended family being scattered across the globe—that was if they were able to find jobs with so many farms downsizing.

"I'll maintain the status quo while I assess the property and the business."

"And then what?"

"My decisions will depend on what I discover about the operation."

"What's to discover? You bought a world-class stable—"

"Hannah," her father interrupted, "Brink will go over the particulars of the agreement with you. All you need to know is that Wyatt has agreed to keep the current staff for a full year unless obvious incompetence leads him to decide otherwise."

Her shoulders snapped straight at the insult. "Sutherland Farm doesn't employ any incompetents."

"Then no one need be concerned," Jacobs said.

Desperation clawed at her throat. "Daddy, please don't do this. I'm sure there's a way you can undo the paperwork. Give me a chance to prove to you that I can run the farm and—"

"Hannah, we closed the deal a week ago. Today was merely the first time Wyatt and I could meet personally to discuss the transition."

"A week ago," she parroted. Her world had crashed and she'd been oblivious. Head reeling and legs shaking, she tried to make sense of the upheaval to come.

"I've already purchased a townhome and the movers have been scheduled," her father added, sending another shockwave rippling through her.

Jacobs stiffened. "A townhome? What about the cottage?"

My cottage! Ohmigod. Where will I live?

Her father's expression turned cagey. "Hannah lives in the cottage."

Jacobs's hands fisted by his sides and anger lit his eyes.

Confused by the exchange, Hannah looked from the interloper to her father. "My home and my job are part of

Sutherland Farm. Where will I go? Where will I live and work?"

Her father sighed and turned toward the bar cart. "I'll let Wyatt explain."

"Luthor excluded the cottage and two acres inside the stone fence surrounding it from the deal. You'll get to keep your house. And, as your father has already explained, like any other employee you'll be kept on staff as long as the quality of your work meets my standards." Jacobs's voice carried about as much warmth as liquid nitrogen.

The man would be her boss.

"Your standards?" From his tone she gathered his standards would be impossible to meet.

Her cottage, the original Sutherland homestead, sat smack in the middle of Sutherland Farm. She'd be surrounded by enemy territory. But at least she'd have a roof over her head.

She swallowed her panic and fought to clear her head. "When is all this upheaval scheduled to take place?"

"I'm taking over as CEO today and moving into this house as soon as your father has vacated."

In other words, life as she'd always known it had ended.

Two

Anger licked along Wyatt's nerve endings like kindling catching fire. Luthor Sutherland had deliberately deceived him.

The man had no intention of "retiring" to the original homestead as he'd led Wyatt to believe when he'd insisted the parcel be excluded from the sale, and Sutherland's daughter was one of the employees Sutherland had been so eager to protect. If Wyatt had known, he would never have signed the employee agreement Sutherland had insisted on.

But if Luthor expected Wyatt to cut his princess any slack, he'd be disappointed. If Hannah couldn't carry her weight, she'd be fired—per the performance clause Wyatt had included.

What incensed him the most was that he knew he had no one but himself to blame for deception getting past him. He'd been neck-deep in closing an international distribution deal and because he didn't have the time, interest or knowledge in running a horse farm, he'd delegated the job of finding a

self-sufficient operation—one that wouldn't require him to
be on-site—to the best buyer's agent in the business.

Sutherland Farm met all his criteria. He couldn't help
wondering if there were any more surprises in addition to the
leggy brunette liability yet to discover. Whatever the issues,
he would find and eradicate them.

He had enough problems without having to deal with a
pampered heiress who had been living out of her daddy's
deep pockets. The snippets of conversation he'd overheard
through the patio door made it clear that description fit
Hannah Sutherland from her silk shirt to her polished high-
heeled boots.

He'd bet his seven-figure investment portfolio that Hannah
had coasted through life on her beauty and pretty-please
smiles. His gut warned him she'd be nothing but trouble. And
his instincts about people were rarely wrong. He didn't need
to see the two carats of diamonds in her ears or the watch
on her wrist so pricey that a thief could pawn it to buy a
car or her short but perfectly manicured nails to confirm her
overindulged status.

"I want every employee's file before I leave today," he
demanded without looking away from the smoky blue eyes
shooting flames at him.

"That's confidential information," Hannah protested.

"Hannah," Sutherland's lawyer interjected, "as the new
owner of Sutherland Farm, Mr. Jacobs has unrestricted access
to employee records."

"But—"

Wyatt nailed her with a hard look. "I'll start with yours.
I have a pretty good idea what I'll find. Private schools.
Sororities. European vacations paid for by Sutherland Farm."

Hannah glared at him. Tension quivered through her
slender, toned body. Her breasts rose and fell rapidly, and
despite his aversion to spoiled women and his anger over his
predicament, awareness simmered beneath his skin.

Something about her got to him. She had a subtle grace

and elegance about her that both attracted him and, because of his past relationships with her type, repulsed him. He'd been burned by her kind before.

"I graduated from an accredited veterinary school," she said through barely moving lips. "My credentials are valid, and since Warmbloods are a European breed, visiting the established and successful breeding farms to study their setups and evaluate their stock for potential matches is a necessary part of my job."

"I'm sure you have references from your previous employers to prove your worth as an employee."

Her chin jerked up a notch and she managed to look down her straight nose at him in the way only wealthy women could—a lesson he'd had driven into him like a railroad spike when he'd been seventeen and green and working at his stepfather's stable. Back then he hadn't been smart enough to know rich daddy's darlings didn't marry boys who cleaned stalls for their stepfathers' stables no matter how intimate the relationship might have become.

"I have worked here since graduating—almost five years. I'm good at what I do."

"I'll be the judge of that."

She folded her arms and cocked back on one of those long legs. "Tell me, Mr. Jacobs, what exactly are your credentials for determining whether or not staff members are performing well?"

"Hannah—" the attorney cautioned, but Wyatt silenced him with a look.

"I'm CEO of Triple Crown Distillery. I employ over six hundred. I recognize incompetents and slackers when I see them."

Anger stained her cheeks a fiery red, proving she'd picked up his implication that he considered her one. "As I've already stated, the Sutherland team doesn't have any weak links. We're a cohesive unit, one of the best in the industry."

"That remains to be seen." Wyatt was beginning to wish

he'd chosen one of the other dozen properties the real estate agent had presented. But as wise as that option now appeared, none of those farms had fit Sam's descriptions and all would have required Wyatt's input as a manager. Input he didn't have the time or inclination to give.

When Sam reminisced about the Kentucky thoroughbred farm he'd once owned, he sounded so lucid Wyatt could almost forget his stepfather was fading away right before his eyes. Sutherland Farm resembled Sam's old farm more than any of the other properties, and Sam deserved to be comfortable, happy and, most importantly, safe for however long he had left. He would be here. Wyatt would make damned sure of it.

And he had no intention of letting Hannah Sutherland prevent him from repaying the debt he owed to the man who'd been a better parent to him than his own flesh and blood.

"Just watch your step, doc. Your father may have indulged you, but I won't. You'll earn your keep if you want to remain employed here. Now, if you'll excuse me, I have files to review and you need to get back to work."

Exhausted, Hannah plodded down the driveway toward her cottage, a hot bubble bath and a glass of wine.

One of her rescue mares kept pace beside her on the opposite side of the white board fence. Hannah found the horse's undemanding company soothing. Unlike people, who were easily disappointed, horses never expected too much.

It had been a tough week. Since her world crashed she'd been juggling her usual duties plus the new ones thrust unexpectedly on her. The staff had turned to her for answers—answers she didn't have.

The mood in the barns grew more oppressive, like an impending summer storm, with each day that Wyatt Jacobs failed to make an appearance. Usually affable employees were on edge and snapping at each other. Even the horses had picked up on the bad vibes and been harder to handle than usual. Hannah wished Jacobs would show up just to break the tension. Not that she wanted to see him again.

The phone on her hip vibrated. The digital display read private caller. Could be a client or, if she was lucky, a wrong number. She didn't have the energy to deal with another crisis or panicking coworker.

She hit the answer button. "Hannah Sutherland."

"Wyatt Jacobs. Come to my office in the house. Now."

Click.

Her feet stuck to the pavement as if she'd stepped in fresh tar. She scowled at the now silent phone then she looked across the lawn toward the main house. A light glowed in her father's—*Wyatt Jacobs's*—study.

The usurper had arrived. And he'd hung up on her. The rude, inconsiderate jerk. Anger charged through her system, riding on the back of a burst of adrenaline. How dare he demand an appointment this late in the evening?

She considered calling back and telling him she was off the clock and she'd see him tomorrow. But according to the clause in her new contract, which Brinkley had pointed out, she couldn't refuse the boss's summons without jeopardizing her job.

She glanced at her stained clothing. If she were truly interested in making a good impression, she'd clean up first.

She wasn't.

She'd done an internet search on Jacobs and found nothing linking him to horses in any way. Why had he bought the farm?

Was he one of those new-money guys who thought owning a horse farm would be trendy and fun? If so, he wouldn't have a clue how much work, money and commitment were involved in a stable the size of Sutherland. If she had to teach him herself, he'd learn, and if she smelled like sweat and horses and other unpleasant stuff, she'd only be furthering his education.

As much as she hated going into the meeting at a messy

disadvantage, he'd have to deal with her dirt. "Welcome to the horse business, Wyatt Jacobs."

Energized by resentment and determination Hannah marched across the lawn and up to the kitchen door. A sideways glance down the patio brought her hand to a halt inches shy of the knob.

An unfamiliar rectangular teak table and chairs occupied the space once graced by elegant glass-topped wrought iron furniture and classic urns overflowing with spring flowers. The sight drove home the reality that this wasn't her father's house anymore, and she didn't have the right to casually enter through the kitchen and feast on Nellie's delicious cooking.

Ten yards away the patio door leading to the office opened, and Wyatt Jacobs's tall, broad-shouldered frame filled the gap. His dark gaze pinned her like a thumbtack stabbing into a bulletin board.

"Come in, doc." He gestured with a sharp beckoning motion of his hand—the same way he would order a dog.

Her hackles rose. Everything about him made her want to snarl and growl and that surprised her. Who was this strange woman with the bad attitude who had taken over her body? It certainly wasn't her. She preferred gracious smiles, gentle persuasion and Southern charm. Kill 'em with kindness, Nellie had always said, and the strategy had worked for Hannah thus far.

Wyatt Jacobs brought out her witchy side. Her churning stomach warned her to handle this encounter with care. Jacobs, the one man she didn't know and didn't care to know, held her future and that of her horses and the rest of the staff in his hands. Being cooperative was imperative.

She'd be damned if she'd let him know how afraid she was of losing everything.

"I'd rather talk out here." Even though she delivered the words with a civil smile, Hannah Sutherland bristled with visible animosity. She pointed to her dust-covered black low-heeled boots. "Since I wasn't expecting your call this late in the day, I've brought barn with me."

Her boots weren't all that was dirty. He noted the smudge filling the hollow beneath one high cheekbone, then a stain on her white Sutherland Farm logo polo shirt drew his eyes to the curve of her breasts. Another dirty streak on her khaki pants ran down the inside of her lean, taut thigh. Her current garb was a far cry from the designer duds she'd been wearing the day they'd met, but she still wore the pricey watch and ice-cube-size earrings.

He caught a subtle whiff of the stables on the breeze. But along with the smell of horses, wood shavings and hay another scent—something feminine and alluring like expensive French perfume—snagged his attention. His heart inexplicably and annoyingly pumped faster.

He'd studied her résumé and bio the way he would a blueprint, searching for flaws and weaknesses, and he'd found nothing to like in her privileged, worry-free upbringing. She'd apparently been given everything she'd ever wanted on a silver platter.

"Other than your years at college you've never lived away from dear old dad or his checkbook, have you?"

Her slender frame stiffened and her smile faltered. "No."

"You never held a job, before waltzing into this one."

"I didn't waltz in. I earned my degree. And I gained experience by volunteering at the university's stables. I wasn't on the payroll because I didn't need the money. I didn't think it fair to take it from someone who did."

Even with, or possibly because of, Sam's help, Wyatt had worked his ass off to get where he was today. Sam might have paid the tuition, but he'd made Wyatt prove himself every step of the way. He'd learned the business from the ground up, and Triple Crown Distillery's distribution and profit margins had increased by sixty percent since he had taken control after Sam's "retirement."

But Wyatt's bitterness and resentment over Hannah's

worry-free life didn't stop the spurt of energy racing through his veins when Hannah glared at him.

"I'm off the clock, Mr. Jacobs. Was there something you needed that couldn't wait until tomorrow?"

The setting sun highlighted the streaks of gold in her brown wavy hair—streaks probably applied by an overpriced hairdresser. Her blue eyes showed no mercy, no interest and no feminine softness. She didn't want him here, and her attempt at hiding her feelings failed miserably.

"Meet me in the stable's business office tomorrow at noon."

"Why?" Her eyes narrowed with suspicion.

"You're going to show me around the farm."

Her stiff shoulders snapped back, becoming even more rigid. She hit him with that hoity, looking-down-the-nose appraisal that reminded him of his first love, first heartache and first betrayal by a woman.

"I can't drop everything to play tour guide for you. Sir," she tacked on at the last minute.

He wasn't used to openly antagonistic females. He would have to be an idiot not to realize his looks and money made most of her gender eager to please. But from the tension and displeasure radiating from her, he would hazard a guess that she didn't give a rat's ass what he thought of her and her disheveled state. Or maybe she'd dirtied up intentionally to make it look as though she worked hard. Yeah, that was probably the case. He doubted Ms. Perfect Manicure ever got her hands dirty.

"You'll report at noon if you value your job."

"I have a full schedule tomorrow. This is the busy season."

"Why?"

She blinked, revealing long, thick lashes he hadn't noticed before. "Why what?"

"Why is this the busy season?"

A pleat formed between her eyebrows. "Not only do we have a lot of boarders showing up to ride on Saturdays, I shouldn't have to tell you we're preparing for the breeding season."

His knowledge of horse breeding was limited. Sam had always given Wyatt more menial jobs—the kind that built character as well as muscle and calluses. Or so Sam had insisted. "Noon, Dr. Sutherland."

"I'll find someone else to show you around, someone who has the time."

"Your father claims you know more about Sutherland Farm than any other employee. I don't want someone else. I want you. That's not negotiable."

"Of course I know the most about the farm. I've lived here all my life, and I've covered every inch of the property. But as much as I'd love to show you all the wonderful things about Sutherland Farm, I have a production schedule to maintain."

Something—maybe a primitive urge to knock her off the pedestal she'd put herself on—made Hannah's resistance both challenging and a turn-on.

That makes you one twisted fool, Jacobs.

A nerve at the corner of his mouth twitched as he fought to conceal his irritation with her and himself. "You're not going to make it that easy for me, are you, Hannah?"

"What do you mean?"

"Per your contract, if you fail to meet my expectations you'll be fired. Make time to show me around or pick up your final paycheck."

Her lips flattened into a thin line and anger flagged her cheeks with red. "You like the power of holding the contracts you made us sign over our heads, don't you? We're all here on a trial basis even though we've been successfully doing our jobs without your interference for years."

"I'm the boss. *Your* boss. That's the way it works."

Her irritated gaze snapped up and down his Armani suit without the admiration he usually received. She heaved an aggravated breath. "I'll be there, but leave the fancy duds behind unless you plan to stay in the golf cart."

She pivoted on her heel with military precision then marched off the patio, her firm, round bottom swishing with each long, angry stride. He couldn't peel his gaze away and his body reacted with unexpected and unwanted appreciation.

Oh, yeah, he'd called it right. Hannah Sutherland with her expensive jewelry, highlighted hair, manicured hands and entitled attitude was going to be nothing but trouble.

Until he got rid of her.

And that couldn't happen soon enough.

Three

The door to Hannah's lab opened abruptly on Saturday morning, startling her. Wyatt stalked in as if he owned the place…which he did, technically. But this was *her* domain—the only place that remained orderly and tranquil no matter what chaos reigned in other parts of her life.

Her muscles snapped taut and the hair on her nape sprang to attention. She'd never experienced such instant antagonism toward anyone before, and the strength of the emotion roiling inside her now surprised her.

"You said twelve. You're early." She tried to keep her tone polite, but judging by his scowl, she failed.

His dark eyes panned the spotless room as if inventorying each piece of equipment before returning to her and examining her as thoroughly. "The rain is predicted to worsen. I want my tour now."

Rain? Hannah blinked and listened. Sure enough, rain snare-drummed on the barn's metal roof. She'd been so engrossed in her tasks and her troubles that she hadn't even noticed the rat-a-tat-tat before now. Usually the sound relaxed her. But not today, thanks to the irritant in front of her.

She stood her ground and returned his appraisal. The hard line of his jaw gleamed from a recent shave and his hair looked damp—either from the weather or a recent shower if he were the type to waste a morning lying in bed. A picture of him on twisted sheets popped into her head.

Where had that come from? She kicked it away.

A black cashmere sweater stretched across his broad shoulders, the white of a T-shirt showing in the V-neck, and faded jeans clung to his hips and long, muscled thighs. Something—most likely aggravation—quickened her pulse. It couldn't be anything else. She didn't like him or his arrogant attitude.

"I still have orders to process before the courier service arrives. Come back at twelve. Please," she added. She wasn't going to let him disrupt her schedule and thereby give him grounds to fire her.

"Reviewing employee performance is part of any new business venture. I'll start with yours. You work. I'll observe."

Anxiety tangled with the coil of exasperation snaking through her. She couldn't throw him out. "Then at least close the door. This is a controlled environment. The room needs to remain dust-free, and the temperature as constant as possible."

"Is it that important?"

"Considering I handle thousands of dollars' worth of product every day, yes, quality control is important."

Curiosity sharpened his eyes. He strolled toward her, encroaching on her personal space, but she kept her boots planted, refusing to surrender her spot by the microscope despite an almost visceral urge to back far, far away.

"What are you working on, doc?"

An odd question from the man who owned everything in front of him. Everything except her, that is. "I'm confirming the viability of the sample before I chill and ship it."

"Sample of what?"

He was kidding. Right? But if so, he did so with a straight face. Hey, she could play along. "Sperm. Want to take a look?"

His short, thick lashes flickered, then he moved forward, calling her bluff and forcing her to yield territory to avoid contact. He bent over the microscope. "Tell me what I'm looking for."

Unsure whether he was testing her knowledge or simply being a pain in the rear, she scowled at the thick, dark strands covering the back of his head. "You're checking to see whether the sample has enough potency to get the job done."

He straightened. Their gazes collided unexpectedly and held. Her thoughts scattered like bowling pins. Tension crackled between them.

"And the answer?"

She inhaled slowly, trying to remember his question, but a trace of his cologne—something hinting of patchouli, sandalwood and cypress—distracted her. He smelled good and looked good. Too bad he was a jerk. She'd dealt with enough overinflated egos over the years to know bad attitude cancelled out any positives.

"Yes, this is a fertile stud, and a good thing, too, since Commander is Sutherland Farm's top moneymaker."

Determined to get back to business, she waved him out of the way and bent over the eye pieces, but his presence disturbed her. She could feel him dissecting and cataloging her every action as if he were waiting for her to make a mistake. When she adjusted the focus her hands weren't as steady as they'd been before his arrival, and it annoyed her that he could rattle her so easily.

"What's the purpose of all the equipment and charts?"

Another odd question from Sutherland's new owner. She lifted her head and put down the pencil she'd been using to make notes. "If I explain, will you go away and let me finish my job?"

"I'm not leaving until you've given me a satisfactory tour."

Not what she wanted to hear. "Are you completely ignorant of the business into which you've invested millions?"

Whoops. Not nice, Hannah. What happened to killing him with kindness and not making waves?

"You mean the business I own, the one that pays your salary?"

He had her there. And if she wanted to continue receiving that paycheck so that she could care for her horses and put food on her table, she'd better dam the resentment pouring from her mouth. "I apologize. The clock is ticking and I really need to get this order ready before the sample is ruined."

"Answer my question, Hannah."

"The shelves are filled with the collection equipment we use. Each stud has his own—" Her cheeks warmed and her tongue tangled. Oh, for pity's sake. Reproduction was her job. Discussing it was routine. So why did explaining it to *him* make her uncomfortable? They weren't discussing *her* personal sexual preferences.

Or his.

An image of him bare-chested, braced on his forearms above her and with passion instead of irritation tightening his features flashed in her mind. Her womb clenched. She inhaled sharply.

Girl, you have been too long without a man's attention.

She cleared her throat and, trying to ignore the unwelcome warmth seeping through her, carefully chose her words. "Stallions have likes and dislikes that could interfere with or assist in production and collection. We get our most successful outcomes when the positive elements are in place, and we keep track of each stud's preferences with the charts."

His eyes narrowed and for a moment the air seemed to hum with tension. "Sutherland Farm has two veterinarians on staff. Your position seems redundant. Why should I continue paying your salary?"

Alarm froze any lingering awareness faster than a liquid nitrogen dip. "You're asking me to justify my job?"

"Correct. Convince me nepotism wasn't a factor in your hiring."

She dampened her suddenly dry lips. "Our staff vet oversees general animal health. I oversee breeding."

"Something animals have managed without assistance or all this equipment since the beginning of time."

"Breeding is Sutherland Farm's bread and butter. Without the raw material, our trainers can't produce champions. We continue to make money off successful mares and studs for years, sometimes even decades, after they leave the show ring."

"And why can't the staff vet oversee that?"

"Developing a winning bloodline is far more complicated than randomly pairing animals and hoping for a pretty foal. It's an intricate mix of genealogy, genetics, biology and veterinary science aimed at producing an animal with optimal traits and minimal deficiencies. It's a science—one at which I happen to excel."

He didn't look impressed.

"Tell me, Wyatt, exactly how much do you know about horse breeding?"

"My knowledge of horses is limited to thoroughbreds."

That explained a lot. "And yet you bought a Warmblood farm. Thoroughbreds are bred naturally. Sutherland Farm does almost everything by artificial insemination."

"Why?"

"There are several reasons. Our horses are too valuable to risk one of them getting injured during the natural breeding process, and artificial insemination allows us to service mares globally and not only in our barns. It's cost-effective and less stressful for the mares than being shipped to the stallion's home stable. Shipping a horse overseas is expensive and often disturbs her cycle. Plus quarantine is a hassle. Shipping semen is less aggravating. We simply freeze or chill it and send it out."

He pointed to yet another chart. "And this?"

Hannah grimaced. She was fond of her charts and graphs. Charts were predictable. They made sense. She could weigh the pros and cons of practically any permutation on paper and erase her mistakes. Unlike life's bad choices.

"That's the stallion schedule. Regular, predictable collection encourages better production. In layman's terms, it's our way of aligning supply to demand so we know where to set our stud fees. And the chart beside it is the pending shipment list—the one I need to get back to before I can give you the tour and before this sample loses viability. So please, Mr. Jacobs, go away and let me do my job."

"Wyatt," he corrected.

She didn't want to be on a first-name basis with him. That implied friendship—something they would never have. But he was the boss and that meant she had to mind her manners.

"*Wyatt*. Sutherland Farm bloodstock has been producing champion jumping and dressage stock for years. Let me show you to the visitors' lounge in the office building. You can have a cup of coffee and look through the catalogue of our studs, mares and foals until I finish here."

His dark gaze lingered on hers until an odd sensation stirred in the pit of her stomach and her toes curled in her boots. "I can find the lounge."

The moment he left the room tension drained from her shoulders, torso and legs as if leaking through her soles. She sagged against the work table, bowing her head and taking a moment to collect her composure.

Damn the man. How was she going to work with him when she couldn't even stand to be in the same room with him? He made her uncomfortable with his long, intense examinations and he was clearly searching for a reason—*any* reason—to fire her.

She'd barely gotten back into the groove when the door opened again. She snapped upright. Her stomach sank as Wyatt strolled in carrying one of the farm's many photo albums and ending her short-lived reprieve. He parked himself on the stool directly across the table from her microscope.

No. "I thought you were going to let me work."

"I'm not stopping you. The sooner you finish, the sooner we can get on with business." He directed his attention to the book in front of him.

Irritation sputtered through her. If he didn't quit distracting her, he'd never get his tour, and he acted as if the delay was her fault.

Determined to ignore him, she gritted her teeth and returned to the job at hand. Every time she looked up from the microscope her gaze slammed straight into his, and each time she felt those dark eyes on her or his body shifted her pulse skipped.

She wanted him gone. From her lab. From her farm. From her life. *Daddy, what have you done?*

Forcing herself to concentrate, she powered through her work with sheer determination. When she finally sealed the last tube in the shipping package, relief coursed through her. Dread trotted close behind. Finishing meant she'd have to spend time alone with her new boss.

Resigned to the torture, she sighed. "Where do you want to start?"

He closed the portfolio and slowly rose, unfolding one smooth muscle after the other. As much as she hated to admit it, Wyatt Jacobs had great conformation and grace in motion, like one of Sutherland's prized dressage champions. "Anywhere."

She swallowed her impatience. She wanted to make this as quick and painless as possible. He wasn't helping. "Narrow that down. We have two thousand acres. Which parts of the property have you not seen?"

"Except for the house, this barn and the office building, I haven't seen any of the farm."

Her mouth dropped open. "You spent millions of dollars without seeing what you were getting for your money?"

"I had pictures, topography maps and the video package the real estate appraiser prepared. Sutherland Farm suits my needs."

She remembered the videographer's visit several months ago. Her father had told her the film would be used for promotional purposes and she'd had no reason not to believe him because they often had photographers on the premises. That meant not only had her father lied, but he'd been scheming to tear her world apart for months. That hurt.

But the past was over. She had to deal with the present, and the present included the testosterone-packed problem in front of her.

"And what exactly are your needs?" She winced when she heard the double entendre of her words.

As if a door slammed shut, Wyatt's face instantly turned inscrutable. "To own a horse farm. What else?"

Wyatt Jacobs was lying through his perfect white teeth. Hannah would swear to it. But she couldn't prove it. And even if she could, what could she do about it? Right now she was nothing but a puppet. And he held her strings.

Hannah didn't believe him, and frankly, Wyatt didn't care. He wasn't here to make friends. In fact, it would suit him better if she got ticked off and quit her job.

Playing chaperone to a spoiled princess had never been part of his plan. He'd bought the farm for Sam and had intended spending as little time here as possible. But Hannah would require more supervision than his planned sporadic visits.

The door to the lab burst open, shattering the standoff between him and the bothersome brunette. A lanky redheaded guy rushed in. "Doc Will's got another one."

Hannah's body language changed instantly from resentful and reluctant to alert and attentive. Wyatt found the switch quite intriguing. She didn't snap at the new guy for keeping the door open, dripping on the floor or tracking in mud. Instead, she wiggled her fingers in a give-me-more gesture.

"He got a call to euthanize, but he decided to give you a look first. He's down at the barn."

Those big blue eyes rounded. "He's *here* instead of calling for a consult?"

"Yep. It's that critical. He hightailed it off the property as soon as the authorities gave him the okay. He says this one will be a real test of your skills."

"He's assuming I'll say yes."

The redhead chuckled. "Hannah, you never say no."

Wyatt tried to make sense of their conversation and couldn't, but he seriously doubted the twentysomething guy meant the words in a sexual context—which was exactly where Wyatt's brain headed when he heard a woman couldn't say no.

He shut down that mental detour and cursed his traitorous libido. Hannah Sutherland might have a rockin' body and a damned sexy pout, but there would be nothing remotely intimate between him and his temporary employee.

"I'm Wyatt Jacobs. And you are?" His question brought both sets of eyes in his direction.

Hannah grimaced. "I'm sorry. Jeb Jones, our veterinary assistant. Wyatt is the new owner."

Wyatt shook Jeb's hand. "Who is Doc Will?"

Hannah ripped off her lab coat and hung it on the hook by the door. "Will is one of our county veterinarians. Your tour will have to wait."

"Are you willing to risk the consequences of refusing my request?" He didn't need to elaborate that she'd be fired, but her quick gasp told him she received his unspoken message loud and clear.

Her defiant gaze drilled him. "You didn't request, Mr. Jacobs. You ordered. And I'm not refusing. I'm postponing your tour until after I've handled this emergency."

Her exasperation came across loud and clear despite the pretty-please smile punctuating her sentence. No doubt that smile worked on most men. Not him.

"Let's go, Jeb." Hannah rushed from the lab.

The kid hesitated, as if trying to decide who was in charge, but then he mistakenly fell in behind his cohort. Taken aback by Hannah's insubordination and the kid's loyalty, Wyatt rocked on his heels. Then he reconsidered. This wasn't the case of a woman standing up for her convictions. Hannah was a spoiled daddy's girl who believed the rules didn't apply to her. He'd teach her and her flunky differently.

He followed the pair, intent on firing Hannah, giving her follower a warning and informing the veterinarian that Sutherland Farm was no longer a dumping ground for unwanted animals of any kind. Hannah might not be able to say no, but Wyatt had no such problem.

Ahead of him Hannah and Jeb raced down the driveway heedless of the rain. They veered off the paved surface and onto a gravel track leading to a building set behind a copse of trees several hundred yards from the main barn. Wyatt climbed into his Mercedes and drove the distance rather than get soaked.

Once he pulled off the asphalt, the uneven ground tested his car's suspension. Considering the pristine condition of the rest of the property, the neglect surprised him. He made a mental note to speak to the manager about ordering a load of gravel to fill the potholes.

A pickup truck with a horse trailer attached had backed through the barn's open doors. He parked beside it and surveyed the stone building through the rain streaming down his windshield. The smaller barn had the same architecturally attractive design as the other barns, but the structure, like the driveway hadn't been as well-maintained as the rest of the farm. Odd.

He climbed from his car, then squeezed between the trailer and doorjamb. While the outside of the building lacked sparkle, the interior was as spotless as a barn could be. The combined scents of fresh shavings, hay and oats ambushed him with memories of happier times with Sam.

The trailer's rear ramp had been lowered into the center hallway. Inside the metal enclosure a horse danced restlessly in the right compartment, its feet thumping hollowly on the rubberized mat covering the steel floor.

Hannah occupied the left half of the trailer, a rib-high divider separating her from the agitated creature. She stroked the animal's withers and back, and spoke calmly. "It's okay, girl. You have nothing to fear. We're going to take good care of you."

Her quiet, soothing tone contrasted with the impatient one she'd used with him each time he'd asked a question this morning.

The horse responded with a panicked sound that raised the fine hairs on Wyatt's body. It had been almost fifteen years since he'd been around horses, but even he recognized the animal's terror.

Firing Hannah would have to wait until she wasn't in physical danger. Distraction in the workplace was an invitation to disaster. "Get out of there."

"In a minute," she replied without raising her voice. "Okay boys, let's ease her out and see what we have."

"You're not gonna like it," an older gentleman wearing muddy jeans and a battered field jacket said as he came from behind the trailer and clapped Wyatt on the shoulder. "Best not to get behind this one, son."

Wyatt flashed back to his teens. He'd heard the same warning from Sam too many times to count when Sam had been at the top of his game and lucid all the time and not just intermittently.

Hannah scowled at Wyatt across the distance. "I'll call you when I'm done."

"I'm not leaving."

"If you stay, you'll end up getting in the way or getting hurt."

"I worked on a thoroughbred farm from the time I was

fourteen until I went to college. But don't unload that horse. It needs to go back to wherever it came from."

Her expression turned belligerent. "That's not an option—a fact the police will confirm if you pick up the phone and ask for Officer—"

"Harris," the veterinarian supplied when Hannah arched an eyebrow.

Her continued defiance rasped against Wyatt's last nerve. "I don't want that animal on this property."

Hannah descended the ramp and didn't stop until they were toe-to-toe, chest to chest—so close he could taste the mint on her breath and feel the heat steaming from her rain-dampened clothing.

He fought to keep his attention from the way her white polo shirt had turned almost transparent. Fought and failed. The wet fabric clung to her hard-nippled breasts and outlined her thin white bra. His hormones reacted the way a healthy man's would and, try as he might, he could not control the sudden increase in his pulse rate.

"Mr. Jacobs, *Wyatt,* if you feel the same way after I've examined her, we'll discuss other arrangements. But for now, please step aside, and let me do my job."

"I thought you were the breeding specialist."

"I only work a half day on Saturdays. In my off hours I wear a different hat."

"Have you forgotten who pays your salary?"

"You're not likely to let that happen. Give me an hour to examine the mare and see what we're dealing with. This could be a matter of life and death. I'm not ready to take a life without just cause. Are you?"

"Are you always so melodramatic?"

"Hardly ever," she answered deadpan.

Her determination impressed him. "Make it quick."

"Thank you." She returned to the trailer, apparently undaunted by the agitated creature's dancing.

Under her direction the trio coaxed the horse down the ramp

in fits and spurts. The mare's hesitant steps alternated with nervous hops and skips, then in a sudden backward lunge the horse launched from the trailer kicking up a spray of shavings. Once the dust settled the wild-eyed animal quivered in the hall, its terror-widened eyes taking in the scene.

Then Wyatt saw what the shadowy trailer had concealed. Open sores and scars crisscrossed the emaciated back, haunches and muzzle. Bloody rings circled the mare's back legs just above the hooves.

She'd been abused. His gut muscles seized and rage blazed within him. "Who did this?"

The vet shook his head without taking his eyes from the animal. "Mean SOB who owned her. I hope the cops give him a taste of his own medicine. A billy club upside his head would be a nice touch."

Hannah handed the lead rope to Jeb then eased around the horse without ever lifting her palm from the animal's dull, scarred hide. Wyatt recognized the trick as one Sam had employed. By never losing contact, the horse always knew where you were and wouldn't be startled.

"You know animal abusers get a slap on the wrist at best, Will." Her frustration came through loud and clear even though she kept her tone low and even. "She doesn't look good."

"Nope. Not much to work with," the vet replied. "She wouldn't have lasted another week in that hellhole."

Wyatt focused on the deep gouges and bloody fetlocks. Now that the fight had drained out of the mare her head hung low as if she were resigned to whatever came next and fighting took more energy than she possessed. She'd probably been a beauty once, but now she was nothing more than a broken shell. She looked ready to collapse. Her spirit seemed broken, her usefulness in doubt.

Like Sam.

The parallel was so strong it blindsided Wyatt. He hated to see anything or anyone turned into a victim trapped in a body that could no longer function or fight back. He turned to the vet who'd brought the animal. "You should have put her down."

"Maybe. That's Hannah's call now."

"Why prolong her misery? Ending her suffering would be more humane."

Hannah bristled, agitating the mare into a side step. "Just because the owner is worthless doesn't mean the animal is. Every life has value, including hers. Her teeth indicate she's less than ten years old. There could be a lot of good years in her yet."

"She's debilitated, terrified and in pain," Wyatt countered, his fists curling in frustration.

"If anyone can pull her through, Hannah can," the vet said.

A muscle jumped in Wyatt's jaw. The horse had been through hell, and someone had to find the compassion and make the executive decision to end her suffering. That someone was him, apparently.

"She's probably disease-ridden and could infect the other horses. And after being abused this severely, her trust in man has likely been irrevocably broken."

Hannah planted herself between Wyatt and the mare. She didn't look like a spoiled daddy's girl now. She resembled a mama grizzly passionately defending her cub. "You can't write her off without giving her a chance."

Her stormy gaze hit Wyatt with a fireball of pain, anger and frustration, the same emotions rumbling through him. The fight in her eyes would cause a lesser man to back down.

"Giving horses second chances is what I do, Wyatt. And if you'd done your research on the farm before you tossed around your money, you would realize it's what you do now, too."

Wyatt stiffened as the barb hit home. He couldn't argue with facts. He'd delegated his research. The agent's report hadn't included anything about Sutherland Farm being a dumping ground for damaged animals, or Hannah Sutherland, who was going to make damned sure he paid for delegating.

"That right rear leg could be broken."

Hannah didn't even glance at it. "It's cut deep from the hobbles. It looks like the brute bound her back legs so she couldn't defend herself when he beat her. But from the way she's bearing weight on it, it's most likely superficial. I'll run X-rays to confirm."

"You mean you'll run up expenses on a lost cause."

She glared at him. "This isn't about money. Find Your Center saves lives. It doesn't destroy them unnecessarily."

"What in the hell is Find Your Center?"

Irritation darkened her eyes to storm cloud gray and tightened the tendons running the length of her neck as she stuck out her chin, making the diamonds in her ears sparkle in the barn's overhead lighting. If she'd been a guy, she probably would have punched him.

"Illustrating once again, Mr. Jacobs, you should have done your homework before your underhanded purchase."

"There was nothing devious about my purchasing this farm. It was for sale. I bought it."

She visibly reined in her temper, taking a deep breath then relaxing her tense muscles. "Sutherland Farm specializes in birth *and* rebirth."

A bird swooped through the open barn door. The horse spooked and jumped sideways, its haunches knocking into Hannah. She stumbled. Wyatt instinctively sprang forward to catch her. His muscles bunched as he banded his arms around her and braced his thighs to keep them both from going down under the ragged, dancing hooves.

Her feet tangled with his as she scrambled for traction and shifted against him in ways that made him excruciatingly aware of the surprising firmness and strength beneath her curves.

"Are you all right?" he asked through a knotted jaw.

Her wary gaze locked with his. Her cheeks flushed and her lips parted. His pulse spiked and heat flooded him, proving he shared something he wanted no part of with the pampered princess.

Chemistry.

"I'm fine. Thank you. Release me. Please." She planted her palms on his chest and pushed, broke his hold and backed away. Keeping an equally watchful eye on him, she circled to the opposite side of the horse.

"I'm sorry, Hannah," Jeb said. "I have her now."

"It's okay, Jeb. My mistake," she offered. "I know better than to turn my back on an unfamiliar animal."

She flashed a brief look at Wyatt as if he were the animal in question, then she bent to reexamine the mare's fetlock the way she'd done everything this morning—with a methodical thoroughness and attention to detail that had frustrated him in the lab because he'd suspected her of deliberately stalling as she checked and rechecked each sample and then meticulously packaged and charted each vial. Slow and steady was very likely her modus operandi and not just a passive-aggressive ploy to get under his skin.

She finally stepped away from the mare and, ignoring Wyatt, approached the vet, who'd been watching Wyatt as much as he had the horse. "I'll keep her."

"She could jeopardize the safety of the other horses," Wyatt objected.

"She'll be quarantined until the test results come back."

The vet nodded. "Thanks, Hannah. I'll take care of the legalities. Can you send me the pictures documenting the abuse ASAP? I took some video with my cell phone and shot that off to the authorities. But detailed still shots will help our case."

"I'll get photos before and after I clean and treat her wounds, and I'll email those and the lab results to you as soon as I'm done."

Wyatt didn't like the way this was playing out. "The mare's suffering should end. Put her down. I'll cover the cost."

Hannah gripped Wyatt's forearm. Her touch burned

through his sleeve like tongues of fire. Heat licked up his limb and settled in his torso.

"If you don't care about the mare, let me put it another way. To stand any chance of making the bastard who did this pay for his heinous crimes and to keep him from hurting another animal, we'll need documentation. Not only was this mare beaten and malnourished, she was obviously living in filth. The judge has to see what a sadist her owner is or the jerk might be allowed to own and torture other animals. No creature deserves to live or die in those conditions. Please, Wyatt, let me do this for her."

When she put it like that how could he refuse? Reports of abuse and neglect had been the top reasons he'd refused to put Sam in a facility. The mare, like Sam, deserved to be treated with dignity.

Her movements slow and deliberate, Hannah approached the mare and smoothed a hand down the white blaze. The horse shied away, tossing her head and almost knocking Hannah over, but the stupid woman wouldn't quit. She kept sweet-talking and caressing until the horse tolerated her touch.

"Look at that face. She deserves a second chance, don't you, girl?" Hannah's eyes, soft and wide, beseeched him. "Give me two weeks. Unless she tests positive for something I can't cure, I'll prove to you, and to her, that she deserves a better life. When I'm done she'll be healthier so someone else might be willing to foster her. Worst-case scenario, her final days will be good ones. She'll be warm and clean and well-fed."

Wyatt couldn't care less about Hannah's bedroom-soft purr or the horse's face. He didn't believe for one minute this spoiled rich girl had what it took to bring the mare back from near-death, but her point about final days got to him. That's why he'd bought the farm for Sam.

"Two weeks. You pay for the costs, and no heroic measures."

Relief softened Hannah's expression. "Wait and see the miracles a little TLC can create."

"I don't believe in miracles."

She shrugged. "Your loss. They happen every day."

"That's Pollyanna garbage."

"Beats pessimism."

The vet's pager buzzed. He pulled it from his pocket and frowned at the message. "Hannah, darling, I have a colic call on the other side of the county. I have to go. Can you manage without me?"

"Jeb and I can handle her."

Hannah flicked her fingers at Wyatt in a dismissive gesture. "You can go, too. I'm going to be busy here for a while. I'll call you when I'm done, and if there's still enough daylight left, you'll get your tour. If not, I'll make time tomorrow."

The liability of her getting hurt on the job outweighed his disgust with the situation, and he couldn't think of a better way to keep an eye on her than to help. "I'm not leaving. You'll be shorthanded without Doc."

Hannah frowned. Her mouth opened, then closed as if she'd considered arguing but had changed her mind. "If you insist on staying, then go into the office and get my camera out of my desk drawer. You can take the before photographs while I get my suture kit. But stay out of my way."

Her bossy tone reminded him that she was probably used to men jumping at her command. She'd learn quickly that he had no intention of being one of her minions.

Four

Hannah could barely concentrate on cleansing the mare's wounds. She wished she could think of a way to get rid of her new boss—one that didn't include angering him and making him renege on their bargain.

Her collision with Wyatt earlier had left her more than a little mystified. His touch had filled her with some weird, almost kinetic energy that she couldn't identify and didn't like. And since then it was almost as if she'd grown antennae that stayed tuned into the Wyatt channel. The constant awareness of him was exhausting. She wanted it and him gone.

His hawkeyed presence made her uncomfortable—something the sensitive mare picked up on and displayed with each nervous swish of her tail. Add in that he had removed his sweater ten minutes ago, revealing a newsworthy set of broad shoulders in his snug white T-shirt, and Hannah was practically salivating over a pair of deliciously defined pectorals.

Pitiful, Hannah. Just pitiful.

She glanced up and her gaze slammed into Wyatt's dark brown one over the mare's withers. Her pulse bucked.

"When will Jeb return?" he asked in that rumbly, make-her-insides-quiver voice of his.

"It'll take him a while to run all the tests. We'll probably finish before he does."

"Does the staff always dump the dirty work on you?"

She couldn't tell if his question arose from genuine curiosity or from the quest for information he could use against her coworkers. She would have to guard every word she said.

"They know I like cleanup detail. It gives me a chance to assess the damage and get to know the horse. But for what it's worth, a number of the employees volunteer their free time to FYC like Jeb is today. Weekends are hectic for most of us. Our trainers are away at horse shows, and the staff left behind is tied up with current or prospective clients."

Despite the crowded farm, *this* barn was empty except for the two of them—something her crazy hormones couldn't seem to ignore.

As much as she disliked the arrogant jerk she needed his cooperation and financial support to keep FYC going. If Wyatt fired her, who would care for her horses? They weren't ready for adoption yet and had little monetary value in their current conditions. She had to take every opportunity to sell the concept of Find Your Center to Wyatt and not only make him a believer, but a willing sponsor.

Making nice wouldn't kill her—or so Nellie always claimed. Afraid she'd choke on the necessary words, Hannah swallowed and forced a smile. "I appreciate your help and the extra set of hands today. You'll see that it's time well spent."

"Doubtful." He capped the antibiotic salve, drawing her attention to his hands—as if she hadn't been fixated on them already. He had good hands. Firm. Strong. Gentle when necessary.

The kind of hands a woman wanted in a lover.

Don't go there.

But she couldn't help it. She would never have anticipated tenderness and patience from the arrogant oaf. "You were good with the mare. I expected squeamishness from a guy wearing cashmere and Gucci, but you applied that slimy salve to her wounds with a deft touch and no gagging."

His appraisal turned suspicious, as if he suspected an ulterior motive behind her compliment. "I have some experience."

"So you've said, but you've left out the details."

He ignored her invitation to fill in the blanks. She smothered a sigh. There was only one way to find out what she wanted to know—by getting to know the boss better. *Not* something she relished, but it was a tactic she'd learned from her more competitive cousin. Megan always found out what motivated her adversaries, then used it against them to trounce them in the show ring.

"Tell me about your years on the thoroughbred farm," Hannah prompted.

Wyatt wiped his hands, slowly and deliberately on a rag, then stepped back to check his handiwork. "Not much to tell. My mother married the stable owner when I was fourteen. He gave me odd jobs to keep me out of trouble until I went to college."

She studied his tightly controlled hair and expression and his traditional attire. "You don't look like the type to find trouble."

His lips flattened. "Are we done here?"

"You avoided answering."

He gave her a level look. "You didn't ask a question, and my personal life is none of your business."

She tried to hide her frustration, but she wasn't admitting defeat so easily. "We're finished for now. We have pictures of her wounds and details on the severity of infection. I'll put her in the quarantine stall and let her rest. She should be exhausted from the travel and all this first aid. Once Jeb has the test results, there will likely be more work to do."

She dropped the irrigation syringe into the bucket, peeled off her gloves, set the pail aside and hitched a lead line to the halter. The moment she released her patient from the cross ties the mare tossed her head, almost dislocating Hannah's shoulder.

"She's going to hurt you."

"And let me guess, you're more worried about the worker's compensation claim than me." *Oops. Shut up, Hannah.*

"Triple Crown Distillery prides itself on running a safe operation. I will expect Sutherland Farm to do the same."

"We do, but this isn't a manufacturing plant. We work with live animals that have personalities instead of stationary vats and casks. The mare doesn't know whether we're friends or foes, and after what we've just put her through she probably thinks we're every bit as bad as her owner. Don't hold her skittishness against her. She'll reveal her true nature as she gets to know us." She stroked the mare's long neck. "Let's go to your new home, girl."

Wyatt blocked her path with a wall of solid muscle and his upper arm bumped Hannah's, splattering her with warmth. "I'll take the lead. I'll be able to control her better."

"That's a chauvinist statement if I ever heard one."

"I'm stronger and I outweigh you."

She surrendered the line. Any bonding he might do with the horse would work in her favor. "She goes in the last stall on the right."

Despite the hour they'd spent working as a team, she still knew next to nothing about her new boss. Intent on finding out as much as she could, she kept pace beside him as they traversed the center aisle. "Your parents are divorced?"

"Yes."

"Father still part of the picture?"

"No."

"Did you enjoy working at the stable?"

"Parts of it."

"Did you like your stepfather?"

"Yes."

"Still keep in touch?"

"Yes."

"Not exactly a conversationalist, are you, Jacobs?" She winced as soon as the words left her mouth.

Don't bite the hand that feeds you, Hannah.

He sliced a sharp glance in her direction. "Do I need to be?"

"Frankly, yes. Running an operation like Sutherland Farm requires you to be equal parts salesman, businessman, diplomat and horseman. From what I've seen, you lack most of those skills. But I can help you."

His eyebrows dipped. "And if I don't want or need your assistance?"

Stubborn jerk. "I think you do. I know a lot of people in the show jumping world. Connections count. I have them. From what little you've shared, you don't. And I speak four languages fluently, which means I can communicate with more of our global clients."

"I'll keep that in mind." He turned the mare into the stall, removed the lead and closed the door. His dark eyes pinned Hannah. "You seem like a detail-oriented person."

Something about his tone set her on guard. Why didn't that sound like a compliment? "I am."

"Then you should have comprehensive records on Find Your Center."

"I do," she offered cautiously.

"I want them."

Not good. He needed to see the good FYC did before he saw the balance sheets. "Let's go to my office. I'll show you the portfolio of the horses we've rescued and placed."

"Financials first. If the numbers aren't good, then the rest is irrelevant."

Her mouth went as dry as a drought-ridden pasture. A bottom-line mindset spelled nothing but disaster for FYC. "What about your tour?"

"It can wait."

"It'll take me a while to pull the reports together. Study the portfolio in the meantime. I'll get the books to you tomorrow."

"Tonight."

She bit the inside of her lip to hold back a grimace. She wasn't going to be able to stall him. "The files are on the computer in my cottage. It's late. I'll print them out after dinner and deliver them to your office first thing in the morning."

"I'll follow you home and get them now."

That sounded more like a threat than a promise. "If you insist."

"I do. And for future reference, Hannah, don't waste my time trying to evade the issue. I always get what I want in the end."

Rain drummed on the car's roof, almost drowning out Hannah's pounding pulse. The short, tense ride from the rescue barn to her cottage couldn't have been more miserable.

Wyatt parked. She debated inviting him inside but his scent enveloping her as surely as the expensive leather upholstery cradled her body muddled her thinking.

Her cottage was the only part of her life he hadn't managed to invade, but if she wanted to persuade him to keep funding FYC despite its dismal bottom line, then she had to endure his presence until she could find another solution. Besides, she had pictures inside that he really needed to see.

Resigned, she reached for the door handle. "Come in while I get what you need."

She shoved open the door and sprinted toward her front porch, but not even a chilly rain could banish the strange awareness of the man shadowing her like a hawk ready to swoop down on a hare. But she wasn't a defenseless bunny. She could fight for what she wanted.

She stepped into her foyer and held open the door. He

swept past her. "Make yourself comfortable. This'll take a few minutes. Can I get you a glass of wine?"

"No thank you." Most visitors paused to study the wall covered with framed photographs, but not Wyatt. He marched between her matching camelback sofas, his boots barely making a sound on her wooden floor as he headed for the stone fireplace and the portrait hanging above it.

"Who's this?" he asked without turning. "You look like her."

"My mother and her favorite horse, Gazpacho. He was a Grand Prix champion many times over and twice a world champion. Gazpacho was a rescue horse. So I guess you could say my mother laid the foundation for Find Your Center by rescuing Gazpacho before I was born."

Wyatt glanced over his shoulder from her to the oil painting and back, his skepticism clear in his expression. "You expect to find another champion in every nag you rescue?"

His sarcasm stung. Now he sounded like her father. "Of course not. I'm not stupid. Champions are rare. Most of our horses go to therapeutic riding schools after they're rehabilitated."

"What is a therapeutic riding school?"

She couldn't have asked for a more perfect opening for her sales pitch. She inhaled slowly, gathering her thoughts and words and trying to put them in perfect, persuasive order.

"Therapeutic riding is a form of physical therapy used to help individuals with disabilities or brain injuries strengthen their core muscles and improve their balance through finding their center of gravity. Hence, our name."

"Putting someone with balance issues on a horse is dangerous and foolhardy. Sounds a liability and an insurance nightmare."

Alarm raised the hairs on her nape. The close-minded were always the hardest to convince. "Our program is well-supervised. We run the classes here on Sundays. You can see for yourself tomorrow. Our instructors and volunteers are trained and our program is accredited. We take every precaution possible to ensure the safety of the participants. We have a long waiting list of applicants because we're so good."

"How profitable are the lessons?"

Ouch. Bull's-eye. He'd hit their weakest spot. She hesitated. "In terms of physical recovery, they're priceless."

His frown deepened. "In dollars and cents, Hannah."

She'd been hoping he wouldn't ask. "We don't charge for the sessions."

"How do you cover your expenses?"

She chewed the inside of her lip. He wasn't going to like the answer. "The farm subsidizes us."

"You're not profitable."

He seemed determined to focus on the negatives. That wouldn't help her cause. She gestured to the photo collection she'd wanted him to see. "This is my Wall of Winners. Each of these horses is a Find Your Center success story that has been rehabilitated and placed in a new home. But to know the whole story you really need to see the book in my office in the breeding barn, which contains the before and after photos. You'll be amazed by the progress."

He crossed the room to study the photographs. Silent seconds ticked past, stretching her nerves even tighter. "I don't see any pictures of you on a horse."

Hannah startled. She hadn't seen that one coming. "I—I don't ride."

His gaze burned her. "You grew up on a horse farm and you don't ride, and yet you're busting my chops for my lack of horse knowledge?"

She bristled. *She* hadn't spent millions on a business she knew nothing about. But being snarky would jeopardize what she wanted—his cooperation and continued financial backing. "I don't have to ride to love horses."

"Why don't you ride?"

Her nails bit into her palms. "That really isn't relevant."

In three purposeful strides he invaded her space, stopping close enough that she could feel his body heat and inhale the intoxicating blend of fresh rain and his unique aroma. That crazy current buzzed between them again, making her nipples tingle and tighten. She folded her arms to hide her involuntary response, then realized the defensive body language gave too much away and lowered her hands to her sides. It took a conscious effort to keep from fisting her fingers.

"Why don't you ride, Hannah?" he repeated, his voice as deep and rough as a rock quarry. His gaze roamed over her chest before returning to hold hers.

"To borrow your phrase, my personal life is none of your business."

"True, as long as it doesn't interfere with your work. But until you convince me Find Your Center is more than an expensive hobby, my checkbook and I are free to leave."

Her heart sank as she stared into that hard face.

"Let me give you a little incentive to talk, doc. From my position it looks like you're a bleeding heart who wastes money, time and valuable land that could be better and more profitably allocated. Your little operation is a high-risk, low-return venture. Convince me I'm wrong—if you can."

His challenge stirred her ire. She'd wipe that superior expression off his face. "My mother died as the result of a riding accident when I was ten. So you'll have to forgive me if I choose to love my horses with both feet firmly planted on the ground."

Instead of scaring him off, interest sharpened his eyes. "How?"

Her throat tightened as the hated movie reel replayed in her brain. "She was showing me how to tackle a water jump. We'd been at it for a while because I couldn't get it right. We were all tired. Her mount—*my* horse—misstepped and they went down. Neither got up."

The one time she'd been determined to win no matter what

the cost, the two loves of her life had paid the price. From that moment on, her life had changed forever.

She struggled to gather her composure. When she dared to look at Wyatt, the empathy and understanding in his eyes— two emotions she would never have expected from him— shook her. He cupped her shoulder. "I'm sorry, Hannah."

As it had in the barn, the warmth of his hand seeped through her shirt and her skin tingled beneath his touch. She tried to shake off the unwelcome response. "It was a long time ago."

"Sometimes the losses of our childhood are the hardest to forget."

"That sounds like the voice of experience."

"We all go through tough times." His fingers squeezed her shoulder, and the air between them changed, becoming charged and thick. His pupils expanded and his lips parted on a slowly indrawn breath.

There was no denying or misnaming the tension expanding inside her until it almost crushed her lungs. Desire. For her boss. Her enemy.

This can't be happening. Not with him.

Wyatt lowered his head. Every cell in her body screamed, *Run.*

But she couldn't.

Mistake.

The word reverberated through Wyatt's head even before his mouth touched Hannah's, but the damned overwhelming compulsion that had steamed through him from the moment they'd met propelled him forward. Then the satiny warmth of her lips snagged him. Stopping wasn't an option.

She stiffened, but before he could react her mouth opened beneath his—whether in surprise or welcome he neither knew nor cared—then she relaxed against him, her soft breasts nudging his chest. He sipped from her lips, but it wasn't enough to satisfy his craving.

Greedy for a taste of her, he stroked his tongue across the lush, moist curve of her bottom lip. Her flavor hit him with the punch of a straight shot of single malt whiskey, making his head spin and his body temperature spike.

Why her? Why did this woman who stood for everything he despised get to him? Hadn't he been burned by her type often enough to learn his lesson? Before he could make sense of her strange magnetism or get his fill of her, she jerked back, eyes wide and wary, and slapped her fingers over her mouth.

"You can't do that. You're my boss."

Reality slammed into him like an oncoming train.

Stupid move, Jacobs.

There was no room for physical attraction in business. His life, work and home were in Asheville. He'd never intended Sutherland Farm to be anything more than a safe place for Sam to live out whatever lucid time he had remaining.

Hannah's presence had already forced Wyatt to spend more time here than he'd intended. But the haunted look in her eyes and the tragic story of her mother's death had resurrected old baggage about losing his father. The difference was his father hadn't died. He'd voluntarily walked away.

"You're right. A personal involvement would be unwise."

But even as he spoke the words he registered her heavy-lidded eyes, flushed cheeks and erect nipples—sure signs that her hormones were pumping as rampantly as his. And as impractical and ill-advised as it might be, he wanted her. He locked his muscles against the urge to reach for her again.

As if she'd read the desire in his eyes, she hitched a breath and retreated. "I won't sleep with you, Wyatt. Not even to save my horses."

Oh, hell. "The survival of your rescue operation depends solely on the balance sheet. We're mature enough to ignore any chemistry between us."

Her expression turned militant, that delicious bottom lip poking out. "There is no chemistry."

A blatant lie. The urge to prove her wrong charged through

him. It would be so easy to take her into his arms, cover that mouth and coerce her into acquiescence. Easy. But not smart.

Fisting his hands and gritting his teeth, he resisted. "Show me your records."

The color drained from her face but determination firmed her chin. "Find Your Center is about so much more than profit and loss."

"Spoken like someone trying to justify a losing proposition."

She pointed to a shelf packed with periodicals. "Our program has been written up in almost every horse magazine on the market, giving the stable free positive advertising globally. You can't put a value on that. You should read the articles."

"Hannah—" He growled her name in warning.

"People relocate entire families to North Carolina to take advantage of our services." Desperation rushed her words.

"I want to be certain you're not taking advantage of my deep pockets to fund an underperforming segment of your operation."

She took a deep breath and stared him down, looking more resolute than ever. "I'm sure you're aware Sutherland Farm makes a lot of money. The farm needs our charitable organization as a tax shelter."

Her evasion was beginning to irritate and strangely, intrigue him. She wasn't afraid to fight for what she believed in, but she didn't do so by throwing a tantrum as he would have expected a pampered princess to do. She argued with nearly logical data.

While a part of him respected and admired her tenacity because he shared the same trait, another part of him wanted the matter settled so he could walk away from her and the unwanted attraction, and from the involvement with suffering horses that reminded him too much of Sam's losing battle.

"An interesting argument, but not my concern."

"Did you know we've been the blueprint for other stables to start similar programs? We've actually trained their managers.

Unfortunately, there are not enough programs around to meet the needs of the special popul—"

"Hannah." He grabbed her shoulders. Her deltoids bunched beneath his fingers, revealing more strength than her slender build implied. His desire instantly resurfaced, simmering through him like thick, hot lava. "Stop with the sales pitch and bring out the financials or you're fired."

She paled, then shrugged off his hold. "I will if you promise to come out and see us in action tomorrow."

Her audacity shocked a laugh from him. "You're in no position to make demands."

"You asked for a tour. FYC is part of the farm. Stop by and watch us work our magic. Interview our students and their families and let them tell you how we've improved their lives. We even have doctors' testimonials—"

"I have other commitments tomorrow. And I'm out of patience *now*. Give me the damned books."

Resignation settled over her features. "I'll print the spreadsheets for you, but I'll need to explain them."

"Excuse them, you mean. I run a multimillion-dollar company. I can decipher a profit and loss statement."

"But—"

"*Hannah*. Stop. Stalling."

She radiated frustration. "You can't waltz in here and strip away everything good about Sutherland Farm. There's more to the business than assets and debits. You're not taking the people into account—the people who work here and the ones whose lives we change for the better with our services."

Give the stubborn woman kudos for being an articulate opponent. If he wanted a spokesperson selling his product, he wanted one with her conviction. Too bad they were on opposing teams. "Who owns the rescue horses?"

She bit her lip and he instantly recalled her taste and the texture of her soft flesh against his. "Once we get all the legalities taken care of, my name goes on the registration papers."

"Not Sutherland Farm?"

Silence pulsed between them and worry darkened her eyes, turning them more smoky than blue. "No."

Interesting. "Why is that?"

She shifted her weight on her feet. "My father didn't want our operation connected to the Sutherland Farm purebreds."

"I share your father's view, and if you don't give me the records now, then I'll get a court order to have your animals evicted from my property."

She sighed heavily. "Fine. But you haven't heard the last of this. Find Your Center is critical to Sutherland Farm's reputation and I intend to prove it."

A threat like that he could handle. It was this crazy desire for her and his admiration for her dedication to the worthless animals that he wanted no part of.

First and foremost, he had to come up with a plan to get rid of Hannah Sutherland and her nags before he did something stupid such as take her to bed to see if she was as passionate between the sheets as she was about her horses.

Five

"My office. Now." Wyatt's clipped command for Hannah's presence via cell phone made her heart skip a beat.

Not a promising start to her Monday.

"I'll be right there." She disconnected the call, slipped her phone into her pocket and trudged toward the house, feeling a bit like a horse traveling down the chute to the slaughterhouse. She'd been dreading this summons since handing over Find Your Center's financials Saturday night. Apparently, Wyatt had taken a look at her files.

And while his kiss might be hotter than a branding iron, she didn't doubt for one moment that the coldhearted bottom-line bastard was going to try to close Find Your Center. If her sales pitch hadn't changed his mind, then she had to come up with something else that would. Too many people depended on her. She couldn't let the students or their families down. And then there were her animals…

She wished her cousin were here. Megan was a brilliant strategist. She knew how to research her Grand Prix opponents and use their strengths and weaknesses against them. But Megan had chosen to ride the European Grand Prix circuit because she avoided anything that would cause her to cross paths with her uncle, and Hannah didn't dare call Megan to ask for help because her cousin would drop everything and race to Hannah's rescue, leaving her horses, her career and her hunky lover behind.

Megan had a chance at success and true happiness that Hannah refused to screw up. She squared her shoulders. If she wanted this situation resolved with the least collateral damage to the people and horses she cared about, she had to win over Wyatt.

The kitchen door opened the moment she set foot on the patio, revealing Nellie. "Good gracious, child, you've lost weight. Can't you feed yourself when I'm away?"

Hannah forced a smile and wrapped Nellie's substantial frame in a hug. "You know I forget to eat when I'm busy, and it is that time of year. How was your vacation?"

"I've discovered Caribbean Island cruises aren't my cup of tea, but I had to try it once especially since the boss was footing the bill."

Wyatt had paid for Nellie's trip? Why? Hannah couldn't believe he'd done so out of the goodness of his black heart.

"Come in, child. I made your favorite raspberry muffins. I'll wrap some for you to take back with you. You need a man to help you remember to eat—a handsome rich one like the boss."

"Don't play matchmaker, Nellie." She couldn't handle it—especially with the memory of that kiss cauterizing a hole in her brain.

"Why not? This is your home. You should be living here, not out in that old house filled with antiques. And it ain't like he's hard on the eyes."

Or the lips.

"Not interested," Hannah denied, averting her face from the eagle-eyed Nellie as she entered the kitchen. The shock of seeing a large Mission-style table in the breakfast nook instead of her mother's elegant dining set—the one where Hannah had spent countless hours doing her homework and eating meals—stalled her steps. She scanned the rest of the room.

The kitchen remained architecturally the same and yet appeared totally different because Wyatt's Southwestern paint scheme stood out jarringly in the once-familiar classic Wedgwood-blue environment. Even the appliances had been replaced with shiny stainless ones.

"You ended your engagement fifteen months ago."

"Doesn't matter. I don't have time for men or the complications that seem to be encoded on their DNA."

Nellie patted Hannah's hand. "The changes take some getting used to, but Wyatt went top of the line on everything while I was away. I 'bout had a stroke when I saw he'd repainted the whole house and replaced my ol' stove."

Nellie's words reminded Hannah that she wasn't the only one facing changes. "Is he being good to you?"

"He is. Doesn't make a mess. Doesn't complain. Keeps to himself for the most part and knows what he wants. He always says thank you. He claims he has no intention of entertaining like your father did, and that's a shame, because this house needs to be filled with people. But maybe that'll come once he stops all his traveling an' settles in. I miss cooking fancy dinners and seeing you all prettied up."

"You're assuming Wyatt would want me to act as his hostess."

"Why wouldn't he? I've seen no sign of a significant other."

Hannah filed that away while she searched Nellie's lined and now tanned face and strained for sounds of the boss. "You'd tell me if he gave you any trouble, wouldn't you?"

Nellie smiled. "Hannah, if you'd fight half as hard for yourself as you do for your causes, you'd be a force to be reckoned with. But I've had no problems with the new boss." She indicated a tray on the table holding coffee and a plate of muffins. "Take that with you to the office when you go, please."

The idea of eating while Wyatt dissected Find Your Center's budget made Hannah's stomach churn. Between his pending verdict and the kiss that should never have happened she had no appetite whatsoever, even though she'd skipped breakfast. That blasted kiss had haunted her for the past thirty-six hours.

She'd forgotten what a man's lips felt like, forgotten how the flesh could be soft and yet firm at the same time, commanding and yet giving. Forgotten the electrical charge—

Check that. She hadn't *forgotten* the electricity. She'd never experienced a jolt that strong before Wyatt.

"How are you and your horses making out?"

She blinked at Nellie's question. "That's what I'm here to find out. That bottom-line bastard wants to shut us down."

"I'm sure you'll find a solution. You're quite resourceful when it comes to your animals."

"Hannah." Wyatt's deep voice from behind her smashed into her. "I'm waiting."

Her skin caught fire. How much had he overheard? She turned and found his eyes focused on her in that laser-like, unwavering and unnerving way of his. His foreboding expression twisted her nerves like hay in a baler.

She tried not to look at his mouth, tried not to recall the texture and warmth of his lips against hers or the strength of his chest against her breasts. But she couldn't help herself. If Wyatt remembered the kiss, he didn't show it by so much as a flicker of his short, spiky eyelashes.

Moot point. The kiss wouldn't be repeated. She wouldn't let it. Wyatt made her want to take risks and she'd learned a long time ago that risks should be avoided at all costs.

"Boss, I made muffins and fresh coffee. Take them with you, and make this girl eat something. She's wasting away."

Wyatt's dark gaze skimmed Hannah from her braided hair to her booted feet, plowing up a wave of goose bumps. Her stomach quivered and her heart banged in her rib cage. Not fair. How could he rattle her with nothing more than one slow inspection?

Surprisingly, Wyatt reached for the tray, then turned for her father's—*his* study. Wishing she could retreat to the comfort of her lab rather than have this confrontation, Hannah followed him. His office presented yet another reminder that this wasn't her home anymore. His taste for clean, sharp lines and his obvious passion for electronic gadgets contrasted sharply with her father's traditional, Old World furnishings.

Wyatt set the refreshments on a square table between the two leather cushioned chairs facing his desk, then snatched up a muffin and circled to fold into his high-backed leather desk chair. "Sit down."

She hesitated. The vertical wooden slats of the Mission chairs reminded her of a cage, making her feel trapped, but she sank onto a chair anyway.

You catch more flies with honey, child, she could all but hear Nellie saying, and dredged her mind for something nice to say. "Nellie tells me you paid for her vacation. That was kind of you. But why would you?"

He bit into his muffin and took his time chewing, obviously not suffering from the same nerves that cramped her stomach. If his goal was to irritate her by making her wait for his answer, he succeeded, but she'd be damned if she'd let on. She folded her hands in her lap and deliberately relaxed her fisted fingers while she noted he had very few personal items on his shelves.

He leaned back in his chair. "I wanted her out of the way while I set up."

"You've made a lot of changes."

"I've only just begun."

That sounded ominous. "If you have big plans, perhaps you should clue in the rest of us."

"The only change that concerns you is that I'm shutting down Find Your Center and ending the free board for your rescue animals. Sell them. Give them away. I don't care how you get them off the premises. Just do it."

The speech hit her like a blow regardless of his words being exactly what she'd expected to hear. "You can't make that kind of decision without having seen us in action. We do too much good to—"

"You lose too much money and your liability is too high. The insurance premiums alone are exorbitant. The barn could be used more advantageously by paying customers. Right now, it's an eyesore."

"That's because my father wouldn't spend money on upkeep."

"You'll pay the standard boarding fees or move your horses."

Panic swelled within her. Her salary wouldn't cover that expense. "Give me three months to change your mind."

"I want the operation off the property by the end of the month."

Dismay raced through her, quickly followed by outrage. "I can't place thirty horses and find a new location for Find Your Center in three weeks."

"Not my problem."

She shot to her feet. Her legs wobbled weakly beneath her. "You're asking the impossible."

The arrogant jerk looked confident that his demands would be met. She had to find a way to fix this.

"I'll give you more time on one condition."

She knew a trap when she heard one, but what choice did she have except to hear him out? "Name it."

He wrote something on a slip of paper, then slid it across the desk before lacing his fingers across his flat abdomen. "Sell me the house and land your father deeded to you. My offer is quite generous. With this amount you can buy your own stable."

Shock stole her breath when she counted the number of zeros. But the amount was irrelevant. She wasn't going to let him drive her away. "My grandparents built that cottage and the wall surrounding it stone by stone from rocks they collected from their fields. This is my home, my heritage. So as generous as your offer is, no thanks."

Surprise flickered in his eyes then his jaw hardened. "Sell me the property and I'll allow you live in the cottage rent-free for twelve months, and I'll continue funding your money-pit operation for the duration. A year will give you plenty of time to find alternative accommodations for you and your animals."

The man had mastered bribery. And while his offer tempted her simply because of the fiscal logic behind it, for the first time in her life a strong competitive urge pulsed through her. She wanted to win—to best this heartless bastard. Failing meant losing everything that mattered.

Searching her mind for alternatives, she tucked her hair behind her ear. The post of her mother's earring scraped her fingertip, reminding her that Sutherland Farm and rescuing horses had been her mother's dream, too. This fight wasn't just about her. This was her mother's legacy and Hannah's way to leave her mark in the world.

"No thanks."

"That's my deal, Hannah. Take it or leave it."

She had to get him physically involved with the students. Seeing the joy and sense of accomplishment on those faces hooked everyone.

Everyone except her father, a voice in her head warned.

And if converting Wyatt to a believer failed, she had to find another way. All of that required time and money—neither of which she had a surplus.

Think, Hannah. What would Megan do?

She'd buy time and strategize.

"I'll consider your offer—" *over my dead body* "—on one condition." She threw his words back at him.

He dipped his head, indicating she continue.

"Give me ninety days to search for a comparable property close enough for our students to continue using our services…

and you have to spend time with us. Watch us in action. Talk to our clients and their families. See the miracles we accomplish."

His eyes narrowed, but not so much that she couldn't see that being backed into a corner had annoyed him. Well, too bad. She wasn't whistling a happy tune, either.

"You're in no position to make demands."

"On the contrary, Mr. Jacobs. I have something you want. That gives me leverage."

A nerve in his jaw twitched. "I could simply evict your horses and outwait you. At the end of the year my contractual obligation to employ you and the other Sutherland employees will be over."

The implied threat against the rest of the staff shocked her, but she held her ground. "You don't seem like the waiting type."

"You're mistaken. I can be very patient when I want something bad enough." Silence stretched between them. "I'll give you sixty days to find a new location. In the meantime, you'll accept no more rescue animals. And you will start covering the expenses for your operation. Is that clear?"

Jerk. She forced a conciliatory smile. "As Waterford crystal."

Before he could change his mind, she pivoted on her heel and bolted through the patio door for the safety and order of her lab. She'd won a brief reprieve of sorts. But that was only the beginning. She had a lot of work to do and very little money to do it with.

"Pretty gal. Your wife?"

Sam's question jolted Wyatt from an unexpected and unwanted attack of lust. His stepfather climbed the stairs from the south lawn to the patio. *Alone.* Where was his nurse?

"I'm not married, Sam."

Wyatt took one last glance at Hannah striding down the driveway toward the barn, her anger giving her hips an attention-getting sway. The fight in her eyes before she'd stormed off had been impossible to miss. And attractive. Damned attractive.

He had to figure out how to get his hands on her land and get rid of her before he did something stupid. Her horses were her most obvious weakness, and he'd expected his offer of free room and board for her and her nags to win him this war. Obviously the lady veterinarian had a higher price tag.

He forced himself to turn away from the tempting and taboo view. "Nellie made muffins. Come inside and have one."

Sam preceded him into the study and grabbed a muffin. "I could have sworn you bought the farm because you had marriage plans. Horse farms are a good place to raise kids. Fresh air. Hard work. Told your mama so."

Sam's confusion only reinforced Wyatt's decision to relocate. He'd hoped getting Sam back in horse territory might result in more lucid moments.

"I was dating someone but we didn't have marriage plans." And she'd bailed the moment Sam had become a significant part of Wyatt's future.

"Lana. Leggy blonde? High maintenance? Bit enamored with herself? No patience with old men?"

"That's her." How could Sam be so astute about some things and completely clueless about others? Alzheimer's didn't make sense. It cast a net, catching random memories and letting others slip through. Some days the weave of the net was tighter than others. The disease defied every rule of logic Wyatt lived by.

"Where's Carol?" Even as he asked the question Wyatt stepped to the door and scanned the hall and foyer. He saw no sign of the nurse who should be shadowing his stepfather.

"Who?"

"Carol. Your nurse."

"Brunette?"

"No. That was the last one. This one is in her early fifties with salt-and-pepper hair." He'd hoped a mature woman would be more diligent than the younger caregiver had been.

Sam's face scrunched in concentration as he ate his muffin. "Is she the one who likes soap operas?"

"I don't know. Is she?" If Carol had let Sam get away because she was watching TV, then she'd be fired on the spot.

"One of 'em did." Sam frowned as if searching his malfunctioning brain. "I think that was the little mousy girl, the one who didn't talk."

"Sam?" Carol's panicked voice echoed through the two-story foyer followed by quick footsteps descending the stairs.

"He's in here."

She hurried down the stairs wide-eyed and breathing hard. "Thank God. Sam, you scared me half to death."

"He was outside. How did he get away from you?" Wyatt demanded. He would fire her on the spot if she weren't by far the best qualified of the applicants he'd interviewed.

Dark flags of color swept Carol's cheeks. "I honestly don't know. I was using the bathroom, and—"

"The suite door wasn't locked?"

She grimaced. "I thought it was. I'm sorry, Mr. Jacobs. I'm not used to having to lock in a client. I must have forgotten to take the key from the dead bolt after Nellie brought up breakfast."

"Confining him is for his own safety. He likes to wander." Wyatt hated caging Sam like an animal, but after the near disastrous balcony incident at his penthouse… Wyatt's gut knotted. He severed the thought of how easily he could have lost Sam that day.

"I understand, sir. It won't happen again." She turned toward his stepfather. "Sam, you've already had two muffins. Are you sure you want another one?"

Sam blinked. "I have?"

"Yes, and eggs and juice, too. You ate quite a big breakfast because we're going for a walk today."

"Where are you taking him?" Wyatt asked.

"I thought it would be nice to let him visit the stables."

Alarm kicked through Wyatt's system. "No. Stay away from the barns. I don't want Sam getting hurt."

"But he stands at the window for hours watching the horses in the pasture. Didn't he used to work with horses?"

"'Course I did and quit talking 'bout me like I'm not here," Sam groused.

"I apologize, Sam." Wyatt surveyed his stepfather, trying to assess today's mental state. Some days Sam seemed as sharp as he had in the old days. Others he was a shell of the man Wyatt had once idolized. "I know you miss the horses, but we don't know these animals well enough to know which ones are safe and which aren't."

Sam puffed out his chest and shoved his hands in his pockets. "I would know. Common horse sense. Just 'cause you made me retire doesn't mean I've forgotten everything I ever knew."

Only most of it. Intermittently. "Let's get settled in first."

"I am settled. Been here a week."

Carol looped her arm through Sam's. "Why don't we walk to the pond and check out that flock of geese that flew over this morning? They passed so quickly we didn't get to count them." She led him toward the door, looking over her shoulder with what Wyatt assumed was supposed to be a reassuring expression.

"Don't let him out of your sight again."

"No, sir. I won't."

Frustration, helplessness and sadness twisted like a corkscrew deep in Wyatt's chest. Over the past two years Sam had been fading away right before his eyes, and none of the specialists Wyatt had consulted could do a damn thing about it. Neither the medications nor the supplements seemed to help much. But he'd be damned if he'd give up without a fight. He owed Sam that much.

Six

Hannah had sixty days to work a miracle.

Panic welled inside her as she studied the new mare. Would that be enough time to change Wyatt's mind?

Sipping her coffee, she sagged against the fence post at her back, stretched her legs out into the grass and watched the birds flying above the tree line.

The mare tossed her head and snorted, looking beyond Hannah's shoulder, then she galloped a few yards away and circled back, pausing with her nostrils flaring and muscles twitching, ready to flee.

"What's wrong, girl?"

"She's afraid of men," an unfamiliar male voice said from behind Hannah, startling her. She twisted abruptly, spooking the horse even more, then slowly rose to face the stranger. He wore jeans, a flannel shirt and down coat even though the sun had long since chased away the morning chill.

"Can I help you?"

"Just inspecting the pastures. My guess is a man is responsible for the bay's scars." He nodded toward the mare.

"You'd be right." Who was he? A prospective Sutherland client? Someone interested in observing FYC's morning session? Or maybe an agent verifying the abuse report she'd filed? After dusting off her hands she reached across the fence. "I'm Hannah Sutherland. And you are…?"

"Sam Reynolds. A little bacon grease will help those fetlocks heal faster."

An old-school remedy, but modern science was her thing. "I'll keep that in mind. Did someone from the office send you to find me?"

"Nope. Found you on my own. Who's in charge of the mare's wound care?"

"I am."

He grabbed the top rail and hoisted himself over the fence. He wasn't frail, but he had the shrunken look older people sometimes got when their lives became sedentary. She saw a lot of that in the newcomers who joined FYC. He wobbled a little at the top.

She moved forward in case he slipped. "Mr. Reynolds, I'd prefer you stay out of the pasture."

"Don't worry, missy. I know what I'm doing." He strode toward the horse surely, rapidly, scaring her farther away, then he stopped.

Apparently not. He was upsetting the mare. "Sir, please leave the pasture."

Hands relaxed by his side, he faced Hannah, turning his back on the animal. "Give her a chance to get to know me."

The horse quivered, attention riveted on her new visitor.

Hannah kept a wary eye on the mare who'd revealed a few bad habits once she'd gotten over the shock of being relocated. The mare's ears twitched forward instead of back like an angry animal intent on inflicting injury. Nose outstretched, she gingerly approached the interloper.

Hannah's breath caught as the mare leaned in for a sniff. "Be careful. She bites."

"You should be working her in a round pen. She has too much room to avoid you here. And sit on the top rail not on the ground. Shows her who's boss without you lifting a finger."

Still ignoring the horse, he paced several yards to the right. The mare trailed him, then he returned to Hannah's side. Again, after a brief hesitation, the horse followed.

Surprised, Hannah could only watch. "I've tried the Horse Whisperer method on her, but it hasn't worked before now."

"I've always had the touch."

"No kidding. Okay, I admit it. I'm impressed at how easily you snagged the mare's attention and cooperation."

He pivoted abruptly. When the animal didn't race off he rewarded her by offering his palm, then rubbing her forehead and scratching beneath her ears—something she hadn't allowed Hannah to do. "Good girl," he addressed his new friend, then angled his head toward Hannah. "It's all in your body language. If you're wary of her, she'll be wary of you."

"I'm aware of that, Mr. Reynolds. I have some experience with horses, but I still think getting you out of harm's way is a good idea."

He patted the mare's neck and raked his fingers through her matted mane. "I've missed this."

"Missed what?"

Before he could reply, a car crested a hill in the driveway at a high rate of speed. The idiot driver was going to get someone hurt. Hannah kicked into action mode, putting herself between Sam and the horse. The sedan's tires locked and skidded to a halt.

A woman threw open the door and sprang from the driver's seat. The mare bolted to the far side of the enclosure.

"Sam, you can*not* keep wandering off."

Who was this woman advancing on them in near hysteria? Sam shook his head. "I wasn't wandering. I knew where I was going. Now look what you've done. I'd just begun to win the bay's trust. Now I'll have to start over."

"Get in the car," the woman ordered, pointing at the vehicle. "Mr. Jacobs will be furious if he finds out you escaped again."

Escaped? Mr. Jacobs? This guy knew Wyatt? "I'm Hannah Sutherland. Could you please explain what's going on?"

The harassed woman parked her hands on her hips. "I'm Carol Dillard. Sam—Mr. Reynolds is not supposed to leave the house without me. Mr. Jacobs specifically ordered me to keep Sam away from the barns."

"I'm not at the barn," Sam added logically.

Hannah focused on the woman. "But Sam likes horses and he's good with them."

The older woman frowned. "Sam is under my care."

"You're a doctor?"

"No. I'm his nurse. He suffers from Alzheimer's."

Understanding dawned, but the diagnosis only led to more questions. "Sam lives with Wyatt?"

"Stop talking about me like I'm not here. Wyatt is my stepson. He worries because I'm a little forgetful sometimes."

Wyatt took care of his stepfather. Imagine that. The jerk might have a shred of decency in him after all. "Are you the one who used to own a thoroughbred farm?"

"I am."

"Wyatt's mentioned you. You should get him to bring you to the stables. If he saw how easily you worked that mare, he wouldn't keep you away. You made more progress with her in two minutes than I have in a week."

Sam smiled. "I'll do that."

Carol tsked and shook her head. "Good luck with that. Now get in the car, Sam, and let's get back to the house before Wyatt calls to check on us."

That caught Hannah's attention. She'd been dreading and anticipating a possible visit and another demand for a tour from the new boss since the first one had been postponed. "Wyatt's not home?"

"He had to fly to the distillery on business this morning."

That meant he probably wouldn't oversee today's riding classes. If she couldn't get him to observe, then how could she win him over?

Sam hoisted a foot to the bottom fence rail, pausing to look over his shoulder at Hannah. "Thank you for your company, Hannah. Meeting you was truly a pleasure."

"You, too, Sam. Bring Wyatt with you next time."

Hannah's skin tingled the way it did when she suddenly thought of a mare-stud genetic combination that couldn't help but produce a contender. She'd found Wyatt's weakness, or more precisely, Sam had found her. And like her übercompetitive cousin, Hannah would have to find a way to use the new knowledge to her advantage.

"Sam, do you ride?" she called as he approached the car.

A sad smile stretched his mouth. "I used to. Before I retired. Haven't been near a horse before today since…" He scratched his head, suddenly looking flustered. "I can't remember. I used to work with horses back in…back when I had a horse farm and a life." His shoulders drooped.

Hannah's heart tugged. "It's okay, Sam. I'll get the details later. And you still have a life. It's just a different one."

She saw a chance to benefit herself and Sam, but especially FYC. She turned her attention to the nurse. "We run a therapeutic riding school on Sundays. Our roster is full, but I'm sure I could pull some strings and get Sam a slot by next week. Why don't you bring him down for a ride?"

"I'll mention your suggestion to Mr. Jacobs, but I don't expect he'll approve. He's overly protective of Sam."

That meant Hannah would have to confront the very man she'd been trying to avoid, the man whose kisses knocked her out of the saddle. "I'll talk to Wyatt."

When she helped his stepfather, she'd not only prove her point about FYC's value, she'd win over Wyatt and at least part of her problems would be solved.

* * *

Anticipation Wyatt should not be experiencing coursed through his veins along with a strong dose of suspicion as he stood on Hannah's front porch.

Why had Hannah invited him to dinner? Had she decided to accept his offer and sell him the property or would the evening yield yet another attempt to milk something from him?

The door opened, revealing his hostess in a peach-colored sweater that clung to her breasts and a black skirt that displayed her long legs to lust-inducing advantage.

Not lust. Approval. There was no room for lust in business.

A tight smile flitted across her lips. "Wyatt, thanks for coming."

Wyatt forced his eyes to her face. She'd done something to her blue eyes that gave them a sleepy, sultry look that he couldn't help but appreciate. Her hair lay like a shiny curtain over her shoulders and breasts, the thick chocolate strands glistening in the overhead light—a far cry from her usual windblown appearance, and try as he might, he couldn't dam the rising tide of his libido.

Life had taught him time and time again that women used their beauty as weapons of coercion. Hannah had to be up to something. The question was what?

"Is there a reason we couldn't have had this conversation in my office?" Where he could have kept the desk between them.

"I thought it would be more relaxing to talk away from work."

The slightly husky timbre of her voice slid over him as smooth and thick as sourwood honey, reminding him of lazy mornings after a vigorous night of sweaty sex. "About?"

Her gaze slid away. "The farm. What else? Come in. Dinner's ready."

He followed her through the living room, his gaze involuntarily drawn to her rear in the snug skirt, then his eyes traveled down her legs to her low, open-backed heels. Nice. Seductive in a rich-girl-next-door kind of way. She hadn't gone for the blatant hard-sell look.

Then he spotted the candles flickering in the middle of the dining room table lending an intimacy to what should be a business dinner and corrected his assessment. "What's going on, Hannah?"

She followed his gaze to the candlelit trap. "I don't cook often and when I do I like to enjoy the effort. Would you pour the wine while I get the food?"

She disappeared through an archway without waiting for an answer. Whatever game she was playing, she'd reveal her hand soon enough.

He lifted the open bottle and studied the label—an award-winning Riesling that sold for hundreds of dollars at auction. After filling the crystal goblets, he scanned what he could see of the cottage. On his first visit he'd been more focused on the financials than decor and then that kiss had blown his observation skills to hell.

This time he noticed the antiques—not reproductions—filling the rooms. Translation: expensive furniture. Like the wine, the BMW Z4 in her driveway, the diamonds in her ears, the watch on her wrist and the crystal on the table. Hannah Sutherland enjoyed the finer things in life—things she shouldn't be able to afford on her salary. That meant she depended on someone else's deep pockets to keep her in the manner to which she'd become accustomed. Her father? A lover? The latter thought kinked the muscles between his shoulder blades.

She returned and set two china plates on the table. "I hope you're hungry. Please take a seat."

He automatically pulled out her chair—some habits were hard to break. Satiny strands of her hair caressed his knuckles, sending a ripple of awareness through him. Her floral perfume—minus the eau de barn additive—mingled with the roasted pork in his nostrils, stirring a hunger that had little to do with dinner. He stepped away and took his seat across from her.

"You have expensive tastes in wine. A gift from an admirer?"

"You could say that. One of our German clients owns the winery. Our association made him very happy, and he sent a few cases of his best vintages as a thank-you gift."

Something about the private smile teasing her lips irritated him like a whining mosquito. His fingers tightened around his utensils. "Was he your lover?"

"Heavens, no." Her surprise seemed too genuine to be faked, but then most women were accomplished actresses. "But we made a beautiful baby together—with his mare and Sutherland's stud. I was engaged at the time."

"*Was* engaged?"

She studied her glass then took a sip, savoring the Riesling slowly—the way she did everything, he'd learned.

Everything?

He derailed the sexual thought, but not before his groin pulsed to life.

"The relationship didn't work out."

"Why?"

She took a bite of asparagus then chewed, swallowed. "Does this fall into the none-of-your-business category or the tell-me-or-you're-fired column?"

"Do you have something to hide?"

Seconds ticked past while she toyed with her food. "My father loved Robert. I didn't. Not enough, anyway."

"Shouldn't you have realized that before you became engaged?"

"Probably. But on paper he seemed like the perfect match."

"On paper? Did you run a financial report on the guy?"

"I didn't need to. Our families had known each other forever. We shared the same background and interests."

"You mean he had money."

Her perfectly arched eyebrows dipped. "Of course he had money. That means I knew he wasn't marrying me for mine."

"Are you wealthy—in your own right?" If she had money stashed elsewhere, he might have more trouble getting rid of her than he'd expected.

"Not that it's any of your business, but no. However, at the time, everyone thought I'd eventually be the owner of Sutherland Farm, which I once believed to be priceless." She shifted in her seat. "Please eat before it gets cold. Nellie managed to teach me a few kitchen tricks. I'm not in her league, although it's safe to say I *probably* won't poison you."

Her teasing smile blindsided him, and an odd feeling invaded his stomach.

Hunger. For food. Nothing more.

But he couldn't deny that despite everything he knew about Hannah, she had somehow managed to derail his usual detachment. She cut a piece of meat, swirled it in the peach salsa and lifted it to her mouth. The sheer eroticism of her lips slowly and deliberately closing around the flatware sent another unwelcome bout of lust rolling over him like a runaway whiskey barrel.

Imagining the slide of the sterling silver tines across her tongue and lips sent his blood sluicing through his veins. He envied that fork, and, as ill-advised and illogical as it might be, the sample he'd had of her mouth had left him craving something more substantial. He wanted to know her taste and texture, and that desire had acted like a parasite gnawing away at him even when he'd been out of town working at the distillery.

What had she done to him? He'd never had a woman get between him and business before. He had to get back on track and out of dangerous territory. Her property was the only reason he'd accepted her invitation tonight.

"Have you considered my offer?"

"I won't deny I've thought about it."

"And?"

She shrugged one shoulder. "Could we save business for later? I'd prefer not to ruin a good meal. Besides, this is practice for you. Remember? I told you that you had a lot to learn about this business? We wine and dine our clients before closing the big deals. It's a courtesy to let them eat in peace before twisting the thumbscrews during after-dinner coffee."

"Are you skilled at twisting the screws?"

"Let's just say my father made sure I knew my role."

He didn't need anyone telling him how to run his business, but he'd abide by her rules—this time—only because he wanted her guard down. He took out his frustration on a piece of pork, pulverizing the tender morsel between his molars.

Candlelight glimmered on Hannah's hair and turned her skin luminescent. Her perfume teased his senses and raised his blood pressure. He needed a distraction.

"What's the status on the new mare?"

"She's coming along. You should stop by and see her. After days of getting nowhere, Sa—we made progress today. But if you're asking whether I'm going to euthanize her, then the answer is no. All of the tests have come back negative. Other than the superficial wounds, she's healthy."

Her lips curved around the rim of the wineglass and he found it hard to swallow. Those secret smiles of hers were something else. He found himself wanting to probe the cause. This crazy obsession with Hannah Sutherland was an aggravation he didn't need. A temporary aberration.

How had she managed to hijack his concentration? She wasn't the most beautiful woman he'd ever met, wasn't the sexiest and certainly wasn't the most amenable. In fact, she might be the most argumentative. Regardless, something about her had snagged his attention.

Something besides a piece of property that put a doughnut hole in his land and devalued the farm. Something besides her faux Miss Goody Two-shoes attitude. He just couldn't put his finger on what it was about her that didn't add up. Yet. But he would.

His rampant hormones couldn't be anything more than a natural response to prolonged abstinence. He'd had a rough few months since his realization that Sam was a danger to himself. The subsequent frantic search for doctors who had provided frustratingly few answers had led to the decision to take responsibility for Sam and the breakup with Lana. Add in the preparation for launching the new ad campaign as well as the property search and Wyatt hadn't had any time for even the most casual encounters.

He was paying for that now with inappropriate thoughts about an employee. But soon she'd be out of the picture and life would return to normal. The sooner, the better.

"Have you looked at any properties?"

"It's only been a few days since you issued your ultimatum. I haven't had time."

Frustrated, he swirled his wine in his glass and inhaled, trying to appreciate the tart green-apple bouquet. Trying and failing. "Do you collect antiques?"

She followed his glance around the room. "Not intentionally. My grandparents started their marriage with what they called hand-me-downs from their families. When they could afford to add pieces they scavenged yard sales—yard sales they often took me to—for items that matched what they already had. This was all here when I moved in after vet school."

"The contents belong to you?" Tens of thousands of dollars worth of furniture—he could thank his greedy mother for his ability to assess value.

She nodded. "I guess you could say the furniture—like this farm—is my family history."

"You can't be ignorant of the value."

She frowned. "I've never thought about it other than the sentimental value."

He didn't believe that for a second. "And the BMW? Did you inherit that, too?"

She stiffened. "Where are you going with this, Wyatt?"

"You live beyond your salary."

"You're determined to think the worst of me, aren't you? The car was a gift from my father, a reward for a record-breaking year last year. It's totally impractical, but I won't deny it's fun to drive."

"It's a long commute to your distillery from here. Too far to drive every day. Why buy a place so far from work? There are beautiful properties closer to Asheville."

She'd done her research. But his reasons for his purchase were none of her business. "I've told you before. The property suited my needs."

"Your sudden burning need to own a horse farm? Neither the staff nor I are buying that since you have nothing to do with the horses. You haven't finished your tour and you never visit the barns."

"Sutherland Farm has a competent management team. Would you prefer I become more active in the day-to-day operation?"

"No. As you said, the staff knows what they're doing."

He pushed his empty plate aside and leaned back in his chair. "What is this evening really about, Hannah?"

Annoyance flashed across her face. She slid away from the table and rose. "You really fail at this setting-the-mood thing. Bring your wine to the living room. I have something to show you."

Setting the mood for what?

Leaving his wine behind because he needed a clear head around her, he followed her to the den, arriving in time to see her bend over the coffee table. The action made her shirt gape, revealing a tempting glimpse of her pale breasts and the white lacy edge of her bra. Wyatt acknowledged his appreciation even while he admitted the move was probably calculated to entice his cooperation.

She sank onto the sofa and her skirt slid up her bare thighs. No stockings concealed her smooth, creamy flesh. She pulled a thick book onto her lap then patted the cushion beside her. "Sit. Please."

The determination in her eyes didn't fit the capitulation he'd expected from her. "Are you going to sell me your land?"

Her eyebrows arched upward. "Your impatience is showing again. You're going to have to improve on that before we have international visitors. They'll be offended by your get-to-the-point methods. Try a little finesse. Ease into the discussions. But to answer your question, no, I haven't decided to sell. I'm still exploring my options."

"If you're hoping for a better deal you won't get one. The price I offered is more than generous, and you can't sell the property to anyone else without giving me an opportunity to match their bid."

"I'm not planning to sell to someone else."

"Then why am I here, Hannah?"

She gave him a patient look. "I'm getting to that."

Gritting his teeth in irritation, he decided to let her play out her hand. Opponents' strategies always revealed more than they suspected about their strengths and weaknesses. He sat. Hannah's scent filled his lungs and the warmth of her body drew him like a magnet.

"This is FYC's story." Her breath fanned his cheek as she leaned closer.

Finally, the motive for the sexy clothing, the wine and dinner became clear. Batter up. Sales pitch coming over the plate. "I don't need to know FYC's story."

"Actually, you do. We have a visitor from Dubai coming soon. He's interested in setting up a similar program."

"I'm not going to promote something I don't believe in."

"You will believe if you just open your eyes and your mind."

"And my wallet."

Flashing him an exasperated look, she spread the large photo album across their laps. Her fingertips made contact with his thigh, sending desire charging through his veins, hot and heavy and drugging.

Her breath caught and her widened gaze found his, telling

him she'd experienced the same jolt. Or she faked her response well. On second thought, she couldn't fake those flushed cheeks and dilated pupils.

Their last kiss in this very room consumed his thoughts. He instantly recalled the feel of her, taste of her, heat and softness of her and he wanted more. His eyes dropped to her mouth. She licked her lush bottom lip—a clear invitation.

He should have known. His experience had proven that women used sex to get what they wanted. Marlie had used sex to get extra care for her horse when she couldn't be at the stable. At seventeen Wyatt had been too naive to recognize the tactic. But by the time Lana had come along fifteen years later and used her wiles to convince him to buy her expensive trinkets and trips, he'd gained enough insight to know exactly what she was doing and he'd given in only when it suited him. He hadn't loved Lana any more than she'd loved him, but she would have been a good asset to his career, a capable and well-connected hostess. That was the only reason he'd allowed her to move into the penthouse.

Hannah had pulled out every element of a good seduction for tonight. Legs, cleavage, candlelight, good food and wine. The question was how far was she willing to go for her horses? And how far was he willing to step beyond his personal code of ethics? It would serve her right if he used her the way she was trying to use him, and then turfed her on her pretty little butt at the first opportunity.

"Is this what you're after, Hannah?"

He speared his fingers through her silky hair and cupped her nape, then yanked her forward and covered her mouth with his. He wasted no time with preliminary get-to-know-you pecks and instead plunged into her mouth.

Slick, hot, sweet and moist, he stroked his tongue along hers. Damn she tasted good, better than he remembered. The stiffness drained from her spine. She leaned into him and kissed him back. His heart slammed approval against his ribs, banging hard enough she could probably feel it against her breast.

Her hands lifted to clutch his forearms, as if she were going to push him away. A moment later, she caressed upward past his elbows, over his biceps and shoulders, leaving a trail of cauterized nerve endings in their wake.

She tilted her head, allowing him better access, and despite the warning bells clanging in his subconscious, he snaked an arm around her waist and pulled her closer, snugging her hot body to his. Instead of teaching her a lesson, the soft crush of her breast pressing his chest and her thigh burning the length of his taught him one.

He wanted her. Ethics be damned.

She felt good against him. Hunger consumed him, making him delve deeper, hold tighter, crave more. Her short nails lightly scored the back of his neck, and a shiver of need racked him.

A thud on the floor vaguely penetrated his subconscious, but Hannah flinched. "Ouch."

Casting a wide-eyed, wary glance at him, she bent and rubbed her foot, then picked up the photo album and clutched it to her chest like a shield. The flush of desire drained from her cheeks, leaving her pale and biting her bottom lip.

"That—that shouldn't have happened."

"Don't play innocent, Hannah. Seducing me into funding your horse operation was your game plan tonight."

Gaping, she bolted to her feet, dropped the book on the table and fisted her hands at her sides. "I didn't invite you here to seduce you, you egotistical jerk. I'd be lying if I didn't admit I need you to continue funding FYC, but the real reason I invited you here tonight was because I wanted to talk about Sam."

Every cell of Wyatt's being snapped to attention. His body went from hot and aroused to cool and on guard in an instant. "What about Sam?"

"*He's* good company, and *his* understanding of horses is impressive."

Wyatt ignored the insults and focused on the more critical issue. "I take it Nellie has been talking."

He'd have to fire the best housekeeper/cook he'd ever had—yet another reason he found himself eager to return to the farm every weekend. That woman could cook. And Sam liked her.

Hannah narrowed her eyes in disgust, and anger vibrated through her. "You should know better than that. You won't find a more loyal employee than Nellie. She keeps confidential information to herself. What happens in that house stays in that house."

"Then how do you know about Sam?"

Her gaze lowered. "I met him."

"When and where?" He'd ordered Carol to keep Sam away from the barns. If she'd defied him, she'd be gone.

"He was out walking Sunday morning. I was in the pasture, and…we met." She shrugged and reached for her wineglass. Her fingers curled around the stem, then stroked up, down, up. Nervous gesture, or intentionally seductive?

Despite his anger, his blood headed south. Did she have any idea how alluring the gesture was? Of course she did. Hannah might be stubborn, but from what he'd seen, she wasn't stupid. Except fiscally.

"Sam's exactly the kind of person who benefits most from our therapeutic riding program."

Her statement dashed ice water over his distraction. He would have to be especially careful about keeping her away from Sam. A woman with her skills could lure an unsuspecting old man down the wrong road.

"You're an animal doctor, not a people doctor. Leave Sam's care to the specialists who know what they're doing."

"Maybe you're seeing the wrong doctors," she retorted.

"I've hired the best in the business."

"Apparently not, or you'd have Sam physically involved in something he cares about greatly." She crossed to a desk in the corner, then returned with a sheaf of papers and stabbed them in his direction. "I printed these out for you. Read what the enlightened professionals have to say. Engaging in physical activity improves mental acuity and coordination. If you really care about Sam and want to help him, then you'll bring him to our riding class Sunday."

"You have the disposition of a leaky faucet. Do you plan to erode my resistance with persistent nagging? We've already covered this ground."

"We haven't even begun to scrape the surface. Read the documentation. Unless you're afraid I'm right. And you're wrong."

He yanked the papers from her hand. He might even glance through them while he was stuck on the plane tomorrow— just so he could discredit her research.

"Wyatt, when I invited you to observe the class before, it was with the abstract notion that you might have a crumb of human decency and compassion for others who are less fortunate somewhere inside your calculator heart. Now that I've met your stepfather, I know Find Your Center can touch *you* personally and change *your* life for the better by improving Sam's. This isn't about you generously helping others any more, Wyatt. This is about helping yourself. Looking out for number one—something at which I'm sure you excel. Sam and FYC will just happen to benefit in the process."

Anger and frustration volcanoed through him. He couldn't believe she'd stoop so low as to use Sam for her own self-interest and accuse *him* of being selfish. He shot to his feet. "Don't try to cloak your agenda behind a feigned desire to help Sam. Mind your own business."

"Find Your Center is my business. It's also yours."

"It's not profitable, and, like any other wasteful expense, it will be cut from the budget."

"You bottom-line thinkers are all alike. You're too blinded by numbers to see that sometimes there's a greater reward than profit."

"This from a woman who lives beyond her means?"

She rolled her eyes. "I have been very fortunate, but I work hard. I don't demand or expect any concessions because I'm the—I *was* the boss's daughter."

"I've seen no evidence of that."

"Give me a chance and you will." Concern replaced the fire in her eyes. "Forget your prejudices and the money for a minute, if you can, and tell me about Sam. He seemed very cognizant when we spoke, and in a span of two minutes he made more progress with the new mare than my trainers and I have made since she arrived."

That was the old Sam. The new one couldn't be trusted not to put himself in jeopardy—a point he'd proven with near disastrous results. Watching his decline helplessly from the sidelines these past few years had to be the most frustrating challenge Wyatt had ever faced. It was one of the reasons he hadn't intended visiting the farm often once he had Sam installed. He couldn't bear to watch.

"Sam has good days and bad. You caught him on a good one. Keep him off the horses."

"Why?"

"He might get hurt."

"I told you we take every precaution to—"

"No riding."

"Wyatt, Sam isn't a cask of whiskey that you can stash in storage and expect him to improve with age. Quality of life is important. Don't take away something he cares so much about. He has an affinity with horses that he should be allowed to pursue. He needs to feel useful. If you want to slow his decline you have to challenge him and keep him mentally and physically engaged. Let him participate in the class."

Her eyes narrowed, then she cocked her head and studied him the way she had the mare's infected wounds. "Maybe you don't want him to get better. Perhaps his decline benefits you and strengthens your role in the company."

Fury boiled inside him at her implication. "I am paying a

damned fortune to protect Sam and keep him comfortable. I am not holding him back."

His voice sounded more growl than human. Anyone who knew him would back off. Not Hannah. She threw back her shoulders. But it would take more than great breasts to distract him.

"And yet you're still losing him. How much worse can it get?"

"You have no idea what you're talking about. You haven't heard the doctors' prognoses or watched Sam fade away right before your eyes."

Compassion softened her face. "No, I haven't witnessed Sam's decline. But I've seen the magic happen for people worse off than Sam. I've seen hope restored to a lot of defeated faces—faces like yours. And Sam's. Riding may not be a cure, but it does buy time in a positive, enjoyable way. Give FYC a chance to work a miracle. For Sam. For you."

Rage against the situation and his helplessness surged through him. He wanted to punch something. He clenched his fists so hard the skin around his knuckles felt as if it would split. He didn't know how much time Sam had left, but he wasn't going to shorten it by letting his stepfather take unnecessary risks.

"I've told you before, I don't believe in miracles. Stay away from Sam."

"But—"

"He's too fragile and unsteady to get on the back of a horse."

"As I've explained, his balance and muscle tone will improve if—"

"I repeat, Sam is not riding. That is not negotiable. Find your new stable and get the hell out of my life."

He turned on his heel and left before he did something to relieve the tangle of volatile emotions she stirred in him. Something like yanking that lithe body of hers close and kissing her manipulative mouth to silence her. But if he did any of those things he wasn't sure he'd be able to stop at kisses.

Without a doubt, he'd end up doing something both of them would regret.

Seven

Jeb blasted through the lab door Monday a little before noon, jerking Hannah from her mental meanderings about a second kiss that should never have happened. And how dare Wyatt accuse her of using sex to sway him anyway.

"There's some old guy in the field with the bay mare. He says his name is Sam and he claims he has your permission to be there."

Hannah's heart jumped. She dropped the packaging tape on the work bench. If Sam got hurt by one of her horses, Wyatt would shut her down with no questions asked. "Sam is Wyatt's stepfather. He lives in the main house. I'll take care of him. Could you finish packaging this last shipment for me? The courier is due in ten minutes."

"Sure."

As soon as Jeb nodded she raced past him and sprinted toward the field. Not wanting to spook the mare she slowed as she neared the pasture and tried to catch her breath. Running wasn't her thing. She'd bet Wyatt ran if the lack of fat on his rock-hard body was any indication. There hadn't been anything soft or flabby about him Friday night.

Sam's nurse stood outside the fence frantically calling, "Sam get out of there."

Sam squatted in a traditional farrier's stance beside the mare's powerful hind quarters. He held a hoof in his hands, but this mare didn't need shoeing. A fist of dread clenched in Hannah's stomach. One sharp, well-placed kick could prove disastrous. "What are you doing, Sam?"

"I brought bacon grease for these fetlocks. Nellie was nice enough to provide it."

She groaned. "Nellie's in on this?"

Beside her Carol nodded. "She said something about letting Sam do a little 'horse healing.' What is that?"

Without taking her eyes off Sam, Hannah replied, "Horse healing is when you need the therapy of talking to somebody who'll listen without a bunch of backchat or judgment, someone who appreciates everything you do. Around here that *somebody* is usually a horse."

"That's crazy."

"It beats paying a therapist hundreds of dollars an hour when all you need is a good listener. Does Wyatt know you brought Sam down here?"

"I didn't bring Sam. He snuck out the door after breakfast. The wily ol' coot is always looking for an escape. When I ordered him to stop, he ignored me. I guess from now on I'll have to keep him locked in his room even at mealtimes."

Shocked, Hannah shot a quick glance at Sam, making sure he couldn't overhear. "Wyatt keeps Sam locked in? Why?"

"He claims Sam's a danger to himself so he installed dead bolts on the suite doors to keep Sam from wandering."

"Is Sam suicidal?"

"No. But there was a near-accident at the last residence. I'm not privy to the details. All I know is that close call got the last nurse fired, and it's one of the reasons Mr. Jacobs is a tad overvigilant."

"You call dead bolts on the bedroom door a *tad* overvigilant? What if there's a fire? Is there any health reason why Sam shouldn't get outside? Other than what looks like mild Alzheimer's."

"None. He's in decent shape for a man of seventy. I'm allowed to take him on walks but not near the barns. However, if Mr. Jacobs hears about this escapade, even that'll change."

"Sam, I'm coming in." Hannah climbed the fence and cautiously moved toward the mare and man. "You know Wyatt doesn't want you near the horses."

"Horses are my life…or they used to be back when I had a life."

She winced in sympathy. "He's worried about you getting hurt."

"I'd rather be dead than incarcerated."

The sincerity in his tone sent alarm jolting through her. She didn't know him well enough to know if he was serious. "You don't mean that."

"I do. Wyatt flies off to work—at the company I started, mind you—and leaves me at home to do puzzles like a school boy. I don't want to live like that."

She hated playing devil's advocate for the jerk, but she didn't want Sam upset. "Puzzles are supposed to exercise your brain."

"My brain isn't all that needs exercising. I need to keep the old ticker pumping. Puzzles put me to sleep."

"I could try talking to Wyatt again…"

But after Friday night's kiss, she wasn't sure she wanted to go anywhere near the man. She'd been tossing and turning each night, restless and itchy and needy and furious, reliving the kiss and cursing his effect on her, even though he thought the worst of her. Thoughts of him had invaded the sanctuary of her lab. She'd been disgustingly inefficient and clumsy.

Until recently she'd been satisfied with her celibate life. Why did Wyatt Jacobs, of all people, have to upset her contentment? She'd thought she had better taste in men, but apparently not. She got hot and bothered over a hunky package with no soul or personality.

"Sam, I'll get your nurse to talk to him, too, but—"

"Carol. Her name's Carol. Some days I don't remember. Today I do. Today I remember a lot of things." He seemed quite proud of the fact. The mare irritably twitched her tail and ears. "Let me finish here before this lady loses patience."

Hannah gripped the horse's halter while he worked and searched for a solution for Sam's predicament—one that could benefit them all.

Sam finished his task and straightened, then wiped his greasy hands on the rag he had tucked into his waistband.

"Mixed a little sulfur in there. That'll fix 'er right up." He tucked the rag through his belt loop.

"Dare I ask where you found sulfur?"

"Garden shed. Passed it the other day when Carol and I were walking."

Sam had thought this out sequentially and planned ahead, Hannah realized, so he wasn't mentally in too bad a shape. She'd seen worse cases in the FYC client roster, and she'd seen those clients improve. Sam would, too. "We'll give your remedy a try."

"Don't care how much pharmaceutical companies spend on product development, sometimes the old ways are the best. She'll be healed by the end of the week. What's her name?"

Hannah blinked in surprise. "I don't know. I haven't received the paperwork on her yet."

"Then I'll call her Phoenix. She's going to come back and be a fine horse. She has spunk and she's smart."

Hannah marveled that the usually skittish animal stayed close, as if wanting more of Sam's attention. "I agree with the spunky part. She's been a handful for us. I'm not sure about her intelligence yet—unless she's been outsmarting us to get out of exercising."

"Let's take her to the round pen and work out some of her excess energy. I'll need a lunge line."

Objections danced on Hannah's tongue.

"She needs to work out as much as I do," Sam insisted before she could protest. "Neither of us is ready to be put out to pasture."

Another band of sympathy squeezed her chest. "Wyatt—"

"Is in Asheville. Won't be back until Friday."

Torn between wanting to help Sam and not wanting to upset Wyatt, she chewed the inside of her lip. If she let Sam spend time with the horse, she'd get in trouble. But how could she send him back to a life he considered worse than death? She'd have to talk to Wyatt about that. One of her high school friends had threatened suicide and everyone had ignored Terri's cries for help—until it was too late.

Hannah knew she couldn't take the risk with Sam. But she still had reservations. Big ones. "Sam, Carol and I could get fired if we let you have your way."

"I'm not gonna tattle. Are you? Besides, the boy told me to stay away from the barn. He didn't say anything about the pens or pastures." Mischief glimmered in the faded blue eyes.

Hannah's lips twitched as she fought a smile. The mare wasn't the only one with spunk. And Sam was right. Wyatt had only forbidden her to let Sam ride. He hadn't said anything about letting Sam lunge a horse.

Semantics. You're looking for trouble, Hannah.

Against her better judgment, she ignored the warning. Maintaining that keen spark of excitement in Sam's eyes took forefront. Normally, the odds of keeping a secret on a farm like Sutherland where the employees were as close-knit as family were slim. But Wyatt never interacted with the staff.

She turned to Carol. "Is Sam this alert and happy at the house?"

The woman shook her head. "I've seen a side of him today that I've not seen before. It's a definite improvement."

That settled it. Hannah had never been a rule-breaker or one to push boundaries before. That had been her cousin's forte.

But this time Hannah had too much to lose by not taking a risk. Sam needed to have a sense of purpose and she could provide it.

"Sam, I'll let you rope me in on this escapade of yours on two conditions."

"Name 'em."

"One, you promise not to sneak out of the house and come down here by yourself anymore. That's really dangerous, Sam. If you're going to be around the horses, I want someone with you who's familiar with their behavior—that means me, not Carol." She wasn't about to let anyone else risk their job.

He rocked onto the balls of his feet with excitement. "Agreed. Next?"

"No riding."

"But—"

"Wyatt forbid me to allow you to get on a horse. I won't go against a direct order from the boss. We're already stretching things."

His shoulders sank. "If you insist."

"I do. I'll go get a line. Meet me and Phoenix at the round pen."

"Are you crazy?" Carol protested as they joined her at the fence. "Wyatt will be livid."

"Sam needs a little mental and physical stimulation. I'm going to provide it in the safest way possible. And apparently this crotchety mare has taken a liking to Sam. I'm trained to work with people with disabilities, and I'll take full responsibility if Wyatt finds out."

"It's on your head."

"Understood and accepted."

"But for what it's worth, I think you're on the right track."

Once Wyatt had irrefutable evidence in front of him of how much Find Your Center could help Sam, he wouldn't be able to deny the benefits of FYC or the funding, and maybe he'd quit trying to run her out of her home.

* * *

A black-and-gold helicopter buzzed the pasture, barely missing the treetops. Hannah ducked. The horses scattered as the craft hovered momentarily over the main barn before moving on.

Crazy pilot. What is he thinking?

"Does that happen often?" the client beside her asked in his sexy French-accented voice.

"It's a first. Our guests usually land at the airport and come over by chauffeur-driven car as you did."

She kept her eyes on the chopper. If he'd flown over the property two hours ago when Sam had been in the pen with Phoenix and the junior dressage students had been circling the outdoor riding ring, it could have proven disastrous.

"He appears to be landing on the front lawn," her client added.

"That's odd." Who would be crazy enough to—

Wyatt.

Her stomach took a nosedive and her heart kicked into overdrive. Wyatt wasn't due to arrive for two days. Why would he cut his trip short and come home early—via chopper, no less—unless he'd found out about her working with Sam behind his back?

She tried to conceal her rising anxiety and focus on business. "Franco, what do you think of these two?"

"Your cousin's faith in you is well-founded. Both the mare and gelding are good choices. Stacy and Natalie will love them. In a few years I'll come back for a mount for my son. At two Theo's too young for anything more than a docile pony."

"I'll look forward to your return." She hoped she'd still be employed here. "Please keep me posted on how this pair works out. Let me escort you to the business office where April can assist you with the paperwork and make the arrangements to transport your surprise gifts home."

They climbed into one of the luxurious golf carts and headed for the business office. A black Mercedes met her on the driveway outside the building. Wyatt's car. For a few heart pounding moments the vehicles faced off like gunslingers in the street. Bracing herself for a confrontation, Hannah exhaled shakily and pulled into the designated space before swinging from the cart on unsteady legs.

Wyatt parked beside her then exited his vehicle and stalked toward them bearing an I-own-the-world swagger and a custom-made black suit. He looked delicious. Hannah pushed her unwelcome appreciation aside and swallowed the lump rising in her throat.

The last thing she needed was a scene in front of a customer—a customer preparing to write a very big check. "Franco, I'd like you to meet Wyatt Jacobs, the new owner of Sutherland Farm. Wyatt, this is Franco Constantine, CEO of Midas Chocolates and Constantine Holdings. He's flown over from Monaco to purchase horses for his wife and daughter."

She couldn't help making comparisons while the men shook hands and exchanged pleasantries. Both were tall, dark and handsome, but while Franco's eyes were a startling blue Wyatt's were fathomless. And Franco's proximity didn't make her pulse stampede—a good thing since he was happily married. But she could see why her cousin found French men appealing.

Wyatt's gaze homed in on her, making her insides quiver. "Hannah, a moment, please."

Phrased nicely in his deep send-shivers-down-her-spine voice, but she didn't miss the steel behind the request. Her euphoria over closing a two-million-dollar deal evaporated.

"I'll meet you in my office after I introduce Franco to April."

"I'll be waiting." The statement sounded like a threat and her fight-or-flight instincts kicked in. But she wouldn't run.

All too soon she'd turned Franco over to the capable sales staff, then with dread miring every step, she forced her feet to carry her to the man whose presence spelled impending doom.

Wyatt stood by one of her charts, hands on hips, aggression in every lean line of his body. She closed her office door for privacy. If she was going to be fired, she didn't want the rest of the staff to hear or try to come to her rescue, thereby jeopardizing their jobs.

She slid behind her desk in an effort to establish a wall of professionalism between them and quickly realized her mistake. Sitting gave Wyatt the advantage. He loomed over her, making her tilt her head back to meet his diamond-hard gaze.

"If Constantine is here to buy horses, why wasn't he talking to our highly paid sales staff?"

"One, because he wanted detailed information about the bloodline and temperament bred into each horse—my specialty since both horses are bred from Sutherland stock. And two, Megan referred him to me."

"Who is Megan?"

"My cousin. She rides the European Grand Prix circuit." She gestured to the framed photo on her shelf of Megan with one of her champion horses.

It seemed ironic or maybe a cruel twist of fate that Megan had inherited Hannah's parents' grace, talent and the aggressive nature required to compete successfully on the Grand Prix circuit. Unfortunately, Megan's competitive instincts hadn't rubbed off on Hannah, even though the two of them had been as close as sisters—especially after her cousin had moved into Sutherland Farm following her parents' and brother's deaths fifteen years ago. The loss of their mothers had linked the cousins in a way no one else could comprehend.

And right now Megan would be telling me to put the enemy on the defensive by striking his weak spot. Wyatt's weakness was his lack of practical horse knowledge.

Only Hannah hadn't told Megan about Wyatt because… she didn't know what to say. The man put her emotions in a blender and churned them into an unrecognizable mush.

Hannah took a deep breath. "What were you thinking to let

your pilot fly that close to the ground? You scared the horses. If we'd had riders in the outdoor ring, as we did earlier, their mounts could have been spooked and the riders thrown."

"I was trying to locate you."

Her stomach muscles contracted. *Here we go.* "Why?"

He parked his fists on her desk and leaned forward, encroaching on her space and making her heart beat double-time and her mouth dry up. "I read the literature you gave me, and then I did more research on the studies and the doctors. Your theories might not be complete snake oil."

Surprise and relief whooshed the air out of her lungs. Wow. A man who wasn't afraid to admit he was wrong. "Really? I mean, of course they're not. I told you I've seen rehabilitation therapy work."

"I've made an appointment for Sam with the doctor leading one of the studies. You're coming with us. You've seen his theories in practice and will know if what he says about Sam has merit."

Problem. If she and Sam spent any time together in front of Wyatt, Sam was bound to let something slip about his work with Phoenix and their secret would be out. As much as Hannah ached to gloat over Sam's progress after only three days' work, it was too soon to prove her point. She had to bide her time until she had irrefutable evidence that even Wyatt couldn't ignore.

And then there was the whole spend-a-night-in-the-same-hotel-as-Wyatt issue. Not a good idea. Not with this unsettling whatever-it-was between them.

"Um…when?" she stalled while trying to think of a good excuse.

"The chopper is waiting to take us to the airport as soon as you pack. Sam's appointment is tomorrow afternoon. We'll fly to Atlanta tonight via the company jet and return Thursday evening."

Tension drained from her, chased by worry at the reason she had to stay here. "I can't go."

His expression darkened. "It wasn't a request, Hannah."

"Wyatt, I'm not refusing for the sake of being obstinate. I really can't go. Not this week…and probably not next."

"You'd better have a good reason for refusing an order."

She twisted a pencil in her fingertips, battling a sense of hopelessness. "One of the mares is about to foal any hour now. I need to be here with her."

"She can't give birth alone or under someone else's supervision?"

"She's older and carrying twins. Twins might be routine in humans, but not in horses. Sable is already showing signs this will be a difficult delivery."

"Why isn't the mare manager handling this?"

He wasn't going to like her answer. "Sable is one of my rescue horses."

The corners of his mouth turned down.

"Don't worry. If the foals survive, there will be horses to sell to recoup some expenses."

"If?"

She bit her lip and pushed up from her desk. "The odds aren't the best. In fact, I need to check the mare's status now. I don't know how you managed to get an appointment with the specialist so quickly when most people wait months, but thank you for agreeing to take Sam. You won't regret it, and I can't wait to hear what the doctor has to say."

She just hoped Sam didn't let their secret slip or she'd be out of a job and her dream—hers and her mother's—would be killed.

Using a flashlight Wyatt checked the brass stall numbers in the darkened barn. As crazy as it seemed, he needed to see Hannah. Tonight.

It wasn't because he missed butting heads with her, but simply because she deserved to know the doctor's findings supported her program. The neurologist believed involvement with horses could slow Sam's decline. The question was how to implement the practices without risking Sam's well-being. Wyatt was counting on Hannah's knowledge of the program to help him develop a safe but effective strategy.

When she hadn't answered the door at her cottage he'd made his way to the stables where he'd run into the security guard who'd told him where to find Hannah.

Wyatt located the stall. A strange energy hummed through him as he approached the chest-high solid wall. An eerie red glow lit the box, but he didn't see or hear Hannah. Two of the smallest horses he'd ever seen lay intertwined on a bed of straw on the far side of the compartment beneath the red lamps. Heat lamps?

Those had to be the twins Hannah had been expecting. But where was their mother and why had she been separated from them? Even with his limited knowledge of horse reproduction, he knew babies fed almost immediately after birth and often thereafter.

And where was Hannah? He'd seen no sign of her in the silent building. Had she taken the mare elsewhere? He swung the beam up and down the dark aisle. No Hannah.

A sigh and shuffle caught his attention. He leaned closer to peer through the vertical slats and spotted boots in the near right corner—boots connected to long, denim-clad legs. Legs he'd recognize anywhere because they'd planted themselves in the forefront of his thoughts lately.

His pulse jumped. Hannah slept slouched in the corner with her head tilted at an angle guaranteed to reward her with sore neck tomorrow.

He eased open the latch, but the click echoed through the silent barn. Hannah jerked upright, her owlish gaze shooting straight for the foals then turning to find him. She squinted at the flashlight beam and threw up an arm to shield her face.

"Jeremiah?"

Her sleep-husky voice zapped him like a shorted wire, jolting his pulse into overdrive.

"No. Wyatt." Who in the hell was Jeremiah and why would

she be expecting him in the middle of the night? He lowered the beam and pulled the door shut behind him while he willed his unacceptable reaction to her away. "What are you doing?

"Keeping an eye on the babies."

"Where's the mare?"

Hannah ducked her head. Her hair fell forward to conceal her face behind a tangled curtain. "I had to put Sable down. I knew the odds were against her, but I was hoping... She's gone." Her voice grew smaller and tighter with each word until the last was barely a whisper. She took a shuddery deep breath.

Irritation surged through him at Hannah's feigned struggle for composure. The women he'd known always used emotional routines to milk sympathy and cash from men. A part of him was disappointed that she had confirmed his initial opinion of her.

Then she leaned her head against the wall and swallowed. The dark strands slid across her pale skin, drawing his attention to the circles of exhaustion smudged like lavender thumbprints beneath her eyes and to what looked to be dried tear streaks on her cheeks. *Dried.* Not freshly generated for his benefit. Something shifted inside him. Her grief was real, not an award-worthy pretense.

She took a deep, shaky breath. "Life and death are routine aspects of living on a horse farm. Age, colic and injuries take horses all the time. When all else fails, putting them down is routine and humane."

The stilted speech sounded like one she'd chanted a hundred times. "Who are you trying to convince, doc? Me or yourself?"

She blinked. "I'm just stating the facts."

But the pain straining her voice was unmistakable, and the way she tried to deny she was upset impressed him a hell of a lot more than crocodile tears or pleas for sympathy would.

Empathy welled in his chest. "I saw you with the other mare. I'm sure you did everything you could with this one."

"I'd like to think I did, but…" Drawing her knees up to her chest and hugging them, she stared at the sleeping foals. "It's never easy to give up. I keep thinking of other things I could have tried."

No, giving up hope was never easy, and watching someone—some*thing*—suffer and fade away was hard, too. "Sometimes it's better to cut your losses and walk away."

She looked at him through spiky lashes. "I never quit when there's still a chance. I didn't know Daisy was pregnant when Doc brought her. When I discovered her condition I had a choice between terminating one of the twins or hoping for the best. The ultrasound showed that the filly was the smaller of the two. She's the one I would have had to—" Her voice cracked. "But she looked healthy and perfectly formed, and I couldn't—"

She plucked at a piece of straw clinging to her jeans. He caught her surreptitiously wiping her cheek on her sleeve and something inside him unraveled. She was trying to hide her tears rather than use them to manipulate him. How totally unlike the women of his experience.

He liked Hannah better when she was ornery and defiant and trying to con him into opening his wallet for her worthless nags. As perverted as it sounded, their arguments energized him. This vulnerable side of her made him uncomfortable. He didn't know how to handle it or like the way it made him feel.

The impulse to put an arm around her stiff shoulders appeared out of nowhere. He locked his knees against the urge to lower himself to the floor beside her. He wasn't into emotional displays and managed to restrain the impulse to hug her. Barely.

He didn't do hugs. His parents had taught him that hugs were meaningless gestures. Sam had been more likely to give him an encouraging slap on the back than get mushy or sentimental. But even without the hugs, Wyatt had known Sam cared—probably more than either of Wyatt's self-involved parents and definitely more than the women who had professed their love to Wyatt over the years.

That's why watching Sam become a shadow of the man he'd once been was so agonizing. It was as if Sam were leaving him one memory at a time, and it was why Wyatt had bought the farm with the intention of only making the occasional weekend visit. He wanted Sam safe, happy and comfortable, but mostly he wanted Sam out of sight, he admitted with a stab of unease between his shoulder blades. Hannah's presence and her rescue operation had derailed that plan.

Though she'd averted her face he could see her blinking furiously to keep the tears in her eyes from spilling over. "I played it safe. I didn't intervene other than to give Sable additional supplements and support. Turns out I made a mistake."

Blame. He understood that, too. Hadn't he repeatedly questioned himself on how and when he'd started missing signs of Sam's battle and what would have happened if he'd paid attention and sought treatment sooner? By the time he'd forced Sam into retirement there had been a few costly errors at Triple Crown.

"Look at that filly, Hannah. She's going to be a beauty. How could giving her life ever be deemed a mistake?"

Surprise and gratitude eased some of the pain from her eyes. Had he been such a bastard to her? Yes, he had. A slow smile curved her lips, and he instantly recalled the texture and taste of her mouth. Damn it.

"You're right. And Sable would want it this way. She'd want her babies to have a chance. Thanks, Wyatt."

"What are the foals' chances?"

When her smile faltered he congratulated himself on severing the feel-good tug between them. "Good if they make it through the first forty-eight hours, better if they make it seventy-two." She checked her watch. "We're approaching the twelve-hour mark."

"Nursing an orphan, let alone two, is a twenty-four hour job. Who's going to care for them?"

Her chin snapped up. She scrambled to her feet and wobbled. He caught her arm to steady her, feeling her muscles flex in his grip before she shrugged him off.

Touching her felt good. And right. But it wasn't. Her employee status made her taboo. And if she was a woman who lived on the edge of her messy emotions, the best he could do was avoid her.

"The foals are my responsibility, but not at the expense of my work, if that's what you're concerned about."

The prickly woman he knew had returned. Thank God. *Her* he could handle. "You can't do it alone. Who's going to help you?"

She raked her fingers through her tangled hair, then absently began to braid it. The action arched her back and displayed her breasts to mouth-watering advantage. What was it about her that made every move a sensual invitation? It took conscious effort to keep his eyes on her face and not her curves.

"A few staff members have volunteered for shifts when they're off the clock, and with the state vet school only an hour away I'll try to recruit students to lend a hand. Twins are unusual, so the mare's pregnancy and the foals' development are of interest. One of the professors has already asked to use my notes as a case study for his class. It helps to know that losing Sable might teach future vets how to get better outcomes in similar situations."

"Could you have gotten a better outcome?"

She shivered beneath her inadequate coat and wrapped her arms around her middle. "Probably not. Anyway, thanks for stopping by. Good night."

"You can't sleep here."

"I couldn't sleep anywhere else," she replied without hesitation.

He pointed to the camera mounted in the corner of the

stall. "If that's video surveillance you could watch them from wherever your monitors are located—somewhere warmer, I'll bet."

Half-defiant, half-exhausted, she glared at him. "I won't leave them, Wyatt. You can't make me."

Her challenge sent adrenaline pumping through him. "The hell I can't."

"Then you'll have to have security haul me out, and I doubt you can convince Jeremiah to manhandle me. He's worked here twenty years."

So Jeremiah was the security guard. Wyatt didn't doubt what Hannah said. In his two meetings with management, he'd learned one thing. The staff was extremely loyal to Hannah. "Why would you camp here when you could pay one of the grooms to do it?"

"You're the one who harps on not spending unnecessary money, remember?" The defiant color drained from her cheeks. "But even if I did have a rich benefactor to foot the bill, I wouldn't leave. I couldn't save Sable. Trying to pull her foals through is the least I can do for her."

The cynical side of him told him this cold, disheveled woman who put orphaned animals ahead of her own comfort seemed too good-hearted to be true. But when he looked into Hannah's eyes her dedication seemed genuine, and as unlikely as it might be, he wanted to believe she was as unselfish and unspoiled as she appeared at this moment.

Had he completely misjudged her? Or had the chemistry between them demolished his objectivity? Had to be the latter.

Whatever the case, it didn't change the fact that she stood between him and his plans for this farm.

He had to get rid of her. But having her die of hypothermia wasn't the way to accomplish his goal. And it would be bad for business.

Eight

Wyatt turned and stalked in the direction he'd come taking his narrow beam of light with him.

"Good riddance," Hannah mumbled under her breath. She didn't want him here anyway. The night had been difficult enough. She didn't have the energy to deal with him. He kept her on edge, and he had a gift for sucking the strength right out of her.

But it had been decent of him to check on her, and he hadn't seemed angry. Sam must not have let anything slip about their adventures during the trip or Wyatt would have been livid.

Forget Wyatt. You have more important things to deal with tonight.

Nearly numb from the cold, Hannah shuffled closer to the heat lamps, trying not to disturb the sleeping foals. Exhaustion weighted her muscles. She should have brought a heavier coat or maybe worn thermals, but the late spring days were so warm she hadn't brought a parka with her and she hadn't wanted to go home to get one. The wind kicking up outside didn't help. It siphoned heat from the barn.

She checked the foals' respiratory rates, then moved back to her corner and started doing knee bends to work some circulation into her legs.

A noise down the aisle made her pause and cock her head. Jeremiah wasn't due for another pass, but he did tend to worry about her. She looked over the stall wall and spotted someone stalking toward her in the darkness. The glare of a bright flashlight beam obscured his features, but she couldn't mistake that confident stride. Wyatt had returned. Adrenaline pumped through her veins chasing away her chill.

As he drew nearer she noticed he carried bundles under each arm. "What is all that?"

"Sleeping bags. Jeremiah told me where to find them. If you insist on bunking here, you need insulation. Open the door."

She did as he asked. "There are four of them."

"Two for beds. Two for pillows."

Her neck prickled a warning. She didn't have to be a mathematician to know—uh-uh. "That's two too many."

"If you're staying, I'm staying."

No! Her internal muscles contracted. "You don't need to—"

"There's only one way to get me out of this stall, Hannah. You leave first."

She didn't want him here, but she could hardly order him off his own land. And she had to admit a tiny part of her was impressed that Mr. Designer Duds would stoop to sleeping in a barn. "Not happening."

"Then you're stuck with me."

No sweet dreams in her future. "You're the boss."

"Don't forget it."

"As if you'd let me," she grumbled and took two of the bags from him. She unrolled one in her corner, then propped the second against the wall for a back brace. Determined to ignore him, she sank into the cushiony softness, slipped into the sack, tugged the warm covers to her chest and closed her eyes.

The air stirred. Her lids popped open as Wyatt's bag fluttered to the floor an inch from hers. *No, no, no.*

"You'll have more room to stretch out over there." She pointed to the opposite corner.

"You'll have more warmth if I'm here."

True, but— "Don't even suggest zipping our bags together. I'm not sharing body heat with you."

He shot her a lowered eyebrow look. "I wasn't offering."

Dread snagged like a fur ball in her throat and agitation skipped along her nerves. It only worsened when he stretched his long legs beside hers and his warmth radiated in her direction, beckoning her closer. She clenched her muscles and fought the urge.

He leaned against the stall wall. "This isn't like any stall I've ever been in. Why are you using rubber mats and fresh straw instead of shavings?"

"Birthing stalls require surfaces we can disinfect to keep the bacteria count down. So you *probably* won't catch anything sleeping here. But if you don't want to chance it…"

"Good try, doc."

"Would have been better if it had worked."

His lips twitched in what could have been a smile if he hadn't checked it, and for a moment Hannah was happy to have his company. Then she came to her senses. If he was staying, he must have an ulterior motive.

Wyatt shifted his attention to the babies in their straw nest. She could have sworn some of the rigidity in his jaw softened. "I've never seen horses this small."

"That's because the usual foal is around a hundred pounds. Each of these weighs roughly half that. The bay colt is slightly heavier than the black filly. She's the one in the greatest danger, but as long as she eats she has a chance."

He turned suddenly and their gazes collided. The boyish wonder on his face made her breath catch. When he shed his arrogant I'm-the-boss-of-you demeanor, she could *almost* like him. Suddenly sharing a stall seemed too intimate, too…close.

He observed her in that lingering, silent way of his, making her want to be somewhere else. Anywhere else. As long as it was away from him. Her toes curled in her boots and her nipples stiffened—unfortunately not from the cold. She tugged the sleeping bag to her chin and cursed her overactive hormones.

Hannah Faith, you are no better than the animals you work with. One whiff of a potential mate and you get all hot and bothered.

Okay, so Wyatt is sexy. Big deal.

And he knows how to kiss. So what?

She wasn't going to let anything happen between them. Because he was a coldhearted jerk and her boss, and she was *not* interested. But her hands grew clammy and her pulse raced out of control.

"Get some sleep," he commanded with his usual superiority.

Did he honestly believe she could calmly lie down and sleep with the enemy when he'd made it crystal clear that he wanted her long gone? "Just because you order it doesn't mean it'll happen."

"Does my presence disturb you, Hannah?"

"Don't be ridiculous."

His hiked eyebrow called her a liar. "Am I being ridiculous?"

She scowled at him. Her body tingled with awareness. Not awareness. Irritation. Heat invaded her limbs and torso. On the upside, she wasn't cold anymore. But on the downside… It had been a tough night. Watching Sable's struggle had brought back horrible memories, and she needed a hug.

But not from him.

His lips tipped in a half smile. "Good night, Hannah."

Cocky, autocratic bastard. "I have to feed them in a couple of hours."

"I'll help."

"Wyatt, you don't need—"

"Didn't we already establish that I'm the boss?"

She clamped her molars shut and silently fumed. She should have known the nice guy wouldn't last. At least now she had her hormones under control.

"I'm not likely to forget who's in charge since you rub it in my face every few minutes. If you want to rough it in a cold, drafty barn, I won't try to stop you."

In fact, she'd even enjoy his discomfort—even if it meant she had to suffer his company. But if he thought he could order her to sleep and she'd blindly obey, he had another thought coming. She would never, ever be able to relax with him nearby—especially now that she'd discovered Wyatt had a crumb of human decency buried somewhere under his thick ogre hide.

"Hannah."

Hannah ignored the voice, snuggled deeper into the pillow beneath her cheek and curled her fingers into the pillow case. Then several things needled her to consciousness simultaneously.

That hadn't been her father's voice trying to wake her for school. Her pillow smelled like sandalwood and cypress rather than her lilac-scented sheets, and the case didn't feel like crisp Egyptian cotton. Her down pillow was hard, warm and thumping.

Thumping?

Awareness of where she was and why and who she had her cheek pressed against thundered through her like a jumper's hooves racing the time clock. She stiffened and her eyes flew open to the dim red glow of the heat lamps. A strong band tightened around her and long, strong fingers curled into her waist, anchoring her in place.

Wyatt's arm. Wyatt's hand.

"Move slowly. Don't startle them." His chest rumbled

beneath her ear, and the vibration traveled straight down her spine, settling like a seltzer tablet in the pit of her stomach.

She shoved her hair out of her eyes and eased upright. Wyatt reclined beside her with his head and shoulders propped against the rolled up sleeping bag and his legs stretched out in front of him. His coat had fallen open to reveal his charcoal grey cashmere sweater—the softness she'd felt against her palm and cheek.

Embarrassment toasted her face. "I'm sorry. I—"

"Forget it. Look."

The softness of his voice snagged her attention, and then he smiled and she couldn't have turned away if flames had been licking at the stall door. Her stomach swooped like a barn swallow.

Wow.

That white smile slashing across his stubble-darkened face was a sight to behold. She'd never seen him smile before. And he looked good. Good enough to make her remember the kisses they'd shared and to want to curl up beside him and experiment with a few more. Her gaze fell to his tenderly curving lips.

Bad idea. Seriously bad idea, Hannah.

But the troublemaker in her head automatically registered the still-dark skylights overhead, which meant the staff hadn't arrived yet. Unless Jeremiah did a walk-by, then she and Wyatt were alone and unlikely to be interrupted.

His gaze locked with hers, and the temperature climbed a dozen degrees. The high stall walls enclosed them in a private world, wrapping them in a cocoon of intimacy. A hundred heartbeats raced past. Then his Adam's apple bobbed and a muscle in his jaw bunched.

"Hannah. *The. Foals.*"

An itty-bitty part of her brain noted his quietly rumbled order, but processing the words was a different matter when her skin steamed and her mind had apparently drowned in a hormonal hot spring.

He cupped her jaw. Desire bubbled up her throat. Her mouth watered in anticipation of his kiss, then his lips hardened. He pushed her chin toward the opposite side of the stall and withdrew his hand.

The sensual haze clouding her vision vanished like a popped bubble. The filly trembled on her haunches, extending one spindly front leg then the other. Everything in Hannah urged her to rush forward and help, but as if he'd read her mind, Wyatt's long, strong fingers closed around her wrist and held her back.

The filly's fumbling efforts rousted the colt. He wobbled and wavered and made it to his feet seconds before his sister, then he gave a triumphant little buck and promptly stumbled and fell.

Wyatt's low laugh startled them all—probably Hannah more than the four-legged occupants of the stall. She stared at him. How had she ever thought his eyes cold? The brown irises glimmered like the tiger's-eye ring she'd bought as a teenager.

Her entire body tingled at the awareness in his eyes. Awareness and restraint. *He* had control of *his* impulses. They shared another moment of silent connection—a connection she didn't want or need *with him*. She tried to shake off her unacceptable response, cleared her throat and twisted her wrist from his hold.

She peeled her gaze from his and spotted the straw clinging to his no-longer-crisply-pressed pant leg. She grimaced. "I'm sorry about your clothes."

He shrugged, bringing her attention to those broad shoulders. Specifically the one she'd slept on—the one with the tiny damp spot where her mouth had been. She'd drooled on him. A fresh wave of embarrassment swamped her.

"They're just pants, Hannah."

"Yes, I guess they are, and if you can afford to spend millions on a farm more or less sight unseen, then I guess you can afford to replace a pair of custom-made pants." She forced out the acidic words hoping to sever the intimacy of the moment. Judging by the way his expression hardened, she'd succeeded.

Strangely, annoying him didn't provide nearly as much satisfaction as she'd hoped.

Then he shook his head. "Seeing this is worth an entire wardrobe."

Her breath hitched in surprise. Who was this man and where had the arrogant bottom-line bastard who'd been her boss gone? She actually liked this version of Wyatt. And liking a man with a calculator for a heart was dangerous territory.

She could *actually* feel her body willing her to move in his direction. Instead, she swallowed and shook her head. "This chemistry between us can't go anywhere. You know that, don't you, Wyatt?"

Wyatt, like Robert, wanted her land and not her. Both were bottom-line, budget dictators like her father, who had apparently forgotten all about the farm he'd once loved.

And yet the knowledge that Wyatt shared traits with the men who'd done her wrong didn't stop her heart from bucking in her chest. A current of electricity hummed from his palm to hers, then traveled up her arm across her breasts and down her torso to settle heavily below her navel.

"At least you're admitting there is chemistry now. And yes, it is inappropriate." If she wanted to break this link—and she did—she'd have to find the strength to push him away.

"What happened with Sam and the doctor?"

Wyatt's expression went blank, but at least she'd broken the push-pull bond. He rose and towered over her. "Isn't it time to feed the foals?"

"In other words, none of my business." Maybe Sam would tell her later.

"It's not none of your business. It's just—" He shook his head and extended his hand. "We need to prepare the formula."

She didn't want to risk touching him again, but she couldn't pretend she didn't see the big, broad palm in front of her face.

Reluctantly, she put her hand in his. His fingers closed around hers and her body, apparently still in loco land, reacted with a skipping pulse and another bubbly burst of fizz.

Why did she react this way to the one man who had the power to destroy everything that mattered to her?

They stood inches apart—inches that seemed to shrink like the formerly spacious enclosure around them. His pupils expanded and his gaze dropped to her mouth, causing it to flood with moisture. The shared hours and kisses encircled them with a tightening lasso of awareness cinching tighter with each passing second.

"Should I stay with them?"

She blinked. At least one of them was thinking. "No. They'll be fine for a few minutes."

Gathering every fading thread of resistance she possessed, she yanked her hand free, and with one last glance at the babies, hurried toward the prep room. Wyatt followed like a dark shadow. His looming, hawkeyed surveillance as she measured and scooped made her clumsy and slow. She had to think through every action as if she were performing the task for the first time instead of the hundredth.

Even then, warm rivulets of formula splashed over the rim of the bottle and her fingers because her thoughts drifted into the taboo territory of what would have happened if she'd unwisely given in to the hunger they were both trying to deny.

Once both bottles were full Wyatt took them from her and headed toward the birthing stall.

"I'll take the colt," he volunteered and, grasping the container awkwardly, offered it. The colt ignored him.

Hannah set down her bottle, grabbed Wyatt's arm and hand and positioned him. "Tuck the bottle into the crook of your arm like this and brace yourself. He's going to pull hard."

Then she realized she was touching him, smelling him, and quickly stepped away. "Offer him the teat."

The colt immediately latched on—a great sign.

Hannah repeated the process with the filly, but the poor

baby seemed too tired from her earlier antics to nurse. Worry gnawed Hannah's middle. "Come on, girl. You have to eat."

But the velvety muzzle wouldn't open. Anxiety and desperation stretched her nerves. She tried again and again, then after several failed attempts the filly latched on with startling suddenness. Hannah's eyes stung, and a sob of relief built in her throat. She bit her lip hard to keep the sob there and turned her head to hide her reaction from Wyatt. The last thing she needed was for him to believe she was too much of a wimp to do her job.

"You don't give up easily, do you?" he asked.

She risked glancing his way and instead of disgust, she found compassion and maybe even a touch of admiration in his eyes. She would swear he—the man she'd deemed a soulless bastard—cared.

"Nellie says when I set my mind to something I can outstubborn a mule. Some days that trait's an asset…and some days a curse."

The colt finished his breakfast first and nudged Wyatt for more. "Now what?"

"Rub him. Pick up his feet. Get him used to being handled."

He frowned. "Why waste the time if they might not survive?"

"For the same reason you're taking care of Sam. You want whatever time he has left to be the best it can be. And if they make it we'll be ahead of the game because we didn't lose an opportunity for training them."

Wyatt's reserve was obvious as he stroked the colt's back. The little guy responded by nuzzling Wyatt's hip, then dancing away and back again. Slowly, Wyatt relaxed. His frown faded and his touch became surer. She even caught a brief smile at the colt's antics.

The filly finished her meal. Hannah raked her fingers through her fuzzy mane and smothered a sigh. Despite their lack of verbal skills, horses were so much easier to understand than people. Their needs and motives were simple. She handled the filly, gently lifting each tiny hoof under Wyatt's watch.

She finally opened the stall and headed for the prep room to clean up. "They'll be okay alone?"

"They'll probably sleep off their breakfast, and my first volunteer is due soon."

Wyatt kept pace beside her. "You were right about Sam. The doctor says he needs more physical and mental stimulation than he's getting. Your horses could be the answer."

Hope swelled tentatively in her chest. "I hear a *but*."

"The studies weren't as controlled as they should have been, and the results are open to misinterpretation. I don't want to put too much faith in this unorthodox approach until I see Sam progress."

A skeptic. Hannah sighed. "I understand your reluctance to believe without proof, but what do you have to lose, Wyatt? Let Sam join the Sunday class."

His obstinate expression returned. "He's not riding. You should understand my concerns. You lost your mother to a horseback riding accident, and I'm sure as a champion athlete she was in peak physical condition. Sam's fragile, and he no longer grasps the concept of danger. He'll take risks and make mistakes. He's getting clumsier. A fall and a broken hip could finish him off. Survival rates after a broken hip are—"

"I know the statistics." She paused by the sink. "And as I've pointed out before, we take every precaution to ensure the safety of our riders. Sam would only be walking his mount around the ring which is covered with six inches of soft sand."

"Are you saying you've never had anyone fall off or sustain an injury?"

She sighed. "No."

"Then he'll work with the horses from the ground or not at all."

"I can arrange that." She already had. But she wasn't volunteering that tidbit. Not yet. But she hated the lie between them.

"Sam will want to see these two." Then his eyes narrowed. "He'll help with the foals."

It was the open door she'd been waiting for. She liked Sam. His wealth of horse knowledge reminded her of her father, but unlike her father, Sam had a warmer and more approachable personality. "That would be great. I'll supervise him myself."

"No, I'll do it. As long as my work permits it, Sam and I will take a daily shift with the foals."

Her stomach sank. "Sam…and you? But—"

"It's a package deal, Hannah. Both of us or neither."

A blessing and a curse. She'd wanted to get Wyatt involved so he could comprehend the importance of FYC, but if she let him hang around the barns too much, he'd surely find out she'd been working with Sam behind his back and that could destroy any goodwill they had developed.

Not to mention his presence would wreak havoc on her concentration and her ability to get her job done. Wyatt Jacobs was definitely a distraction. She didn't know what to make of his less hostile side or if she could trust it. He'd stated very clearly that he wanted her land. Was he trying to lure her into acquiescence?

The only way to determine his real character was to treat him like one of her rescue animals and spend time with him. But she'd have to tread carefully—the same way she would with any unfamiliar animal.

She didn't want to think what would happen without animosity to keep them apart, but she'd find a way to ignore the attraction, keep Sam quiet and make it all work. She had no choice if she wanted to keep her home and her horses.

"You've got yourself a deal."

Exhaustion clouded Wyatt's thinking and infused his shoulders with a dull ache. His condition had little to do with last night's makeshift bed on the barn floor and everything to do with a certain leggy brunette.

It had been months since he'd slept beside a warm body, and

Hannah's soft curves curled against him combined with her silky hair teasing his chin had kept him awake. And aroused. *Very* aroused.

He needed a shower—preferably cold—and a bed, but more than anything, he needed distance from the woman whose scent clung to him.

Hannah crossed to a chart on the wall. "If you and Sam take a shift with the foals, you'll need to log in the feeding time and the amount each consumes."

"Got it."

She faced him, shifting uneasily on her feet. "The least I can do to repay you for your help is make you a cup of coffee."

Every cell in his body screamed a warning. "Are you inviting me back to your place?"

Her lips parted, then she shook her head. "There's a coffeepot in the lounge."

He should refuse and head for the safety of the house before he crossed a line he shouldn't cross—one that blurred more every minute. Hannah tempted him too much with her flushed cheeks and sexy disheveled hair. But if he wanted to find a way to convince her to sell her land, then he needed to take advantage of her guard being down to pump her for information.

"I could use a cup." The caffeine might clear his head and give him back his edge. Against his better judgment he followed her toward the office suite in the main barn.

She headed straight for the small but well-equipped kitchen provided for Sutherland clients. She didn't detour by the luxurious guest bathroom to waste time in front of the mirror as he would have expected of her. But he was beginning to see Hannah was much more complex than he'd originally surmised. She might be her daddy's pampered princess, but she also appeared to be as dedicated to her horses as she was to her expensive toys.

Unless she was giving one hell of a convincing performance.

He prowled the lounge while the fragrant brew perked. A

shelf containing multiple leather-bound volumes lured him
across the room. The one with *Horses by Hannah* inscribed
in gold on the spine caught his attention. Wyatt opened the
cover to a glossy mare's photograph.

A chart beneath the picture listed the dam and sire as well
as the animal's numerous wins to date. He flipped the pages
and found more of the same on subsequent entries. As he
studied each data sheet something became clear—something
he wished he could deny.

He'd underestimated Hannah. She hadn't exaggerated her
expertise in equine genetics. In five short years as Sutherland
Farm's breeder, she'd racked up credentials. Valid, impressive
credentials. She bred winners. And that complicated his
situation.

"Wyatt?" Hannah stood beside him holding two tall
insulated mugs bearing the Sutherland crest. She glanced past
him toward the door as if she couldn't wait to be gone. "Help
yourself to cream and sugar."

"I take it black. Thank you."

She rocked in her boots. "Thanks again for your help last
night. I have to get going. Please tell Sam I said hello."

"I will." If this was one of Sam's more lucid days, he might
even remember her. Sam's decline since Wyatt had forced
him to retire had been rapid. So rapid Wyatt dreaded the first
encounter with his stepfather each day because he never knew
which Sam he'd see—the wise man or the shell.

Hannah hustled from the lounge. Her butt in snug jeans
wasn't a sight Wyatt needed to appreciate at the moment, but
the sensual sway pulled his gaze like a tugboat nonetheless.
It took far more effort than it should have to concentrate on
the remainder of the photos in the album while he drank his
coffee.

He closed the cover, his conclusion unaltered. Unfortunately.
With Hannah's talent for breeding champions, getting rid of
her would be a bad business decision. Whenever Sam no
longer recognized his surroundings Wyatt would move Sam to

a more restricted environment and put the farm on the market. Hannah's position as the breeder on staff was undeniably an asset that would make the stable more desirable and valuable.

That meant he couldn't run her off, even though every iota of common sense he possessed urged him to cut her loose. He had to find a way to keep her on board but stay away from her, and still use her skills to help Sam. And he had to control the flow of cash into her money pit. Though the doctor's research showed the validity of such programs, FYC ran deep in the red. That had to change.

Finding a solution required a clearer head than he had at the moment. His concentration was shot. He needed food and a couple hours' sleep.

He left the building and stepped into the empty parking lot. The absolute silence of the farm at 5:00 a.m. settled over him like a heavy, dew-laden blanket.

When he'd begun working for Sam years ago, Sam had insisted Wyatt accompany him on his sunrise inspections of both the barns and later the distillery. During those early hours Sam had dispensed his wisdom and guided Wyatt on life. Back then, Sam would have been able to identify each birdsong and every animal footprint.

Wyatt missed those quiet moments now as much as he'd resented them when Sam first started dragging his ass out of bed before sunup and making him participate. After Wyatt had joined Triple Crown's team, he and Sam had made it a practice to walk the distillery floor together every morning before the machinery roared to life and shattered the silence of the night. Wyatt still prowled the concrete floors each morning, but it wasn't the same without his mentor by his side.

That reminded him he'd neglected to ask Hannah which shift she wanted him and Sam to take with the foals. He scanned the horizon and caught a smudge of movement in the Charleston-style lampposts lining the driveway. Hannah was too far away to shout for her. He dug out his cell phone and dialed. It dumped straight to her voice mail. She must have turned off her phone.

By the time he'd climbed into his car, started his engine and backed out of the parking space she'd disappeared. He steered toward her cottage, but failed to locate her in the headlight beams ahead of him.

He reached a V-shaped opening in the fence and a line through the damp grass caught his attention. He slowed. In the dim light he could barely make out a path leading toward distant trees. Hannah ought to have sense enough to know it was too cold and dark for her to wander through the woods alone. He pulled over and parked, then grabbed the flashlight from under his seat and followed.

Dew dampened his boots and the cuffs of his pants and slickened the stones underfoot. He'd yet to tour the property beyond the buildings and driveways and had only a vague idea from the topographical maps that an old rock quarry now filled with water lay in this direction.

Wishing he had on his hiking boots, he made his way carefully through the shadowy woods with the aid of the flashlight beam. He didn't see or hear Hannah ahead of him as he descended a hill and rounded a bend.

He reached a clearing and stopped. The brightening sky illuminated a pond, its surface disturbed along one side. Hannah sat on the end of a small dock in front of a white structure that resembled a boathouse. Despite the cold bite of the morning air she had her pant legs rolled up and her feet kicking in the water. She looked young and carefree— something he hadn't been in a long time.

A twig snapped beneath his foot as he closed the distance and she startled, twisting his way with her hand to her chest. "Wyatt, you scared me."

"You shouldn't be wandering through the woods alone in the dark."

"I know this property as well as I know my own skin."

Becoming familiar with Hannah's skin was not a path he

needed to travel. "It's a rough trail. If you had slipped on the wet rocks, no one would have known where to look for you."

She shrugged. "I needed a minute to clear my head."

"You could do that in the warmth and safety of your cottage."

She stared at the pinkish-orange glow emerging above the pine trees lining the sheer rock wall at the far bank of the lake and tinting the water with the same sherbet hues.

"This is…tradition. My mom and I used to come here every time we lost an animal. She always said this place reminded her that the end of anything was always the beginning of something else."

"A philosophy that makes loss a little easier to swallow, but it's not always true."

"Says you. Mom was a fierce competitor, but she had another side that only Dad and I were allowed to see. She was a pushover for any injured or orphaned critter. She rescued cats, dogs, birds, rabbits, squirrels…just about any living thing."

Hannah swirled her feet, sending fresh ripples across the surface and drawing his attention to her sexy red toenail polish. "This was the place where we set the wild ones free or said goodbye to those that didn't make it. I've kept up her practice of coming here to say goodbye to stock and students."

"Stock and *students?*"

"FYC's clients often have health issues. A few have passed away while still enrolled." Her drawn face said more than words.

"And you mourn them all."

"Of course."

He couldn't fathom lining up for dose after dose of pain. He'd learned the hard way from his father, his mother and a parade of lovers that relationships always ended. He'd found it easier to keep his emotional distance.

Hannah's connection to this land was another factor working against him. That made finding a solution to his problem more complicated. "You could save yourself a lot of heartache if you didn't get attached."

She flashed him a look of disbelief.

"I couldn't do it any other way. If I give my time to something, usually a little piece of my heart goes along for the ride. Every life, whether human or animal, teaches us something and we're richer for having experienced it. Like the cliché says, I'd rather love and lose than never feel anything."

"Do you honestly believe that nonsense?"

She shook her head. "That sounds cold and unfeeling, Wyatt, and we both know you're neither. If you were, you wouldn't go to so much trouble for Sam and you wouldn't have helped me last night. Nor would you have followed me down here to make sure I was safe."

He stiffened at the accusation. He was no damned bleeding heart. "You're mistaken. We both know I'm a bottom-line bastard."

She winced. "You heard that, huh? I'm sorry."

"Did you mean it?"

She shifted her bottom on the dock, tucking her hands beneath her thighs. "I did at the time."

"Then don't apologize. First impressions are usually the correct ones." A fact he needed to remember. "Don't try to paint me as some kind of hero, Hannah. The only reason I bought Sutherland Farm for Sam was because my mother screwed him royally when she divorced him. He was forced to sell his thoroughbred farm to pay off her part of the divorce settlement. I owe him."

"Your mom sounds lovely," Hannah replied sarcastically. "I suppose I'll get to meet her when she comes to visit."

"She won't visit unless she runs out of money or men." Why in the hell had he volunteered that information? Hannah had no need to know his personal business.

She checked her watch. "I'm sure you have a busy day ahead. Don't let me keep you."

"I'll follow you out."

"Afraid you can't find your way?"

Her sassy comeback caught him off guard. He was beginning to like her quick tongue. "I'm not leaving you here alone."

"Then you'd better pull up a chair." She picked up her coffee mug and sipped, ignoring him. "I'm here to watch the sunrise."

She was calling his bluff. He decided to take her up on it, and since there were no chairs, he'd have to join her. He had a fleeting thought as he kicked off his shoes and tugged off his socks that his time could be more valuably spent going over the new Triple Crown ad campaign. Even if he couldn't be in the office, he needed to get some work done.

He sat beside her and the cold water enclosed his feet. He whistled in a sharp breath.

"Keep your feet moving and it won't be so cold."

A fish splashed along the bank. Birds chirped all around him. A bat skimmed along the water's surface. He couldn't remember the last time he'd done anything so laid-back and… wasteful as kicking his feet in a pond. But he couldn't work up any regret. The peacefulness of the setting enveloped him, easing the ache from his shoulders.

The sun crested the trees, illuminating Hannah's face, the flush on her cheeks and the dampness of her lips. Hunger rekindled in his gut—hunger he wasn't sure he had the reserves to deny.

As if she sensed his acceptance of the inevitable, she turned her head. Their eyes met and her feet stilled. Awareness crackled in the air between them, parting her lips, widening her pupils and lifting the fine hairs on his body like the static charge of atmospheric electricity before a lightning strike. If he had any sense, he'd leave before he did something he'd regret.

He didn't get involved with employees and he'd sworn off silver-spoon women. And yet he didn't move. The longer he remained stationary, staring into those smoky blue eyes, the stronger the magnetic pull between them tugged.

"Hannah, if you don't get out of here now, I'm going to kiss you," he threatened in a Hail Mary effort.

Her lashes fluttered. She bit her lip. Then the wariness faded from her expression, replaced by resignation.

"You can't scare me off, Wyatt. Not from my home. Not from my horses. Not from you. I'm made of sterner stuff than that."

Nine

You're going to regret this.

But Hannah knew she'd regret it more if she didn't kiss Wyatt. The man had something—something that lit her up like a string of Christmas lights—and it was her duty as a scientist who studied winning genetic combinations to figure out what made the him-her connection so much more stimulating than anything she'd experienced before.

Once she figured out that secret, she'd be able to insulate herself against it…whatever *it* was.

So when Wyatt cupped her cheek in his big, warm hand to pull her closer, she leaned across the gap and met him halfway. His mouth collided with hers, hot, hard and hungry. He took control from the get-go. His tongue penetrated her lips and tangled with hers, gliding, stroking, unraveling her reservations.

She knew she was in over her head immediately and debated breaking away, because no matter how she dissected it, until a few short hours ago, she hadn't even liked Wyatt.

And one day did not a relationship make. But she couldn't pry her lips from his.

Last night she'd discovered a caring side of him—one the hard-edged tycoon fought hard to hide from the world. And today he'd come looking for her because he feared for her safety. She found Wyatt's softer side extremely attractive.

His fingers wove through her hair and curled around her nape. He sucked her bottom lip between his, lightly grazing the tender flesh with his teeth. Her senses overloaded and her head spun. Any objective analytical ability she might have possessed dove right off the dock.

How could she figure out how he did whatever he did when she could barely think? Barely breathe. In a last-ditch effort to recapture her diminishing reasoning skills she planted a hand on his chest, but the wild bump of his heart beneath her palm only exacerbated the irregular rhythm of hers.

His fingertips glided from her cheek to her neck, dusting over her sensitive nerve endings in a featherlight caress that sent ripples of pleasure across her skin like a rock skimming the lake's surface. She shivered as the sensation skipped to the pit of her stomach.

He caressed her shoulder then her upper arm, trailing his thumb along the inside of her bicep and wreaking havoc with her concentration. She tried to focus on his technique. What made his approach so much more effective? Was it the gentle tug of his lips? The inflaming slide of his tongue? The unique taste of him? The texture of his hair between her fingers? Pheromones? His…um… Mmm.

Dizzying desire made it impossible to keep a clear head. Then his arm banded around her, urging her closer. His thigh seared hers, and all she could do was revel in the soft, firmness of his lips and the strength of his arms.

She'd never been the sexually aggressive type, but the craziest urge to straddle his lap and mash herself against him from zipper to collar blindsided her. She needed to get closer. Much closer.

Just one more minute and you'll have this crazy connectivity all figured out.

She tilted her head and met him kiss for kiss, stroke for stroke and sip for sip. The muscles of his shoulders bunched and flexed beneath her palms as he smoothed the curve of her waist, rhythmically and hypnotically stroking up and down between her hip and rib cage. She mirrored the movement, feeling the leashed power beneath his clothing.

Then he covered her breast, accurately finding and buffing her nipple through her shirt and bra, and everything inside her sizzled like a hot branding iron hitting cold water. Desire curled through her like wisps of steam. It's a wonder the water lapping at her ankles didn't boil. She moaned approval into his mouth.

He broke the kiss, sucked a sharp breath and rested his cheek against hers. The mild abrasion of his morning beard rasped erotically against her skin.

"This is not smart." The movement of his lips and the whisper of his breath against her ear made her shiver.

She searched for the willpower to pull away. Searched… and didn't find it. "No. It's not."

He grasped her shoulders and held her at bay for a moment. The hunger in his eyes incinerated her. Then with a muttered curse, he yanked her in for another reservation-wrecking kiss. When he lifted his head again, she dug her nails into his thick biceps and whimpered in disappointment.

"I want you."

The gravelly words vibrated through her.

This would be the right time to come to your senses, Hannah.

Who was she kidding? Even if he hadn't anchored her with his firm grip, she was honest enough to admit she'd already lost the battle. She wanted this. *Needed* this. After last night she needed to feel alive, needed to feel sexy and desirable and not like a failure. And Wyatt, for whatever reason, seemed to be the only man up to the task. But…

Sex with him was wrong on so many levels. She gulped air, hoping to inhale a little sanity, then tilted her head back, taking in his passion-darkened eyes, *ravenous* eyes that fanned the flames of her own hunger. "I want you, too, but I don't have protection."

"I do."

Her tummy fluttered. So much for reason, because there was no way she'd say no. "The boathouse, then."

He shot a glance over his shoulder at the structure, then rose with that athletic grace of his and offered his hand. When Hannah curled her fingers around his a sense of rightness and purpose washed over her.

How could passion this strong be a mistake?

He lifted her to her feet and their chests gently collided, sending a current of sensation from her breasts to her toes, and then he lowered his head and kissed her again, this time raking his hands through her hair and unraveling her loose braid, then down her back to grip her bottom and press her hips against his. The thick column of his erection burned her. She shifted restlessly and blood pulsed to the contact site.

Hannah broke the embrace to gasp for air and led him toward her sanctuary. Their bare feet made no sound on the wooden dock, or maybe she simply couldn't hear their steps over her thundering heart. She opened the French doors and warmth enfolded her. Solar panels on the roof kept the small space balmy year-round. She entered the room, trying to see it from a newcomer's eyes.

Her father had left all this furniture behind in the girly summer house that her mother had decorated in whites and pastels. Twin daybeds draped with colorful quilts and lacy pillows flanked the tile-floored room with a white iron table between them.

She'd never shared this space with a man—only her mother and Megan. She could almost hear Megan cheering her on.

You go, girl. Get you some of that delicious man.

But Hannah wasn't Megan and sexy trysts had been few

and far between in Hannah's life. She'd always been more comfortable with horses than humans. Second thoughts edged in, slowing her steps.

Wyatt closed the door behind her, then his arms encircled her. His front blanketed her back with heat. He nuzzled her hair aside. Then his warm breath on her neck preceded a hot, openmouthed kiss. His tongue danced over her wildly beating pulse point, pouring fuel on the fire burning deep in her belly. His palms slid under her shirt, scorching a trail across her abdomen. A short fingernail raked along the waistband of her jeans, making her muscles contract involuntarily, then he flattened his hands on her belly.

"Mmm." Her lungs emptied and she wallowed against him. Oh, yes, she wanted this. How could she not?

The combination of his teeth tugging on her earlobe and the ever-widening circles he drew on her torso sent her head spinning like a centrifuge, leaving her limbs weighted and her head light. She let her skull rest on his shoulder as he unfastened the button of her jeans, loosening the fabric, allowing room for a much-needed inhalation.

The rasp of her zipper gliding down vibrated through her body, and need swelled inside her with each pendulum-like sweep of his fingers slowly descending across her skin until he reached the edge of her bikini panties. Anticipation stole her breath. Then he delved beneath the lace band and her lungs filled on a gasp.

He combed through her curls, sliding lower and lower until he found moisture, moisture he used to graze over her center. The intimate stroke struck her with a lightning bolt of desire, and her knees buckled. He caught her around the waist then lifted her arms and looped them around his neck. "Hold on to me."

The position arched her spine, pushing her bottom against his hardened flesh and thrusting her breasts upward in invitation. She lifted her heavy lids and her reflection stared back at her from the large mirror hanging opposite the doors.

Passion flushed her face and parted her lips. She'd never seen herself like this. Wanton. Hungry. Sexy. And surprisingly, it added to the urgency of the moment instead of making her turn away.

Wyatt's gaze met hers. Dark color tinted his cheekbones. He captured her nipple with his left hand, rolling, plucking, flicking. He matched the motion with his right across her most sensitive spot. Arousal bore down on her like an approaching storm. Her skin turned hot, humid, damp. Her lids grew heavier. With each slide across her center he coaxed a deeper response from her, and having him watch her increased her arousal, multiplied the eroticism of the moment tenfold.

His mouth burned her neck, ears and jaw, sucking, nipping, licking, as his fingers teased her pleasure points until she quivered in his arms. Pressure built, straining her muscles, making her quiver. She tried to keep watching him, but then release exploded from her core with such shocking sudden ferocity that her lids slammed shut and her head lolled back. She curled her tingling toes against the tiles as the sublime feeling quaked through her.

When the waves of pleasure relented her body went limp. She hung on Wyatt's supporting arm, waiting for the strength to return to her legs. She'd never ever experienced an orgasm that powerful—and with her clothes still on no less. And yet as amazing as it had been, it wasn't enough. She craved more. She needed to feel the full potency of Wyatt's passion.

She forced her eyes open and found the same hunger reflected in his expression. He shoved her jeans to the floor. Cool air skimmed her thighs as she stepped out of them. Then he whipped her shirt over her head, grasped her hand and turned her around.

The eyes she'd once thought cold burned over her like a welder's torch. His nostrils flared as he took in her lacy bra and panty set. Then he bent and brushed his lips across the swell of her breast, first one, then the other. She caught her breath and let the soft caress undulate over her.

He unfastened her bra and pulled the lace away. Her nipples puckered, shamelessly begging for his attention. A low growl rumbled from him seconds before he swept her into his arms and laid her on the nearest bed. He paused to retrieve the condom from his wallet, then dropped the black packet on the pastel quilt beside her.

He reached for the hem of his sweater, spurring her into action. "Wait. Let me."

She knelt on the bed, grasped the soft cashmere and the T-shirt beneath and pulled both over his head simultaneously. She wanted him naked. The sooner, the better. She tossed his clothing aside and sat back to admire the taut flesh she'd uncovered.

Wyatt was all lean muscle from his broad shoulders and ropy arms to his washboard abs. His pants rode low on his hips, revealing a dark trail of hair from his navel to the leather belt encircling his narrow waist. A thick bulge pushed against the fabric of his trousers, sending a fresh bolt of hunger through her. She rested her hand over it momentarily, savoring his rigid length and his sharply indrawn breath.

Then impatience took over. Her hands shook as she eagerly worked leather from the brass buckle, then tackled the hook and zipper. She looped her fingers beneath the band of his boxers and pants and eased them over his erection. His size sent her pulse skipping faster with anticipation.

She pushed his pants down his thighs. Then, wanting to share the pleasure she'd received, she curled her fingers around him and stroked his hot, hard, satiny heat. His breath turned choppy and a milky drop appeared on the thick head. A shudder of pure, animalistic need racked her.

She bent to taste him, but before she could make contact his fingers plunged into her hair, cradling her skull and lifting her for another voracious kiss. Their hot torsos melded for a heart-stopping moment, then he eased her backward and whisked away her panties before following her down. The wiry hair on his thighs tickled her tender skin in the most erotic way as his knees separated hers and his chest burned her breasts.

She wound her arms around him, dragging her palms over the muscles bunching and flexing in his back. His head snapped back, ending the tangle of tongues and teeth with a hiss. He quickly donned the protection, but instead of driving inside her and filling the void the way she wanted, needed, *craved,* he bent to capture her nipple in his mouth.

White-hot heat enclosed her. He sucked, grazed, tugged, and her womb twisted tighter with each pull. She squirmed beneath him, impatient to ease the building pressure. His hands steadied her, gripping her knees before ever so slowly gliding upward with his thumbs, sweeping an electrifying path closer and closer to where she needed his touch the most. And then he bumped over her center, flicking the swollen flesh back and forth. Raw desire ripped through her, making her gasp.

His lips worked magic on first one breast then the other, pushing her closer and closer to the edge. Her back bowed off the mattress. Her leg muscles locked and trembled as the void inside her yawned wider. He lifted his head, and she whimpered in disappointment, but the press of his arousal between her legs cut short her protest. His thumb circled again and again, holding her gaze with those hot espresso-colored eyes.

"Please, Wyatt."

"Wait for it." His passionate, deep voice rasped over her.

Her lungs filled as she teetered on the verge of climax. Then Wyatt plunged deep inside her, catalyzing an orgasm so intense the first one paled by comparison. Each of his powerful lunges carried her higher. She clung to his shoulders until the last spasm faded and her vision cleared.

Wyatt's hands fisted in the quilt beside her head. Dark swatches of color stained his cheeks. Hannah caressed his chest, savoring his supple, hot skin, his bunched muscles and tiny taut nipples, then his strong arms, back and buttocks.

Unable to satisfy her need to touch him, she skimmed his thighs and lifted her hips to take him deeper. The moment she did she felt it again—the promise of impending release.

Surprised by her over-the-top response, she met him thrust for thrust. Her heart raced. Her skin dampened. Wyatt's pace increased. And then another climax rocked her and she didn't care about anything except the heat pulsing through her. His groan filled her ears, then seconds later he eased down onto her. His flesh, hot and slick, molded hers. His heart slammed so hard she could feel it through her breasts.

Wow. Wow. Wow.

She melted against the mattress, buried her face in his shoulder and gulped for air. They'd come so far from their initial animosity to the most explosive sex of her life. Wyatt definitely wasn't as cold-blooded as he liked to pretend, and a relationship this passionate had to have potential. "That was… amazing."

His body went rigid. He pushed up on his arms, and his arctic eyes chilled her to the bone. "This won't change our business relationship. Don't expect any extra concessions for you or your horses."

Anger geysered up her spine. How dare he accuse her of trading sex for favors when his body was still buried deep inside hers? She'd forgotten what a jerk he could be.

"I didn't have sex with you for my horses." She saw disbelief in his eyes and shoved on his chest. "This was a mistake. We don't even like each other."

She waited for him to contradict her. Instead, his silence spoke volumes. Regret and humiliation swamped her. She pushed harder on his shoulders. He disconnected from her, rolled off the bed and reached for his pants.

She suddenly couldn't bear the thought of being naked in front of him. One whiff of the man, and animal instinct had overridden intellect. She saw it happen with studs all the time, but she'd thought herself smarter. Apparently not.

Cursing herself for letting chemistry make her stupid, she

sprung from the bed and grabbed her panties, stepping into them quickly before snatching up her bra and stabbing her arms into it. She kept her back to him, but it didn't help—not with the mirror reflecting his every move.

His gaze met hers in the glass. "What time do you want Sam and me to help with the foals?"

She blinked in surprise at his change of subject, then fought a cringe as realization sank in. How could she avoid him now without hurting Sam and abandoning her plan to prove FYC's value? She couldn't.

She clutched her shirt to her chest. "Anytime is fine. You're the boss."

His eyes narrowed at the sarcastic bite she hadn't managed to suppress. "Sam and I will take the next feeding. Go home and get some sleep."

His implication couldn't be clearer. "In other words, don't be there."

"That would be best."

"I'll post a schedule outside my office door. After today please work around the other volunteers' times." His scrutiny remained steady, making her muscles tense and her heart rate erratic. How could he go from volcano-hot to North Pole–cold so quickly?

"Don't let me keep you, Wyatt…unless you can't find your way out."

His eyebrows dipped at the challenge, but instead of hurling another barb her way or insisting she go first, he turned on his heel and stalked out of the boathouse. She heard him pause to put on his shoes.

The moment he left the dock, her knees buckled. She fumbled her way onto a chair at the bistro table and dropped her head into her hands. For the first time in her life, she wanted to take a page from her cousin's book and run away from home. But as she'd told Megan repeatedly, running from your problems never solved them.

She had to stay and fight if she ever wanted her life to

get back to normal—or whatever normal was now that a Sutherland didn't own Sutherland Farm.

Life would be so much easier if she could avoid paying for her mistakes, Hannah decided as she entered the barn. But hiding out in her cottage until her pride quit stinging wasn't an option even if Wyatt had ordered her to stay out of his way.

She had to ensure the foals' formula was properly mixed. At this stage, mistakes could be fatal. If all went according to plan, she could prepare the formula and escape before Wyatt and Sam arrived.

Butterflies swarmed in her stomach at the memory of making love with him this morning, and even if she wanted to forget, the fatigue lingering in muscles she didn't use often wouldn't let her. But the intimacy was over. No encores on the books.

And she was okay with that.

Mostly.

She'd survived the messy endings of intimate relationships before, but this one felt different. She'd never reacted as viscerally to any man as she did to Wyatt. Ignoring a connection that powerful wasn't going to be easy. But if life had taught her anything, it was how to say goodbye.

She deliberately kicked the unpleasant thought aside. The foals needed one hundred percent of her attention to pull them through. It had been only a couple of hours since she'd left them, but so much could happen in that short time span at this critical stage. She had to be extra vigilant.

She stepped inside the barn and a voice carried down the aisle. Sam's voice. "Been a long time since I saw foals this small," he said.

Her steps slowed. If Sam was here, so was Wyatt. An hour early. So much for her plan to avoid them. The sawdust on the floor sucked at her feet like quicksand, and her stomach filled with lead-like dread as she approached the stall. Their early appearance also brought up a second sticky issue. She prayed Sam wouldn't let anything slip about their secret rendezvous.

A low chuckle—*Wyatt's*—made her heart beat unevenly.

"Likes to buck, that one," Sam said. "He's going to be a handful."

"If he makes it."

"He'll make it. He's a fighter."

"You can't be sure, Sam. There's no point in getting attached."

"Son, nothing in life is guaranteed. But you can't live life long-distance. You have to get down and dirty and sample everything—even if it might be a bitter brew. Do you know how many failed attempts Triple Crown had before we hit on the right recipe?"

"One hundred forty-seven. You've told me."

"That means one hundred forty-six failures. But the success was worth it. Henry Ford believed failure was an opportunity to begin again with more knowledge. Sometimes you get a gut feeling about whiskey or animals or people and you just have to trust it. My intuition tells me this fella will make it, and so will the filly. She's a mite timid and small, but there's an alertness in her eyes that says she's gonna try to stick around."

Hannah inched closer, positioning herself where she could see into the stall without being seen. Wyatt had shaved away his sexy beard stubble and tamed the hair she'd mussed with her fingers. And though the morning was still cool, only a snug black T-shirt and jeans hugged his supple muscles—muscles she'd mapped with her hands, tasted with her tongue.

Within the smothering confines of her jacket her body steamed from embarrassment and lingering arousal—arousal that would be denied if she had a functioning brain cell remaining in her body. Her attraction to Wyatt made no sense—the explosive sexual chemistry even less so.

Sam briskly rubbed the colt, then turned his attention to the filly. He rambled on about conformation, but Hannah barely registered Sam's words. She couldn't peel her attention from

Wyatt. He looked so different with his shoulders relaxed and the rigid control missing from his expression. He'd brought no trace of the stiff bottom-line bastard into the stall. Instead, he seemed likeable. Approachable.

Like the man who had tempted her instead of repelling her.

The easy camaraderie between the men was something she'd never had with her father who'd been more likely to order and criticize, trying to get her to be the one thing she never could be—her mother. Her father's lack of communication since he'd left the farm and her behind only confirmed the emotional gulf between them.

"Good-looking foals," Sam concluded. The filly latched on to his finger, trying to nurse.

"And hungry," Wyatt responded with a smile in his voice that made Hannah's knees weak. "We need to feed them."

Not wanting to get caught spying, she took a bracing breath, gathered her courage for the initial awkward encounter ahead and stepped into view. Wyatt's head snapped up. His shoulders went rigid, and his dark eyes speared her.

Every cell inside her jumped like a spooked herd. "Good morning, Wyatt, Sam."

She gave herself a mental pat on the back for keeping her voice level when her nerves and knees quivered like gelatin. Wyatt didn't need to know that her palms were damp or that her mouth watered from the memory of his passionate kisses. Nor did he need to know that despite the asinine way he'd acted after their encounter, her body still lit up like a Fourth of July salute for his.

Wyatt scowled. "I told you to sleep in."

"Some of us have to work for a living. Besides, I didn't show you how to prepare the formula last night."

"I can read the directions on the container."

"I'm adding additional nutrients since they're underweight."

If what had happened between them haunted him the way it did her, then his cool eyes and tone didn't reveal it. Didn't he remember each kiss, each touch, the feel of their bodies coming together? Or was she just another woman in a long line of them? That possibility bothered her more than it should.

But why? Was she actually developing feelings for a guy who slept with her then shoved her away? Surely she had better sense?

Then his gaze slowly raked over her. He looked at her differently now—in a way that said he'd seen her naked, had his mouth on her breasts and his body deep inside hers. The respective intimate parts awakened in response, and when his eyes lifted to hers again it was all she could do to avoid hyperventilating.

Apparently she wasn't smart enough not to have some lingering connection to him.

"Beautiful babies, Hannah. Sorry you lost the mare."

Sam's comment provided a much-needed and sobering distraction. She met his gaze only briefly, hoping he wouldn't let anything about their secret slip. "Me, too, Sam."

The click of the latch as she opened it sounded as loud as a rifle report, and for some silly reason her legs quivered as if she'd run a marathon as she joined them in the stall. The square seemed as cramped and stuffy as a closet with the three of them inside.

Focus. "I need to do a quick exam before we feed them."

"We'll step out," Wyatt said coolly.

"Need any help?" Sam said simultaneously, his need to feel useful impossible to miss.

"Thank you, Sam. You could hold their heads while I take their temperatures. If they have any fever, I'll need to start antibiotics."

"Will do. Wyatt will block their haunches to keep 'em from moving away."

Wyatt's reluctance to be anywhere near her couldn't be more obvious, but he moved into place. She quickly took each foal's temperature and did a cursory exam with the weight of his dark, watchful, judgmental gaze on her. Finishing was a relief and not only because neither foal had a fever.

"I'll get the formula."

"Show me how to mix it," Wyatt ordered.

"Y'all go ahead." Sam waved them on. "I'll stay with these two. Nothing like a young'un to put some life in an old body."

Wyatt hesitated, clearly debating Sam's safety. Needing to get away from him, Hannah hustled toward the prep room. He followed. The uncomfortable silence between them as she mixed the powder into warm water made her edgy, but she couldn't think of anything to say to break the tension.

When she set the spoon aside Wyatt passed her a bottle and the funnel. Their fingers brushed, sending a jolt of electricity through her that suctioned the breath from her lungs.

She scrambled for a distraction. "You said your mother did Sam dirty when they divorced. But that doesn't explain why you're taking care of him."

He positioned the funnel and held the bottle for her to fill. Was he ignoring her or choosing his words?

"I owe him," he said a full minute later.

"Because…?"

Another long silence filled the air. "He treated me like a son, paid for my education and gave me a job at Triple Crown Distillery when I graduated. Sure, he made me start at the bottom, but he mentored me. And then I stole the company from him."

Shock rippled through her, chased by disgust. Wyatt really was a heartless bastard.

Wait a minute. "If that were true, then Sam wouldn't like and trust you."

Wyatt's eyes narrowed. "What makes you think he does?"

"You're very comfortable together."

"He could be senile."

"He's forgetful sometimes but not senile. If you took the business from him you must have had a good reason—one he understands and accepts."

Wyatt's eyes narrowed with suspicion. "That's a big assumption for someone who's only met him once before."

Oops. "I have a lot of experience working with Alzheimer's patients, and assessing their abilities is crucial to their progress." True, but of course, not the whole truth. "What happened with Sam to make you seize control of the company? And before you tell me it's none of my business, you made it my concern when you brought Sam in to take care of my animals."

"At first he misplaced things. His reading glasses, his favorite pen, his car. Then he had trouble remembering names, meeting times and verbal agreements with distributors. As second-in-command I covered for him until the day he got lost on the way home from work and ended up calling for help when he ran out of gas two states away. He'd become so unreliable that I forced him into retirement and took over as CEO."

He capped the bottles. "Sam lived for two things—his horse farm and Triple Crown Distillery. My mother took the first. I took the second. The least I can do is assume responsibility for his care."

"Doesn't Sam have any other family who could help?"

"No. He and his first wife never had children."

"You have alternatives to letting him live with you."

Anger flared in his eyes. "He deserves better than to be shoved in a facility and ignored."

"I wasn't suggesting you do that."

"Others have."

"Tell me, Wyatt, what would have happened to Triple Crown if you hadn't taken control of the company?"

"That's irrelevant. I didn't allow that to happen."

But it was relevant. It proved Wyatt was capable of seeing beyond the bottom line to the people involved. "If you were the heartless bastard I initially believed you to be, you would have institutionalized Sam and walked away without a second thought."

"Is that what you'd do?"

"No. I'd take care of him as long as I could. And I'd keep

his dream alive the same way I'm keeping my mother's alive by continuing to rescue horses."

Their gazes held in a connection that wasn't in the least bit sexual but was satisfying nonetheless. It went deeper and filled Hannah with the hope that they could work through their awkward situation. Then he blinked, and the distrustful expression she'd come to associate with him returned.

"My mother left Sam the moment he was diagnosed. She said she wasn't wasting her life playing nursemaid to a man who was regressing to childhood. My last girlfriend ended our three-year relationship when I told her I'd be assuming responsibility for Sam. She didn't want to be saddled with his care, either."

Hannah wanted to hug him more than anything at that moment. And she knew the gesture wouldn't be welcome. "Not every woman bails when the going gets tough."

"It's not just women, Hannah, it's human nature to look out for number one. *Love* only lasts as long as it's convenient. When it no longer serves a purpose or becomes a burden, love and the people involved in it are discarded like three-day-old fish. That's why there will never be another woman in my life other than the temporary kind. If you can handle that, fine. But don't try to plant a white picket fence around me."

She flinched. And then it was as if a light bulb went off in her brain. Wyatt had a lot in common with her rescue horses. He snarled and bit because he'd been hurt before. If he pushed her away with his verbal attacks, it was only because he was afraid to trust, afraid to love. Afraid to be let down. Again.

But if anyone needed his trust restored in people, it was Wyatt. With a little TLC, he could become a decent human being.

But was she woman enough for the task? Or was this rescue beyond even her capabilities?

There was only one way to find out. She'd have to save Wyatt from himself, and doing so would be her biggest—her riskiest—rescue challenge to date.

Ten

Summonses to the house were nothing new, but today the butterflies in Hannah's stomach multiplied with each step. Given the explosive chemistry between her and Wyatt, the course she'd chosen was a risky one strewn with emotional pitfalls.

Rather than face Nellie, who could read her like a book, Hannah crossed the patio to Wyatt's office. She spotted him through the French doors sitting behind his desk, his attention focused on his laptop computer. Then he looked up and the impact of his gaze hit her, scattering the butterflies.

He looked every inch the successful millionaire in his white silk dress shirt with the neck unbuttoned and the sleeves rolled up to reveal his muscular forearms and his platinum Breitling watch. She struggled to fill her lungs without looking like a gaping guppy.

He closed the computer, rose and crossed the room to open the door. "It's about time you got here."

Textbook case of growling to warn her to keep her distance.

But she didn't scare so easily. "I was working with the studs. That's not something I can interrupt without throwing off everyone's schedule."

"Come in." He stalked away, leaving Hannah to follow.

She studied his broad back and the black trousers outlining his firm buttocks—buttocks she'd dug her nails into when she'd pulled him deeper into her body. Her heart banged faster and her mouth watered.

Wyatt stabbed a finger at the visitor chair, then sat behind his wide desk and rocked back in his seat. His gaze rolled over her in that knee-weakening way of his.

She sat. "Why the urgency?"

"Your visitor from Dubai called Nellie and informed her he'd be arriving in two days. When I told her I'd be out of town and asked that the sales staff handle him, she insisted I talk to you."

"Didn't she explain that Mr. Shakkar is too important to pawn off on the sales staff?"

"When I bought the farm I was assured the staff could handle day-to-day operations. Why not this?"

"Mr. Shakkar is a long-term customer who has spent millions on Sutherland horses in the past, and he's likely to buy more on this trip. He's very influential both stateside and on the European circuit, and he's sent a lot of business our way. My father always—"

"I'm not your father."

"I know that." Boy, did she ever. "But as I was saying, my father always gave repeat customers the VIP treatment. It encourages them to be loyal to us.

"Don't worry about it. I'll take care of Rashed. He's been interested in opening up a therapeutic riding clinic for a while. I'll walk him through FYC's practices, then cook dinner for him at my place afterward."

Wyatt's expression turned thundercloud dark. "I've experienced one of your business dinners. I wouldn't want him to get the wrong impression. Unless, of course, that is your plan."

She stiffened at the accusation, then forced her fingers to relax. *He's only snarling as a defense mechanism because he's afraid to trust.* She couldn't blame him. The attraction between them was scarily powerful.

"Just because you misunderstood my intentions doesn't mean he will."

He shot to his feet and paced to the window, hands on hips, spine stiff. "You take care of the client during the day. I'll get back in time for dinner *here.* You'll act as my hostess for the evening as Nellie tells me you did for your father. But business is as far as it goes, Hannah."

The harder he fought, the sweeter the success of winning him over would be. She bit the inside of her lip to stop an anticipatory smile. For now, she had to work on getting him to lower the drawbridge he kept closed tightly around the fortress of his heart. Only then could he heal.

"You don't need to warn me off again, Wyatt. You've done an excellent job of that already. I'm well aware you regret our…encounter. I'll talk to Nellie about the menu on my way out."

"I'll handle it. Sutherland Farm is now a Triple Crown property. From now on we do things my way."

Where in the hell was Hannah?

Wyatt checked his watch as the limo he'd hired to pick up their guest approached the house. As his hostess, she should have been beside him to greet Shakkar. But she'd failed to make an appearance, and she wasn't responding to his text messages or calls. He'd managed to make it back from Chicago on time, but she hadn't made it a half mile up the driveway punctually.

Did she believe sex with him gave her permission to be irresponsible? If so, she'd learn differently.

Triple Crown ran a first-class operation and international

visitors were common. He knew his way around entertaining, but he'd been counting on Hannah's familiarity with the guest and horse lingo to facilitate the evening. He'd obviously misplaced his trust, which only reinforced his belief that women used sex to bend the rules to suit them.

Masking his irritation, he descended the stairs to meet the limo at the end of the sidewalk. The rear door opened before he could reach it. Instead of a suit-clad middle-aged man emerging, a drop-dead sexy black do-me stiletto attached to a shapely feminine limb emerged from the dim interior. Even while he appreciated the sight, Wyatt mentally adjusted to the change in head count. Shakkar hadn't mentioned bringing a guest, but Nellie could make it work. Nellie could make anything work—as he'd discovered through her calm handling of several of Sam's crises.

Wyatt forced his gaze upward over the shiny black fabric outlining curvy hips, a narrow waist and sweet breasts, then he encountered Hannah's sexy, smoky eyes. Surprise stopped him in his tracks.

She looked beautiful with her ruby red lips and short, form-fitting strapless dress. Lust hit him like a bullet train. Her gaze ran over him in a slow visual caress and her pupils expanded. Reciprocal embers of desire ignited in his groin, despite his decision to avoid any future entanglements with her.

She turned her attention to someone in the car behind her, snapping the connection. Wyatt attributed the oddly deflated sensation sweeping him to relief that she hadn't stood him up but had been seeing to their guest.

While she was distracted, he took in the rest of her. She'd pinned up her dark hair, leaving her neck and shoulders bare. Kissably bare. Silver earrings dangled from her lobes, dancing against her neck with each movement. His mouth watered for a taste of her pale nape. He crushed the thought, but acknowledged the surplus of creamy skin on display would be a distraction tonight and a test of his control. Digging deep for composure, he took a slow, measured breath and released it.

A man with olive skin and black hair graying at the temples exited the car. The older guy eyed Hannah with a lap-her-up appreciation that set Wyatt's teeth on edge.

Hannah said something in a language Wyatt couldn't identify, but the familiarity and warmth in her tone scalded him like acid. Their guest caught her hand and carried it to his smiling lips. "Hannah, you are a true blessing. A feast for the eyes as well as the soul."

Wyatt's molars gnashed at the effusive flattery. "Good evening."

Hannah's bright smile transformed into a tense stretching of her lips as the duo faced him on the sidewalk. "Rashed, I'd like you to meet Wyatt Jacobs, Sutherland Farm's new owner. Wyatt, Rashed Shakkar."

Tamping down his instant hostility, Wyatt shook hands. "Welcome. I trust Hannah gave you a satisfactory tour this afternoon?"

One that didn't include a visit to her cottage, her bed or the boathouse. The words burned like a lit fuse through Wyatt's brain.

"Hannah is a wonderful hostess. Her knowledge of horses is outshone only by her beauty."

A ruby the exact shade of Hannah's lips twinkled on a thin chain between her breasts drawing Wyatt's gaze like a magnet. With substantial effort, he forced his attention back to his guest. "Come in. Nellie tells me she's prepared your favorites."

"Ah. Nellie. Another Sutherland treasure. Her cooking is always one of the highlights of my visit. She is as much a magician in the kitchen as Hannah is with her horses."

Wyatt tamped his irritation and led his guest inside. It was going to be a long night if he had to listen to this bombast all evening.

Ninety-two agonizing minutes later, Wyatt decided he had

to end this evening. His jaw ached from clenching his teeth. He ordered his taut muscles to relax as Nellie cleared the dessert plates.

Hannah had charmed their guest throughout the meal, playing Shakkar like a Stradivarius, drawing him into conversation and making him laugh at her stories. Wyatt's custom-tailored dinner jacket chaffed like a straitjacket, his tie squeezed like a noose, and the desire to get rid of Shakkar was quickly becoming a compulsion.

Shakkar laid his napkin beside his plate. "Wyatt, do you realize how fortunate you are that Hannah stayed on after her father's retirement? I assure you, I am not the only one who would like to lure her away."

And not only for her horse-breeding skills, Wyatt concluded. The man wanted Hannah in his bed.

"I'm well aware of Hannah's value as an employee."

And as a lover.

Wyatt set his brandy snifter aside. Perhaps he'd been too hasty in dismissing a relationship with Hannah. They had a sexual connection like no other he'd experienced. She was intelligent, worked hard and had an undeniable loyalty to the farm. She'd be a dedicated custodian of the property and would allow him to focus on Triple Crown as long as he controlled her expenditures on her rescued animals. And she treated Sam well. In fact, she might be more knowledgeable about Sam's condition than Wyatt was.

The most important selling factor of a relationship with her was that when he decided to sell, she'd insist on staying behind. There would be no emotional goodbyes or ugly scenes. She'd be nothing more than a chapter in his life—a short, passionate one—with a preset ending.

Establishing Hannah as his mistress could prove quite advantageous for each of them. He could pacify her love for material things with the gifts he could bestow upon her, and with her beauty and poise she'd be an asset to his business and an excellent hostess, not to mention sharing his bed when he came home to visit Sam. He could even use her Grand Prix connections to ink a sponsorship deal and tap into a new market.

Decision made, Wyatt pushed away from the table and stepped behind Hannah's chair to pull it back. As soon as he dispatched their guest he'd make his proposition. With all she stood to gain, how could she refuse?

Shakkar covered Hannah's hand on the table before she could rise. "Hannah, thank you for devoting your day to me, and thank you, Wyatt, for allowing her to entertain me. I regret I cannot stay longer. Hannah, my dear, before I return to my hotel I have a small gift for your horse rescue operation."

Shakkar reached into his jacket pocket and laid a check on the table. Hannah quickly covered the paper, but not before Wyatt saw the amount. Twenty-five thousand dollars.

Warning sirens screeched in his head. Had Hannah been charming the old goat to get money out of him? Would Shakkar expect favors in return for his gift? *Sexual* favors.

Wyatt's mother had made a career out of charming her "gentlemen friends" into supporting her after she'd dumped Sam. Was Hannah formed from the same mold as his mother? He'd begun to believe otherwise, but now... Hannah's flushed cheeks and sweet smile knotted the muscles along Wyatt's spine.

"Rashed, you're very generous. Thank you. And as I promised this morning, I'll keep an eye out for suitable horses for your rehabilitation program."

"You could sell him some of yours," Wyatt said to interrupt their little mutual admiration party.

Hannah stiffened, then she slowly rose and turned toward him. "I don't have qualified horses to spare at the moment."

Shakkar stood. "Just as well. Now I have a reason to keep in touch. You have my direct line should you need to contact me for any reason."

Hannah beamed and nodded. "I'll be in touch."

"Now, regretfully, I must take my leave. I would like to

stay longer, but I have monopolized your time and prevented you from breeding your future champions. I look forward to the delivery of mine. You will notify me close enough to the date for me to make arrangements for an extended stay?"

"I'll let you know. For now, pencil in late January."

By then, Wyatt intended to have her firmly entrenched as his mistress. And he would not share.

Rashed linked his arm through Hannah's, ignoring and irritating Wyatt. The duo walked through the foyer and onto the columned front porch. Humid night air clogged Wyatt's lungs and clung to his skin, making his collar feel tight and abrasive. Hannah started to descend the stairs. Wyatt grabbed her free hand and anchored her by his side where his hostess—*his woman*—should be.

Shakkar paused. His eyes dropped to Wyatt and Hannah's linked hands, then rose to Wyatt's face. His wizened expression said the old guy knew how much his attention to Hannah had annoyed his host.

"Mr. Shakkar, I hope you have an uneventful flight home," Wyatt spoke with what he hoped sounded like genuine courtesy.

Shakkar dipped his head ever so slightly to acknowledge Wyatt's claim, then released Hannah's hand. "Thank you. I wish you many years of enjoyment from Sutherland Farm, Mr. Jacobs."

Shakkar descended the stairs, then stopped by the limo door the chauffeur had opened. "Hannah, take care until next time, and please give my regards to your father. And remember what I said. If you decide you would like a change of climate, there will always be a position for someone with your considerable talents at my stable. And for Nellie, of course."

The bastard was trying to steal Hannah *and* Nellie right in front of his face. Wyatt's supply of civility vaporized. "Good night."

With a bow, their guest ducked into the car—not a moment

too soon. Wyatt waited until the limo rounded a curve in the driveway and the taillights winked out of sight.

"For what delivery is he planning to return?"

"Rashed made a one-point-eight million dollar deposit on one of Commander's yet-to-be-born foals today. You've given the staff the authority to operate as usual, so you weren't consulted." She tugged her hand from his. "It would have been polite for me to escort him back to his hotel."

"So you could thank him properly for the twenty-five grand?" Damn it. That had sounded like jealousy. And he was not.

Her cheeks reddened. "Does being obnoxious come naturally to you? You do it with such skill."

"You had him eating out of your hand."

The ruby pendant glistened in the porch light as she took an angry breath, drawing his attention to the soft swells of her breasts. Swells he yearned to touch, to taste.

"It's my job as your hostess to be charming, and that's easy to do when someone is as gracious, knowledgeable and entertaining as Rashed."

"Gracious? The man flirted with you throughout the meal. Perhaps because of your dress."

Her eyes rounded. "What's wrong with my dress?"

Besides the fact that Wyatt wanted to peel it from her? "It's provocative."

"Oh, for pity's sake. I—" She shook her head. "Never mind. Good night, Wyatt." She pivoted.

This wasn't going as planned, but Hannah, damn her, had the ability to shatter his composure. He recaptured her hand and pulled her around, knowing even as he did so that detaining her now was a mistake. He was too on edge after watching her work their guest all night. He would do better to make his pitch tomorrow—after he'd calmed down.

"You look inviting, Hannah. I wouldn't want Shakkar to get the wrong idea."

"So you've said. But I never once implied to Rashed that I was available in that way."

"Aren't you?"

She grimaced. "He's almost my father's age. And believe it or not, contrary to my recent actions, I am usually extremely selective about who shares my bed."

Once again, she jerked her hand free. Not liking the out-of-control feeling boiling through him, he let her go.

She took two steps away then faced him again with her hands curled into fists by her sides. "What is your problem, Wyatt? You don't want me so you don't think any other man should?"

He should have known Hannah wouldn't act as expected. Thus far she'd done nothing but surprise him. "I never said I didn't want you, Hannah. In fact, I do want you. Very much. I believe we could come to a mutually beneficial arrangement."

"What kind of arrangement?" she asked suspiciously.

"Our chemistry is too potent to be denied or ignored. Become my mistress and you can keep your job and your home and I'll continue funding FYC. The only difference will be that when I'm here, you'll spend your nights in my bed."

Wyatt's mistress.
Nights in his bed.

Hannah's breath shuddered from her lungs, forced out by her pounding heart. The switch from Wyatt's cool and distant demeanor during dinner to the request for her to become his mistress made her head spin.

Not his *lover,* but his *mistress.* That distinction defined their roles quite explicitly, pulling her in and keeping his distance simultaneously. Like an animal whose trust had been abused.

The air between them crackled with electricity and awareness—the way it had each time their gazes had met across the dinner table tonight. So yes, maybe she'd tried a little harder to entertain Rashed, been a bit more talkative, laughed too much and sipped a bit too much wine all in an effort to hide the effect Wyatt had on her. Her face ached from all the smiling she'd done.

"Wyatt, what do you really want? Do you even know? You claimed you wanted a horse farm, and yet you've shown no interest in running one. Then you said you wanted to help Sam, but your overprotectiveness holds him back. And now you say you want me in your bed, and yet you've insulted me at every opportunity."

"I want you. I want this." He hooked a hand behind her nape as swiftly as a striking snake. His mouth slammed over hers and he took, greedily, aggressively mashing his lips against hers and ravaging her tongue with his. But his hunger only magnified her own.

He tasted of after-dinner coffee, brandy and…Wyatt. Delicious, seductive, sexy Wyatt. Adrenaline blasted through her veins. The man knew how to kiss. But to be his mistress? She couldn't imagine going into an intimate relationship knowing it would be temporary.

With her lips tingling and her body weakened by want, she made a last-ditch attempt to reclaim rational thought by wedging her hands between them and pushing against his chest. "I don't know if I'm mistress material."

Wyatt's gaze burned with hunger. "That's all I can offer, Hannah."

Given the way his trust had been violated in the past, she couldn't blame him for being leery of relationships. But his dedication to Sam proved he had the capacity to bond deep in his wounded wary heart. All she had to do was prove it to him.

Wyatt had so much potential. The invitation to become his mistress was like the door to a perfect opportunity opening a crack. If she could earn his trust and gently break past his barriers, he would be whole again.

With each thump of his heart against her palm, heat pulsed up her arms then settled heavily in her belly. She wanted him, craved him, ached for him, yearned to relive that cataclysmic rush of desire they'd shared. But more than that, she wanted Wyatt to realize that it was okay to trust and care and open his heart to love.

A voice in her head urged her to back away and guard her heart. But what better way to teach him to trust than to open herself to him? It was risky. Very. Very. Risky. But for his sake, for Sutherland Farm's and FYC's sakes, she had to try. She would simply have to make sure to hold a bit of her heart in reserve because the time would come—as it did with every rescue—to let go.

She gulped down her doubts and took a deep breath. "I accept your terms."

His strong arms banded around her, molding her torso to his. Even before their lips met urgent desire drenched her like warm honey. As he lowered his head she rose on tiptoe to meet him and wound her arms around his waist, digging her fingers into his hard muscles. The unleashed passion in his kiss trampled her, filling her with urgency.

There were too many barriers between them. She needed to strip him down—physically, emotionally. She fumbled with the buttons of his shirt until she found hot, supple skin. While their tongues tangled, she splayed her fingers over his pectorals and impatiently shoved fabric out of her way without breaking the kiss that melted her insides. Her fingers bumped over his tiny beaded nipples once, twice.

His groan of approval vibrated through her and her womb spasmed in anticipation, then he tore his mouth away, hissing a breath between his teeth. "I want you in my bed."

"Then take me there."

He grabbed her hand and towed her through the front door. Without turning on the lights he led her up the stairs. She'd traveled this path countless times when she'd lived here so she had no trouble recalling each tread in the darkness.

He led her to the double doors that had once been the entrance to her father's suite. Uncertainties about the wisdom of this choice flickered through her. She'd come across a few animals in her time whose trust could never be regained. What if Wyatt was one of them?

But then he backed her against the door frame and kissed her again. His hands skimmed over her hips, her waist, her breasts, stealing her breath, making her dizzy with desire and vaporizing any reservations she might have had. He cupped her bottom and pulled her hips to his. The thick column of his erection against her tummy made her ache for his possession. She threaded her fingers through the springy hair at his nape, and a shudder racked him.

He swept her into his arms, kicked the door shut and crossed the inky dark room. Not even a sliver of moonlight penetrated the window coverings. She couldn't see anything, but that only magnified her other senses. A trace of his cologne lingered in the air mixed with that certain something unique to Wyatt. His breaths teased the hair at her temples, tickling her in the most erotic way.

He released her legs, easing her feet to the floor in a slow, seductive slide of her body against his. Her feet sank into deep carpet. His fingertip traced the ruffled edge of her bodice, then dipped into her cleavage. He touched her pendant, circled it, flicked it, rolled it between his fingers.

"This has been driving me crazy all night. I wanted to taste you here."

The sexual nuance in his voice rumbled over her skin like a sandpaper caress. Her nipples puckered as he bent to brush his lips across the spot his fingertip had marked.

He reached for her zipper. Then, in a frantic tangle of arms and legs, they undressed each other. She splayed her hands on his chest, mapping his muscles with her fingertips. She traced his collarbone, his broad shoulders, the veins cording his big biceps, then stroked down his sternum and circled his nipples. His breath roughened, quickened.

Her fingers bumped over the valleys between his abdominal muscles, then he caught her upper arms and snatched her forward. Bare skin slapped bare skin. Every naked scalding inch of his chest, belly and thighs branded hers. His teeth sank into the side of her neck—not hard enough to hurt, but with enough pressure to make her squeak in surprise and tremble with desire. His tongue swirled a teasing pattern across her shoulder and goose bumps lifted her flesh.

Deft fingers found her nipples, pinching and rolling with the perfect amount of pressure to make her weak in the knees. His ability to know exactly when and how and where to touch her to drive her wild couldn't be sheer luck or just skill. It had to be more—like the rare magical winning combination of a champion mare-stud combo. A meant-to-be union.

He tweaked and caressed until she squirmed impatiently. Then his fingers dug into her hair, releasing the clip. Cool strands rained down onto her shoulders, teasing like sensual feathers. She shivered and reached between them to wrap her fingers around his thick erection. Hot. Hard. Satiny. She stroked his length, up, down, up again, savoring the guttural encouragement her caresses elicited. His hands covered hers, stilling her.

"Wyatt, I can't wait to have you inside me," she whispered.

He swept her into his arms again, carried her across the room and lowered her. The cool fabric of his bed against her overheated skin shocked a gasp from her. Before she could recover, he whisked her panties away. A drawer beside her opened, then closed. The mattress dipped, then blazing heat enclosed her nipple. Wyatt sucked her, grazed her with his teeth, laved her with his tongue.

The sensations building inside her were so stupendously wonderful she didn't want him to stop. She speared her fingers into his hair and held him close. He transferred his attention to the opposite breast while his fingers outlined her waist, hips, thigh, then ever so slowly scraped along the inside of her knee before heading upward at a snail's pace.

Torn between urging him to hurry and wanting to savor each second and make it last, she tensed in anticipation as he inched near her center. And then the slightly rough pad of his finger moved over her, making her gasp and jump at the slash of desire ripping through her.

He simultaneously teased her with his mouth and his hands, until her muscles contracted and her back arched as she strained for release. She massaged his shoulders, digging her nails into his thick muscles as her climax neared.

"That feels...so good," she managed to say in a broken whisper. He lifted his head. A moan of disappointment spilled from her lips. "Please don't stop."

"One of the things I've noticed about you, Hannah, is that you take your sweet time with everything—until we're in bed. Then you rush."

"I can't help it. You make me—" She bit off the confession. He didn't need to know that she'd never felt anything even remotely as profound as she did with him.

His breath steamed the skin at the base of her breastbone, then traversed down her midline. His tongue dipped into her navel, then cruised lower. He palmed her legs apart. Then his hot tongue flicked over her. She jerked and cried out at the almost unbearable intensity of the pleasure assailing her. And then he stopped.

She fisted her hands in the sheets in frustration.

"I make you what, Hannah?"

"Want. You." *Forever.*

No. No. No. Not forever. Only until he's healed.

"The feeling's mutual." He dipped his head and set a rhythm destined to drive her insane. She focused on that rather than her crazy thoughts, and he made it easy. Each sweep of his tongue jacked up her response. Each sip of her flesh emptied her lungs. Pressure built, like an inflating balloon, then she exploded as orgasmic shock waves rocked her.

The pulsing waves receded and her tension eased, but before she could catch her breath Wyatt began his assault anew, relentlessly pleasuring her. The second orgasm hit harder, faster, before she was ready.

Decimated, weak, spent, she hooked her hands under his arms and tugged. "Wyatt, please, I need you inside me."

"Not as much as I need to be there."

She couldn't see his face in the darkness, but she could feel his heat, hear his raspy breath and the hunger in his voice and that stoked hers. He rose over her then, the thick head of his erection nudged her opening. He paused, but she couldn't wait. She lifted her hips to meet him and used her hands to guide him. He sank deep in one smooth plunge, filling her completely. His groan rolled over her, then he withdrew.

She gripped his hips and pulled him back, relishing the contractions of his buttocks as he returned. She wound her legs around him and locked her ankles behind his back. Only then did she realize she still wore her heels. The knowledge made her feel a little bit naughty, a tad kinky and very, very sexy.

Each thrust rekindled her passion, carrying her along on his journey to yet another climax. And then he rolled over, pulling her on top so that he lay on his back and her legs straddled his hips. She braced her hands on his pectorals.

"Ride me, Hannah," he ordered hoarsely. He covered her breasts, tweaking, teasing, tormenting, as she lifted and sank over him again and again until her thighs burned and her muscles strained for relief. Then his thumb found her spot. The combination of his deep penetration and deft touch, the blackness of the room and the echoes of lovemaking hurtled her over the edge. Spasms of ecstasy racked her.

Even before her body quit quaking, Wyatt's fingers dug into her bottom, holding her close as he plunged harder, deeper and faster. Then he groaned and went still beneath her.

Drained, she melted onto his bellowing chest and rested her ear over his booming heart. She'd never been so perfectly attuned to anyone. And she was very, *very* afraid she'd crossed the point of no return and let herself get too attached.

Eleven

An unfamiliar sound jolted Hannah awake from a dead sleep. She squinted at her clock, but it wasn't there. Her room was dark. Too dark. Power outage?

Then she heard steady breathing beside her and remembered where she was. *Wyatt's bed.* She'd agreed to become his mistress.

A bolus of adrenaline raced through her system, erasing all traces of sleepiness. Doubts assailed her. What did she know about being any man's mistress?

She turned her head. She couldn't see him, but she could hear Wyatt beside her, feel his heat beneath the sheets and smell the heady aroma of their passionate night.

An overwhelming urge to escape beset her. She wasn't ready to face him. Not yet. Not until she understood the rules and boundaries of her new position and charted a way to get past his guard and teach him to trust again.

She eased onto her elbow. The red digital clock on his side of the bed read 5:06. Hannah bit back a groan. Nellie would be up and about, starting coffee and tinkering with whatever recipes she'd chosen for the day. If she caught Hannah slipping out of the house, Hannah would never hear the end of it.

While Nellie might play matchmaker and push Hannah in Wyatt's direction, Nellie was too old-fashioned to accept a sex-only arrangement and Hannah didn't want to disappoint her.

She cautiously felt her way to the edge of the mattress and slid her legs over the side, all the while listening and thankfully not hearing a change in Wyatt's respiratory pattern. The sheet dragged across her bare, hypersensitive skin, stirring a hormonal response that should have been exhausted last night.

Her feet landed on something sharp. *Ouch.* Her shoes. Wyatt had removed them last night—sometime during the second round of Braille sex in the dark.

Her pulse jumped and her skin prickled at the memory of that slower and even more intense last session. She'd been so sated afterward her brain had shut down, and instead of leaving as she'd intended, she didn't have the slightest recollection of what had happened after he'd tucked her head into his shoulder.

Scooping up her shoes with one hand, she inched blindly across the thick carpet toward where she thought Wyatt had dropped her dress. She found her bra first, then the crumpled Shantung silk, and eased each on, wincing at the sound of the zipper tearing through the room. Shoes in hand, she shifted on her feet. Now what?

How was she going to make her escape? The front stairs seemed too exposed. But the back staircase passed directly by Nellie's suite. That left only one option. The hidden staircase between Hannah's old room and her parents' suite led directly to the garage. Surely she could slip out undetected from there?

She sent up a silent thank-you that her mother had been an avid devotee of historic houses and European castles with their secret passages and rooms and had insisted the architect incorporate a hidden staircase in their home.

Hannah crept toward the concealed door, hoping Wyatt hadn't blocked it with furniture. She'd loved playing in the passageway as a child, pretending she was a European princess hiding from the dark knight who'd come to kidnap her and make her his bride.

Did Wyatt know about this exit? Running her hand along the chair rail, she felt for the telltale seam in the wood. When she found it, she pushed and the spring-loaded panel clicked open. She paused, ears straining for any sound from the bed, but Wyatt's breathing remained slow and steady.

Cool, slightly stale air drifted over Hannah's bare skin. She hesitated, yearning to spend a few more moments in his arms, but knowing she must go. Then she slipped inside, gently closed the door behind her and stopped on the landing to get her bearings.

She hadn't used this passage since her senior year in high school when she and Megan had missed curfew. Hannah had been terrified that her father would find out and ground her for the rest of her life.

She was tempted to open the door on the opposite side and visit her old bedroom, but she didn't know which of the four suites Sam and his nurse were using.

Without turning on the light because she didn't want to risk the faint trace around the door to Wyatt's room alerting him of her escape, she carefully descended the stairs, counting down. Twelve, eleven, ten… She'd made it to six when she heard something below her and froze. A footstep. A human footstep.

Heart racing, she gulped and listened and heard another shuffled tread. "Who's there?"

"Hannah? Is that you?" a quiet masculine voice replied.

The familiar tone pulled the cork on her fear. It drained from her like water from a rain barrel. "Sam?"

"Yep."

The overhead light flicked on. She blinked at the sudden brightness. Sam stood at the bottom landing. He wore his usual jeans and a flannel long-sleeved shirt and heavy down coat despite the predicted high temperatures for later in the day.

"What are you doing here, Sam?"

"I live here. What are *you* doing here?" he parroted.

Her cheeks burned. "Going home."

"Sneaking out, you mean. I'm sneaking in."

"Is this how you've been getting out of the house without Carol or Nellie seeing you?"

"Shh. Whisper. Yep. Wyatt can't keep me locked up like a prisoner."

She sighed. "He believes he's protecting you. I'll talk to him again. How have you been? Phoenix and I have missed our workouts with you."

"Phoenix hasn't missed me. I can't leave during the day when Wyatt's here or Carol's hovering, so I've been seeing Phoenix every night."

Uh-oh. "Alone?"

"Yep."

That explained the horse's improved behavior. Hannah and her staff had been amazed by the mare's rapid progress now that her wounds had healed.

"How have you managed to avoid security?"

He shrugged. "I learned the guard's schedule."

A good sign cognitively, but a bad one as far as Sam's safety was concerned. "Sam, you promised not to go to the stables alone."

"I did? Oh. Yeah. Guess I did. But you promised to let me work with Phoenix. So I did."

"I promised to let you work *with me* and only with me."

He eyed her clothing. "You're all dressed up."

"I had dinner with Wyatt and a client last night."

"And you stayed. With Wyatt."

Another blush worked its way from her chest to her hairline. She stalled by descending the last few steps.

"His room and mine are the only ones at the top of this staircase," Sam pointed out.

"Yes. I stayed with Wyatt. I don't mean to be rude, but I need to get home. I have to be at work soon." She laid a hand over Sam's forearm. "Sam, as much as I appreciate what you've done with Phoenix, promise me you won't go to the barn alone anymore. It's incredibly dangerous for you to be there without anyone knowing where you are. And if Wyatt finds out I've encouraged you to work with the horses behind his back, we'll both be in trouble."

Sam tilted his head and put a finger to his lips. "Shh."

The door beside them opened unexpectedly, revealing Nellie with Wyatt right behind her. Hannah's stomach dove to her bare feet. This was not going to be good.

"Land's sake, child, I thought we had talking mice. What are you doing in here?"

"Yes, Hannah. What are you doing?" Wyatt asked, his voice and eyes ice hard and showing no signs of last night's intimacy as he took in the duo huddled in the stairwell. Jeans and a white T-Shirt outlined his lean, muscular form to mouthwatering perfection.

"I didn't want to wake anyone on my way out."

Lame, Hannah. Staying in bed with him would have been less awkward than this.

Wyatt leaned into the stairwell to examine the space, crowding her against the wall. The smell of their lovemaking still clung to his skin, and his nearness made her body flush hot from her scalp to her toes. A delicious beard stubble darkened his scowling face. Fighting the urge to test the roughness of his jaw, she tightened her fingers around her shoes until a heel dug into her palm.

Wyatt's eyes pinned Sam. "Is this how you've been getting past Carol?"

Sam shifted on his feet. "I wouldn't have to slip out if you didn't keep me caged like a rabid dog, son."

"That's for your safety. Remember the penthouse?" Wyatt's attention shifted to her. "In my office. Now."

A lump rose in her throat at the fury in his eyes. "Wyatt—"

"Now, Hannah. Unless you want to be fired before you've had a chance to make excuses for your deception."

Her gasp echoed up the stairwell. How could he threaten to fire her after last night? She couldn't ask, not with Nellie and Sam listening to every word.

Who was the real Wyatt Jacobs? This coldhearted bastard? Or the man who cared for his stepfather and made Hannah's body sing?

The first she could hate. The second she could lov—

No. No!

She couldn't love Wyatt. She didn't know him well enough. Or did she? A sinking sensation provided her answer. She'd fallen for the man he was deep down inside—the one he tried to hide from the world.

Head and heart reeling, she stared at Sam, torn between fighting for him and self-preservation.

"Hannah," Wyatt threatened in that low tone that rumbled over her like thunder.

Sam patted her shoulder. "Go on, child. I'll be fine. Wyatt's more bark than bite."

She hoped Sam was right. She risked a glance at Nellie. Surprisingly, Nellie looked cantankerous rather than disappointed, as if she were more than willing to go to bat for Hannah, thereby risking her own job. Hannah couldn't have that.

She headed for the office and reckoning. The once familiar room now seemed like foreign territory. Enemy territory. How could her life have changed so much in barely over a month? She'd gone from gliding along in a contented rut to life on the edge of disaster and loving a man who might never heal enough to be able to love her in return. If she couldn't find a way to fix this, she could lose her horses, FYC, her job, her home…and her heart.

Wyatt's deliberate footsteps approached and her mouth went dry. He entered the office and slowly, precisely closed the door, his controlled movements revealing his anger more clearly than shouted words.

He stopped inches from her. His eyes weren't cold. They burned with fury. "You knew my concern for Sam's safety and you encouraged him to work with the horses anyway."

Guilty. "He didn't ride."

"Can you be sure of that, Hannah? Were you with him each time he visited the stable? From what I overheard, you weren't."

How long had he been listening? "No. I can't be certain. But he promised and I trusted—"

"You trusted him? Sam's memory is like a sieve, and his reasoning is faulty. How long have you been lying to me and working with him behind my back?"

The anger and betrayal in his eyes stung like disinfectant on a fresh wound. She swallowed, struggling to find words to make him understand. "It was only a few times. But I knew if I could show you the value of horse therapy, you'd realize FYC is an important part of Sutherland Farm."

"You lied to me and you selfishly jeopardized Sam's safety."

She cringed. "Maybe you should tell me about the incident at the penthouse so I'll understand why you're so overprotective of him."

His lips flattened in refusal and seconds ticked past. "The only reason I am explaining something that is clearly none of your business is to make you realize how stupid you've been. Sam took a bar stool from inside my apartment out onto the patio to change a lightbulb in the eaves."

She frowned, not understanding. "And that's a problem why?"

"We were forty stories above the ground. One slip and he'd

have gone over the wall and landed on the concrete below. He was inches from death on a wobbly stool."

Nausea rolled through her. "Did he not realize—?"

"No. That's the point. Sam saw a task that needed doing but not the big picture. Poor judgment, as you should know, is only one symptom of his condition. Usually his errors are as innocuous as dressing inappropriately for the weather or forgetting he's eaten, but other times he makes life-threatening miscalculations like crossing the street without checking for traffic. Some days he's the stepfather I remember. Others he's as careless as a three-year-old and needs a keeper."

She hadn't realized the range of Sam's behavior. As Wyatt had said, she'd been so worried about herself and her horses that she hadn't considered Sam might have issues she'd yet to see.

"I'm sorry. I should have asked for his medical records the way I would for any of FYC's students. But each time I've been with him he's been quite lucid—except for the clothing mix-up."

Wyatt's eyes narrowed. "Were you befriending him in hopes of finding another sugar daddy for your horses?"

Surprised, she blinked. "No. I— Why would I do that?"

"Don't play the innocent, Hannah. I saw the way you worked Shakkar. The man was practically salivating over you. And we both know you've done your research on Triple Crown Distillery. You're too smart not to know Sam's net worth."

"I didn't." But Wyatt's disbelief was clear on his face. "How can you accuse me of being mercenary? Especially after last night."

His hardening expression told her bringing up last night had not been a wise choice. "All women use sex to manipulate men into giving them what they want."

Ouch. She might have underestimated the depth of his emotional damage. "Maybe you've been associating with the wrong women."

He stalked to the French doors. "You lied to me. I can't trust you. And I can't trust Sam. I had planned to keep this place until Sam's no longer cognizant of his surroundings. That's no longer an option."

Shock flowed over her like an iceberg. "Wait a minute! You bought Sutherland Farm and flipped my world upside down with the intention of turning right around and selling the property?"

He pivoted with rigid control. "Sam spends most of his time reminiscing about his farm, and he's most coherent when he discusses horses. I wanted him to be comfortable for however long he has left. But not at an increased risk to his safety."

That he'd spent millions of dollars to make his stepfather comfortable touched her. "Because you love him."

Wyatt recoiled as if she'd slapped him. "No. Because considering what my mother and I cost him, I owe him. It's a debt to repay. Nothing more. Nothing less."

She didn't want to believe he considered Sam a duty, but the coldness in his face and eyes was irrefutable. Clues she'd ignored suddenly formed a picture so clear she couldn't miss it.

"That's why you guaranteed our jobs for a year. It wasn't altruism. It was apathy. You never had any interest in Sutherland Farm at all. You planned to dump it at the end of the year."

"It could have been longer, depending on Sam's condition. But not now."

Her stomach hollowed out and her legs folded. She plopped into a leather chair across from his desk and stabbed her fingers into her hair. This wasn't just about FYC or her world imploding anymore. This was so much bigger.

"You never tried to get to know the staff because you don't give a damn about the farm, its mission or its people. All you care about is the bottom line and making the business as profitable as possible before dumping it on the market once it's served your purpose. That's why you were so determined to shut down FYC and to buy my little piece of land—to make Sutherland Farm a more attractive package for the next buyer."

"There's nothing wrong with cutting waste and improving profitability."

How could he be so clueless? "Not if all you care about is money. But I keep telling you, Wyatt, money isn't the only measure of success. Even if you haven't bothered to attend any of FYC's classes to see how we help dozens of others, you've seen Sam's progress when he works with the horses. Every day his balance, coordination and thought processes are clearer. His plotting to work with the mare at night when he wouldn't get caught is proof of that. My gosh, he even memorized Jeremiah's schedule."

"What good is thinking more clearly if he ends up dead?" The ice in his voice sent shivers up her spine. He had a point.

"And what about us? Was I only a temporary convenience, too? One you'd shed when you sold the farm? Do you have no feelings for me at all?" She wanted the needy words back the moment she heard them. But it was too late.

His unblinking gaze drilled her. "I asked you to be my mistress, not my wife."

She flinched and cursed herself for the telling reflex. "No. Marriage wouldn't be *profitable*. Would it?"

There sometimes came a painful point during a rescue when she had to admit she couldn't save an animal and she had to let it go.

Like she had with Sable.

And now with Wyatt.

She'd been wrong about him. He was one of the few whose trust could never be regained. And in becoming his mistress she wouldn't be earning his trust. She'd only be fooling herself into believing they had a future. Wyatt would never open his heart enough to love anyone.

The pain in her chest pulsed outward. Needing to escape before he discovered how badly the discovery hurt, she forced herself to her feet.

"I have to get to work and earn my keep. I'd hate to be responsible for the slowing of the money train. But you'll have to find yourself another mistress. I'm no longer available."

"Good thing we learn from our mistakes 'cause letting that gal walk out was a doozy," Sam said from the open patio door. The rising sun illuminated the lines in his face and the droop of his once proud shoulders.

"Hannah jeopardized your safety."

"She gave me a purpose for living. Working with that mare reminded me there's something I'm still good at."

"Sam—"

"Wyatt, I know your intentions are good, son, but I'd rather be locked up in an old folks' home where all I can smell is disinfectant and dirty diapers than be incarcerated here where I can see the life I'm missing."

Consternation rooted Wyatt to the rug. "You don't mean that. You love horse farms."

"I love being part of a horse farm, not looking through the windows at one like I'm watching TV. I know I have days when I forget stuff. And sometimes I overlook important details—or so you keep telling me. But being locked up isn't living."

Guilt twisted inside Wyatt like a knife. And if anyone understood the pain of being discarded, Wyatt did. But what else could he do?

"Give it time, Sam. You'll get used to the farm and I'll visit as often as work allows."

"Time is the one thing I don't have. My life is over. Might as well be dead. Told Hannah as much. At least *she* understood."

Alarm kicked through Wyatt. "You told Hannah you'd rather be dead than here?"

"Yep. That's why she let me work with the mare. I'm the one who broke the promise I made her by sneaking out. But I forgot. Or maybe I wanted to forget."

No wonder Hannah had intervened. "She should have come to me with her concerns instead of going behind my back."

How could he trust anyone who would do that?

"Would you have listened?"

Probably not.

"Much as I love you, Wyatt, you can be one stubborn son of a bitch when you set your mind to something. That ambition is good in business, but it doesn't work so well with people."

Wyatt flinched. "I'll make sure you get more time with the foals."

"I want to do more than play with babies. I want to work with horses that try to outsmart me. Like that mare. If I can't do that, then I want to go home."

Sam's passionate words were a jarring reminder of why they were here in the first place. "You can't, Sam. You sold your house before you moved into the penthouse with me. Remember?"

Sam frowned. "I do, now that you mention it. But this ain't my home and it never will be if I can't be with the people I love and enjoy the things I love doing while I still can."

Frustrated, Wyatt watched Sam storm out. He'd done everything he could to make Sam comfortable here. And Sam would calm down as he always did after one of his emotional outbursts and things would be fine.

Hannah, on the other hand, had betrayed him. She had to go.

Hannah stood on the unfamiliar doorstep of her father's town house, wishing her first visit to his new home could be under better circumstances and hoping he'd give her the answer she sought.

Her father, wearing only his bathrobe, opened the door. His eyebrows shot up, then he glanced briefly over his shoulder. "Hannah, this is a surprise."

"We need to talk."

"It's 6:00 a.m."

"This can't wait."

"It's all right, Luthor. Let her in," a recognizable woman's voice said from inside, spurring Hannah's heart into a racing beat.

Hannah gasped. "Is that Dana?"

The door opened wider, revealing the registered nurse who had been volunteering for FYC for almost a year. She also wore a robe and her tangled hair suggested she'd just climbed from bed. Not a pleasant realization.

"Good morning, Hannah. I need to get to work, so give me five minutes, then I'll be gone and you can talk."

Flabbergasted, Hannah's gaze bounced from the forty-something blonde to her father. He had a girlfriend? She couldn't remember him ever dating anyone. "Dad?"

"Come in, Hannah. There's fresh coffee in the kitchen." He turned and headed in that direction. Dana trotted up the stairs.

Hannah entered cautiously, not sure she could handle another shock this morning. She passed a den containing the leather sofas that had once occupied her father's office. In the kitchen he indicated she take a seat at a table that hadn't been in the old house.

He filled a mug and set it in front of her. "What brings you here so early without calling first?"

"I didn't realize I'd be interrupting something."

Her father's cheeks turned ruddy. "I have a life now. One that doesn't revolve around horses."

"You could have told me you were seeing someone."

"I wasn't sure how you'd handle it."

"I won't deny it's a surprise, but Mom's been gone a long time, Dad."

A little of the tension eased from his shoulders.

Dana breezed into the room wearing pink hospital scrubs. She kissed Hannah's father square on the mouth. "Gotta go, love. I'll see you tonight. And Hannah, I'll see you Sunday." Then she was gone.

"Does she live here?"

"No."

"How long have you and Dana been seeing each other?"

"About six months."

"Is she the reason you sold the farm?"

He sighed and sat. "She's not the reason, but Dana was my wake-up call. Life was passing me by while I chased your mother's dream."

"It was your dream, too. And mine."

"It was more your mother's than mine, but I loved her and wanted to support her in any way that made her happy. I lived out her vision long after she was gone, even though my heart wasn't in it. At first I carried on because I didn't know what else to do. I missed her and working with the horses kept her memories close. But it wasn't the same without her."

Her throat tightened. He had never let his grief show before now. "You never told me that."

He shrugged. "Hannah, I don't want you to make the same mistake of forgetting to live *your* life while you're living her dream."

"I'm not."

"You were always so enamored with her diaries, her charts and her books. I should have done something sooner." He cleared his throat and fidgeted for a moment. "The accident wasn't your fault, Hannah."

She'd needed to hear that from him for so long. "If I hadn't been so determined to make that jump—"

"You inherited that persistent streak from her. She was just as determined to see you succeed."

Her chest tightened. "Her death wasn't your fault, either, Dad. I never should have accused you of murdering her when you discontinued life support. I'm sorry."

"You weren't ready to give up hope. Neither was I. Signing that form was the hardest thing I've ever done. But it was the right thing to do."

Tears stung her eyes and burned her throat. "I know that now."

"It doesn't matter how many nags you rescue, Hannah, nothing is going to bring her back. We both have to move on. I don't want you to wake up in twenty years and realize there's a list of things you never got around to doing, like having a life and a family, because you were always nursing your nags."

"They're not nags," she defended automatically, then took a breath. "So you left me to sink or swim." She couldn't keep the hurt from her voice.

"I told you I won't be around to support you forever. You have to learn to stand on your own feet."

"Couldn't you have had your relationship at Sutherland Farm?"

"This is not about my relationship with Dana. It's the all-consuming Grand Prix lifestyle. I'm tired of eating, breathing and sleeping horses. I want more and so should you. Even if that weren't the case, that was your mother's house. She designed every inch of it. I would never dishonor her memory by taking another woman there." He set down his mug. "So what brings you here this morning, Hannah?"

She blinked as reality returned. She and her father had covered more ground this morning than they had in the past nineteen years. But in light of what he'd shared, her reason for coming might not matter to him. But she had to try.

"Wyatt bought the farm you and mom devoted your lives to as a temporary investment. That's why he guaranteed the jobs. Because he has no interest in running the business. He plans to dump the property as soon as it's served its purpose."

Leaning back in his chair, he folded his arms. "What do you want me to do?"

"Buy it back!"

The corners of his mouth dipped and he shook his head. "And then we'd be right back where we started. I'm through with horses. If staying in the business is truly *your* dream, then you'll find a way to make it work."

"But Dad—"

"Believe it or not, Hannah, I'm doing this for your own good." He rose. "I love you too much to help you."

If she couldn't sleep, she might as well work.

Hannah zipped her coat to her chin and stuffed her hands into her pockets to ward off the middle-of-the-night chill as she strode through to darkness toward the barn. The weight of her day weighed heavily on her shoulders.

The confrontation with Wyatt and the dissolution of their relationship had left her feeling empty, confirming she hadn't just been rescuing Wyatt for his own good. She'd been saving him for herself. Not a good thought.

After her visit to her father she'd decided that if Wyatt insisted on selling the farm, he might as well sell it to her, and she'd spent the afternoon on the phone fruitlessly searching for financial backers. But after calling several banks and everyone in her address book, she hadn't found anyone willing to back an inexperienced stable owner in the current financial climate. She couldn't call Rashed because with hindsight she realized Wyatt might be right. Rashed did seem interested in more than a business relationship. And she wasn't going to sell herself to anyone—not even to save Sutherland Farm.

A metallic screech caught her attention. She turned and spotted the gate to the small paddock swinging in the breeze. The *open* gate. Alarm shot through her. Phoenix!

Had the mare escaped? Hannah broke into a run, stopping when she realized the pen was empty. Heart racing, she scanned the shadows between the puddles of light cast by the lampposts, but she didn't see the horse.

Sam. Had he snuck down here even after this morning's fiasco? The sinking feeling in her stomach told her Sam and Phoenix were together. She dug her cell phone out of her pocket and dialed Wyatt.

"Jacobs." Sleep graveled his voice, sending a thrill through her—one she wished she could ignore.

"Is Sam there?"

"Hannah, it's one in the morning."

"Wyatt, the bay mare is missing. Please check to see if Sam is in the house."

He cursed. Then she heard the swish of sheets and pictured them sliding over his skin. "His bed and suite are empty. Damn it. This morning Sam told me he wanted to leave the farm. I didn't take him seriously."

A chill that had nothing to do with the cool night temperatures shuddered over her. "Check the rest of the house. If he's not there, call the sheriff and get him to issue a Silver Alert. I'll get Jeremiah to help me search the grounds."

Maybe Sam had taken Phoenix to the indoor arena to work her. Hannah slid open the heavy door and flipped on the lights, but the cavernous space was empty. No Sam. No Phoenix. No indications they'd been there recently. She sprinted through each building, ending up at FYC's barn, checking to see if Sam had visited the foals. He wasn't with them, either.

A sound made her turn. Her hopes fell when she spotted the security guard. "Jeremiah, have you seen Sam or the new bay rescue mare?"

"No, Miss Hannah. It's been real quiet tonight."

Her heart bumped its way up her throat. "Get into your truck and look for either of them, please. Let me know if you see anything—anything at all—out of the ordinary."

What felt like an aeon later, Hannah's fear turned into full-blown panic when she discovered an empty saddle rack in the tack room. She heard Jeremiah's truck in the driveway and ran outside. Wyatt's Mercedes skidded to a halt right behind him.

"Did you see anything?" she asked the security guard.

"Gate's open to the back pasture," Jeremiah said. "No sign of Sam or the mare as far as my spotlight could see."

The back pasture bordered the river. "There's a saddle missing. I think Sam has taken Phoenix and run away."

Wyatt's face looked pale and drawn in the murky moonlight.

His hair was a rumpled mess. "We'll take a truck and go after him."

"We can't. The terrain is too rough in that pasture, and there's no road." There was only one option, and it terrified her. "I'll saddle up a horse and see if I can find him."

"You haven't ridden since your mother died," Wyatt pointed out. "You don't have the experience. Let the sheriff's team lead the search."

"It'll be hours before they can assemble a team of riders and truck the horses here. It's too cold to wait."

"I'll call the chopper pilot."

"A helicopter might spook the mare. Wyatt, I know this property better than anyone. My mother and I used to ride the trails, and I still hike them. If anyone can find Sam, it'll be me."

Wyatt's expression turned even more determined. "I'll go with you."

"Two inexperienced horsemen won't be better than one."

"You're a liability out there alone in the dark. If something happened, no one would know where to look for you and we'd have two casualties instead of one. I'm going."

The stubborn set of his jaw warned her not to waste more time arguing. "Jeremiah, round up anyone who can help."

She turned to Wyatt. "A couple of the rescue horses are docile and trail safe. We use them with the most inexperienced FYC students. We should be okay."

Hannah hurriedly saddled the horses. Because of her experience with helping FYC's students, preparations went too quickly and yet far too slowly when every minute counted. She handed Wyatt a headlamp. "Put the elasticized band around your helmet."

Dread crawled across her skin like an army of ants as she released the crossties and handed one set of reins to Wyatt.

"Wyatt, you don't have to go with me. You can stay here and talk to the sheriff. Fill them in on Sam's condition and show them the topographical maps."

"To paraphrase you, I can't do anything else. Let's go."

She stuck a foot in the stirrup and swung herself into the saddle. She'd forgotten how dizzyingly high being on horseback felt. Her legs trembled wildly as she placed her feet in the irons and tried to get her bearings. Fortunately the placid gelding didn't seem to mind her agitation. "Ready?"

Wyatt sat in the saddle, his carriage every bit as perfect as she'd once suspected it might be. "Let's go."

She urged her mount out of the brightly lit barn and down the dark driveway toward the open gate. Once they entered the fence and left the lampposts behind, they had only the moonlight and the thin beams from their helmet lights to guide them.

The urge to gallop after Sam thundered through her, but the darkness, the uneven ground and her rusty riding skills kept her at a safer, albeit slower, more frustrating pace. She tried to focus on the basics and could practically hear her mother's voice. *Heels down. Back straight. Hands steady. Eyes ahead. Trust your horse, Hannah.*

"If Sam gets hurt, I hold you responsible." Wyatt's voice low and scalpel-sharp, sliced through her. "If you hadn't encouraged him to work with the mare behind my back in a selfish attempt to weasel funding out of me for your damned nags, he never would have pulled this foolish stunt."

Hannah flinched. The truth of his words stung like the lash of a bullwhip. "I was trying to help him."

"You were trying to help yourself. If we find him—"

"When," she corrected and prayed they would find Sam before it was too late.

"*When* we find him you're fired. I want you and your horses off the premises immediately. Other than cleaning out your desk, I don't want you anywhere on my property."

Hannah gasped, then gulped. Wyatt's decision was nothing less than she deserved. She'd known the risk going in and acted anyway. Nellie had always accused her of having tunnel vision where her horses were concerned.

They rode in tense silence, the cold humid air penetrating Hannah's clothing and chilling her to the bone. She tried not to think of what she'd do, where she'd go or if she could find another job breeding horses in the current economy. She had to focus on finding Sam. She'd worry about her future later.

"Look," Wyatt's voice pulled her out of her misery. "There's a trail through the dew. That's how I tracked you to the boathouse."

The boathouse. That perfect moment seemed like a lifetime ago. With hindsight she acknowledged she'd probably fallen in love with him that morning when the *heartless bottom-line bastard* had helped with the foals, then followed her to make sure she was okay.

She aimed her beam, following the trail, worry taking over. "He's headed toward the river. There's a shallow, rocky crossing upstream from here."

"And then?"

"Highway. I wish I knew how much of a head start he had on us." The idea of Sam riding along the interstate on horseback in the dark— She urged her mount into a trot and clung for dear life until her body relaxed into the motion, finding the horse's rhythm and remembering how to post with it. "I'll call Jeremiah and get him to have the sheriff patrol the highway side."

She slowed long enough to make the call. Wyatt kept pace beside her, monitoring every word. Five minutes later, he pulled his mount to a halt. Hers stopped automatically. "Is that the river I hear?"

"Yes." And she didn't like the sounds of it. The recent rains had created small runoff streams on the steeper slopes, and from the dull roar ahead, Hannah suspected the river would be swollen and flowing faster. But she didn't want to burden Wyatt with that news.

Her mount sensed her tension and took it as a cue to go faster. She rounded a bend. A downed tree blocked the trail ahead. Hannah quickly scanned the area and spotted Phoenix, the saddle on her back empty. Fear closed her throat. She pulled her gelding to a stop. The leafy top of the tree divided a small channel of water flowing fast enough to carve a path on each side of the broad trunk. A water hazard. Like the jump that had killed her mother and her horse.

Nausea rolled through her. She swallowed it. Where was Sam?

Please, please don't let him be lying on the other side of the tree.

From the saddle, Hannah did a cursory check of the horse which looked unharmed, its legs shaped as they should be, as far as her narrow beam could make out. Then she surveyed the dense bamboo forest surrounding the blocked path. The only way Sam could have continued was to go over the obstacle. Had he tried to jump and the mare refused, tossing him over her head? Sam wasn't fit enough to crash-land without injuring himself.

The image of her mother, twisted and unconscious and her horse struggling to rise with a severely fractured leg, flooded Hannah's mind, making her heart pound and her muscles freeze in terror.

"Hannah." Wyatt's tone indicated he'd called her more than once. He rode up beside her, his calf bumping hers.

She blinked away the grisly mental picture, reined in her fear and dismounted. Her legs trembled like leaves in a gale-force wind as she tried to find the courage to approach the tree.

Wyatt joined her. He scanned the scene, his light landing on the mare, and his face paled. "Sam!"

He lunged forward, but Hannah stepped into his path, planting a hand on his chest. "Stay with the horses. I'll let you know if he's there."

"Get out of my way."

"Wyatt, you don't need to see—"

Comprehension dawned on his face. "You stay here. Sam might need my help."

What if Sam was beyond help—as her mother had been? She bit her lip and tasted blood. "You're not going without me."

She jogged through the water beside him. Each step felt like a mile through mud. They leaned across the trunk simultaneously. No Sam. Air rushed from her lungs, making her dizzy with relief. She sagged against the downed trunk. "He's not here. That means he's able to walk."

"Sam," Wyatt shouted again.

Only the gurgle of water answered, then a twig snapped in the distance. Pulse-pounding seconds later, Sam entered their narrow spotlights—walking normally. "You found me. Too bad. I was hoping for a little more adventure."

Hysterical laughter bubbled up Hannah's throat, cut short by Wyatt vaulting the trunk and sprinting toward Sam. He stopped a yard short, clenching and unclenching his hands. Then he grabbed his stepfather in a bear hug. Sam patted Wyatt's back. She could see his lips moving, but couldn't hear his words. Only then did she notice Wyatt's shaking shoulders.

Everything inside Hannah turned to mush, and tears stung her eyes. She'd been right about Wyatt. He wasn't a coldhearted bastard, though he pretended to be one. And he might deny it, but he did love Sam. He just didn't, or couldn't, love her.

And who could blame him after this? She'd inadvertently put Sam's life in danger with her self-absorbed tunnel vision.

Her throat clogged. She had to stop trying to rescue people and horses, because her father was right. No matter how many she saved, she couldn't bring her mother back. And she might get someone else hurt. Or worse.

That left her with only one option. She'd have to sell her cottage to Wyatt and walk away from everyone and everything that mattered to her. Her home. Her history. Her mother's legacy.

Twelve

Too overwrought to sleep, Wyatt sat in his dark office and fought off the lingering remnants of panic.

He'd almost lost Sam. And it would have been his fault. Not Hannah's. *His.* Because he'd pushed his stepfather away when Sam had needed him most.

While listening to Sam reminisce during the horseback ride home an hour ago, Wyatt had been ambushed by memories of the good times they'd shared, and he'd realized he wasn't ready for the past to be the sum total of their relationship. He wanted to bank more memories, and the only thing preventing him from doing so was his misconceived attempt at protecting himself from the pain of eventually losing Sam. He had Hannah to thank for that uncomfortable insight.

Hannah. He'd completely misjudged her. And he owed her an apology.

A hint of pink on the horizon lured him to the French doors. He stepped onto the patio outside his office. The beginning of a new day hovered beyond the distant treetops.

The landscape looked the same and yet totally different because today he saw Sutherland Farm for the first time not as a multimillion-dollar investment he couldn't wait to unload, but through Hannah's eyes.

The rolling green pastures and stone buildings held the history of her family, a tradition of breeding champions, and imbued a sense of belonging and renewal. When he'd purchased the property, he'd robbed Hannah of all that. Despite that, she'd made room for him and Sam in her life, and last night she'd faced her fears for them.

First by climbing on a horse for the first time since her mother's death, and then, even after he'd fired her, she'd tried to save him from the pain of finding Sam's body on the other side of the tree. From her deathly pallor when she'd planted herself in front of him, he guessed she had been remembering and reliving the day she'd lost her mother and horse. But she'd wanted to spare him.

Such generosity confounded him. He always looked out for number one, whereas Hannah tried to save and protect everyone but herself. He'd encountered many women willing to hurt him. But hurt *for* him? None. Until Hannah.

Her actions last night had revealed the depth of her character in ways nothing else could. The woman he'd deemed too good to be true was the real deal, and it shamed him that he'd been so blinded by his prejudices and the superficial glitz that he'd missed the truth even though it had been right in front of his eyes all along.

Hannah's father had showered her with material possessions, but she hadn't become the spoiled, pampered princess Wyatt had assumed her to be because she dealt in a different currency—a more personal, more valuable one. She doled out chunks of her heart like coins to anyone or anything in need despite the emotional cost that inevitably followed.

Her courage humbled him. She invested herself in her

causes while he took the easy way out by paying other people to handle the messy, emotional details of life.

He'd been convinced that having Sam out of sight would equate to having him out of mind. He'd been wrong, and his emotional cowardice had not only robbed Sam of his dignity, it could cost Wyatt his relationship with the man who'd been more of a father to him than his own flesh and blood.

And it could cost him Hannah. It surprised him to discover how much that bothered him. He'd completely blown it with her. He didn't want to let her go. But he didn't deserve her. Or to put it correctly, she deserved better than a man who'd treated her badly and tried to run her off. His only excuse was that the feelings she stirred in him scared the hell out of him.

Life had taught him that emotionally investing in someone led to pain and disappointment. But when things got messy, Hannah rolled up her sleeves and waded in with her heart wide open. She took on cases that others had written off as lost causes even though she knew she could fail.

The least he could do was try to match her courage.

A flash of movement caught his attention. Hannah emerged from the crop of trees surrounding her cottage and leaned against the stone wall facing the barns a quarter mile away.

Firing her had been a mistake. She belonged here far more than he did.

She turned in the opposite direction. He considered calling her back, but with the wind rustling the leaves she might not hear him. Besides, this was a conversation best had somewhere besides the driveway. With the staff due to roll in, there would be too many interruptions.

He descended the steps and followed her. His feet sank deep into the thick emerald lawn and it brought back memories of running barefoot on Sam's farm, of lazy days fishing beside his stepfather. Even though Sam had had a stable and a distillery to run, he'd always made time for Wyatt. It was time for Wyatt to return that favor.

Hannah ducked through the fence and headed down the path to the boathouse. The secluded spot was as good a place as any for his apology. He had to slow his steps when he entered the still shadowy woods and by the time he reached the clearing, Hannah was already on the dock. But this morning she hadn't removed her shoes and she wasn't paddling her feet in the water. She stood staring at the horizon with her shoulders slumped and arms wrapped around her middle.

He knew the exact second she became aware of his approach by the tension invading her body. The platform rocked beneath his feet and the wooden boards creaked as he joined her. "Good morning, Hannah."

"Are you going to have me arrested for trespassing?" Her pallor accentuated the shadows beneath her eyes and the urge to brush the purple smudges with his thumbs almost overwhelmed him.

"No. I'm sorry I lost my temper last night. You're not fired. You're an asset to Sutherland Farm. I don't want you to go."

Her lips parted as if she were going to speak, then she turned back to the water. "How's Sam?"

Typical of the woman he'd discovered her to be, she showed concern for someone else rather than herself. "Sleeping off his exciting night. Why aren't you doing the same?"

"I couldn't sleep." She wrapped her arms tighter around her middle and stared across the water.

"Same here. I hate to think what would have happened if you hadn't helped me find Sam last night. I know it was hard for you. Thank you."

"You're welcome." She still didn't look at him.

He swallowed. Opening up wasn't easy, but if he wanted to convince Hannah to give him a second chance he had to make her understand why he'd made bad decisions. "You accused me of being a bottom-line bastard. And you were right. I was pushing Sam away because I was afraid of losing him…like I did my father."

Her head whipped in his direction. "Your father's dead?"

"No. He had an affair. When his lover became pregnant, he discarded Mom and me without a backward glance and started a new family. It was as if Mom and I had never existed."

Sympathy darkened her eyes. "How old were you?"

"Almost fourteen."

"That must have been hard. You don't keep in touch?"

"I haven't seen him since the day he walked out. I didn't mind for me, but for my mother... She became cold and distant, someone I didn't know."

"You lost both parents at the same time."

"It felt that way. And then she met Sam, and for a while she became the mom I remembered. Then Sam was diagnosed and she turned her back on him the way Dad had us."

"I'm sorry."

"I'm not asking for pity. I'm trying and not doing a good job of explaining why I fought so hard not to let myself care too much. After my father left, I promised myself I wouldn't love anyone else ever again. It wasn't worth the pain. But Sam got past my defenses. Then I started losing him one memory at a time. I bought Sutherland Farm as a place to dump him so I wouldn't have to watch his decline. I was leaving him before he left me." A lump swelled in his throat. He swallowed.

Hannah squeezed his arm. "I know how difficult it is to watch someone you love fade away. That's what happened with my mom. She held on for a week before Dad took the doctors' advice and discontinued life support."

He swore. "Hannah—"

"It's okay. In the end, her organs allowed four people to have extra time with their families. She would have wanted it that way."

"Your ability to always see the positives is mind-boggling. I envy that."

"Yeah, well, sometimes that's harder than others." She ducked her head and stubbed the toe of her sneaker on the dock. "My father is right. I have no head for business. I've never tried to learn the financial side of the operation because sticking to a budget meant cutting expenses, and cutting expenses meant making difficult decisions about which students and animals I could help and which ones I had to turn away."

She fisted her hands until her knuckles turned white. "My inability to say no put Sam in jeopardy. I'm going to dissolve the school and rescue operation and ship all my horses to Rashed for his program."

The defeat in her voice twisted something inside him. He'd done that to her—crushed her spirit and taken everything she loved away. "What about the people and horses you help here?"

"And as you've pointed out more than once, FYC is a high-risk, low-return venture and, regardless of the precautions we take, if I operate it long enough someone is going to get hurt. Last night—"

"Hannah, last night was not your fault. It was mine. Sam acted out because in my fear of him getting hurt I'd caged him like an animal. Don't let my mistakes shake your confidence and kill your dream. You do good work here."

She shook her head. "I've decided to accept your offer to buy my cottage."

Her voice broke on the last word. Desperation rose inside him. He wanted—no, needed—to find a way to make her stay. He needed Hannah in his life to show him that some battles were worth fighting.

"My purchase offer's no longer on the table."

Eyes wide, she swung toward him. "B-but this is what you wanted. You've been trying to get rid of me ever since you bought the place."

"And now I want you to stay. What would Sutherland Farm be without a Sutherland?"

"It'll be whatever the next owner calls it."

The idea of Sutherland Farm without Hannah's presence repelled him. His life without her in it appealed even less. Her damned Pollyanna attitude had gotten to him and he was addicted. "I'm not selling the farm, Hannah."

"But—"

"I have a different proposition for you."

Suspicion pleated her brow. "What is it this time?"

"I'll deed the entire property over to you if you'll allow Sam to live in your cottage and work with the horses as long as he's able. Afterward all of the property—all two thousand two acres, including the main house—will be yours."

"What's the catch?"

He took a deep breath. It was time to lay his cards on the table and risk rejection. "You've shown me that success isn't limited to numbers on a balance sheet, and the time I have left with Sam is worth far more than dollars and cents. I want to be a part of his life. And yours, Hannah.

"You've proven denying my emotions doesn't eradicate them, and you've taught me what true selflessness is and what it means to open myself up—no matter the personal costs. You dream big, Hannah, with the vault to your soul wide open. You're not afraid of hurt or disappointment and I envy that."

"Of course I'm afraid, Wyatt. I get hurt like everyone else and I fail sometimes, too. But I don't choose to let the negatives keep me from searching for the positives."

"It's that ability to see the potential in every man or beast you encounter that makes you unique and special. I like the me you see, and I want an opportunity to become that man— the one who is not afraid to admit that—" The words jammed in his chest. He cleared his throat. "I love Sam."

Her tender smile twisted something inside him. "That wasn't so hard, was it?"

"No, I'm getting to the hard part." His heart hammered like a knocking piston against his chest. He experienced the same dizzying sensation he'd felt when he'd looked over the forty-story apartment balcony and realized how close he'd come to losing Sam. But to be worthy of Hannah, he had to take the risk.

"I've fallen in love with you, Hannah. You're a woman who can't say no to lost causes. And I'm hoping you won't say no to the biggest one of all—me."

Her mouth parted in a gasp, and for several seconds she gaped at him, searching his face as if doubting his words. Tears filled her eyes, and his gut burned like hot metal. Then a weak smile twitched her lips. "I never called you a lost cause. I may have thought it, but I never said it."

"It doesn't change the fact that I was one. But I can change." He captured her cold hands in his. "Rescue me, Hannah. Help me become the man that you see—the one who has the capacity to open his heart and not just his wallet. The one who's not afraid to feel."

"You're not nearly as hard as you think you are, Wyatt. Your love for Sam proves that."

Her words filled him with hope. He moved closer and cupped her soft cheeks. "Let me love you. And learn with you. Let me hold you in my arms every night, not as my mistress, but as my wife, as the woman who keeps me grounded in what really matters."

A lone tear trailed down her cheek, spilling over his thumb. "That's a pretty tall order. But I can't think of a better place to be. You are lovable, Wyatt. Sam loves you." She rose on tiptoe and briefly pressed her lips to his. "And I love you."

He banded his arms around her, hugging her close and covering her mouth. He couldn't get enough of her taste, her scent, her warmth. When he finally lifted his head, their panting breaths mingled. "You won't regret giving me a chance."

Her swollen lips curved upward. "I know I won't."

He laced his fingers through hers and led her into the boathouse. "I'll make you a deal. I'll teach you how to run

FYC as a business and help set it up as a charitable operation. That will enable you to help more people and more horses. In exchange, you keep reminding me that life's about more than a balance sheet. But later. Much later. Right now I need your skin against mine."

Her cheeks flushed and the corners of her eyes crinkled. She held out her arm, revealing goose bumps. "I only get those when I've come across a champion combination."

* * * * *

A sneaky peek at next month...

Desire™

PASSIONATE AND DRAMATIC LOVE STORIES

My wish list for next month's titles...

2 stories in each book - only £5.49!

In stores from 16th March 2012:

☐ Enticed by His Forgotten Lover – Maya Banks

& The Billionaire's Borrowed Baby – Janice Maynard

☐ Reclaiming His Pregnant Widow – Tessa Radley

& To Touch a Sheikh – Olivia Gates

☐ An After-Hours Affair – Barbara Dunlop

& Millionaire Playboy, Maverick Heiress – Robyn Grady

☐ Much More Than a Mistress – Michelle Celmer

& Bachelor Untamed – Brenda Jackson

Available at WHSmith, Tesco, Asda, Eason, Amazon and Apple

Just can't wait?

Visit us Online

You can buy our books online a month before they hit the shops! **www.millsandboon.co.uk**

0312/51